The Shy Avenger

Reader's Comments:

Daphne Ellman, S.W.A. Isle of Wight. U.K.
'I have to tell you what a fabulous read I found 'The Shy Avenger' to be. It grabbed me right from the start – the prologue left me wanting to know more. Whilst the start was the image of the gentle idyll and beautiful people you had the sense that all was not well. As it continued the tension grew, I couldn't put the book down, it had me totally believing and I physically shrieked once. It was like being on a roller coaster ride of twist and turn of surprise. It is a great imaginative story and whilst it's an amazing read, I can also see it as a film, the special effects would be fantastic! So don't stop here I want more!!
Thank you for such a wonderful spell of entertainment.'

Kate Kemmis. Adelaide, Australia.
Have to say, I loved this book. I was pulled in right from the start and couldn't put it down (and that does not happen to me with books). Can't wait for the next one.

THE SHY AVENGER

By

Geoffrey Scardthomas

The Shy Avenger   Scardthomas

This book is a work of fiction. All persons are the product of the author's imagination. Any resemblance to actual persons, living or dead is purely coincidental.
Fictional names have been used in the immediate topography, although some nearby geographical and architectural sites were used as models for reference.

Copyright 2019.   Geoffrey Scardthomas. All rights reserved.
ISBN. 1706979258

No part of this book may be reproduced, stored in a retrieval system, or transmitted by any means without the written permission of the author.

Previously published in 2010 using the title Brother. This revised edition entitled The Shy Avenger first published 2019. Edit carried out February 2023.

To Bex

With love & best wishes

GS

3

CONTENTS.

PART ONE.   1975

PROLOGUE.

CHAPTER ONE.   Arrival at Yewhurst - June 1975.

CHAPTER TWO.   "Must be a child," she said.

CHAPTER THREE.   "There is something that bothers me."

CHAPTER FOUR.   "I may be able to help you there."

CHAPTER FIVE.   'Where the joy of now had been born.'

CHAPTER SIX.   It was all very odd.

CHAPTER SEVEN.   "Are you from these parts?"

CHAPTER EIGHT.   "Somebody's got your number."

CHAPTER NINE.   "Were you an only child?"

CHAPTER TEN.   And down went the hammer.

CHAPTER ELEVEN.   "You are a clever doggy."

CHAPTER TWELVE.   Her day would come.

CHAPTER THIRTEEN.   The Secret Pond.

CHAPTER FOURTEEN.   "Where is it now?"

CHAPTER FIFTEEN.   "We may be very grateful to him."

CHAPTER SIXTEEN.   "If you notice any change..."

CHAPTER SEVENTEEN.   "Are you absolutely sure about that?"

CHAPTER EIGHTEEN.   She sensed something in that sigh.

CHAPTER NINETEEN.   "Sorry – must have missed it."

CHAPTER TWENTY.   "Have you ever seen anything like that?"

CHAPTER TWENTY-ONE.   "Well – that answers that."

CHAPTER TWENTY-TWO.   Headline News.

CHAPTER TWENTY-THREE.   One guest was directly involved.

CHAPTER TWENTY-FOUR.   "Same subject – I'm afraid."

CHAPTER TWENTY-FIVE.   "There is nothing remotely like them..."

CHAPTER TWENTY-SIX.   "We have a mystery."

CHAPTER TWENTY-SEVEN.   This was something new.

CHAPTER TWENTY-EIGHT.   The last touch with her world.

CHAPTER TWENTY-NINE.   "There is only one thing they can do."

CHAPTER THIRTY.   "You could say that."

CHAPTER THIRTY-ONE.   "Must ask him about that."

CHAPTER THIRTY-TWO.   "Unless – that someone was known to him."

CHAPTER THIRTY-THREE. A happening never before witnessed by mankind.

CHAPTER THIRTY-FOUR.   Unusual – for a pine.

CHAPTER THIRTY-FIVE.   She would never have envisaged.

CHAPTER THIRTY-SIX.   "Shame he never made it."

CHAPTER THIRTY-SEVEN.   The unexpected visitor.

CHAPTER THIRTY-EIGHT. "She does not wish to speak with you."

PART TWO.   1976

CHAPTER FORTY.   "And what is the matter with you, Mr Anti-Social?"

CHAPTER FORTY.   "You mean – he's a thief?"

CHAPTER FORTY-ONE. "Witness to what exactly – water divining?"

CHAPTER FORTY-TWO.   "Seen any fish in here?"

CHAPTER FORTY-THREE.   "Now – it doesn't matter anymore."

CHAPTER FORTY-FOUR.   "It's been nicked?"

CHAPTER FORTY-FIVE. A police matter.

CHAPTER FORTY-SIX.   She absolutely knew.

CHAPTER FORTY-SEVEN.   Seemed to accentuate all his senses.

CHAPTER FORTY-EIGHT.   Both men gazed at each other.

CHAPTER FORTY-NINE.   "Was it magnificent?"

CHAPTER FIFTY.   She was not aware of it.

CHAPTER FIFTY-ONE.   "Now ... rest in peace."

CHAPTER FIFTY-TWO.   "What did you do that for mister?"

CHAPTER FIFTY-THREE. So that was what that look had been about.

CHAPTER FIFTY-FOUR.   "We salute you both."

CHAPTER FIFTY- FIVE.   "I take it – that is no?"

CHAPTER FIFTY-SIX.   "I'm very pleased you did."

Poem: THE SILVER BIRCH RUN.

Story Poem: JOHN THE RED. (THE RED ADDER OF YEWHURST. 1947/48)

PART ONE

1975

PROLOGUE

What is it that makes a man follow-up on a mysterious message from his past – even though the undertaking may involve serious risk?

Due to several weeks of uncharacteristically warm and dry weather, some parts of England's green and pleasant land were rapidly turning into various shades of pale umber, as areas became parched through lack of rainfall.

It was just coming up to noon on Friday, 6th June 1975.

Suspended in a vast azure sky the pale golden sun, haloed in shimmering ivory, cast its brilliant rays to the flora below: a forest area nestling under chalk downs not far from the City of Winchester. The atmosphere was infused with dappled light and palpable dryness, invaded by the buzzing of countless pollen-searching insects.

Around a bend, on a little used woodland pathway – wandered a man. His gait was more of a plod than a walk, and he progressed slowly, intently watching as each footfall cast up miniature fountains of dry sandy soil, to fall over the toecaps of his boots. From his appearance, he looked to be old. His face; lined and dirty, was framed by a shaggy mop of greyish hair, descending in long whisker like strands onto the collar of a distressed coat. His hands were thrust deep inside the coat pockets, and his head was hunched into his shoulders.

Coming to a short rise, he stopped and looked upon a broad mighty oak growing a little way off to the left of the track. As his head tilted upwards, the intense midday sun shone through his untidy brow, and caught the vivid blue deep in his eyes, suggesting, perhaps, a very different earlier life. Turning his back on the tree, he sat down on the long grasses by the side of the path, fixing a gaze somewhere among a row of conifers close by, lined up like giant camouflaged soldiers.

This morning, his mind had reflected a great deal. It was hard to believe that once he had been a courageous young captain in the Royal Marines. Today, thirty-one years ago, he had been leading his troops to bloody glory on a heavily fortified beach in northwest France.

With a distinguished service record, he left the marines at the end of the war to try his luck in the world of commerce. But commerce did not need honourable brave leaders. Over a period of years and disillusionment, due to being unfairly used again and again by senior management; often made a scapegoat for errors that were none of his responsibility, our once dashing army officer became a middle-aged non-entity.

His romantic life, too, had been treacherously unkind to him, preferring in his tastes the very women he should have avoided. Frankly, they were too good looking for him to handle. Now, nearing old age he had resigned himself to ... what? ... He did not know – or care. There were no immediate relatives. Friends had been carefully shunned and gradually discarded using a masochistic screen of shame.

He rose shakily to his feet, turned off the path and headed straight under the great oak tree to seek shade. Suddenly, as if by an unseen command, all sounds from neighbouring wildlife ceased. Most noticeably, the birds stopped their busy calls. Occasionally, the blanketed sound of a vehicle travelling along a road could be heard; it bounced off countless trees imitating isolated gusts of wind. The strange silence lasted for no more than a minute or two, until, abruptly, a startled cry came from the direction of the man under the tree. This was followed almost immediately by a dreadful scream, which seared and shattered the silence echoing horribly into the depths of the forest. It was a scream hurled from the throat of a person that had been radically shocked by sudden, intense pain. Then – all fell quiet. After some moments, gradually, the soft woodland chatter returned.

CHAPTER ONE

ARRIVAL AT YEWHURST - JUNE 1975.

A Firecrest, one of the British Isle's smallest birds, was making its way upwards from the lower reaches of a six- hundred-year-old oak, through the bark of centuries, searching for small insects. The flash of orange feathering on the top of its head stood out vividly against yellow and black border stripes on each side.

Nearby, just a few steps over a gentle mossy bank, a young beech tree was trying to make a presence in the crowded woodland. It was surrounded by a thick mass of dead leaves several inches thick. The feeding bird ceased all movement and fixed a stare at this deposit of last year's autumn debris. The reason was because, in a soundless undulating motion, those leaves appeared to be moving. Immediately, with a sudden flick of its wings, the Firecrest was gone. It flew in a low rapid wave-like motion, a few hundred yards through a sizeable copse of silver birches, weaving around the trunks, before alighting on a fragile garden gate at the back of an uninhabited thatched cottage. The little bird emitted a short high-pitched warbling whistle to announce his arrival. What it could not know – was that soon, for the second time that day, its territory would be violated.

Less than an hour later, on this pleasant Saturday morning, Christine Westward went to join her husband, Timothy, who was looking over a low hedge enjoying the extensive views over the countryside. They were both wearing blue jeans and white cotton shirts. Christine's denim was more faded than Tim's, and, by the look of it, the shirt she was wearing looked suspiciously like one of Tim's discarded items of office clothing. Her husband glanced at her as she walked towards him and thought, admiringly, that it looked a great deal better on her than it had on him.

It was a fine day giving a distant haziness. Above their heads, the sky was the palest of blue fading to off-white by the time it reached the horizon. Everywhere was dry, but the lushness of the recent spring was still evident in the crops growing in the fields, and the copse lying haphazardly on the slopes of the downland below them.

"Can you see our village?" asked Christine. Her voice had a middle-class Surrey-ness about it, but not overly so.

Tim smiled and looked over to the left-hand viewpoint. "Nnn-o," he stretched the word out. "It's somewhere over there," and he pointed in the rough direction. Unexpectedly, Tim felt a kind of undefined premonition: not a pleasurable one.

Reading something in his facial expression, Christine asked,

"What's the matter?"

Tim blinked hard and shook his head. "Absolutely nothing," he said giving her a reassuring smile.

They were parked on the summit of the chalk escarpment known as Cheesefoot Head. Tim was driving a medium sized van containing household possessions, and Christine was using their own Morris Minor. It had been pre-arranged that they would stop at this scenic outlook for a rest and a drink of coffee from a vacuum flask. The time was now eleven o'clock.

That morning these two very excited people had left behind their rented, semi-detached house just off the Purley Way; a busy thoroughfare not far from the southern districts of London. They were on their way to a three-bedroom thatched cottage, nine miles to the west of Winchester. This was to be their home for the foreseeable future. It was situated well back from the road and surrounded on three sides by forest.

Tim was twenty-four, tall and slim with sandy coloured hair, hazel eyes and an infectious grin, which had been so well used that already the right side of his mouth seemed a touch higher than the other. He was a likeable man.

Christine, a beautiful woman, twenty-two years old, had natural blonde hair and oval blue-green eyes. She stood five feet seven inches tall with the sort of figure that most men everywhere turn their eyes to. Her lips were full and slightly pouting. It had the effect that when she smiled her whole face went with it; but these gifts had not spoilt her kind nature, suggesting that good looks had come to her in late adolescence.

Tim had acquired a temporary clerking job in London after three years as a student geologist in Edinburgh University, where he obtained a degree with honours. For the last eighteen months he had joined the morning and evening rush-hour traffic to and from London's Edgware road, accompanied by numerous irate failed Grand Prix drivers. He did not like the work at all. It was so boring he found himself looking forward to the lunch break far too soon. However, to pay the rent, it had been necessary so that he and his wife could be together while waiting for suitable employment in the field of geology.

Recently, Tim finally achieved a position with a firm near Winchester. Certainly, a job that he enjoyed, and an improved salary were important, but more than anything else he desired a nice home. Nothing overly grand: just a peaceful situation with a garden. He wanted this especially for Christine; and now, at last, it was going to happen.

The environmental change that they were about to experience was extreme. Living alongside the Purley Way caused gross pressure on the mind trying to find peace. The general traffic noise from numerous cars and the thunderous power of heavy trucks together with horns used, it seemed constantly, threatened to drive the pair of them crazy.

Contrast this with what they would be likely to experience tomorrow. If they woke early, it would probably be due to the sound of the birds' dawn chorus. Alternatively, they could sleep through this event, and, later, all they might hear would be the drone of a solitary bumblebee as it flew past the bedroom window.

Their car, a Morris convertible was already ten years old when Tim bought it; however, it had been sufficiently restored. The car's body had a deep cream colour and he was quietly pleased with its appearance. Although she was frequently worried that it might brake-down at the wrong moment, Christine loved the motorcar. In fact, despite its age, it was proving to be a reliable vehicle. For the current journey, Christine had decided to travel with the hood up, preferring not to be exposed when driving alone, as she found that her blonde hair and good looks attracted the wrong kind of attention, even though, like her husband, she was a definite fan of open-air motoring.

They had made this journey several times during the last couple of months, a trip that took over two hours, to view and decide upon the purchase of a house. Both were more than glad that this was the final one.

The coffee was enjoyed in a sort of impatient silence. Both of them were anxious to continue, despite the scenic beauty.

The destination was the village of Yewhurst, situated seven miles to the west of Winchester. Their new home, Beech Cottage, lay two hundred yards off a road on the edge of a wood bearing the same name as the village. With a bit of work, the dwelling could be the all-round picturesque, thatched cottage in an idyllic setting. It had the lot: old oak beams, once part of a seventeenth-century naval vessel, an inglenook fireplace, low ceilings, and mind-your-head doorways.

A mere half-an-hour after leaving Cheesefoot Head, the new occupants arrived. "Come on love. We have to do this properly," said Tim. Whereupon he put his left arm under his wife's knees, and while supporting her with the other tried to carry her over the front door threshold.

"Oh! Careful Tim! Ow!" She cried out in pain as her knee collided with the door frame. Her husband expressed apologetic concern while Christine gave her bruised knee a vigorous rub. Then she ignored it. Nothing was going to spoil her enjoyment as they wandered from room to room – savouring this much-awaited, special moment. To give the place an airing they opened all the windows, except one in the kitchen that simply would not budge. Tim was relieved to see that their new refrigerator and cooker had been delivered.

After a snack lunch, they unloaded the hired van and quickly returned it to the rental office in Southampton, also fitting in a visit to a small supermarket.

Later, back at the cottage, they were in the process of surveying the garden, when they were interrupted by the voice of a strange old lady peering at them over the front gate. "Yer've got some werk to do tharn," was her introduction spoken in a broad southern England rural dialect. The elderly woman was wearing far too many knitted garments for such a hot June day, but she seemed completely at ease, apart from a slight head nodding movement.

Her shoulders were a little hunched. Untidy grey hair billowed out from her craggy features, and dark eyes peered at the young couple behind full eyebrows. There was a large mole just below her right temple, and tight lips starkly framed what little teeth she had. A rather grubby looking spaniel was snuffling next to her trying to get under the gate. Standing there, looking at the two of them, the woman exuded an air of country living.

"Oh ... hello," said Christine. "Do you live near here?" Tim gave the old lady a half-welcoming grin, together with an uncertain – do I want to know you look?

"Oi does," replied the woman but adding nothing further on that subject. "Stayin' long is yer?"

"Yes, we hope so," replied Christine. "We've just moved down from Croydon today. Lovely country around here, isn't it?"

"Some say so. Yer'd betta watch out fer Jahn if yer goes walkin' tha."

"Er, Jahn?" queried Tim.

"Yer – Jahn, he be still abaat fer sure. I knows what I be talking abaat. Yer mark me werds!" As she said this, she jabbed her walking stick at the woods, over to the left-hand side of the cottage, several times. Her eyes seemed surprisingly alert for her age. Their trajectory constantly flicked in and around the scene in front of her, especially into the depths of the forest to the side and behind Beech Cottage. Neither Christine nor Tim said anything. They were both confused. "Well – Oi must be aff. Nice ter greet yer." With that, she shuffled off into the woods, her spaniel taking the lead. Christine noticed the lady was wearing an old pair of men's brogues. Turning, she lamely waved a hand in goodbye.

After a suitable pause, Tim said, "Well – what did you make of that?"

Christine giggled before making the comment. "Our first neighbour!"

"More like the local witch," joked Tim.

Five years before, the cottage had been derelict, but its recent owners had carried out a programme of renovation. It had been re-thatched so that it now sported a new soft-gold hat. However, there was a considerable amount of work to undertake in the decorating department. Tim's sister, Suzanne, who lived with their parents in Somerset, had agreed to come and spend a few weeks with them to help. She was due to arrive the following morning.

For the remainder of the afternoon and the early evening, Christine and Tim set to work unpacking early requirement items.

By seven-thirty in the evening, they were both exhausted but content with their efforts, and on Tim's suggestion they decided to sit in the back garden and sip a long, cool beer; a drink they both enjoyed at this time of year. At one time the back garden would have been a thriving vegetable plot abruptly ending where it backed onto thick woodland.

Although Yewhurst Wood was now the responsibility of the Forestry Commission, and had been extensively planted with conifers, some of the peripheries had been left with their natural screens of silver birch, and it was a crowd of these delightful trees that Tim and Christine looked upon. A rickety old gate gave a hint of a disused path going off into the forest. Silver birches happened to be Tim's favourite trees, and right now they were in full leaf, but he knew there were many delights in store: the ochre and sienna colours of autumn, and the small bright green leaves of spring sheltering the fresh hanging catkins, especially looked at under a clear blue sky. The evening sun still found a spot to shine by the back door, and there was an old wooden bench conveniently placed there.

What occurred next made Tim choke on his beer and caused Christine to jump out of her seat. Just a few yards beyond their boundary, a large cock pheasant, in full plumage, let go a deafening alarm call, and, with a loud thudding beat of its wings, struggled through some young birches, before disappearing from sight over the treetops.

"The delights of country life!" exclaimed Christine, recovering her composure. "Come on Tim, let's go and explore."

"Hold on, I'm enjoying my beer."

"It'll keep," she persisted.

"No, it won't. It'll get warm." Never-the-less Tim gave in and followed his wife to the gate, which had collapsed on its hinges. "Another job requiring my attention," he muttered.

The pathway was so overgrown that they had difficulty in making any progress. Bracken wrapped itself around their ankles and birch twigs kept whipping across their bare arms and face. Eventually, they broke free onto a dense vivid green grass covered path. From here there was not much of a view in either direction. The track meandered and soon got lost in the forest. It had, however, a beauty of its own because there was obviously running water somewhere near, which would account for the richness of the growth under their feet. The trees immediately on the edges of the track were taller than the rest. This had a closing in effect, but in the evening light it was both cool and comforting.

Suddenly, out of nowhere, came a distracting sound. Everything was still except for the bird's evensong, so the disturbing noise was startling. It came from some way away: a distant, high-pitched, shrieking intense sound, similar to that made by old trains releasing excess steam at a station. Both of them looked in the direction from which they thought it came. Tim wore a perplexed frown on his forehead, and Christine visibly shuddered, opening her eyes wide with the effect. It had been so out of place. They looked at each other, mystified.

"What was that?" said Tim. Christine could not say anything. She was swiftly a little apprehensive. Without explaining, she started to head back to the cottage. Her husband followed.

Later, a little deeper into the woodland, behind Beech Cottage, a small tortoiseshell cat walked quickly along a narrow pathway enclosed on both sides by bracken and young fir trees. She was at the extremity of her territory, and in a hurry. Due to the large area she covered she was able to fend for herself. However, this evening's hunt had been without success, so not only would she have to return to her owner's home for something to eat, but the first signs of dusk were arriving, and although she had no fear of predators during daylight; twilight brought the possibility of an encounter with a fox, or worse, a badger.

She had come to a small clearing that lay before the base of a chunky oak tree, when she unexpectedly stopped with one paw raised off the ground. A couple of feet away from the trunk of the tree, a man lay in the foetal position. No feature of his face was visible – only a mop of dishevelled grey hair. Initially, he looked to be fast asleep. The cat's wariness was not acute, for she had often encountered vagrants in these woods, especially in the summer months, and they were usually kind to her. There had only been one occasion when one of them, in a moment of temporary insanity caused by excessive consumption of alcohol had hurled a small log in her direction.

It did not take her long to realise that the present encounter was different – very different. She did not need to investigate. Her senses told her. She slunk further into the growth on the far side of the track and went on. She knew – that the man lying there – was lifeless.

Not long after, following a substantial plate of bacon and eggs, Tim and Christine finally sat down properly in their new living room for the first time. The furniture consisted of a two-seater sofa and single armchair, which did not match. Also, in place were a coffee table and an old bookcase. The large inglenook fireplace dominated the room.

For the kitchen, Christine's mother and father had given them the new fridge and cooker, but they were short of furniture for the bedrooms. One double bed and a camp bed were not sufficient. A dressing table and full-length mirror for Christine were on the urgent list. They had so many plans to make, and it was gone ten o'clock before one of them stopped talking.

When they laid their heads on the pillows, they were both very glad that their first job, on arrival, had been to make up the bed, because sleep, for the two of them, was virtually instant. However, their bodies were close. They always were.

CHAPTER TWO

"MUST BE A CHILD," SHE SAID.

Sunday morning, the next day, again brought sunshine and they awoke early to the finale of the dawn chorus. This was a sound that neither of them had heard to such intensity for some considerable time. So, they lay in bed for a while enjoying the experience, and Christine tried to renew a childhood skill of putting the name of the bird to its song. But, after all, she could only be sure of the wood pigeon. "My toe bleeds Betsy," she uttered.

"You what?" her husband queried.

"My toe bleeds Betsy," repeated Christine. "Listen ... that's what the pigeon is saying. There ..." as one conveniently made its call ... "see?"

"No, it isn't. It's saying it's your turn to make the tea."

"Cheeky!" she said before bopping him over the head with her pillow. She was wearing a short nightdress, creating an alluring picture as she took herself down the narrow staircase; her golden hair catching the morning sunlight through the little window halfway down.

Tim propped himself up on one elbow. Their bedroom was a reasonable size for a cottage, but the other two rooms were positively tiny. Christine had drawn back the curtains, and Tim could see the thick young thatch overhanging the diamond leaded windows. He sighed with satisfaction.

Suzanne, Tim's sister, was due to arrive at Southampton rail station at eleven-thirty that morning.

Later, after cleaning chores, Tim said, "We'd better get going. Mustn't keep Suz waiting."

"Yes – and be nice to her. I don't want any of that sibling rivalry."

"I'm *always* nice to her," he countered. "She's the pain in the bum."

"Oh Tim, that's not fair... I'm on her side."

"Typical – come on then, quick wash and brush up. You don't need to put on a face; the current one will do."

"I shall do as I please! Go on – out of the way. I want the bathroom."

Before they left, Christine announced. "Half a mo'; I must set the oven. We are stopping for a drink on the way back, aren't we?"

"No. I've turned teetotal," replied Tim

"That'll be the day! Just be sure you have some money on you," she said, over her shoulder, as she strode through to the kitchen.

Christine knew this silly mood of Tim's. She knew it as surely as she knew he was very happy.

Southampton was quiet currently on a Sunday morning. There were several cars loaded with luggage, heading presumably for the ferry terminals.

They arrived at the station in plenty of time to meet Suzanne's train, and, after checking that it was on schedule, sat down on a bench to wait and watch the comings and goings.

Suzanne Westward was just twenty-one and carefree in attitude because her childhood had given her plenty of feelings of security. She was petite, while erring, just a little, towards the fuller figure, but this tended to enhance her cheerful personality. Her nut-brown eyes were always twinkling, and they highlighted an enchanting and frequent smile. Over the years, her family had become familiar with the sparkle in her eyes. A family pet cat took to her when she was nine years old, and it always used to sleep just above her head on the pillow. When it died three years later – that sparkle disappeared for days.

She was totally different in appearance to her brother. Tim took his mother's side, and Suzanne – her father's. Her hair was jet black, only in bright sunlight could a sheen of the darkest brown be detected.

As the train of many carriages neared Southampton, she fidgeted in her seat with an obvious excitement that her fellow passengers could not fail to notice. She was dressed in a light blue sear-sucker blouse, with pale denim jeans and blue suede flat shoes. When the train began to slow, Suzanne jumped to her feet and grappled with the larger of her two suitcases on the luggage rack. A middle-aged gentleman took his eyes away from the sight of her well-rounded derriere and helped her. He opened the carriage door with a polite smile as the train squealed and grumbled to a halt.

"There she is!" shouted Christine, above the clamour of the station. They embraced each other with a big hug.

"Hello Suz," greeted Tim. He received a wet kiss on his right cheek.

"Hi both," Suzanne took a step backwards. "You look fantastic! Must be the effect of your new home." Tim picked up his sister's big case and they made their way to the car park, with the two girls walking in front chatting amiably.

On the way back, they stopped off at the Cowherd's pub on Southampton Common for a drink where they managed to find a vacant table outside. Suzanne was eager to catch up on their news and family gossip. Eventually, Christine recounted the tale of the meeting with the old lady at their garden gate.

Suzanne was intrigued. "Well, have you found out who the mysterious John is?" she asked.

"No," said Tim, "And it's not John, it's Jaan. They all laughed at Tim's pathetic attempt to imitate the local country dialect... "Probably just some tramp who lives in the woods," he added.

"Ugh," exclaimed Suzanne, "I hope I don't meet him. He's bound to be smelly."

"Hmm, I expect you'll hum a bit when we've put you to work," said Tim mischievously.

"Hey, I'm not your slave you know – brother dear." They laughed again as Suzanne made a sour face. "But, while we're on the subject – what's to be done? I've brought some old clothes. Well, they are not that old, but I wanted an excuse to get rid of them." Tim and Christine told her about their plans.

Suzanne informed her brother that their mother and father wanted to know when they could visit. "Heck, hold on, give us a chance," Tim said quickly. "I'll ring them this evening. Also, don't forget Christine's parents want to come as well. That right love?"

"Yes – but whatever will-be-will-be," replied Christine with a shoulder shrug.

As they climbed back into the Morris, it did not escape Tim's attention that his wife and sister were attracting a lot of attention from various male university students enjoying a lunch time drink.

When they arrived at Beech Cottage, Suzanne went into raptures over, "The beautiful little place," as she called it. She produced a bottle of wine to go with their lunch, and they enjoyed the meal in the back garden.

"Will have to get ourselves organised with a barbecue," said Tim.

"Tim wants to build a proper brick one," added Christine.

"Doesn't surprise me," commented Suzanne. "Actually, he is rather good in the do-it-yourself department, I seem to remember. Probably gets it from his dad."

They were enjoying a cup of coffee after lunch when Christine suggested that they go for a walk. "There is an interesting church about a quarter of mile from here, with a pretty churchyard. We can get to it easily through the woods. Do you fancy strolling up there Suz?"

"Yes, okay," Suzanne answered. "Are you coming Tim?"

"No, I'm going to make a start on the garden. You two go. I'll see you later." Following a lengthy inspection, he thought he would delay major work for the moment. A lot of it would need his wife's input, such as what to cut down and what to leave or trim. It had been so dry recently that normal weed growth had been severely retarded, making his present task considerably easier.

When they finished their coffee, the two girls set off. The afternoon sun was still hot, and the shade cast by the various trees was welcome. They made their way along a path that ran adjacent to the road.

The Forestry Commission had planted large areas of Yewhurst Wood with conifer trees. The later plantings were still young and therefore small in stature. The public were asked to stick to marked pathways when enjoying its recreation, in order to avoid unnecessary damage to the saplings. The path Christine and Suzanne were taking formed the southern-most boundary of the forest and wound its way in and around mature beech trees, part of the various areas of deciduous trees that had been left in place.

At length, they reached a copse of yew trees and the track petered out joining one of the main wide pathways that ran north-south through the plantation. These clearances were designed to cause a break in the event of a forest fire and were considerably wider than any of the other paths. They climbed over a stile and waded through a patch of last season's dead bracken, until they found themselves among some dark-leafed bushes that looked over the church car park.

A double bank of rhododendron, on two levels, bordered the churchyard, which was perched on top of a small hill.

"Wow!" exclaimed Suzanne referring to various mature ornamental plantings scattered at various points in the church gardens. "I wonder how high that big tree is?"

"No idea," said Christine.

They were so busy admiring the scenery and chatting that they did not notice a lady sitting on a wooden seat, underneath the tree recently referred to. As they walked up the gravel path towards the church itself, the lady unexpectedly remarked. "Are you lost?"

Both Christine and her sister-in-law started with surprise. Christine was the first to answer. "No ... I don't think so. We were just looking at the church." Then she briefly explained that they were new to the area.

The lady seemed a pleasant person, somewhat aristocratic, but not pronounced. She was dressed in a summer skirt of royal blue with a pale lilac blouse. They blended nicely. Her blue rinsed hair had been cut to a curl just above the shoulders. In her lap she cradled a large ball of burgundy coloured wool.

They entered into polite small talk before introductions were made. The lady was obviously pleased to have someone to talk to. "Julia," she announced when it was her turn. She had a joyful way of speaking, putting an emphasis on the initial syllable of the first word from each sentence. "Where is your new home?"

"Do you know Beech Cottage?" answered Christine.

"Oh yes," replied Julia. "Such a pretty place," she paused. "Although – it was rather run-down."

Christine spoke positively, "Fortunately the last owners did most of the renovation work."

The lady recollected something. "You know, now there was a funny thing – those previous occupants. Never did get to the bottom of that: a nice couple. They put in so much work on the place, and then, abruptly up-ed and left."

"We never met them," said Christine with one eyebrow raised. "An agent handled everything. What were they like?"

The Shy Avenger   Scardthomas

"Perhaps they had to move. Job or something," interjected Suzanne.

"Possibly – I think the wife was with child as well. I'm afraid I never met either of them though, so I can't enlighten you," said Julia. "Let's hope Ma Hessil didn't scare them off."

"Ma Hessil?" queried Christine.

"Yes, that woman is always at it – spreading stupid rumours."

A thought occurred to Christine, and she told Julia about the old woman who had spoken to them over their front gate.

"That's her, that's her," she repeated, wagging a straight finger at nobody in particular. "What did she say to you?"

"She told us to watch out for somebody – a man called John. Who is John?" asked Christine.

"T'tch, you don't want to take any notice of that. John is supposed to be some sort of deadly snake. It's all a load of scare mongering. I mustn't be too hard on her though. She lost her son due to snakebite – way back – about 1948. Turned her mind some folk reckoned. There were two very long hot summers – nineteen forty-seven and forty-eight. For some reason the adder bite was extremely venomous around here at that time. Normally, an adder's bite is not life threatening and a very rare occurrence, but during those two years – quite the opposite. It was very sad: happened not far from here. You see that house over the road." Julia indicated the dwelling with her right hand. "Well – there's a cart track that runs down the side of it. Somewhere beyond the end of that apparently. They say the same snake bit her son's fiancée at the same time. She died as well."

"How awful!" exclaimed Suzanne.

The two girls remained silent. "Anyway, we don't want to talk about such a depressing subject on this glorious Sunday afternoon," said Julia.

"No fear," said Suzanne. "I'm not too keen on snakes."

"Well, don't you worry dear. Since the forestry people have been about, the snake population around here seems to have disappeared. Dr Andrews, my doctor, was only telling me the other day; it has been years since he had last seen an Adder. They used to be much more common. In the fields of late summer, you would often see snake skins hung over the fences, where farm workers laid them out to dry for use in crafts."

Julia offered to show the girls around the church. She got up, slowly, but not awkwardly as she half turned to place her knitting on the seat. Then she took them up the gravel path to the church entrance. Inside she showed them around pointing out plaques, vases, urns, and other objects representing past historical matter. Of particular interest was the stained-glass window above the altar. It was considered a great work of art due to its ability to portray wonderful colour when the sun's rays penetrated. She was extremely knowledgeable on all matters concerning this church, mainly due to the years of service she had given in voluntary help to the administration of the village in general.

Christine and Suzanne must have created a good impression for they were invited to tea at Julia's home on the following Tuesday afternoon. They accepted and took their leave, thanking Julia for the tour. She wished to stay behind to water the flowers at the altar before returning to her knitting.

On the way out of the churchyard, by a junction in the paths, Christine stopped by a small, unmarked grave. It was in shade under the lower boughs of an ancient yew. In fact, some of the tree's roots looked ominously close to the small mound and its stone surround. "Must be a child," she said. "I sense great sadness."

"Yes – wonder why there is nothing to say who it is?" Suzanne remarked with a puzzled expression on her face. It was odd because while the gravestone was substantial enough, the head had no inscription whatsoever. Nothing. The burial must have taken place many years ago. It was not just the weathered look of the stone which suggested this; all recent graves had been dug on newly consecrated ground at the far end of the churchyard.

That evening Tim erected the camp bed in the smallest of the spare rooms, which had just enough space for Suzanne to be comfortable. There was a small built-in wardrobe for her use, which should be sufficient for her temporary needs. While making up the bed with Christine, she made a point of saying she was quite prepared to "rough it."

Over a light supper of Brie cheese, crackers and sweet pickled onions, they brought Tim up to date on the revelations about 'John', which they had gleaned from the lady in the churchyard. Christine had the distinct impression that her husband was not convinced about the deaths supposedly caused by snakebite, all those years ago. He was quite sure the European Common Adder would not have a bite that venomous.

On Suzanne's prompt, Tim telephoned his parents. It was agreed that they would come and visit later in the summer.

About this time, just a mile away, a tall broad-shouldered man, just out of young, dressed in blue denim walked quickly towards the main fire-break route, which ran up to Yewhurst Church from the deepest section of the woodland. He was good-looking, but there was something else: a sort of physical charisma. What this was due to could not easily be identified. It had a great deal to do with his height and general physique – yes, but together with this; he exuded a confident power of masculine fluidity of stride. Close to his right heel, pacing gracefully was a magnificent male Tri-colour Rough Collie.

The first signs of dusk were approaching, and the man wanted to be back by the road before it got much darker. In wooded areas, the sunset shadows seemed to approach faster than in more open spaces. Neither of them had eaten any dinner, and the pangs of hunger were nagging.

What had kept them out later than usual was a considerably longer walk than their normal exercise routine, in order to catch sight of an area of the forest that had a grand growth of bluebells, before the blooms faded with the advancing season. It had been worthwhile. In the evening light, under the branches of young deciduous trees, the faint mauve tinge upon the blue had gone, to be replaced by mind alluring French ultramarine. The most vivid sights existed where the sunlight penetrated through in streaky layers of transparent gold dust, as though spot lighting the stars of the show.

While the collie wandered off, the man remained admiring the scene for some time. His alert, deep-blue eyes seemed to be exploring every aspect, perhaps mapping out something in his brain. He took a long menthol cigarette from a packet in his denim shirt pocket and lit it, periodically blowing puffs of tobacco smoke into the trees. One foot was raised on a log; half obscured by bracken fronds, with the other firmly planted on the hard, excessively dry woodland soil. When, eventually, he glanced at his wristwatch, his face showed surprise and he called his dog to him.

As their fast walk propelled them homewards, the man turned a questioning face to the collie, for he sensed sudden stiffening in the animal. The dog was still to heel, but with his head lowered and inclined towards the left side of the pathway, where a large growth of hazel trees had choked out everything else. Without checking his pace, the man studied him. With twenty-five times more receptors than his master, the dog's sense of smell had picked up a horrid presence. His owner would have no knowledge of this – or that this presence was causing great fear to his canine friend.

"What's up boy?" the man asked with concern, in a clear, relatively deep voice. But the dog just kept up the sideways walk. They had reached the wide pathway before his stride returned to a brisk confident pace; only then did he give a reassuring lick to his master's trailing hand.

Several hundred yards farther on, they were nearing the top of a rise before the route ran down to a large wooden five-bar gate by the road. At this point both master and animal broke into a casual run that took them along the track adjacent to the road. The athletically built man had to constantly bend his knees and swivel his hips over the undulating ground. At the same time, he frequently lowered his head to avoid overhanging branches covered in beech leaves, which obstructed the path.

Rounding a bend, the first of the two cottages on this side of the road came into view. A light was clearly visible in an upstairs window. 'Must be new occupants,' thought the man. He slowed to a more sedate walk calling after his dog to do the same. The collie grunted in disappointment coming to a slithering halt, turning his head to pant and await the approach of his owner. At this point, they crossed the road to go down behind the Claymans Heron hotel, and along the border of a field, before coming back up to some old farm labourer's cottages on the other side.

At Beech Cottage, they all went upstairs to sleep fairly early. Tim was off for the first day of his career first thing in the morning, and the girls wanted a prompt start for a shopping trip. Fortunately, there was a bus stop within walking distance.

Suzanne's makeshift bedroom looked over the woodland at the back of the house, and, before getting into bed, she could not resist leaning out of the window and gazing, absent-mindedly, over the birches that stretched away in front of her, finishing on a dark line of conifers that formed part of the main forest plantation. Set right in the centre of all this – was a magnificent mature oak. It towered overall, silhouetted in the fading light. She was naked and welcomed the slight cool breeze on her skin.

A strange noise interrupted the late evening bird song and silenced it at once. It was like an enormous hiss, but with the simultaneous addition of a lower note, making it feel sinister. It came from somewhere deep in the forest. Then there was silence for a while, before the birds started to sing again. Suzanne wanted to go and ask her brother what it was, but tiredness and the inclination to leave them alone, won. She climbed into bed and instant drowsiness put the strange occurrence, for the time being, out of her mind.

CHAPTER THREE

"THERE IS SOMETHING THAT BOTHERS ME."

Tea with Julia proved a pleasurable experience for Christine and Suzanne. The lady lived in a typical period Hampshire house complete with a tall chimney. The red tiled roofing and dark sanguine coloured bricks of the building were a perfect complement to a well-tended cottage-style garden. They ate dainty cucumber sandwiches and drank Earl Grey tea.

The next day, in the sitting room at Beech Cottage, Christine and Suzanne were putting the finishing touches to the doors, window frames and skirting boards with cream gloss paint. Tim was due at any moment to join them for lunch.

His new employment as a geologist was, so far, all that he had hoped for. Currently, they were working with a small team establishing ground geological details for a major engineering construction site near Cheltenham.

Currently, he was on his way home. As he drove the Morris over the hill by Olivers Battery, admiring the countryside around him; he gazed, with appreciation, at this stretch of road and its open fields pulling away in both directions. The long hedgerows made it easy for an artist's eye to take in the perspective; up over another hill, round a couple of bends and he entered the rural community of Crowsley. After passing through this village, he turned sharp right and followed the road for a couple of miles before a gradual climb brought him to Yewhurst. The Claymans Heron hotel lay on the left, with Beech Cottage lying three hundred yards further on the other side of the road.

It was not Tim's normal practice to come home at lunchtime but today was an important one in his calendar.

Christine had heard the car arrive and stood at the front door. Her old jeans and light blue denim shirt were now liberally covered in paint. This morning, she had managed to get even more than usual in her hair, due to starting the day by giving the sitting room ceiling its second coat with the aid of a roller. She never could manage to prevent it spattering in specs all over her head, arms and shoulders.

Tim came through the gate casually spinning a packet in his right hand. His wife grinned sheepishly at him. "Happy birthday, darling," he said, and deposited a kiss firmly on her lips.

At breakfast time, he had been grilled in an attempt to pressure him into telling her just what this present was. Tim had to explain that it would not be available until mid-morning. Although he had arranged to collect the item in time, a minor alteration had been necessary.

Suzanne had brought her mother and father's present for Christine, plus her own with her, but a few more, together with several birthday cards had arrived with the postman during the morning. Christine was blessed with many relations, and, also, quite a few friends from school and college days.

She studied his face and crinkled up her nose. Tim handed her the gift-wrapped parcel. They passed through into the front room and Christine set about tearing off the decorative paper. She came to a medium sized, dark red velvet box. "My! – What is this?" she said. She pulled open the lid on its hinges and there, nestling inside on white satin was a beautiful amethyst pendant. "Tim! It must have cost a fortune!"

"Just a bit," said Tim in a warm tone. "Let's just say, it's special. That is – it's special to me." He gave no further explanation.

She looked into his eyes before giving him a firm embrace. Then Tim took the pendant out of the box and placed it around her neck. "There you are. The best turned-out decorator in the business."

Just then Suzanne entered the room. "Let's see?" she demanded, curiously. "My goodness – isn't that lovely?" she said staring at the amethyst. "Oh Christine, it ... really suits you." After admiring herself wearing it in a mirror, the birthday girl put it back in its box, stroking the velvet as she closed the lid, a smile of pleasure on her face.

They all tucked into sandwiches and salad prepared by Suzanne, then relaxed for a short while; the girls approving their own handywork before Tim had to return to his office.

Not far away, a young woodpecker was practising his, rather late in the year, courtship display. High in a towering beech tree, on a branch under young pale green translucent leaves, he drummed his beak faster than the human eye could follow, sending the rapid rat-tat-a-tat sounds

The Shy Avenger   Scardthomas

deep into the forest for as far as a quarter of a mile. He was a splendid, great spotted male with his plumage of black, red and white. It would take something very unusual for him to stop what he was doing. It did. The loud hammering ceased abruptly. A movement low down on an old yew tree, adjacent to the beech caught the bird's eye. What he saw was not so much unusual in itself: it was the atmosphere that suffused at the same time, causing the bird to crouch and close his wings fast to his body. He stayed like that for a full minute, watching – with a steadfast gaze.

The strange being completed the climb up the gnarled yew trunk and commenced a traverse along a branch; glimpses of its body were shown to the observing bird in between obscuring dark green foliage. Enough: silently, the woodpecker lifted off – and flew away.

At about half past four in the afternoon, the door knocker sounded. Suzanne was having a well-earned soak in the bath while Christine was writing a letter to her mother. She rose and went to the door, still in her painting clothes. Standing politely on the doorstep was a man dressed in grey trousers and wearing a short sleeve clergy shirt.

"How-do-you-do? Paul Sanders, I am the vicar for the parish of Yewhurst. Thought I would call and welcome you to our village."

Christine's first reaction was to gape at this man smiling at her over his white clerical collar. He looked considerably younger than his age and possessed a ruddy complexion with a neat, angular nose. His eyebrows were dark and trimmed. It was only in his hair that his true years could be discerned, for there were tinges of grey across the temples, and flecks showing against the darker tones all over the top of his head. His blue eyes and gently smiling mouth took in the picture of the girl on the doorstep before him. She recovered herself. "Hello. Please excuse my appearance," she greeted him with a quiet chuckle in her voice.

"Oh – I will take you as I find you. I expect you have a lot to do." It was not a question, but a statement of fact.

"Christine Westward," she said offering her hand.

He exhibited a warm smile and Christine found herself taking to this well-mannered member of the Church immediately. "Julia Thornton was telling me of your meeting with her last Sunday."

"Oh yes. She very kindly asked us to tea." This was the first time Christine had heard the lady's full name. "We went to see her yesterday at her cottage."

"Ah, so you are getting to know the neighbourhood?"

"I think they call that part of Yewhurst – Chapp – don't they?"

"Yes. You will find all the little hamlets around here have names, whether they are attached to a village or not." The conversation swung, accordingly, through the locality and finished with Paul asking about Christine's husband and his line of work.

Suzanne appeared, refreshed from her bath, and wearing clean casual clothes. She had on a white blouse and her shoulder length black hair shone audaciously against it. Her endearing face made Paul beam at her. She was just in time to be introduced to him before he left. "One more visit to make: the old chap who looks after the churchyard isn't well, so I must pop in and see him and his wife. Talking of wives, I'd better get a move on, or I will be in the doghouse when I get back to the vicarage."

Soon, the vicar departed walking in the direction of the church along the pavement by the road. Shortly afterwards, while the two girls were still standing by the open front door, they heard a commotion coming from that direction. Overhanging trees on a bend obscured the exact cause. They went to investigate. After rounding the bend, they found themselves witnessing a strange spectacle, which was taking place some one hundred yards ahead of them.

Situated on the pathway running parallel to the road, old Ma Hessil was standing, wobbly legs astride, with her arms held as high above her head as her stooped shoulders would allow. In her right hand was a worn, gnarled stick. The old woman was facing the forest and shouting at the top of her voice in a high-pitched tone. "So, yer've cum baack Jahn! Oi knew it! Oi knew na that there be na rain fer the paast month! But yer can't finish it can yer. Yer wan' us to live darn you. Oi curse yer Jahn! Oi curses yer as yer cursed Oi! Damn yer! Damn yer." Her pitiful screeching gradually died away until she dropped her stick and bent her tired old head into her shoulders, sobbing continuously.

Paul Sanders was by her side trying to console her. The two girls went towards them at an unsure pace. The vicar put an arm around the distressed lady's shoulder and started to whisper something to her. By the time Christine and Suzanne arrived the sobbing had become more muted.

Suzanne noticed a black Cocker spaniel lying with its eyes closed against some new growth of bracken. She gasped at the sight. The animal looked so utterly vulnerable. Suzanne knelt by the dog. Its hair was unkempt. She could not take her eyes off the sad-looking face. "Be careful; Mrs Hessil says a snake has bitten it," said the vicar quickly. The warning went totally unheeded. She was one of those many women whose maternity instinct over-rode caution. Placing her hands under the dog's body, she raised it up and cradled the lifeless form in her arms.

"What's up?" Christine recognised her husband's voice. He had just arrived home and had come to investigate practically following his wife and sister.

"Hello darling … A snake has bitten this lady's dog," she informed him.

Tim took in the scene. He noted the strange old woman who had spoken to them on their first day. The man by her side, he did not know, but spotting the clergy shirt thought he might be the local vicar. Christine quickly introduced her husband so that they could attend to more urgent matters.

"Let me accompany you home," said the vicar, helping Ma Hessil to stand upright.

Christine gave Tim a familiar, prompting look. "Where does the lady live?" he asked.

"In the centre of the village," answered Paul. "About quarter of a mile – if that."

"I'll get my car along the road – opposite. It won't take a minute."

"Ah, thank you." Paul glanced in the direction they had to go. "Meantime, we will make our way to meet you," he added. Tim nodded and went off at a run. Paul, with his arm supporting Ma Hessil, slowly led the way over the rough terrain towards the road. Christine picked up the old lady's stick and Suzanne followed behind, still cradling the dog.

It only took Tim a few minutes to drive the Morris down to the most accessible point. Now came the tricky problem of getting the troubled woman into the back of the car, but they managed, and Paul climbed in beside her.

Suddenly Ma Hessil began rambling. "T'is staarted agin, t'is staarted agin."

The vicar attempted to comfort her. "Now, now – there is nothing to worry about – we'll get you ...."

"Tha be everthin' ter worry abaat," she pleaded. "Yer must stop 'in! Some'un 'as got to kill 'in, an' make sure he be burnt to ashes this toime." She looked appealingly at the vicar. "Tis ne good. You dun believe ... Will no un tak 'eed? Oh, me God." Then she began to sob again.

Suzanne placed the spaniel on the front passenger seat as gently as she could. She leant over and whispered in her brother's ear. "I think it's dead." Tim looked at his sister's face. There was an unashamed single tear falling down her right cheek. He was used to her sentimentality in certain situations. Considering this was the first time she had seen the dog, it had to be one of those times – but – that was the way she was.

Christine retrieved Ma Hessil's stick and passed it through to the rear of the car. Tim nodded to his wife. "Be back soon," and after checking that the road was clear, drove off.

With the vicar's guidance he located Ma Hessil's cottage and parked outside. They both helped the old woman indoors, who was now passively silent. The character of the house immediately struck Tim. It had been built over a hundred years ago. The ceilings were incredibly low, to the extent that both men, being fairly tall, had difficulty moving about. After placing Ma Hessil in a chair of her choice they went outside for a discussion.

"I don't think there is any point calling a vet," said Paul. "The dog is obviously dead." Tim agreed and they both decided to ask her what she would like done with the body.

Eventually, Paul broached the subject with Ma Hessil. "Yerd better lay 'im in shed at bottom of gardin," she said, tearfully. "Oi'll get moi nephew ter bury 'im later. "Well – one thin' for sure – he can't tae nuttin' else offer me, cause Oi ain't got nuttin' else to tak." The old lady paused for breath and placed her hand on the vicar's arm. "If you wouldn't mind doin' that for me, Oi'd be most grateful. Oi'll be alright after thaat."

Tim found an old blanket in the small rickety garden shed and laid the dog's body out between some flowerpots, on what looked to be a perfectly dry wooden floor. No doubt Ma Hessil would make her own emotional visit later.

Back in the lady's front room, Tim found himself next to a mantelpiece, which had a few small frames containing sepia-coloured photographs arranged along it. He noticed that some of them appeared to be of a boy going through the stages of growing up. In the middle of the collection was a larger photograph, framed in the black and gilt Hogarth style, of a young man in army uniform. The soldier was displaying a wide and very cheerful looking smile. 'Was this, perhaps, her late husband?' thought Tim.

Shortly afterwards, as the men were getting ready to leave, Tim could not resist asking her. "Did you see the snake actually bite your dog, Mrs Hessil?"

"Na, but Oi see'd 'im go. It were John alright. He 'ould 'ave attacked from the skoi thaat's for sure." Tim did not have the remotest idea what she meant by that.

After ascertaining that the old woman was comfortable, or at least in a sufficiently calm state to be left alone, the two men departed. Outside, Paul thanked Tim for his help and then asked him if he had heard about John the Red?

"John the Red. So that is the beast's full title. Yes. My wife and sister were told about it. Mid nineteen-forties – I believe?"

"Yes. Look …I feel it would be wise not to mention this to anyone. If this episode gets out, the terrible fear that swept the neighbourhood just after the last war will begin again. Especially as that story started with the death of a dog by snakebite – and a spaniel at that! But still – I won't plaque you with any more details just now – you'll be anxious to get home. However, my point is this; I should be wary who you talk to about this. We can't stop the old lady spreading rumours, but I'd rather not compound the problem."

"There is something that bothers me," said Tim. "The dog could survive an adder bite, surely?"

"We only have Ma Hessil's word for it that there was some kind of snake 'attack', as she calls it. Perhaps the dog pounced onto it? Perhaps it was a figment of her imagination? Who knows? There again – the dog *was* getting on in years. Maybe it had a heart condition."

"I see," commented Tim. "Anyway, I won't hinder you now. I'm sure my wife and sister will be wondering where I've got to. Oh, and I'll tell them 'mum's the word'," he finished, putting a vertical finger to his mouth. "It was nice to meet you, Vicar." He held out his hand.

"Paul – and you likewise Tim – thank you again," he said, returning the handshake. Paul declined a lift. It was only a short walk to the vicarage, and he still had that one last visit to make.

Back at the cottage, Tim brought Christine and Suzanne up to date.

"What about this John the Red business," commented Christine. "How does it affect things today?"

"Maybe there is a larger than usual adder with a more venomous bite – out there," ventured Suzanne.

"Look – whatever it is – please promise me that you won't go walking in those woods without boots on," Tim blurted out.

Suzanne blew a raspberry at him. "Haven't got any."

"Well buy some. I'm serious. Please!"

"Oh Tim – in this weather?" Christine joined in.

"Please, just until we get to the bottom of the matter. Suzanne can wear that old pair of yours. You both have the same shoe size – don't you?"

"Oh, all right, if it makes you happy," said Christine.

CHAPTER FOUR

"I MAY BE ABLE TO HELP YOU THERE."

After a supper of gammon, new potatoes and runner beans with a cheese sauce, Tim and the girls decided to walk over to the Claymans Heron for a drink.

It was a bright, beautiful early summer evening and the air felt pure as they strolled along the path by the road, before crossing over opposite the hotel. Being early June the new leaves on the trees still had a green luminosity, and the tall deciduous beech, oak and chestnut showed off their new coats to full effect. It was Suzanne with her youthful zest for all things lovely who remarked, "I don't think I have ever seen trees looking so gorgeous before. Is it something to do with this part of the country?"

"No idea," said Christine. "But I agree. Aren't we lucky Tim – to have all this?"

"Bit of an improvement on the Purley Way," he muttered, dryly. At the entrance to the main bar, Tim held open one of the double doors and said to his sister. "Your round Suz. I'll have a champagne cocktail."

"Get stuffed," was the reply. "You'll have a beer and lump it," Suzanne countered with a tight expression on her face.

"That's nice," he turned and grinned at his wife. "Actually, can I have a pint of lager with lime? I need something to quench a thirst: must be the gammon." They all agreed, and Suzanne ordered the drinks from the uniformed barman. Then they took their beverages over to a booth with an adjacent double open window.

The Claymans Heron hotel, restaurant and pub was one of the largest thatched roof buildings in the country. It had the appearance of a giant coaching inn. Set well back from the road to allow for a generous gravelled car park, it possessed a magnificent frontage of white rendered brick and a massive roof. The first-floor windows peaked out of the thatch to finish off the effect.

Suzanne's attention was caught by a handsome man with wide shoulders and dark hair walking along the footpath beyond the hotel car park. A magnificent collie, head held high, was a little way in front. Glancing back at the man, Suzanne felt the end of her toes curl sensually as she studied his tall, athletic physique, and long lean striding legs. Christine gave her a secret kick under the table. They shared a soft knowing giggle, which escaped Tim who was concentrating on the thirst-quenching satisfaction he was getting from his pint of beer.

Christine lowered her chin and cradled her birthday pendant. "I do love this," she said, twiddling it about to catch the light.

"So do I!" said Suzanne. "I am so amazed at my brother's taste. It's usually rubbish."

"I shall treat that remark with the contempt it deserves," said Tim peevishly. Secretly, he was overjoyed at his wife's pleasure with his gift. A sudden memory flashed into his mind: the first time they met. He had gone to a tennis club dance while staying with some friends near Guildford, and there she was – sitting at a table, fingering a brooch and wearing a plain mid-blue, summer cotton dress, similar to that which she had on now. He had not been able to take his eyes of her.

Fortunately, one of his friends arranged an introduction. He will never know what gave him the courage to ask her out: whether it was the effect of alcohol, or, as he believed, nature prompting. Anyway, he had been even more amazed when she accepted, so much so that he forgot to pick up the beermat on which he had written her phone number. His friend did not know her surname and the receptionist at the tennis club was not very helpful. Fortunately, just two weeks later the same friend ran into someone who knew where she lived. Luckily for him, she was still keen. Over a period of two years, they had seen each other whenever possible while Tim was home from university, and, a couple of times, Christine had gone to Edinburgh for a weekend to visit him. Finally, after Tim graduated with his degree, he proposed to her while staying with his parents in Somerset. They got married four months later.

Suzanne decided to liven things up, "Happy birthday!" she announced and raised her glass. Immediately, her brother did likewise,

The Shy Avenger   Scardthomas

except that he started to sing, "Happy birth…" That was as far as he got before Christine silenced him with a well-aimed kick on the shin, and the song turned into a cry of pain. Christine hated having attention drawn to herself, publicly, on her birthday.

"Bad luck Tim, a couple more bars and I would have been with you." Suzanne grinned impishly at Christine.

"That's okay," said Tim, rubbing his bruised leg. "Wait for the cake! I've asked them to light the candles before they bring it over." This was Tim all over – he could not resist a tease when he should know better.

"Tim! You haven't ordered a cake!" Christine appealed desperately. "I'll murder you!"

"Might have."

Christine narrowed her eyelids. She pointed an accusing finger. "You! … Tell me you haven't … please!"

"Might have."

"Right – I'm going home," and she made as if to get to her feet.

"All right – all right – only kidding." Tim gave her a pleading smile and she looked mightily relieved.

"Stop teasing me you two. Whose birthday is it anyway?"

"Okay. Okay. Sorriee…" said Suzanne. Her brother just smirked.

Inevitably the talk drifted back to Ma Hessil and her unfortunate pet dog. "What was its name?" asked Suzanne. She directed her question at Tim.

"I wondered that," he replied. "Ma Hessil never referred to it by a name."

Like Suzanne, Christine had a common distaste of most reptiles and some large insects, but something fascinated her about this matter. "Why John the Red?" she suddenly asked.

From the next table booth behind her, a man's voice disturbed their privacy. "I may be able to help you there." The voice belonged to a gentleman who was peering at them in an agitated manner. "Forgive me for intruding but I couldn't help overhearing." He rose to his feet, a man of lowly height, and came around to their table. He was dressed in a herringbone suit and as it was exceptionally warm, carried the jacket. The knot in his maroon tie had been pulled down and the top button of his shirt was undone. His face was a little flushed from the heat. He had a fair complexion, creased by time, with a full head of blond hair, which did not appear to have a trace of grey in it. His eyes were pale blue, and they gave off a feeling of penetrating alertness. The eyebrows were not immediately visible due to their bleached appearance. His nose was large and bulbous, seemingly out of proportion to the narrow lines of his lips. "I am a – now retired – vet," he said, raising an arm almost apologetically. "I know quite a lot about John the Red."

Christine was a friendly soul. She would talk to most people, trusting to her instinct of first appearances to get the measure of them. "Oh good," she said. "You can help us clear up the mystery, and then we won't have to wear boots while walking in the woods."

The Shy Avenger   Scardthomas

"Boots in the woods?" queried the man – a slight frown on his face.

Tim looked at Christine who gave him a cheeky half smile in return. Then he explained how he had asked his wife and sister to be careful when walking in the forest, due to recent events.

The man did not query this. He told them that he used to have a veterinary practice in Eastleigh, and how he had been consulted in the summer of 1947. This was in connection with a dog that had been killed. "I'll tell you the facts," he said. "That is if you have the time. I'll be as brief as I can."

"As long as it's not too much trouble?" said Christine.

"I hope it's not gruesome," remarked Suzanne. "At the rate things are going, I shall be seeing snakes behind every bush!"

The stranger introduced himself as, "Allen Haddle," and indicated with his left hand the space at the end of their table. "Of course," said Tim jumping up to locate a chair and then letting him know their names in return.

Allen put his jacket over the back of the chair and retrieved his drink, a long whisky and soda. Seating himself he said, "Well now, it was May 1947 ... we were enjoying a glorious spring I remember. My wife and I are very fond of walking, so we took full advantage of the dry weather. There are some lovely routes around about, whether you like open farmland or woodland; it is all in the immediate vicinity. Anyway, I was at my practice one morning, going through the usual surgery routine, when a telephone call came in from a lady who lived not far from here. Do you know The Great Mile?" Tim looked at Christine and they both shook their heads. "Right at the other end of Yewhurst, heading towards Stockbridge, the road enters some woods at the top of a hill. It bends round to the left, and you find yourself in a sort of giant tree tunnel, which goes straight as an arrow – for about a mile."

He paused to take a drink. "Right, where was Oi?" This was a momentary lapse into a Hampshire country dialect, which seemed out of character. "Oh yes, the telephone call. Well, it appeared their Springer spaniel was very ill, and would I come and have a look? Their six-year-old daughter found it lying prostrate in the woods by the side of a lane. As luck would have it, I had to be in Stockbridge by lunchtime, so I said I would call as it was on the way. I got to their house about twelve o'clock.

When I arrived, a woman and three young children were there, all in a very distressed state. I'm afraid I wasn't able to alleviate their sadness. The dog was dead. I could not immediately determine the cause, so I asked permission to take the body off their hands. They agreed – reluctantly, I felt." Allen shifted in his chair.

"That evening in my surgery I carried out the post-mortem. Death was due to blood poisoning, easily recognisable by the blue-black colour showing beneath the animal's coat. It was not long before I discovered a worse area of discolouration on the dog's back. Also, there were penetration marks that looked – well – looked like fang bite incisions. Some snakes kill their prey by means of venom that attack the nervous system, which, in turn, paralyses those centres that control the heart and breathing mechanisms. However, not so the viper family, of which, the adder, our only poisonous snake, is one. Their venom attacks blood vessels. Now – even allowing for the fact that the dog had been bitten during the morning, it was not feasible that virtually the entire blood cell population of the animal's body would have been infected. Not from an adder bite. Yet it was. The evidence was before my very eyes." He took another drink, his throat becoming dry. Then he continued, a slight flicker under his right eye becoming noticeable. "I decided to get the blood analysed. It meant a trip to Southampton the next morning, but I had the result quickly." He paused for a moment to make sure that his next sentences would have the fullest effect. "Those results confirmed that the venom was that associated with the viper family of which the adder is a member. But it was of such an incredibly potent intensity that not even the North American rattlesnake could compare. I calculated that this venom would cause death in a dog, of average size, within a minute! In some cases, it would be considerably quicker than that!"

"And to a human being?" said Tim, almost in a whisper.

Allen gave a casual shrug of his shoulders before replying. "Half an hour – maybe less – but that is a guess. I'm not qualified to say." Christine and Suzanne visibly shuddered. Allen continued. "So, you can imagine the thoughts that ran through my mind. Here was inescapable proof that a snake possibly more deadly than anything known to mankind – was probably at large on The Great Mile."

"Heavens, what on earth did you do?" interrupted Christine.

"Good question," he said, pushing his hands out and away from him. "I informed every authority I could think of, local government, hospitals, the police, fire brigade – you name it. I was deeply concerned that the next victim might well be a person." Allen paused and sighed; a long, deep sigh that made both girls' frown. "It was to no avail, and I have to admit, as some very responsible officials pointed out, they did not really know just what they were looking for. Nothing had come to light in the immediate area where the attack took place. Nobody had seen the reptile, so no-one knew what it looked like. It might be similar in characteristics to our common adder. Naturally, there was no point in starting a panic, with the newspapers in on it and what have you. What did concern us was the extent of the problem. Was there only one snake possessing this deadly venom – or were there more?"

"What happened next?" Tim could not resist the interruption.

"The following Sunday, a man was attacked by a snake on The Great Mile. Please note that I say *attacked*. This was not the usual – *trod on by mistake* – event. He and his family were having a picnic. They say he was dead before the ambulance arrived."

"Let me get you a drink," suggested Tim, getting up without apologising for stopping the flow of the tale. "I need one. What about you two?" He glanced towards his wife and sister. Both had at least half a pint left in their glasses and declined.

Allen offered up his glass. "Are you sure? That's – that's very civil…"

"Not at all. Whisky and soda?"

"Thank you … errm … Bells, if I may?"

"Okay. Could we have an interval while I'm at the bar?"

"Of course, dear fellow." So, while Tim was away, they indulged in small talk.

When he returned carrying the two drinks, Allen carried on. "About this poor chap who had been enjoying a family picnic. We now had a witness, the fellow's wife. She had suffered the horrible experience of seeing the whole thing. Three interesting facts came from this. One, the snake attacked from a tree. This would explain how the spaniel had come to have fang marks on its back. She stated that she had seen the thing land on her husband's back, and that it appeared to have launched itself from the oak tree they were seated under."

Suzanne could not resist it. "Better get us some hard hats Tim. Boots won't be much use." The two women laughed.

"Ha, ha," chuckled Allen showing a line of false upper teeth as he smiled. He continued, "Secondly, the snake was bright red. Thirdly, it was about four feet long."

"Ah – John the Red!" said Suzanne. "But it doesn't explain the reason for 'John'?"

"There you have me," said Allen. "The term came into being the following year. Started by some woman in the village – I believe."

"I think we have met her," interjected Christine. "Would it, by any chance, be a lady who goes by the name of – Hessil?"

"No – no, no, I can't recall her name. Anyway, she died about fifteen years ago. Now – the only thing *this* snake probably had in common with our native adder was the layout of its fangs. I'll explain that further. A viper does not need to actually bite its victims – more of a stab really. May I demonstrate, and he made to take hold of Suzanne's wrist?"

"Oh, of course," she held out her arm – not at all sure what was coming.

"Right," Allen paused and held up the thumb and fingers of his right hand in the rough shape of a snake's head. Then he simulated opening the jaw by dropping his thumb. "Non-Viper," and he closed the shape all the way over Suzanne's wrist. Releasing the grip, he said "Viper," and with crooked thumb and forefinger, this time only opening them up an inch, stabbed the result at her arm. "You see the fangs of most snakes are at the back of their mouths, but in the case of the viper, they are nearer the front… Got it?" They all nodded. Suzanne resisted the desire to rub the area of contact. "Two other things were odd about this incident. Although a viper will always be ready to strike, it does not deliberately do so, preferring to avoid man if possible. In this case, it appears, it aggressively attacked having no regard for its own safety. We did consider the possibility that the husband had disturbed a nest of young, but there was no evidence to back it up. Secondly, it struck from above, a practice unheard of by an adder."

"Couldn't the snake have simply fallen from the tree?" asked Tim.

"Not according to the widow. She, quite clearly, was convinced that an attack was launched upon her husband, and don't forget the dog was presumably struck from above as well." Allen took a long drink from his glass. "Now, nothing else happened until the early summer of the following year. A young boy, only ten years old, was found dead by the side of his bicycle, not far from where the picnicker had met his end. The same powerful venom was the cause. This was very sad. A lovely lad – you know – the cheerful sort. Always had a smile for you. He was from the same family who lost their dog. They moved away after the tragedy. Who could blame them?" Allen made a small cough to clear his throat.

"How dreadful!" exclaimed Christine. They were all beginning to find the whole thing depressing.

"It finally sparked officialdom into action. A hunt was carried out from one end of the mile to the other. But they found absolutely nothing. No trace of snakes, not even the common adder. Some busy body ordered a few trees, in the prime area, to be cut down and thoroughly examined. It was to no avail. Think they had a giant bonfire after that."

"What for?" asked Tim.

"To scare the thing away. Couldn't see the point of it myself. Didn't solve the problem, and now we didn't know where it was. And sure enough, about a month later, a courting couple were killed not far from here actually…"

"Now – that was Ma Hessil's son, wasn't it?" interrupted Christine.

"Yes – how do you know that?"

"Do you know Julia …Thornton, I think her surname is?" she replied.

"Yes – I have attended to her cats on a few occasions. She has lived in Yewhurst for longer than I can remember. She told you, did she? I didn't think she liked talking about John the Red."

"We rather got that impression," agreed Suzanne.

"The tragedy of Peter Hessil and young Susie Maybourne was quite terrible. A young couple, out courting on a summer's evening and to die like that! Awful business! A couple of days later, a fellow who was co-owner of the farmland claimed to have killed the snake, and there were several witnesses. Apparently, he chopped a large red snake in half with an axe when it was about to attack his wife. They say it landed on the ground – having flown down from a tree. One of the witnesses said it had wings of a sort along its body. Trouble was, there was no definite proof. No body. Just the stories. However, that was the last attack and there have been no sightings since: one or two rumours, particularly during heat waves. As for instance – it appears – now. What was that you were saying about Mrs Hessil's dog?" Tim told him all that they knew about the lady's Cocker spaniel. When he had finished Allen said, "Perhaps I ought to try and get a look at that dog."

Tim thought for a moment before saying, "To be honest, I would not like to be the one to ask. Why don't you have a chat with the vicar?"

"I will," said Allen, positively. "What does he think about Ma Hessil's story?"

"Doesn't believe in the snake attack bit – I know that," replied Tim.

"I don't suppose – when you buried the dog that you noticed any skin discoloration under its hair anywhere?" Allen asked.

"No – but I wasn't looking for anything like that, and it was a *black* dog."

"Good heavens! You don't think there is something serious to be alarmed about, do you?" Christine asked, looking perturbed.

"The original John the Red, even if it wasn't killed by the farmer would be what?" Allen appeared to make a hurried calculation in his head shutting one eye, "Twenty-eight years old ... I don't think so," he said with a smirk on his face. They all laughed at this. "However, I think it my duty to check into the matter. It was fortunate I overheard your conversation."

"When you picked up the animal you didn't notice anything unusual did you Suz?" asked Christine looking at her sister-in-law.

"No – all I remember," she replied, "is that sad little face. It is something I shall never forget."

Allen looked at her. "Of-course dear – don't bother about it."

"There is a little matter that *bothers* me," said Tim. "I did say to the vicar – we would keep this afternoon's event to ourselves."

"Don't worry," said Allen. "I'll have a word with him. I know Paul Sanders very well. Now I must be going," he said, casting an eye at his watch. "I'm sure you good people have far more cheerful matters to talk about – such as, for instance, someone's birthday." As he said this, he smiled at Christine. "Happy birthday, my dear."

She coloured slightly and said a muted, "Thank you." Tim and Suzanne grinned.

"Just one thing," quickly asked Suzanne before Allen rose from his seat. "What sort of noise, if any, did this snake – John the Red make?"

Tim eyed his sister sideways. 'Strange question,' he thought.

Suzanne was almost embarrassed by the direct stare Allen gave her in response. "I really do not know. You mean a hiss – the warning. That is the only noise adders make," he finally said.

Suzanne gave a slight nod regretting asking the question. "It was really super meeting you."

"Likewise, likewise," said Allen looking at them all in turn, then he rose and left, muttering a goodbye to a member of staff behind the bar.

They talked of other things for a while before deciding to make their way home. On the way back, Christine blurted out. "Well – Mr John the Red isn't going to spoil my opinion of this countryside, or our new home." She took her husband's arm.

"No fear!" agreed Tim.

Suzanne suddenly felt devilment come over her. She waited until

Tim unhooked his arm from Christine to jump a ditch, and then pitched into him at exactly the right moment. Seconds later, Tim was lying in the bottom of the ditch. It was the sort of thing she had done to her brother when the opportunity presented itself from the age of seven or eight onwards. She knew it thoroughly annoyed him. He rose, cursing with an old catkin hanging from one ear, and a glint of anger in his eyes. Suzanne shrieked with laughter and ran for it. Tim clambered out of the ditch and tore after his sister shouting abuse. Unfortunately for her, she was not gifted at running fast and Tim caught up with her before she made it back to the cottage. The result was that she was unceremoniously picked up and dumped in a pile of dead grass cuttings. Christine laughed out loud at the spectacle of her sister-in-law attempting to remove bits of hay from her clothing and hair. "I'll get you for that, Timothy!" she spluttered.

"Oh, come now, you deserved it," said Tim. "Call it quits." Suzanne made a face and followed them inside.

CHAPTER FIVE

WHERE THE JOY OF NOW HAD BEEN BORN.

On the following Sunday evening, after their supper, Tim, Christine and Suzanne decided to take a stroll along one of the lanes they had not yet explored. An old school friend of Tim's and his girlfriend had called on them for the afternoon. They were on their way to the West Country and had pre-arranged the visit. Both were very complimentary about Beech Cottage, and Tim's friend muttered something about him being, "A lucky so and so," just before they left.

Crossing over the road the three of them started down a wide gravel lane. There were a few large houses in evidence set well back with ample front gardens.

They were about to discover that the top of this lane was a place where frequent chance meetings took place between local residents. Not only was it a favourite crossing place to Yewhurst Wood used by dog owners, or others enjoying its recreation, but, also, it adjoined an entrance drive to the Claymans Heron pub and restaurant.

By the gate of the first domestic residence, which was located close to the road, a man and woman were approaching a pristine looking Jaguar saloon car. They were saying their goodbyes to a gentleman whom they all recognized, Allen Haddle. He spotted Tim and the girls.

"Hello!" he greeted them.

"Hello," returned Tim followed by Christine and Suzanne. They hung back from the gate not wishing to intrude as they made to pass bye. Allen was just about to open it to let his guests out. He decided to introduce them to the new village residents.

Dr David Andrews and his wife Dorothy were both in their early fifties and in good health. For a country doctor, David did not exactly look the part. Today, he wore black trousers, black patent leather shoes and a crisp white shirt. Beneath his blond fringe were exceptionally large silver spectacles. Dorothy, however, did look more like a rural doctor's spouse. She wore a light summer tweed skirt with a subtle green blouse. Before introductions could be made, Allen's wife, Jean, appeared from the passage that ran down by the side of their garage. Jean Haddle was an absolute joy to know, possessing an infectious jubilant personality. She was delighted to be meeting the new young occupants of Beech Cottage. Tim thought he could detect the lilt of a slight Welsh dialect. Nobody seemed to be in any kind of hurry, and they all stood around chatting by the gate enjoying the early summer evening. Eventually, the subject got onto the weather, and why they were having this remarkable tropical spell.

"I was talking to a meteorologist the other day," said the doctor. He possessed a pleasant voice with good diction and a confident manner. "The fellow was telling me – an anticyclone came in from Europe some time ago, lingered over us for a couple of weeks, then drifted back towards the Baltic Sea. Apparently, it changed its mind and came back again for another visit."

"Great stuff," said Tim with a chuckle.

"And to whom are you regaling with your crackpot theories," said a strange, deep-toned voice out of nowhere. It belonged to a man who looked as though he had just been enjoying a strong beverage in the Claymans Heron. He was middle-aged, portly; dressed in baggy canvas trousers and a mildly grubby cream shirt. Despite untidy greying hair, the broad smile on his countenance more than made up for it. Dark blue eyes twinkled at the same time. He puffed enthusiastically at a cigar.

"Thomas – good evening!" David Andrews answered. "And where have you been?" he accused, ignoring the criticism directed at him.

"Mind your own bloody business," was the abrupt reply. Suzanne noticed there was dry mirth in his tone. Also, he seemed familiar.

"I suppose I had better introduce you to this *gentleman*," said David with an undisguised but friendly hint of sarcasm. You had to give the doctor credit. He got all their names right, even though he had only just met them. Thomas Hurn was an actor. He was the type of thespian whose face would be recognized all over the country, employed mostly on the small screen. Christine recalled seeing him in a part he had played in a television series a few years earlier, which she had very much enjoyed, and she said so. Thomas was obviously delighted in the flattery, even though he had been praised for that performance many times and had won several awards.

A little dark tortoiseshell coloured cat appeared from nowhere and started rubbing up against Suzanne's legs. The cat chose the right person, probably by instinct. Suzanne knelt to stroke the animal and it made dainty four-footed leaps accompanied by little mew sounds in acknowledgement. "That's Beam," said Jean with enthusiasm. "Lives next door – she's a poppit."

"Our new neighbours have had an encounter with old Mrs Hessil," said Allen.

"Talking about that …" Tim was reminded of something. "Did she give you permission to dig up her dog?"

"Err; I'd rather not discuss that. I'm surprised the whole village didn't hear," said Allen in an exasperated tone. "When I went to see her, she shouted and screamed at me as soon as I made the request. Went and on and on exclaiming 'farcts be farcts' – sorry, can't do her accent very well. Told me to believe her for a change."

David Andrews had been made aware of the happenings involving Ma Hessil, from Allen, but Thomas had not. "And what is all this about?" he enquired. Tim suddenly remembered about his pact with Paul Sanders, when he gave his word that he would keep the incident of Ma Hessil's dog to himself.

Allen read it in his face. "It's all right Tim. I've spoken to our vicar."

"Oh … thank you. Did he understand?"

"Absolutely – there isn't a problem as long as it's kept among responsible people."

"Well – that rules out Thomas," David jumped in. The two of them frequently entered into this sort of banter when they met.

"Thank you," said the offended man. "However, I am bursting with curiosity, so I am sorry." He pointed two outstretched fingers with a crooked thumb at David. "If you don't tell me, I'll shoot you between the eyes."

"Oh – all right," said the unarmed man. "But I think these good folk had best tell you." He beckoned at the three new arrivals. Between them they told him of their encounter with Ma Hessil and about the unfortunate death of her dog.

When they had finished, Thomas asked them all if they had ever read the poem about the events of 1947 and 1948. David and Dorothy had, Allen and Jean said they hadn't. The Westwards, obviously, were ignorant of the poem's very existence. Apparently, it appeared on the scene in the shape of a few foolscap copies sometime after the snake attacks of 1948. The author was unknown. Thomas, on the appropriateness of the moment, asked them if they would all like to come and hear him recite it.

"Sounds fascinating," said Suzanne. David and his wife looked at each other. Neither of them could see any reason to depart just yet, and the Haddles agreed that tasks waiting for them at home could be done later. Thomas beckoned for them all to accompany him. Beam followed a little of the way before turning to go under the gate where her owners lived.

The actor's house was the last but one along the lane, fronted by a mature beech hedge with a large wooden five-bar gate opening onto a tarmac drive, which was liberally dotted with clumps of weeds that had burst through. It sloped sharply down to the house. Built in the 1950's, the dwelling had a veranda style porch and the deep red brickwork expanded out on both sides, with a low-tiled roof that dipped over the first-floor windows. A garage built in natural round cuts of chestnut stood on the right. It did not look as though it was used to shelter a vehicle. There were two skylight windows in the roof and the door was very substantial with what looked like an expensive Chubb locking system. Thomas showed them in through his front door, which had been left unlocked.

"You're very trusting," remarked David.

"Left the radio on," said Thomas as though that was quite sufficient explanation. "Now – first of all – who would like a coffee?" Judging by the general affirmations it seemed most of them did.

"Let us make it for you Thomas," said Jean. Take the men into the lounge and we will be along soon." This was not as strange as it might sound. A few years ago, Jean had been very friendly with Thomas's wife before she passed away, suddenly, after suffering a rare form of cancer. Subsequently, she had frequently comforted the thespian, who had remained in a profound and deep grief for some time.

"Oh – thank you Jean," said a grateful Thomas. "I'll entertain your men folk in the meantime."

Jean beckoned to Dorothy, Christine and Suzanne to follow her and she led the way off to the left-hand side of the hallway, flanked on both sides by framed black and white photographs of Thomas performing in well-known dramas, through to a large farmhouse style kitchen.

This was a big house for someone who lived alone. Thomas showed the three men into his lounge. It ran the full width of the house, with a good-sized fireplace in the centre of the outer wall. He went up to an old-style radiogram and turned it off. Music that had been playing as they entered the room abruptly stopped. French windows looked out over a back garden of about a quarter of an acre. Unusually, it was still laid out in the same design as that used during the Second World War.

There was very little ornamental about it. The two glass doors opened out onto a rough patio area. Right in the middle of the garden lay a lawn, which was virtually square. On one side of this lawn was a line of Coxes apple trees, and on the other, strawberry plants under protective netting. At the back of the lawn stood an orchard with cooking and sweet apples, damson and Victoria plum trees. Deep into the rear, on the left, was a fruit cage housing raspberries, red and black currant bushes, gooseberries and some others that harvested the very best blackberries. The whole garden finished in a copse of ancient yew trees.

Thomas opened the doors of the French windows. As his quests stood looking out, he urgently started to ascertain whether they would all like some of his special malt whisky, uttering something about it being wasted on women.

At that moment, Dorothy entered the room. The conversation stopped dead. She wished to find out how many of them would like coffee. Looking at the scene, she noticed Thomas's concealing air. "Interrupting something? What are you discussing?" she asked.

There was a short pause before Thomas uttered, "Budgerigars." Everyone looked nonplussed, none more so than Dorothy. "Thinking of getting one ..." Thomas added. In fact, it was one of the last things he wanted.

"Oh," said Dorothy and returned to the kitchen after learning that only three of them required a hot drink.

When the ladies came through to the lounge, with Christine carrying a green pot of freshly made coffee and Suzanne with a tray bearing cups and saucers, the four men were ensconced in easy chairs with a large glass of malt whisky in their hands, looking like Lords of the manor. Thomas invited the women to take seats saying, "Didn't think you would want any of this stuff. Bit rough you know. Can I get you something else, sherry, port or a liqueur?"

Dorothy and Jean said no, but Christine noticing the smug expression on her husband's face asked what liqueurs he had? "Green Chartreuse, which is probably not to your palette, but I tell you what, I do have some very nice cherry brandy." Both Christine and Suzanne agreed that would be lovely.

"How are you Thomas?" said David. "Haven't seen you for a while. Been getting the sun, I see."

"I've been enjoying this marvellous weather," the thespian answered. " I am a very lucky man. Resting, you see. So, I can take advantage of it." While Thomas located a couple of liqueur glasses and poured the girls their drinks, they discussed which part he would be playing next. This was of great interest to Christine and Suzanne. They were intrigued by his deep voice. It made him charismatic and was delivered marginally slower than normal speech. The cigar, although not finished, now lay dead in an ashtray. He held up an ugly carved pipe. "Any of you ladies object," he said with a raised eyebrow. No one did. Suzanne had the feeling that if anyone had, he would have carried on regardless. She confessed to liking the aroma of pipe tobacco.

After a few more minutes of general conversation, David invited Thomas to commence the reading. "Right," he said. He got up and went to the other end of the lounge where there was a splendid oak corner bureau. He pulled out two weight rests and lowered the lid. After studying the contents briefly, he said, "Hah, there it is," and took out some sheets of paper. Returning to his armchair, he switched on an angled overhead lamp, saying, "Just to provide the right atmosphere." He settled himself in his seat and made sure the papers were in the correct order. "When I first got a sight of this poem – I thought that it might have been written by someone – young – maybe a teenage boy. I don't think a girl. It is a poem without metre, although it does have a kind of rhythm."

All his guests waited in respectful silence. "The main title is John the Red, and it has an alternative title written underneath in brackets, The Red Adder of Yewhurst."

Dusk was starting to descend as Thomas placed his pipe in the ashtray and began to read in a slow, normally pitched voice:

"There is a straight mile of road run along by oak and beech each side,
That lies beyond Yewhurst Hill where the Red Adder does reside.
It was a hot summer's day and the snake lay high among the trees,
Looking down on mossy way through the pleasant myriad of leaves.
Tom, the spaniel, was padding softly along the path,
Easy walk for an old dog over the short aftermath.
(Thomas raised his voice.)
A flash of red cast through the air! It came from out of the sky,
And old Tom howled his last … then lay down to die."

The reader paused before continuing. Evening shadows had entered the room, the solitary light shining behind his head, created an eerie effect. This was a desperately sad tale and the atmosphere abruptly became leaden. Over the next twenty minutes, the frivolous feeling they had all enjoyed outside in the lane, vanished. Thomas read the rest of the fifteen verses, altering the pitch and depth of his thespian's voice to suit the writer's words. It was a story poem, and the actor, using his own interpretations, captured the drama perfectly.

He read through the events of 1947 and on to the next year: the awful killing of the young boy and the double tragedy of Peter Hessil and his fiancée. Essentially, the Red Adder ruined four families' lives.

Outside – night fell.

During the final verses, when the farmer known as Big Harry was trying to protect his wife, Lucy, the actor's voice became extremely loud at times. A quick glance from David towards the rest of the audience revealed Suzanne wide-eyed with three fingers of her right hand in her mouth. Christine was sitting bolt upright with whitened knuckles gripping the edge of the settee, and Tim was openly chewing his fingernails.

Thomas continued:

"At that time Lucy did not know what made her jump and start.
A dire feeling told her something evil was approaching lightening fast.
   (The reader's voice grew louder.)
She froze – rooted to the ground! John landed two feet away!
Her mind was in a daze and her body started to sway.
She tried to scream but her voice had gone, lost by shock and fear,
As John made to make the strike: her death was surely now so near.
   (Thomas Hurn started to literally shout.)
Out of the air, a mighty arm wielded the axe incisively true!
Crashing it to the ground! There lay John the Red – in two!"

Sounds of relief could be heard from the listeners. Still reading loudly but ceasing to shout Thomas started the last verse.

"A great cheer rose from the hill; it was heard for miles around.
The curious went out to meet the workers – homeward bound.
(Thomas lowered his voice and the depth of the tone seemed beyond human possibilities. He read slowly)
But Big Harry stopped and retraced his steps.
'Folk must see John's body,' he thought, 'face to face.
Then we'll be free from the dreaded viper we all feared.
We will burn him on this piece of land that we've just cleared.'
(The final two lines were read in a low but perfectly audible whisper.)
But – when he came up to the place where the joy of now had been born.
He gazed in disbelief ... for the two parts of John ... had gone."

It was not that the poem was of any great merit, and they were all familiar with the story; – it was the delivery that stunned them into an unnatural silence. The open doors of the French windows now looked out onto an ebony night, and a cool breeze from nowhere – invaded the room.

CHAPTER SIX

IT WAS ALL VERY ODD.

Over a week later, well on into the Thursday afternoon, Julia Thornton, in her usual place – the seat by the Wellingtonia – raised her eyes from her book attracted by a slight sound some way off. Jack Path, the elderly man who tended to the grounds, had just come into view beyond the rear of the church. He always took the same route to enter and leave via a gate that came from a pathway leading to the hamlet of Chapp. Julia immediately closed the book, 'Westward Ho!' by Charles Kingsley. It had been her father's favourite novel and she had always intended to read it. She was now well into the long narrative and, consequently, was finding it hard to put down. She got to her feet and went to intercept Jack.

The dry and warm weather was continuing unabated. Being just past the longest day of the year, the sun was still strong for the time of day, and as Julia drew near, she could see Jack had quite a bit of perspiration on his brow. As far as she knew, this was the first time he had put in an appearance at the churchyard for quite a while, due to his recent illness. Needless-to-say, with the growing season well and truly under way, his services were very much in need. The vicar had used the mower a couple of times, but the grave areas and borders were desperately in need of attention.

Jack was a small man, both in height and stature, but he always had a grin about his countenance and his eyes smiled with it. The face was bronzed from his convalescence in the sun, but there was a redness about him that was not usually there. In truth, he did not care too much for hot weather; it did not suit him. He only ever wore suits and the older the suit became; the more it was used for gardening and other activities. He was not wearing a jacket, but he did sport a grey waistcoat, and although unbuttoned, a watch chain was clearly visible looping from one side pocket to the other. His shirt was the type to which you could attach a collar. A collar had not been worn with this shirt for some time, and it lay opened at the neck where the stud would have been. His black boots were heavy and looked as though they might have metal toecaps hidden beneath the leather.

Julia intercepted the gardener on his way towards the shed where all the tools were kept. Despite the heat affecting him, he acknowledged the lady's presence with one of his warm smiles. "Jack – how nice to see you up and about. I hear you have been quite poorly?"

"Ah," he made a slight nod with his head. "It were one o' them viral things – you knows."

"What? The flu – in this weather?"

"Dunno, doctor says it were viral – that's all Oi knows. But it were a right B an' no mistake!"

"Dear me, the vicar said you were laid low. I am sorry. How is your wife?"

"She be fine. Strong as an 'orse – that-un."

"Ah good. Now you won't overdo things will you Jack? Best to take it easy to begin with – aye." Julia was genuinely concerned. Jack was showing his age. Before he could reply, she suddenly turned around and looked towards the gate on the far side of the church grounds. "Good heavens!" she exclaimed. "Jack. Do excuse me. I have just seen something that needs an explanation. Must dash. See you soon, and mind what I say."

Jack turned around to watch her. He could see nothing unusual in the direction she was headed and wondered what she might be about. Julia was half walking, half running in a kind of sideways motion, all the while holding her hat in place with her left hand and clasping the book in the other. Soon, she disappeared behind some rhododendron bushes.

Jack could not have been aware then ... He would be the last known person to see her.

July arrived and still there was no rain. The appropriate authorities in various areas throughout the country brought in water restrictions. However, this part of Hampshire had good underground reserves in the chalk downs, and the local inhabitants suffered far less than in other areas. Nevertheless, Tim and Christine found it irksome that they could not use a watering hose. Their garden was parched brown, but there was a bonus: weeds were not growing in the profusion normally applicable to an English country garden – so less work – more time to enjoy the sun.

The effect of Thomas Hurn's reading of that poem had given both girls nightmares. Walking in the forest had been avoided, mainly due to the hot weather. Whenever they relaxed, it was usually lying prone in the back-garden sunbathing. By now they were both possessors of a deep tan from crown to toe. Christine had gone an attractive golden brown, but Suzanne was considerably darker, almost to the extent of having the same skin tone as an Asian girl, complimented by her dark hair.

Apart from some odd touching up here and there, most of the decorating had been completed inside the cottage. Before starting on the exterior doors and window frames, they decided to treat the interior wooden beams against worm.

Christine and Suzanne were working on this one Wednesday morning. Tim was away for the day over in the Mendip Hills on a field trip for his firm. The radio had just announced it was eleven o'clock when the doorbell rang. Christine clambered down from a stepladder, and because she had been applying treatment to ceiling support beams, let her arms hang down by her side in relief. She went to the door and opened it. Standing there with his blond hair neatly parted; craggy face jovial and wearing a smart suit was Dr David Andrews. He had one of those jaw structures that rarely showed his teeth when he smiled, the lips being drawn in a straight line, slightly ballooning his cheeks.

"Good morning," David announced. "Thought I would call and see how you are settling in?"

"Hello," greeted Christine cheerfully. "Sorry about the pong. It's wood treatment stuff."

"Ah, know it well. We have acres of oak beams at our house. Mind you – it's worth doing. Can save you some nasty problems." Suzanne came to the door having recognized the visitor's voice. She gave him a welcoming smile.

"You must have smelt the coffee. Would you like some?" asked Christine.

"Yes ... please!" answered David stepping into the hall at Christine's beckoning hand. "I must confess I'm ready for a cup. How have you both been keeping? You seem to have progressed well with the paintbrushes."

They intimated that they were in fine health. While Suzanne finished making the coffee, David admired and congratulated Christine on all the work they had accomplished. They were both on the stairs looking at the woodwork when Suzanne called to say their hot drink was ready in the sitting room.

When seated, David explained the reason for his visit. "I thought I ought to call and tell you the results of my enquiries with the forestry people at Chapp. I know your husband was interested."

"To be honest we didn't know anything about it," said Christine looking at Suzanne for confirmation.

"Ah, that is the consideration your husband shows. Probably didn't want to alarm you," commented David.

"Oh, did he?" said Christine. "Wait 'till I speak to him."

"Now please ... you will get me into trouble," said David, a slightly perturbed expression on his face.

"Don't you worry Doctor Andrews; I shan't involve you," said Christine.

"And now we are back to surnames?" David looked at her quizzically.

"*David,* I mean." Christine explained that she found it strange to call a doctor by his first name.

"Times they are a changin'," quoted David from the Dylan song. "No, but seriously, I am sure your husband merely didn't wish to alarm you unnecessarily."

"I suppose so," Christine acknowledged. She suddenly looked up. "Why – is there something to be alarmed about?"

"Yes. What happened when you went to see the forestry people?" asked Suzanne, wide-eyed.

"No. There isn't anything to be alarmed about: absolutely nothing. In fact, I made rather a fool of myself. I asked some of the Forestry Commission workers whether any of them had seen any unusual snakes, and this man pipes up and said that indeed he had!"

"What!" exclaimed Suzanne.

"Exactly my reaction," said David. "I enquired further. He completely floored me when he blandly said that he had recently seen a red adder!"

"Oh no!" Christine exclaimed, amazed. "But you said there wasn't anything to be alarmed about?"

David nodded profoundly. "It appears," he said, looking abashed, "that there is such a snake as a red adder. It is no more than an *ordinary* adder, normally a female, with different skin pigmentation. Apparently, they are a coppery-red colour, with the usual zigzag marking on their backs. The forester was most enthusiastic. He said that it was the first red adder that had been seen in these parts for years. He even went as far as to describe the thing as beautiful. Anyway, to cut a long story short, I took the matter up with Allen Haddle. He confirmed that it was quite usual for adders to have a different colouring to the mottled brown tones they are normally associated with. He said he had personally seen a black one."

"And what about Ma Hessil's dog?" asked Suzanne.

"I'm inclined to agree with our good vicar on that," said David. "She must have made it up. Her dog, presumably, suffered a fatal heart attack or something equally drastic. After all, nobody else witnessed seeing a snake in the vicinity, and Ma Hessil is well known for her phobia about John the Red. Mind you – it doesn't seem to affect her habits. She is always taking walks in the forest – come rain, hail or snow: even fog – I've been told. If she was scared out of her wits, it figures that she would not go near the place."

"Hmm – It does seem rather strange," agreed Suzanne. "Considering she lost her son to snake bite, I can understand her being afraid, but how long has it been a phobia?"

"Ever since 1948 when it all started, I understand. She used to blame her next-door neighbour for it by all accounts."

"Why would she do that?" asked Suzanne, allowing time for David to take a sip of coffee.

"I don't know," he replied. "From what I've heard, the Hessils lived next door to another couple – John and Doris Head. They had no children; John was killed in the war during the D-Day invasion. For some odd reason the widow never got on with her neighbours afterwards. She died from a coronary condition at the age of forty-five. Very young for that: especially in a woman. There is no doubt that deliberate malnutrition brought it about by weakening the heart. When the strange snake killed Peter, Ma Hessil's son, they say she openly blamed it on Doris."

"But why?" persisted Suzanne.

"Well, I think I am right in saying it was Doris who originally coined the title, 'John the Red.' Perhaps it has something to do with that," David answered with a sigh, before taking another drink of his coffee.

"Ma Hessil's husband?" said Christine. Nobody had mentioned him before. She presumed he had passed on.

"I was called out on that case myself," said the doctor, realising her dilemma and placing the cup back on the saucer. "He was out strolling in the woods not far from here. The year would have been" – he thought for a moment – "19 ... 59. Poor man had a stroke, although he wouldn't have known much about it: killed him outright. I do remember his facial expression – frozen in unmistakable horror. Ma Hessil blamed it on John the Red. That year was one of those rare, long hot summers.

"Were there any sightings of a strange snake?" asked Christine.

"No, no, no – not to my knowledge," he replied. "Now - I must go. May I leave it to you to pass on the info' to Tim?"

"Yes, we'll tell him," said Christine as they showed the doctor to the door.

"What do you make of that lady's disappearance in the village?" David asked, without turning his head, as he passed through the front doorway.

"Pardon?" said Christine. Suzanne just gaped.

"Sorry – don't you know. Her name is Julia Thornton: one of Yewhurst's oldest residents. Most extraordinary – just vanished!"

Christine gasped. "What?" exclaimed Suzanne. "But we had tea with her not long ago."

"How long ago?" David suddenly looked serious.

"Oh – before we first met you," replied Christine. "What do you mean – disappeared?"

"Well – put it this way. The last person to see her was Jack Path, the man who keeps the churchyard tidy, about two weeks ago. The first anybody knew about it was when one of her cats begged for food from a neighbour. The police broke into her house. Nothing appears to be missing, except the lady herself. A niece, her only known relative, can't shed any light." David shrugged his shoulders sorrowfully.

"Well ... I never," said Suzanne. "How absolutely awful. What can have happened to her?"

"Let's hope there is some explanation. Gone away on a secret trip – perhaps. We shall just have to wait and see," said the doctor.

"Julia Thornton doesn't strike me as the sort of person who would leave her cats to starve!" said Christine. David was well aware of this. His ruse had been to try and alleviate the distress for the two women. He agreed with them but, nevertheless, hoped that however unlikely, an explanation did exist which would bring the lady back to the village alive and well. They discussed the matter further for a while before the doctor departed.

That evening they gave Tim this news. He seemed at a loss to suggest anything, bearing in mind that he had not actually met Julia. He questioned his wife and sister for as much information as possible. It was all very odd.

Later, almost as a bye the way, Christine told Tim about the copper-coloured adder seen by the forestry worker, and Dr David Andrew's opinion that there was nothing further to worry about with regards to the Red Adder.

CHAPTER SEVEN

"ARE YOU FROM THESE PARTS?"

With the arrival of the weekend came definite signs that it might rain for the first time in eight clement weeks.

On Saturday afternoon Tim, Christine and Suzanne were travelling in the old Morris to a local beauty spot called Farley Mount. Turning off the main road to the left from the small hamlet of Standon, they found the narrow road that led up to a chalk down. Farley Mount marked the highest point in the surrounding countryside. It was very popular with families for picnics. The lane wound its way up through wide fields, already well on in growth for the hay crop. The tarmac stopped abruptly someway before the summit. Hedge screened car parks had been landscaped for the public's use.

Tim's new work colleagues had told him of the fine views to be seen from the top of the hill, and about the monument that marked the place of burial of a famous white horse. Rain appeared to be threatening at any moment, judging by the low scudding clouds, but none of them had bothered to bring a coat. To get wet from soft summer rain can be a pleasurable experience.

The dubious weather kept the usual Saturday crowds away from the down, and Christine, Suzanne and Tim Westward found themselves alone as they walked up the grassy track towards a monument. Despite the cloudy sky, a mighty panorama of Southeast Hampshire lay behind them, stretching over the chalk downs towards Chichester on the coast, and the highest point in the county, Butser Hill, which was clearly defined against the horizon. They had to turn sharp left off the track to walk the final few hundred yards to the top. The monument stood on the summit of a large mound, and a narrow path wound its way up to the entrance. Tim led the way. They entered a cave like opening in the pyramidal shaped structure and found themselves confronted by a tableau. Tim read it out aloud, his voice echoing in the confined space. It gave some details concerning a famous horse that in 1733, while foxhunting, had leapt into a twenty-five feet deep chalk pit, with its rider on his back. The horse went on to become famous for winning a major steeplechase. Presumably, this was also the animal's burial site.

"Have you noticed anything?" said Suzanne.

"What?" asked Tim. "Can't say I can see anything unusual."

"Nor me," said Christine. "What is it Suz?"

"It doesn't mention that the horse was white," she answered them.

"Why should it?" said Tim in an irritated manner. "Anyway – it was."

"And how do *you* know?" his sister provoked him.

"Because it is a well-known fact. Everybody says so."

"That doesn't mean a thing. Everybody says so – ha ... I bet it was a dark one."

"You're a dark one, that's for sure."

"Oh, shut up you two" quickly intervened Christine. "What does it matter anyway?" And she led them out saying, "Come on – let's look at the other side."

They found their way blocked by a beautiful Tri-colour Collie. He was not the usual sable and white combination, instead possessing a deep black back that faded away to a tan colour, with white legs and under body. The proud looking head, with its elongated jaw was studying the three of them. He was panting comfortably. Suzanne let out a squeal of delight and started to cuddle the magnificent animal. "You are a pet, aren't you – eh?" The collie took an immediate liking to her and made to lick her face.

"Isn't he gorgeous? He is a 'he' – isn't he?" said Christine joining in the stroking.

A low but audible whistle sounded from the other side of the mound and the collie hurriedly disentangled himself from the gushing women, and ran off towards the sound, disappearing behind some stumpy trees.

"Must be his owner," said Suzanne. "What an obedient doggie."

The three of them stood for a while admiring the view looking west over the New Forest. In this kind of situation there can be an advantage to a cloudy sky; it invariably provides clear visibility unlike the distant haze occurring on hot days. The horizon today just went on and on. They could even see the Isle of Wight, quite clearly, on the other side of the Solent Sea.

Coming back down from the mound, they were navigating their way between some dwarf yew trees, when they came across the owner of the dog. He was standing with his back to them looking out over the downs, and in his right hand he held a notebook and a pencil. The collie sat obediently at his side – gazing over his shoulder at the approaching threesome.

Something made Suzanne stop in her tracks. This tall man, who must have heard them coming, did not turn around. His mind was quite obviously engaged on some other purpose. He just stood letting the breeze run through his clothes, billowing them slightly. He wore a dark blue denim shirt and blue jeans with a generous black belt. He turned to face them. Suzanne, who was not five yards away, found herself looking into a tanned face with a shock of dark brown hair lying carelessly over one eyebrow. Clear blue eyes looked kindly upon her. Wide square shoulders gave his slim frame the appearance of being athletic. "I hope Fly did not bother you?" he asked of them all in a pleasant voice, raising the eyebrow, which was not hidden by hair, as if in question.

Suzanne was struck dumb. It was Christine who answered him. "Fly ... what an unusual name?" He nodded in affirmation, at the same time displaying a warm smile. "No – he didn't bother us. We think he's lovely, don't we Suzanne?"

Suzanne spluttered something unintelligible, and much to her chagrin, started to blush. Christine gave her a suspicious look before asking. "Are you from around here?" She was quite certain that she had seen both the dog and the man before.

He flicked the offending curl of hair away from his left eye. "Yes – but it is some time since I last visited this place. And you?" He asked politely.

Christine nodded. "Uh huh. We are new residents in the village of Yewhurst. This is the first time we've been to Farley Mount."

The stranger pushed the notebook and pencil into a back pocket. He had a handsome face and there was no hardness to it. The high cheekbones should have made him look classical, but they did not. He appeared to be of a gentler disposition.

Fly went up to Suzanne, tail wagging expectantly. She petted the dog muttering words of endearment. The stranger spoke to her. "You know – when I see girls making up to Fly – I think to myself – he's got something I haven't." Suzanne smiled shyly.

The man took a few steps towards his dog. "Well Fly – aren't you being made a fuss of then?" He smiled – his gaze locking onto Suzanne eyes.

She knew she must say something. "I think he is the most beautiful dog I have ever seen. How old is he?"

"Just two," was the reply. It was now the stranger's turn to be dumbfounded. He had never seen such a face before. It seemed to represent his dream of the perfect young women. This girl before him, who had earlier been so shy, now looked straight at him. She was the possessor of features, which illustrated nothing but lovability. Her eyes: they were so bright. It was almost as though they had lights in them.

In mutual understanding – they smiled at each other. Her teeth came visible as in a wave, confident in their pearl-hues under her natural rosy lips. Visible below her eyes were some tiny dark freckle-like spots – few in number. They added to her cuteness and within the overall smile seemed doubly enhancing.

Then it began to rain. Not hard enough to make them dash for shelter, but a steady fall that persuaded the whole group to start back down the hill. One thing Suzanne observed was that although she, Christine and Tim pulled the collars of their jackets about their ears, this man did not. True – he was only wearing a denim shirt, but he made no move to protect himself. He held his head high and seemed to walk at the rain, rather than through it.

The conversation was brisk all the way back to the car park. Tim explained to their new acquaintance about their recent move to Beech Cottage. "You know," spoke the man, "I thought you said Yewhurst earlier on, and now you say you live at Beech Cottage. We live about five hundred yards away from each other."

"You're joking! Do you really? Where?" asked Christine.

"The left side of the Claymans?" He said this in the form of a question.

"Oh," said Tim. "We haven't been over that way yet. Took a stroll down the other side of the hotel the other day." The discovery of the proximity of their dwellings immediately opened up the way for possible friendship. The rain began to ease as they arrived at the parking area.

"By the way – I'm Tim Westward. This is my wife, Christine. He placed an arm over her shoulder.

"Dalmar," said the tall man. It had become obvious to him quite early on that Tim and Christine were together, by the subtle body language between them. "Dalmar Hunter," he enlarged.

"This is Tim's sister, Suzanne," said Christine.

"Hello," acknowledged Dalmar with a slight bowing of his head. Suzanne smiled coyly in return.

It now dawned on Suzanne that this was the man she had seen walking his dog, from a Claymans Heron window, some weeks ago. She was not going to let it go at that. "Dal-mar. That's an unusual name. How do you spell it?"

Dalmar spelt out the letters slowly, but he made no comment on its unusualness.

Suddenly Christine came out with an unexpected statement directed at their new acquaintance: "We were thinking of going for a drink at the Claymans this evening. Are you doing anything?"

Suzanne turned her head to look at her sister-in-law mouth agape. Tim was amazed, but not displeased.

"Only a bit of work with my typewriter," answered Dalmar.

"Wondered if you would like to join us? It would be a chance for us to get to know another neighbour." Christine deliberately kept the invitation low-key.

"Well – umm – that would be nice ..." he replied, hesitantly.

A sudden thought had sprung into Christine's mind. It occurred to Suzanne almost at the same time. "Do you have someone you ... wish to bring with you?" asked Christine.

"No, no," answered Dalmar. "Unfortunately, I can't bring Fly – not allowed."

"Well," she said. "About eight - that suit you Tim?" She realised that her husband had not been consulted and tactfully brought him in.

"Sounds good to me," said Tim. "Look forward to more conversation this evening." He looked Dalmar's way, with a grin.

"Eight it is. I'll see you in the bar. I've got the T.R. over there. I'll let Fly have a run." He pointed to the next car park along. "Like the Morris by the way Tim." He strolled off, whistling Fly away at a fast run.

Suzanne stared as he went. The damp, dark brown locks of his hair curled into themselves on the back of his neck, glistening in the dull light. He walked with long purposeful strides, and she noticed for the first time that he was wearing moccasins.

CHAPTER EIGHT

"SOMEONE'S GOT YOUR NUMBER."

As it turned out, things did not work quite to Christine's plan, in that none of them got to know much about Dalmar because they ended up talking to various other people during the evening. The bar was crowded, and Dalmar was already involved in a conversation with some other local inhabitants when the Westwards arrived. Nevertheless, during the couple of hours they were there, she did learn enough to know that he seemed a likeable man, and there was no doubt that Suzanne thought so – she could not take her eyes of him. Having confirmed that his last name was Hunter, Christine did not leave matters there. She checked with her husband first, then she looked up his telephone number in the directory and rang him the very next day, late in the afternoon, asking him if he would like to join them for an evening meal on the coming Wednesday. After checking that it was all right to bring his dog, he readily accepted.

On that evening, a great deal of preparation took place at Beech Cottage, prior to Dalmar's arrival. Despite the fact that Christine had intimated in her invitation that it would be just a casual supper, flowers miraculously produced from a devoid garden appeared on the dining table. The two girls kept up an almost continuous chatter, Christine saying, "He could be just the man for you Suz."

And Suzanne coming back with the comment that, "He would probably not be interested in her. Not his type," she suspected.

It was five minutes past eight. Sometime before this, it had stopped raining and very quickly became quite warm and humid. Christine kept glancing out of the window. They were all sitting in the front room waiting for the doorbell to ring. Tim was helping himself to a small beer, when the back-door knocker sounded. This was unexpected and made them all start. Tim put down the drink and went to answer it. Dalmar stood there holding a bottle of Pouilly-Fuisse in one hand, a rubber torch and Fly's lead in the other. The dog, tail wagging furiously, stood obediently behind him. "Hello," said Dalmar smiling, "I've just taken this out of the refrigerator."

"Oh, thank you ... Welcome," said Tim. "Come on in." He placed the bottle in the kitchen and, pointing out the low beams, started to lead his guest through to the sitting room.

Christine intersected them. "Why did you come to the back door?" She asked Dalmar with a big smile of greeting.

"Hello. Thought I'd better bring the dog in that way. Just in case there was any dirt on his feet - better safe than sorry. May I put these down somewhere?" He indicated Fly's lead and the torch. Christine said,

"Of course," and pointed to a small table by the back door, before giving Fly a pat of welcome on his nose. What puzzled her was how their guest had managed to get around the cottage without anyone noticing.

"Hello Dalmar – nice to see you again," said Suzanne coming up behind her sister-in-law. Fly, unlike most dogs that bound into strange houses making a fuss, had been trained not to. Naturally he would like to make a big scene, but instead, contented himself with forceful tail wagging and putting his head out to whoever would oblige him with a pat. Suzanne was there in a flash.

Within a few minutes, they were all seated in the front room. Tim had poured them a drink and Fly was curled up on the hearth mat. Suzanne noted with pleasure Dalmar's mode of dress. He now wore a smart pair of deep blue denim trousers, and a white short-sleeved cotton shirt that highlighted the suntan around his neck and arms. As before, he was wearing moccasins, though a newer, less scuffed pair. Although the rest of them were dressed in a rather more sophisticated mode, Dalmar did not look out of place. He took a packet of American menthol cigarettes from the breast pocket of his shirt and offered them around. Christine and Tim did not smoke, and Suzanne, only on rare occasions. This was one of them. Dalmar produced a solid silver Dunhill lighter from a trouser pocket and lit her cigarette, and then his own. Suzanne noticed that his hands looked neat for such a tall man. They were strong while having a piano player's quality about them.

"Did you finish your typing last Saturday," asked Christine, casually.

"No, I'm afraid not," he answered. "I couldn't get it right, so I decided to leave off – for the time being."

It puzzled Tim that Dalmar should have to do typing. "Is your secretary on holiday?" He queried.

"Oh no, you misunderstand. It has nothing to do with my work. From my experience you get absolutely no thanks whatsoever for grafting in your spare time." He changed the subject. "I'm working for a modest-sized firm, at the moment, and they are good employers. I used to be an assistant to a personnel manager of a large London concern. My god, when I think of the hours I used to put in, quite productively I thought, and my reward – nothing." He made a circle in the air with his cigarette.

"Is that why you changed to a smaller company?" asked Tim.

"Only partly. To be honest I didn't have much choice. Made a couple of mistakes at the time redundancies had to be made, so I turned out to be one of them. Lucky not to have been sacked really."

"You sound as though you are happier now?" commented Christine.

"Yes, well it did get me out of London. I think the capital is a great place to visit, but not to live in. There is an argument that says I ran away from competition. Personally, I prefer peace of mind to competing in a world of what I term – corporate bitchiness."

"You have had more experience than I have, but I feel we both left The Smoke for much the same reasons," said Tim.

"Here's to us then." Dalmar raised his glass. Turning his attention to Tim's sister he said, "Are you working, Suzanne?" She was smartly dressed in a pale blue blouse, and dark blue suede trousers. She had applied lipstick of a shade that seemed just right for her. Dalmar felt flutterings and knew what they could mean. Very soon he would see only beauty in everything she did, and he had absolutely no desire to stop it. Naturally, right now, he needed to know more about her social life.

"I've just finished secretarial college."

"Ah, then I know where to come if my secretary leaves. But I expect you would be too expensive for our little concern." He said smiling at her. She grinned back and then explained to him that she was only staying here for a few weeks during the summer, to help her brother get things ship-shape in the cottage. "I shall think about starting work when I get back to Somerset."

After this, Christine went out to check on the meal. Meanwhile, Tim related to their guest how he earned a living. Then he returned to the former subject. "What did you mean when you referred to – what was it? Corporate bitchiness?"

"The reason is quite simply desire for advancement by any means. The system is okay – I think; it is its misuse that's wrong. The two men then proceeded to try and put the world of business morals to rights, while Suzanne excused herself to go and help her sister-in-law. Eventually a call came from the kitchen. "Grub up – come and get it!"

On the way through Fly looked up and was about to get to his four feet when Dalmar put out an arm and slightly held up his hand. The dog seemed grateful and stayed where he was.

The dining room was small but in the shape of a neat square that made it look larger than it was. The table was laid for the meal, and lit candles had now been added to compliment the flowers in the evening light. Tim opened the wine and they all tucked in to a first course of pork chops with vegetables. The visitor got to know his three new neighbours a great deal more.

Whether it was the wine or not, Christine did not know, but she managed to summon up the courage to ask Dalmar how old he was.

"Forty-two," he said, gazing at a plate of cream-laden apple crumble with a completely straight face. The effect was electrifying. Suzanne stared at him open mouthed, spoon held in mid-air. Christine was aghast, looking straight at her husband as though it was his fault. A tiny little grin started to grow on Dalmar's face. Tim noticed, realised, and started laughing.

"Oh, come on – you're not?" said Suzanne with an expression of mixed feelings.

"Don't be such a tease," pleaded Christine.

"Well – perhaps I exaggerated a bit. You know how it is?" He looked at both the girls, then screwed up his face as though he was about to tell some awful truth – "Fifty-one." Christine threw the wine cork at him which he managed to catch in a reflex action. "Alright, all right, I surrender ... I *am* thirty-one."

Eventually Dalmar learnt all their ages as well, although he had to go through a guessing routine. He underestimated with Christine, which was totally successful tact. Got it spot on with Tim, and suggested Suzanne might be sixteen, which resulted in her brother going into further convulsions of laughter. He tried to get out the words, "She certainly acts like…," but Suzanne had retrieved the wine cork and got him right on the end of his nose before he could utter the complete sentence.

When the meal was finished by all, Christine suggested they have coffee in the sitting room. "You two men go on through. Suz and I will bring it."

"Don't you want to wash-up first?" queried Dalmar. "I am really quite good with a tea towel."

"No thank you. Tim, take him along. Go and keep your dog company." The two men did as they were bid.

Out in the kitchen Christine whispered, while plugging in the coffee percolator, "Don't you think he's dishy?"

Suzanne smiled. She had expected that. "I bet he has a steady relationship going. Someone that good looking – must have."

"So – you do fancy him?" Christine had a knowing grin on her face. Suzanne hid her face over the coffee cups. They heard male voices getting louder. "Ssh ... he'll hear you," Suzanne whispered anxiously. They listened to the two men in the hall. Tim was showing their guest the location of the cloakroom. Fly wandered into the kitchen and watched the two girls curiously.

After a few moments the toilet flush sounded, a door closed, and Christine peeped out of the kitchen into the hall. Dalmar was making his way to re-join her husband. As he passed the telephone on a table by the front door, before entering the sitting room, he hesitated. Christine thought that for one awful moment he was going to turn around and catch her spying on him. But instead, he took a couple of steps backwards and picked up a pencil that lay by a pad of paper near the telephone. He took a cigarette packet out of his shirt pocket and wrote something on it. Then he replaced the pencil and went in to see Tim.

Christine went up to Suzanne, who had not noticed her sister-in-law's indiscretion. "Someone's got your number," she whispered.

"What?" said Suzanne.

"Dalmar has just made a note of our telephone number. If you want proof, get a look at his packet of fags." Suzanne could not disguise the thrill she felt on hearing this. She hunched her shoulders and wrung her hands. They grinned at each other as Christine gathered up the tray. Fly followed and parked himself next to Suzanne. He received the cuddle he had been expecting.

The two men were talking about motorcars for which they both had a natural weakness. They stopped, politely, when the girls arrived.

"Have you heard of a snake called John the Red?" Christine asked Dalmar.

The expression on his face changed. Even when discussing serious matters there had always been warmth in his countenance. Now – there was none. He looked extremely uncomfortable. "Err... yes ... I have. Why?"

"Do you know Allen Haddle?"

"I know there is a vet by that name ... lives near the Claymans."

"Yes, that's him. He overheard us talking about a snake in the pub." Christine then told Dalmar about Ma Hessil and their subsequent introduction to David and Dorothy Andrews, and Thomas Hurn's reading of the poem.

"You seem concerned," Tim said, looking in Dalmar's direction.

"I am," he replied. "Very." Then he made a slow – low sigh. "Actually – it is not my favourite topic of conversation."

Suzanne came to his rescue. "I couldn't agree more. After hearing that poem, I had nightmares for ages afterwards." As she said this, she got up to leave the room and visit the cloakroom.

Before dropping the subject, without registering any queries as to 'the poem', Dalmar looked up to ask his hosts, "Have you heard any strange noises coming from the woods?" Tim and Christine looked puzzled.

"No, don't think so." Tim put the question to her, "Christine?" His wife thought about the odd sound coming from the distant forest that had perturbed her on their first evening at the cottage. But as she had not heard anything similar since, she said nothing and just shook her head. "Why do you ask?" said Tim.

Dalmar shrugged his shoulders. "Probably not important," he said. "Heard something the other day I couldn't make any sense of."

"What was that?" Christine was curious.

"Don't know really ... just odd. Sorry." He smiled at his lack of explanation. Truthfully, he was regretting having raised the matter.

"Oh, and what about Julia Thornton?" said Christine while they were on subjects of local interest.

"Is that the lady who has vanished?" asked Dalmar.

"Yes."

"I think I may have seen her on the odd occasion. Does she sometimes occupy a bench in the churchyard – in fine weather – reading?"

"Probably," Christine confirmed, "Although, when Suz and I first saw her, she was knitting." She thought for a while in a closed lip pose before saying. "Still no news – I suppose?" She asked this of both the men. Tim had heard from someone that the police had carried out a thorough search of her house, but that was all.

They engaged in mostly humorous conversation for the next hour or more.

Around eleven o'clock, Dalmar took his leave saying how much he had enjoyed the evening and thanking them for the dinner. Instead of going straight home he decided to give Fly a walk and turned towards the church. Being late in the evening the rural traffic had died away on the road, so he stuck to the path beside it, although this necessitated keeping his dog on a lead, who padded quietly along by his master's side.

Dalmar halted to light a cigarette. "S'truth!" he said to himself, "It is warm." The air was still – so very still. The humidity had deadened any sound, and everything was hushed. Even his footfalls were silent, partly due to his mode of footwear. The only noise was Fly's soft panting.

Coming to the entrance to the churchyard, they made their way up the gravel path. Now and again, Dalmar had to use his flashlight to make sure of his way: the night was ultra-dark. He turned sharp left and stood for some time by an unmarked grave, the dog sitting quietly by his side. Then, he took the route between two rhododendron hedges, and walked down into a miniature valley to an old drinking well at the bottom. He opened a gate and started back along the roadside. Everything was silent and even the church spire was swallowed up by inky blackness. Visibility ended somewhere near the top of the far rhododendron hedge. Despite the heat, Dalmar shivered slightly due to the eerie atmosphere.

Suddenly, Fly abruptly stopped walking, almost causing his owner to trip over him. "Oh Fly! ... What's up boy?" he said. The dog went into a crouching position, his fur standing up all along his back. His owner had never seen him like this before. Usually, when he was alarmed, he would bark loudly and continuously until pacified. But now it was as though he had been possessed by some evil presence. He quivered all over, but otherwise remained quite still staring straight ahead of him. Dalmar followed the dog's line of sight. A giant Wellingtonia, with its considerable height of two hundred feet plus, could just be seen against the black heavens.

At first, he saw nothing unusual. Then he held up the big rubber torch and switched it on. The lower crescent-shaped boughs of the giant pine leapt out of the darkness. Dalmar slowly raised the penetrating beam of light upwards, exploring the deep shadows in the inner depths of the tree on each side of its massive trunk. The higher it reached, the shorter the branches became, and the less he had to move the torch from side to side.

At about a hundred feet off the ground, he passed over what looked like a pinprick of light coming back at him. He moved the torch slowly downwards again until he found it. Two yellow eyes appeared to be looking straight at him. "Christ Almighty!" he blasphemed aloud. They were like those of a cat caught in the glare of a car's headlights. There was no movement in them; they just appeared to be staring. Then an explanation came to him. "Fly – you silly mutt; it's only an owl." He switched off the torch; took one last inhalation on his cigarette before extinguishing it in the verge, and then patted the dog on his head reassuringly. But Fly made no move and continued to quiver at the same time not taking his sight from that part of the tree where the eyes had been seen.

Eventually, Dalmar with much cursing had to pick up the encumbering animal and carry him, trying to hold onto his torch and the dog's lead at the same time. Fly made no objection. They climbed to the top of the rise, passing by the tall tree. It was then that Dalmar knew. They were not being watched by an owl. He broke into a casual run and did not stop until they reached the point where the forest ended just before the Claymans Heron. Breathing heavily, he put the dog down, who immediately recovered and licked his master's hand in gratitude. They quickly crossed the road, jumped the ditch and carried on at a jog towards their home.

Dalmar did not get to sleep for several hours that night, but it was not the eyes in the Wellingtonia that kept him awake. Very definitely, it was due to persistent thoughts about a certain young lady. He desperately tried to convince himself that a twenty-one-year-old might accept a date from a thirty-one-year-old bachelor. Doubts raced through his mind over and over again. Had he not learnt from the past that to chase after attractive women, always ended in sadness for him? Time and again in his late teens and throughout his twenties, he had been close to a lasting relationship, only to find that he did not have what it takes to win such women. Short-lived, lustful affairs would follow each break-up, with the poor unfortunate girls involved eventually discarded for pastures new. There was something else which compounded Dalmar's sensitivity to rejection, something he could do nothing about, because it all happened – a long time ago.

CHAPTER NINE

"WERE YOU AN ONLY CHILD?"

Two hours after dawn the next day, about half a mile into the centre of Yewhurst Wood, a vixen stirred in her den. Some three feet below ground under the upturned roots of a giant fallen beech, slept a family of red foxes. The male dog fox had provided well during the night for his vixen and three cubs. Also asleep, soundly, sharing the den was an older dog fox, no longer dominant, a member of the family who had to fend for himself. The cubs were at a stage of their development where their fur was fully grown, and each had a good set of milk teeth, so they were able to eat the same food as their parents.

What caused the vixen to stir, she did not know. Even in deep slumber an alarm bell had rung inside her. She opened one eye, followed almost immediately by the other. Then she raised her head. Suddenly she was fully awake, standing, with her ears at their most alert. Slowly and soundlessly, she made her way along the narrow passage that took her up to the tangle of dead roots and – daylight. To put this in perspective, the vixen had not risen at such an early hour since giving birth to her cubs, and that was in late February. So why had her sleeping brain become agitated enough to rouse her? The small but incredibly sensitive nose, enclosed on both sides by white fur, sniffed the air long and hard. Slowly her dark ringed eyes peered out. Before she saw anything at all, the vixen became aware of a powerful presence. Over to the right a large area of pale, lifeless long grasses showed movement from something making its way beneath. Whatever it might be was not visible. But judging by the meandering motion, it was fairly long. The fox froze into temporary immobility – her gaze unerring. She became aware that her mate was alongside. He was no longer asleep because his senses had picked up her acute signals. Now, he too became concerned. Both of them watched the snake-like motion in the grasses – a mere half a dozen feet from the opening to their family den. They observed, without moving a single muscle, until the anomaly got lost from view, going away, as it reached a copse of hawthorn trees. Making up their minds in unison both foxes edged backwards, before disappearing into the depths of their den.

A snake such as the common adder or grass snake would be of no concern to a fox. However, as vixen and dog re-joined their still sleeping young, they both had only one thing on their minds. There would be little sleep for them today. The cubs must be moved to another den on the other side of their territory, and the old dog fox must be persuaded to help. Such was the power of whatever it was that they had been witness to.

The wet weather ceased within a few hours on Thursday.

Tim Westward went off to work by bus that morning. Hopefully, he would be coming home in another vehicle, which would be primarily for his wife's use.

About mid-morning, Suzanne answered the telephone. A rather nervous Dalmar was calling from his office. Nevertheless, he did manage to ask her if she would like to go out for dinner with him one evening. Suzanne was overjoyed and made no attempt to hide the fact. They made a date for the following Friday. Dalmar found himself very taken with the captivating tones of her voice. Some of the girls educated in a Roman Catholic convent, during these times, developed a very engaging personality with an infectious sense of humour. This was probably due to a sense of security, coupled with the desire to have a dig at the strict discipline imposed by these institutions.

That evening Tim arrived home in a rather old Ford estate. Tim boasted that he had picked it up for a song, although he knew the risk he was taking mechanically. Anyway, Christine and Suzanne were delighted. No more laborious bus journeys and struggling with shopping bags. They decided to give it the first run the following morning.

Suzanne grew more and more excited as her dinner date drew nearer. She was only a little apprehensive, sure in her judgment that Dalmar had a balanced personality. Her main concern was the extent of her wardrobe. This possibility had not occurred to her when she packed for her stay at Beech Cottage. Christine eventually managed to persuade her that judging by Dalmar's appearance up to now, he seemed to prefer casual clothes. While shopping in Winchester, she purchased a new pair of light blue trousers and a white blouse with frills on the cuffs. Currently in fashion for lady's shoes were thick heeled, platform styles. Suzanne was not comfortable with them. Her preference was for the daintier type. Fortunately for her purse, she was not able to find the pair she was looking for. Eventually, she settled for a pair of navy-blue shoes she already owned. Jewellery was not something she possessed a lot of, being tender in years. But there was one item of which she was very proud: a deep royal blue, sapphire brooch, which had belonged to her grandmother, who had passed away two years before. To compliment this, she inserted a medium-blue velvet Alice band just above her forehead. The effect was lovely: simple but beautiful.

At seven-thirty Dalmar turned off the T.R.6's engine outside Beech Cottage. He liked the masculine design of his motorcar and had made sure of getting home early in order to give it a clean. As he cast an appreciative glance over his shoulder, the brilliant white paintwork gleamed back at him. He was dressed in a pair of dark blue trousers, and virtually matching open-necked long-sleeved cotton shirt, with black casual lace-less shoes.

Tim and Christine greeted him. He declined the offer of a beer, electing to wait until they got to the restaurant.

"Do you happen to be free – tomorrow morning?" Tim asked him in a matter-of-fact tone.

Dalmar thought briefly. "Nothing that won't hold. Why?"

Christine took up the subject and talked in a seductive tone with her big eyes upon him. "Well, you see, there happens to be this auction of furniture and things at Alton, and we wondered if you would like to come with us?" She finished with a slight pout, lowering the tone of her voice at the end of the sentence.

A smile gradually grew on Dalmar's face as he saw through the ruse. "In other words, you could do with an extra pair of hands to help with certain items of furniture – perhaps?" He squinted one eye in her direction.

Tim chuckled and said, "That is roughly the idea." Christine looked expectantly at Dalmar.

"No problem at all," he said. "There is just the question of my fee?" He put a suitably mean expression on his face and rubbed his hands together.

Christine grinned. "Would lunch be suitable – Sir?"

"Utterly," and then he added. "I'm at your service. What time do you want to get away?" Tim explained that the auction started at eleven in the morning and that they wished to get there early for a look around. This meant leaving at about nine-thirty.

"Sure," agreed Dalmar. "I can take Suzanne in the Six – that is – if she is accompanying you?" He pushed his hands outwards but did not wait for a comment. "Leaving you with space for anything you want to bring home. Is that what the estate is for?" The new arrival had been obvious to him when he drew up.

"That's my jalopy," answered Christine. "Lousy colour, but I'm not complaining."

Just then Suzanne came downstairs and walked into the room. Dalmar fought to prevent a gasp. She was so darn pretty, dressed in her new clothes, with her shoulder length near-black hair setting off the beauty of her dusky skinned face. Yet he found himself drawn again to those intense dark brown eyes that shone out of her presence. The deep, partially transparent, blue of the brooch, set adjacent to her white blouse was a kind of obscure distraction from her enchanting features, and it helped prevent him from staring into her eyes for too long. Her hair band enabled him to see more of her smooth forehead, than hitherto.

"Hello – tall man," the face said.

"Hello." And they smiled at each other. Tim alleviated the charged atmosphere by asking Dalmar what restaurant they were going to.

"It's an old pub, actually. The lounge bar bit is now a very fine restaurant. The Fox and Hounds at Crawley."

"Eh?" said Tim. Both he and Christine looked incredulously at him.

Dalmar realised their misunderstanding. "Not Crawley town in Surrey. There is a village of the same name, not far from Winchester."

"Oh, thought you had gone off your rocker for a moment. Driving seventy odd miles to go to a restaurant," Tim said with a smirk.

"I thought I was about to be abducted on an airplane at Gatwick," said Suzanne, looking hopeful.

"Then he would have gone off his rocker. Who would want to abduct you?"

"Shall we go Dalmar? We'll leave my brother to his fish fingers." She said tartly, at the same time opening her eyes wide in mock horror.

Tim growled at her. "Oh, go on Dalmar take her away. Don't worry if you have forgotten your wallet, she is absolutely the tops at washing the dishes, less a broken plate or two." Christine managed to stop the sibling baiting and get the two hopefuls off on their date.

Alone together for the first time there was a bit of an embarrassing silence, apart that is from the deep throb of the roadster's engine. Experience had taught Dalmar never to force this to end, and to naturally let it reach its own conclusion.

"Do you like this car?" To many this question from Suzanne might seem daft, but not so with her. It was just an honest query.

"Ye-es, I do," he replied with slight mirth in his voice. "However, can't say I am that fastidious about it. For instance – take a look at the dog hairs in the back." Suzanne looked over her right shoulder and let forth a really genuine, giggly laugh.

The ice broken they chatted comfortably. After passing through Crowsley village, Dalmar turned off the main road and drove down a narrow lane, which Suzanne recognized as the way to Farley Mount. But before the road started up towards the down, he kept straight on through the delightful village of Sparsholt, and out and across the Stockbridge to Winchester road. As they descended the hill immediately before Crawley village, Suzanne let out a small cry of pleasure on seeing a pond lined on the far bank by period thatched cottages. It was an appealing sight. They stopped and watched the ducks for a while. Mother duck was shepherding her new brood and cute little ducklings were darting hither and thither over the water, just like little children refusing to go to bed.

The Fox and Hounds Tudor architecture leans out over the road as if to say 'stop – you have arrived.' Dalmar parked the sports car in the car park at the back of the building, and they entered the cocktail bar by the rear door. The cheerful girl in the pub welcomed them. Suzanne decided to have a glass of wine to calm her nerves.

After a pleasurable half an hour studying the menu and consuming their drinks, they were shown to a table for two in a cosy medium sized dining room. Wine racks, complete with dusty bottles, lined one wall and polished wood tables butted-up against the other. Above head height there were little recesses displaying various period items of porcelain and copper. Only six other diners were having a meal. On a Friday night it was usually booked up; although, even when full the small number of tables available prevented the place becoming overcrowded, or the service unmanageable. They began their meal with prawn cocktail and requested the wine they had ordered to be served straight away.

The Shy Avenger — Scardthomas

"Dalmar," started Suzanne, her voice echoing inside her wine glass as she took a sip, "the first day we met you, on Farley Mount, you said you had some typing to do. And when we questioned you about it, you never actually said what it was for. Do you write or something?"

"Yes," he replied, with a shy smile. "Actually, it is just a hobby; I try to write poetry."

Suzanne looked sincerely at him, small fork in hand. "I love poetry."

"Honest? ... You are not just saying that?" When he spoke, she noticed, properly, for the first time, that he had nice teeth. The upper one's downward arched pleasantly, but where they were supposed to be straight, in the front, they were not – quite.

"Cross my heart." And she made a suitable sign over her breast. "Why so surprised?"

He thought for a moment. "There are the obvious exceptions like 'I wandered lonely etc' but most folk don't care for poetry today. They are fascinated by the famous, of whom some happen to be poets." For the first time, Suzanne received confirmation of her suspicions that there was more to this man, other than a good physique. She learned a great deal by the time they had finished the main course.

Over coffee, Suzanne talked about her childhood explaining that she had been sent to a convent school in Taunton. She had been on two family holidays to Spain and a trip to the Norfolk Broads. "I'm afraid my knowledge of the outside world is limited."

At this Dalmar said, "Easy up, there is plenty of time for you. Do you want to travel?"

"Oh yes. Lord knows how though." Feeling she might be hogging the conversation, she said, "Anyway that's enough about me; let's have your story. Tell me all – particularly the dark secrets." She smiled with her eyes twinkling, at the same time showing off an endearing dimple on either side of her mouth.

"Rather tame really. Oh – there is the little matter of my six kids on the island of Natkatchafushi." He managed to keep a straight face.

Suzanne pouted at him across the table. "Oh yes! ... and I am a Ward of Court. Stop teasing."

"Okay," he said laughing. "Actually, I was born not far from here. I don't remember much about it, my parents moved away by the time I was five years old."

"Were you an only child?"

"No, I have an elder sister. She and her husband are out in Rhodesia."

"How fantastic. Have you been to visit them?"

"Never really thought about it. We write to each other now and then. She says it's a beautiful country."

"You ought to really. It's a good excuse to go there. I would. Go on, what did you do on leaving school?"

"I joined the Cunard shipping company as an assistant purser. I was nineteen then. Served for five years."

"Wow and here's me talking about travelling. You must have seen lots of countries all over the world."

"Seen them – yes. Got to know them – no. Cruise passengers like a good time on board the ship, while visiting as many places of interest as possible. If you really want to get to know a culture, you won't do it in half a day. I sometimes think that the showing of photographs to friends, after a holiday, is more important than the actual experience, for some people."

"Yes - and boasting about it. But still you must have done an awful lot of things that most of us only dream of."

Dalmar cast a knowing look at her. "Water skiing – skin-diving – that sort of thing. Give me a mask, snorkel, and a pair of flippers near a coral reef and you won't see me for hours."

"There you are then?"

Prompted by Suzanne he went on to tell her a couple of amusing stories, which occurred during his time at sea. Flushed by the pleasure of each other's company, good food and wine, they left the Fox and Hounds.

On the way back in the car, Suzanne asked Dalmar if his parents were still alive. She put it that way because they had, as yet, not been mentioned. "No," he replied. "Actually, that is why I left the Merchant Navy. They both died within a few months of each other, and there was a great deal to see to, so I decided to call it a day."

"How old were you then?"

"Twenty-six. I had older parents than most. My mother was forty-two when she had me."

"Even so, she was quite young when she ..."

"Yes – I guess."

"How did you get into personnel?"

"It's one of the things you pick up as a purser. So – had to start fairly low down, but actually got promoted very quickly – too quickly."

Suzanne took a cigarette out of the packet Dalmar had placed on the dashboard, lit it, and passed it to him. "Don't you have any relatives living around here?" She noticed that he wore a simple gold watch on his wrist, which was different from his usual daytime chronograph.

"None at all. But that is not necessarily a disadvantage." He turned slightly in the driving seat and winked at her.

Suzanne felt a distinct quiver go down her spine. She summoned up the courage. "What about current girl friends?" She kept her face down.

Dalmar smiled to himself. He decided not to tease and felt a warm feeling of pleasure at her question. "Nothing serious," and he left it at that before saying. "What about *current* boy friends?"

Suzanne giggled. "Oh," she said, "so many – I don't know which way to turn." The infectious lilt in her voice became most pronounced as she said this.

He took up the challenge. "Well, tell them they might have some serious competition."

"Okay," she said demurely, and then, deliberately changing the subject asked, "Does your dog get lonely, left alone?"

"Let's face it – most dogs do," he replied, "But he is very good about it and usually greets me when I arrive home. Sometimes though – he hides – gets the sulks – but I can never fathom why? Just one of those things," he finished with a small shrug of his shoulders.

"Why did you call him Fly, or was that his name before he came to you?"

"No ... the very first time I saw him, at the age of six weeks, he was half squatting a foot or so away from his brothers and sisters. A bluebottle was perched on the end of his nose, and he was trying to look at it all cross-eyed." Suzanne chuckled and the more she thought about it, the more she laughed. "Although, the character meaning is also appropriate," he added.

"I'm not surprised!" Suzanne still had a chuckle to her voice. "In fact – that's what I thought it was about."

Soon, they arrived at Beech Cottage. Suzanne invited Dalmar in for a coffee, but he regretfully suggested that they call it a night so that he would be on time tomorrow morning. At this point, it occurred to him that it would be polite to check that she had intended to come to the auction with her brother and sister-in-law. She said, "I wouldn't miss it – should be fun." He leant across and kissed her on her lips, gently, and said how much he had enjoyed the evening. "So have I," she replied in a whisper and then added, "See you in the morning." Before she could extricate herself from the car Dalmar made to get out his side and go round to open the door. But he was stopped by a gentle hand laid on his left arm. Suzanne smiled at him and as gracefully as the low seat of the sports car would allow climbed out.

CHAPTER TEN

AND DOWN WENT THE HAMMER.

The Saturday morning broke back to the brilliant sunshine of ten days ago, only this time it was even warmer.

Dalmar disturbed the Westward's breakfast, so he begged some coffee while they were getting ready. Setting off in convoy with Fly sitting proudly in the back of the open top Triumph, enjoying the breeze and frequently petted by Suzanne, they made good time to Alton, and managed to find a couple of parking spaces fairly near to each other. Fly was placed in the estate car with all the windows partially wound down. Dalmar knew he would have to give him a break after about half an hour, even though their vehicles were in a shady spot. They located the auction house in the market square and joined the crush of people having a preview of the sale.

Having acquired their catalogues, Tim suggested that they go to the outside section where carpets were to be sold before the main event. Christine located two Indian rugs in reasonable condition, with several years of wear left in them. They were lots 10 and 11, and soon, the auctioneer came to them. It was explained before the commencement of the bidding that whatever the winning bid for the first carpet, the second would be offered to the purchaser at the same price. Tim found himself bidding against a dealer and decided to stop when the lot reached eighteen pounds. He mentioned to Dalmar that he wanted some bedroom furniture, which Christine had already earmarked.

All the carpets having been sold everyone returned to the main auction room. From his rostrum the auctioneer commenced his repertoire. "Figurine of a lady. Give me two pounds. Two pounds I'm bid. Two-fifty. Three. Three-fifty. Four pounds. Four pounds I'm bid. Five pounds. Did I hear five pounds? Yes, five pounds. Six pounds I want. Five-fifty. Six. Six I have, on my left... you are at six pounds... Six pounds it is..." And down went the hammer.

Christine and Tim had eyes on lots 96, 97 and 98. They were a natural walnut wardrobe with matching dressing table and cabinet. All were just the right size for their bedroom.

To Tim, Christine and Suzanne's surprise, Dalmar suddenly joined in the bidding for lot 57: four, very pretty silver on glass miniature vases.

With his height he hardly had to bat an eyelid to attract the auctioneer's attention, and he acquired the set for eight pounds.

"What did you buy those for?" asked Suzanne with a curious expression on her face.

"For my Chinese room," replied a straight-faced Dalmar.

"Your Chinese room. How fabulous, I didn't know you had one?"

"Neither did I," he replied.

"What are you talking about … you're mad," she said dragging out the middle syllables of the word mad.

The auctioneer had started on the next item and someone behind then said, "Shush!" loudly, in obvious annoyance. Suzanne started to giggle, and to make matters worse, Dalmar tickled her ribs. She burst out laughing trying to push his hands away. Her plight was made worse by the fact that she was hemmed in and could not seek the sanctity of the open air. The shushing grew louder, and more people joined in.

The auctioneer stopped in mid-sentence, looking extremely annoyed. "Perhaps we could share the joke?" he demanded raising his voice and glaring in the direction of Suzanne. She immediately felt awful and her cheeks started to go red.

Her confusion was saved not by Dalmar, who had started sniggering himself; together with Christine, but a very rotund gentleman nearby who shouted in the loudest voice of all, "Some ones likely farted!" proceeded by a guttural chuckle. A sudden hush ensued followed by a gasp from a tight-faced lady, and then by Dalmar who broke into loud strings of uncontrollable laughter.

When Dalmar really laughed, he did so uncontained. Loud, "Huh! huh! huh!" sounds emanated, it seemed from the depths of his chest. It was extremely infectious, and, eventually, a large part of the auction's participants joined in. Some people became convulsed with hysterics. Even the auctioneer eventually had to give in, starting a loud cackle.

The hilarity lasted for quite a few moments before normal business could be resumed; the auctioneer making the comment, "Perhaps the next lot should be an air freshener," in a remarkably posh voice, followed by dubious laughter.

Dalmar chose this moment to go and see if Fly was all right. It would be his third such trip. Suzanne stopped him, volunteering to go herself. Tim gave her the car keys and she pushed and eased her way out.

Lot 96 eventually arrived, and this time Tim found himself on the right side of the bid. He acquired the walnut wardrobe for eighteen pounds, and the matching dressing table and cabinet for thirteen and ten pounds respectively. Christine was overjoyed.

Meanwhile, Suzanne, after paying a hasty visit to the lady's toilet, had been comforting Fly. Eventually, she decided to take him to the auction. The trouble was that she had not quite mastered how to control him. The dog kept leaping up at her in his joyous freedom, while she was still trying to put on his lead. "Down Fly – sit!" she tried unsuccessfully.

The Shy Avenger

Scardthomas

However, she managed to get him to the back of the crowd at the auction room, attach his lead, and he instantly calmed. Unfortunately, the collie spotted his owner's moccasins deep inside the throng of people. At that moment, Suzanne relaxed her grip on his lead thinking he would just sit and wait. In front of them were a couple of benches piled loosely with items of crockery. The crowd was closed in on this from both sides. Fly could only see one route forward. He leapt with a neat bound right into the middle of the plates and cups and saucers, scattering them in all directions as he frantically tried to keep upright. The resultant noise of the smashing china and people's uproar obviously attracted the attention of everybody. When Dalmar saw Fly trying to make his way towards him, his facial expression changed from curiosity to outright horror. Thinking fast, instead of calling the dog to him, he pushed his way out of the building, coming across a distraught Suzanne. He beckoned to her to follow and ran off in the direction of their motorcars. She went after him but failed to understand quite what was going on. Once they were a safe distance out, Dalmar let go a shrill whistle.

Back at the auction house, Christine and Tim witnessed an amazing scene. The auctioneer completely let go of all reason. "Get that hound out of here!" He shouted as loud as his lungs would allow. Fly had lost sight of his master's legs and was looking around puzzled. Broken crockery littered the stone floor near the entrance and a bench was upside down. Someone got hold of the collie's collar, but quickly let go when the dog turned snarling teeth at him. Fly started to bark repeatedly as if in panic, then he heard his master's whistle and bounded off with his lead trailing and the chaos he had caused behind him.

The harassed looking auctioneer called a halt for a lunch break. Tim and Christine made their way back to the car park to find a pensive looking threesome of Dalmar, Suzanne and the collie. Fly had been pacified but his master did not look too happy.

He and Tim went to pay for their purchases. When it was his turn, Dalmar gave his lot number and then said to the chap at the desk, "And you had better add on that crockery over there." He nodded in the direction of the now swept up pile in the corner. "That was my dog's fault." The man called over to the auctioneer and the two of them whispered a few words on one side.

The auctioneer eventually approached Dalmar and said, "It was good of you to own up, but don't worry about it. We put that on one side for the charity shop. That is why it was where it was, ready for collection. It wasn't worth much."

"In that case," said Dalmar, "Give this to the charity shop;" and he handed over two five-pound notes.

"Thank you – thank you *very* much," the auctioneer said in his aristocratic dialect. "Oh, and by the way, next time you come, can you bring that laugh of yours? It's extremely good for business." And they all jollied the matter away. Dalmar felt much relieved, and his face muscles relaxed again.

Following this came the task of loading up the furniture. Tim had put a roof rack on the station wagon the evening before, so they placed the wardrobe on it and roped it down. The other items went inside – just.

They decided to call in at the Bush, an inn near the village of Ovington, for a drink and snack.

On the way there Suzanne felt drunk with happiness. The open top car was particularly refreshing on such a hot day. Every now and then, Fly, from the rear rather confined seating, nuzzled her right cheek as though sharing her contentment. Dalmar was enjoying the closeness of the girl beside him – very much.

The Westward's had never been to the Bush Inn, and a day such as this was an ideal time to appreciate its surrounding scenic beauty. Just where the dual carriageway commenced after Alresford, Dalmar navigated them off to the right down a narrow road by the eastern bank of the river Itchen. They parked the two vehicles around the back of the pub and said hello to a white horse in its stable. Then the Westwards entered the bar while Dalmar took Fly off for a quick walk.

Inside, there were period paintings hanging on the walls and horse brasses on the low oak supporting beams. A large six-foot wide fireplace dominated one wall.

They ordered a ploughman's lunch for all of them before taking their drinks out to the garden area to find a free table. Dalmar and Fly rejoined them, the dog settling himself into a prostrate position by their side.

A tributary of the river ran along the bottom of the lawn and ducks of many different types seemed to have taken up residence. Young wildfowl were in evidence all over the place, completely oblivious of the two great Danes who lolled lazily in the early afternoon heat.

"Have you got anything on this evening?" Dalmar broke the other's reverie.

Christine grinned and said, "Did you hear that Suz? Told you he would need watching."

Suzanne joined in. "All in one day. Not only does he cause major disturbances and breaches of the peace, but also arranges naturist gatherings as well."

Dalmar looked at Tim, seeking support, only to find him grinning unsympathetically. The embarrassed man held up his hands in mock surrender. "What I meant was…"

"We know what you meant you dirty devil," Christine interrupted him, enjoying his confusion.

Dalmar bowed his head and scratched at his wavy hair. He took a cigarette out of a pack, put it in the corner of his mouth and lit it, letting the smoke drift slowly upwards.

"As I was trying to say…" Dalmar waved his hand still smiling at himself. "I wondered if you would all like to come to my place this evening? I could go to bangers and mash."

This appealed very much to Suzanne. A great deal of it was

curiosity, naturally, to view the interior of his house. She offered to come over earlier and help, which was gratefully accepted. Tim thought it would be a good end to the day.

After the crusty bread, cheddar cheese and pickled onions, they left the Bush and went for a short walk on the other side of the river, crossing by means of a narrow wooden bridge. The main waterway, a chalk stream, looked to have a lower level than usual, but was still running fast. Long, bright green weeds trailed off the banks and up from the depths into the current. This was mesmerizing to look at and gave the four of them a tranquil feeling. They came across a pair of swans with their cygnets: a family of the river, their glorious white plumage advertising their status. It was a wonderful setting for an afternoon's stroll.

Afterwards they made their way home and Dalmar helped Tim unload the new acquisitions at Beech Cottage, before going to his house to start preparing for his guests that evening.

Late in the afternoon, Jack Path was putting away his tools in the garden shed at the back of Yewhurst churchyard. He tended to most of the tasks involved in keeping the burial areas, lawns and pathways neat and tidy. It had been his part-time job for many years and, currently, his retirement occupation. They did not pay him much, but his reward was more in the doing and the satisfaction achieved. Having recovered from his illness and now being as fit as ever he would be for his age; he was trying to make up lost time. 'It had been a hot afternoon,' he thought, and he looked forward to a refreshing cup of tea. His wife would have the kettle on by now. Walking back towards the main gate he turned around to survey his work. The freshly cut appearance of the lawns and the smell of grass juices in the air – pleased him.

His mind strayed to the last time he had seen the lady who used to speak to him from her seat by the Wellingtonia, Miss Thornton. Although they were from different ends of society, she had always been courteous and kind to him. He enjoyed their chats. "Where be you got to?" he mumbled thoughtfully, scratching his head, trying to dislodge some annoying midges.

Unexpectedly, his attention was drawn by a movement in the sky above the church steeple, between two large pines. A long thin shape, motionless in itself, sailed through the air from the top of the left-hand tree, and landed somewhere among the branches of the other... Jack stood still. For some time, he stared at the spot where the oddity had disappeared. "Well bless my soul," he said. "That were strange."

CHAPTER ELEVEN

"YOU ARE A CLEVER DOGGIE."

Perfumed and looking lovely, Suzanne left Beech Cottage at six-thirty. Her dark hair glistened in the evening sunshine, and her mind was full of anticipation for what was to come.

She followed Dalmar's directions and was soon gaily walking up a gravel path bounded on both sides by lawn, with a solitary apple tree to her right. His house was one of a pair of farm labourer's cottages, joined together. A central chimney flue served the two properties. There was once a small communal courtyard with washhouses and toilets. In modern times, this had been split in half using a high wooden panelled fence to privatise each area. The old washhouse on Dalmar's side was now used as a garden shed, and the former outside lavatory had become a log storage shelter.

As the cottages had been built prior to the days of the motorcar, they now found themselves back to front. When the road was laid alongside the Claymans Heron in the 1940s, residents of the cottages started to enter their homes through what was then the back garden. The original arched front door and porch-way in Dalmar Hunter's half was left locked up most of the time. This entrance would have been used when access was gained from a farm track, many years ago.

Suzanne rang the doorbell. Fly came bounding into the kitchen and jumped up, placing his front paws on the top of the bottom half of a stable door, which had been left ajar. Suzanne was able to liberally pet his head.

Dalmar appeared at the entrance to the kitchen, wearing a towelling bathrobe. "Sorry about this. I decided to mow the lawn and forgot the time. Come on in," he said with a lilt of humour, pulling back the bottom section of the door.

Suzanne stood, looking mischievously at him. She nearly said something cheeky but went shy of it. "Dalmar, that honeysuckle scent is absolutely gorgeous!" She pointed to the full flowering bush above the glass porch.

"Yes. Actually – it's nearly over. But maybe we'll get a second bloom: sometimes happens. Fly – that'll do!" The dog was still trying to get as much attention from Suzanne as possible.

"Oh, you know I don't mind – do I lovey?" she said fussing over the dog further. Dalmar had to explain to her about the front door – back door situation. There was no dining room as such, just a sitting room with a bay window that looked out over a large field towards a farmhouse. The property had a quarter of an acre of garden, and its owner kept it reasonably tidy – most of the time. Just to the right of the bay window, a few yards out from the front porch grew a magnificent silver birch in its prime. At the base of the trunk a sizeable mound had formed. Growing on this mound were some scarlet poppies in full bloom.

He left her looking out of the window while he went up to his bedroom to finish dressing. Her attention soon strayed from the view to the room's interior. There were a couple of photographs on a shelf in a small display cabinet, which was set in a recess. She went across and studied them. One, the larger of the two, was of a middle-aged couple standing in a garden, backed by a good-sized Georgian house. The lady had similar features to Dalmar. The other showed a teenage girl with a shy smile. Suzanne wondered if that was Dalmar's sister. There was only one picture hanging on the walls: a medium sized photographic study of Burnham beeches in full autumn colouring.

Within a few minutes, her date came back down. "Like to look upstairs?" he asked.

"Of course!"

He took her up the tight spiral staircase and showed her the three bedrooms. None of them were particularly large, and they were all very simply furnished. The nicest room was the smallest one, possessing a single bed and some cute cottage style furnishings.

Dalmar's room had the same view from the window as the lounge downstairs, except that you could see a further distance over farmland. There was nothing staggering about the house, and compared to Beech Cottage, it was no match for period architecture, but what it did have was an intoxicating homely atmosphere: an unusual achievement for a bachelor pad. More than likely, this had something to do with past farming community, family occupations.

They talked about various things. "Who looks after Fly when you are at work?" Suzanne asked him. This had puzzled her for some time.

"He stays next door with Joe and Janice. I checked it out with them before I got Fly. Joe works for a local horticultural firm, and Janice doesn't mind. A paying arrangement you understand?" Suzanne nodded. "When Janice goes shopping or something, Fly house guards. Fortunately, as yet, they haven't been on holiday, so he hasn't been kennelled at all."

"Well, while I'm staying with Tim and Christine, I don't mind taking him out if you like," Suzanne said expectantly. There was a small smile on her face. "And I'll do it for free;" she finished smiling broadly.

"Well – thank you," said Dalmar. "Fly – you are getting too popular." The dog knew they were talking about him and wagged his tail enthusiastically.

They returned to the kitchen and set about preparing the evening meal. While the potatoes were boiling and they were sitting in the bay window enjoying a cup of tea, Suzanne asked Dalmar if she could see some of his poetry. He took down a black folder from a high shelf and left her with it, while he laid the table.

After a while she suddenly spoke. "Oh, I like that, 'Concerning Christianity.' It is applicable to so many people – including myself." She read aloud:

"I am afraid to say
I do not believe,
because of what I feel.
Yet, I'm afraid to say
that I believe,
because of what I know.
Therefore, I remain a cowardly in-between
and take consolation, in that, I am one of many."

The poet gave a shy smile in acknowledgement.

The doorbell rang to announce the arrival of Christine and Tim. Dalmar was about to put the manuscript on the shelf when Suzanne placed her hand over it, saying with sincerity. "I'd like to look at some more – later."

The sausages, mashed potato and gravy went down well, and the wine flowed. Dalmar always kept a few bottles in stock. After the meal, they played a game of Scrabble, which Christine won easily. Suzanne then made coffee and the host produced a bottle of Cognac. They whiled away the last hour listening to records and chatting.

Round about eleven-thirty, Christine turned to Tim and said, "I think we had better make a move ..." Tim agreed. Dalmar decided to walk over with them and so give Fly some exercise. Suzanne had the volume of poetry in her hand and she coyly asked the writer if she could borrow it, promising to take great care. He said that of course she could. He felt flattered.

Tim and his wife walked on ahead leaving the other two and the dog some fifty yards behind. "Why didn't Fly bark when Tim and Christine arrived earlier?" asked Suzanne.

"It's uncanny actually. When the doorbell rings, or there is a tap on the door, he seems to have the ability to know friend or stranger. Believe me, if it is a stranger, he barks the ruddy place down."

"You mean, because he knows us, he didn't bark?"

"Uh huh."

"That's fantastic: absolutely fantastic. You are a clever doggie!" she said calling ahead to Fly.

Before she crossed the main road, Christine turned and shouted. "Thanks, Dalmar... Goodnight!"

Tim turned, smiled and waved. "Thanks for your help at the auction!"

Dalmar raised a hand to both of them. "Pleasure – goodnight!"

By the time Dalmar, Suzanne and Fly had arrived at the gate, the front door of Beech Cottage was closed, and there was no sign of life. Even the porch light was extinguished.

The night was a clear one. A full moon made vision up to a hundred yards relatively easy. But apart from Fly snuffling at their feet, Suzanne and Dalmar felt conspicuously alone. "Thanks ever so much for helping," he said as she put a hand on the gate. They were very close and that old magnetism from a million yesterdays started to pull their two bodies together.

"Oh, that's okay – I enjoyed it – and come to think of it, I never really thanked you for last night..." She broke off, looking up into his face. He slowly raised his right hand and very gently stroked the hair partially curled under her cheek. It felt sensually soft and tingled against his skin. She did not move – her eyes hypnotised by his. They came together in a very gentle kiss, although she felt power from his arms during the embrace.

"See you soon – I'll ring you tomorrow." he whispered in her ear. The deep tones resonated within her head.

"Okay," she said in a hushed voice. The kiss had had such an emotive effect on her, she was finding it difficult to keep calm.

Fly was looking up at them with his head on one side, and a look of puzzlement in his eyes. Their hands trailed away until just their fingertips were touching, then she opened the gate and attempted to half-skip up the path. She stumbled on the porch step, but whether it was due to the effect of the kiss, or the fact that she had just spotted Christine peeping from behind a curtain, she alone knew?

CHAPTER TWELVE

HER DAY WOULD COME.

The following day, at dusk, the light gold body of a barn owl could be seen gliding along the hedge that bounded the eastern border of Yewhurst Wood. It lifted in a soft air current, showing its white feathered under body, before landing on a fence post adjacent to the blackthorn hedge. This male had already hunted successfully, having started his quest late in the afternoon. He had young to feed and leaving matters to night-time could result in a sparse result. Changing his mind, he lifted off and climbed with delicate flaps of his wings to take him to a perch in an old oak tree that grew just off the edge of the field. From here, his binocular vision could see over to the barn where the nesting site was situated.

As the feathers along his body settled, the fair, heart-shaped face turned a full three hundred degrees to look back along the branch on which his talons were firmly locked. The slightest of movements from another being had caused him to do this. The exceptionally large pupils of his eyes became fixed onto what appeared to be a snake. It was not a snake that this owl had ever seen before. It was much bigger than anything he had ever come across. Also, he had never encountered a reptile of any description coiled around the branch of a tree. But that was not what held the owl's gaze. It was the adverse aura that this strange being gave off. The barn owl's vision, although excellent for long-range sight, was in monochrome, and what he now looked upon brought intense misgiving. Without warning the odd reptilian life form raised its head and returned the stare. The barn owl waited no longer, and, without bothering with his usual silent take off, quickly, with rapid wing movement took to the air. Those eyes that had looked upon him seemed to be burning within. During the remaining years of his life, the barn owl never perched in that tree again.

While lying in bed enjoying her secure world during the twilight of sleep, Suzanne would frequently think about Dalmar. There were thoughts of pleasure concerning his masculinity. Of most appeal to her was the way he moved. It seemed to sum up the most able physique for the hunter: the provider of yesteryears. There were thoughts about his persona – a charisma of male charm with high values of integrity. There were thoughts about his selflessness, illustrated in his care for his dog, and, she suspected, a caring father waiting in the wings. Most of all she loved the way he looked at her sometimes, with a shy expression of want. Passion showed in his eyes, while his lips remained closed.

The next week scorched its way through time. Temperatures reached the nineties in some parts of the country.

The Shy Avenger   Scardthomas

Tim and Christine, Dalmar and Suzanne had arranged to go to a quiet beach on Sunday that Dalmar knew of, in the eastern part of the county of Dorset. The plan was to avoid the early morning traffic and set off about mid-morning. All being well, they would stop for lunch at Corfe, a village of some appeal, and go on to the beach at their leisure. But instead of returning with the majority of traffic in the late afternoon, they thought it would be a good idea to stay on the shore until well into the evening. Dogs were not allowed on the particular beach they were going to, so poor Fly had to stay at home. His owner would have to leave plenty of food and water, for it would be a long time for him to be left alone. However, Janice from next door had agreed to take him for a walk during the afternoon.

All four of them could fit into the Morris with a certain degree of comfort. So, at eleven o'clock, they set off, hood down, on a perfectly glorious sunny Sunday. Very little traffic was on the road. They passed through Yewhurst, down a long hill, up again on the other side, round a bend and into a tunnel of overhanging trees, where in the far distance you could make out a pinpoint of light. This was the Great Mile.

Tim, with his hands firmly on the steering wheel, glanced above him before looking to his left and then to the right into the woodland on either side. Large houses with their gardens of abundant rhododendron and azalea dissolving the treescape at regular intervals.

They made good time through the northern extremities of the New Forest before traversing across country to Wimborne Minster and down to Corfe. Parking in the little square with its buildings of Portland stone, they walked around the corner to a bookshop with a cafe. At the back of the restaurant was a garden with a few tables and chairs laid out on a green-grass lawn.

The onlooker looks upon one of the finest views of interest in the area. The ruins of Corfe Castle are right in front of you and take up three-quarters of the picture transmitted to your eyes. In sunshine, the light is at its best and the blue-sky background makes the scene a star performer in the county of Dorset's high spots. The distressed, cream coloured giant stone walls and fallen buttresses stand out starkly against the tufted, variegated green grass which grows all over the undulating area. From this vantage point the scene is made all the more special, because there is only a small audience at any one time.

They sat at a white metalwork table with matching chairs, and on Dalmar's suggestion ordered Welsh rarebit for all of them. Apart from words of appreciation for the beauty of the place, their conversation was sparse: there was no need of any. The scenery was the entertainment, coupled with a desire to learn more about the history of the castle. Tim purchased a small booklet in the shop, which they all studied together.

Happy with the experience of Corfe, they set off over a section of the Purbeck Hills towards the sea. Arriving at a suitable point, they stopped in a lay-by to admire the panoramic view over Poole Harbour and the river Frome's estuary. Then they drove down to Studland Bay,

Dalmar giving directions to a private beach. They had to pay a small charge before parking in a tarmac area that had a light covering of wind-blown sand. There were a lot of cars, some with trailers for boats, but this did not seem to worry Dalmar and they soon found out why. Gathering together their swimming gear, they undertook a short walk over ample sand dunes to the beach, which stretched for two miles in an easterly direction, and a mile or more to the west. It looked surprisingly sparsely busy. Dalmar led them along the water's edge for a few hundred yards before cutting inland. He found a spot, which was not totally private, because a footpath was visible not far away, but it was good enough.

They took off their outer clothes and put on swimming costumes with the aid of modesty towels. With the exception of Tim, they were ably tanned; Dalmar because he had been swimming in the sea several times this summer, and the girls because of their idle moments in the back garden of Beech Cottage. Tim knew he would have to be careful and, sensibly, he kept his sports shirt on to protect his fair skin.

They all headed for the sea. The beach was covered in pale beige coloured sand. The old port of Poole lay to the east and on the horizon the white chalk cliffs of the Needles, off the Isle of Wight, could be clearly seen. There was a great deal of small boat activity, and in the middle distance a good-sized yacht race was in progress, but it looked to be very slow due to the calm conditions. Having taken the heat of the day, they approached the water with varying degrees of anticipation. Suzanne ran for it closely followed by Dalmar. He could not help but admire her in a bikini, which was decorated in multi shades of blue and contrasted alluringly with her dusky skin tone. She looked charming and curvy, rather than classically beautiful.

That day proved to be one of those that its participants would preserve in their memory. It was quite simply perfect. The weather stayed hot and the skies kept clear. It was a day of laughter, relaxation and games in the water.

Only one small moment worried Suzanne. She looked up from her book while sun-bathing in the middle of the afternoon. It had been some time since Dalmar said he was going for another dip in the sea. She went to the top of the dune and scanned the foreshore and the shallows. After a while she said to the others. "Where has Dalmar got to?" Christine looked up from her prone position with a questioning expression. "He said he was going for a swim," Suzanne said anxiously. Tim came and joined her. He looked further out to sea. "Tim – I – I just can't see him," his sister said. After a moment he tapped her on the shoulder and pointed a couple of hundred yards straight out to sea. A tiny dark mop of hair topped a bobbing head. In a few moments it could be discerned as a fast breaststroke swimmer coming towards them. "Thanks Tim." There was relief in her voice.

It was at times like this when Suzanne felt pangs of insecurity over her relationship. She knew that she was in love. But what were Dalmar's feelings towards her. True, he had often been complimentary over her appearance, but he had not told her that he loved her or anything near it.

Christine got a big boost to her ego when she went to get them all ice creams. She passed a crowd of fellows, all in their late teen years, resting from a beach soccer game. The wolf whistling directed at her was piercingly loud, but then, she was a very beautiful woman. Her blonde hair hung square over her shoulders, and had that crinkly look, having dried naturally following immersion in the sea. Her bright pink bikini, hugging the soft-light-brown-sugar colour of her body, accentuated the sway of her hips as she walked. She smiled with embarrassment.

They left the beach at nearly eight o'clock in the evening. Once again, they duped the heavy traffic. On the way back they stopped at the High Corner Inn: an isolated hostelry in the open area of the New Forest. Wine for the girls and a pint of real ale for Tim and Dalmar, together with a light bar meal finished off their day. It was still warm enough to eat outdoors in the evening light. Forest ponies grazed the meadow nearby, and several rabbits darted hither and thither, kicking their back legs out in a frisky moment.

The long day in the open air and the light burn of the sun sent them all to bed early. Their bodies were tired, and their minds were relaxed. Two of them, who slept in different houses, dreamt of each other and hoped that the other was thinking about them. A piece of paper fell onto the floor from Dalmar's bed, on which were scribbled some lines of verse scrawled in uneven letters.

Dalmar took Suzanne out twice in the next week, once to the cinema, and a couple of days later for a drink at a bar by a yacht marina. On the Friday evening, all four of them went to the Fox and Hounds for an evening meal.

It stayed hot. Cricket pitches all over the country were parched brown, and so were private lawns because hosepipe bans were still in operation. Such weather made England, un-English. The press made comparisons with the summer of 1947, and numerous statistics were published. Nevertheless, it had been, and still was very hot, very dry and very dusty. The weathermen saw no sign of a change in the immediate future.

After a long hard-working day, four forestry workers in Yewhurst Wood were sitting in a safe area, away from the woodland, enjoying a well-earned smoke. They were at the top of a rise, at the end of the track that led directly to a logging region. In front of them lay a tarmac road, the way back to Chapp and their cottages. All of them were liberally coated in sawdust, not just on their clothing, but also under their shirt collars and in their hair. The chain saws had long since been put away, but there had been a considerable amount of clearing up to do. This meant that it was now past nine o'clock and the twilight shadows were lengthening rapidly. They were not talking much, preferring to enjoy their

The Shy Avenger   Scardthomas

tobacco while listening to the evening forest sounds.

Abruptly, utterly pervasive, came a strident hissing sound from a dense part of the woods, which was not too far away. "What the 'ell was that?" exclaimed one of the men. As if in answer, it was repeated, this time backed by a low, strange roaring noise.

"Du'n'no," uttered a red-haired man. "But it ain't the first time Oi heard it." He paused for a moment before adding. "It always 'appens in the eve'nin – just about dusk like – usually way off – o'er on the eastern side of the forest look."

"Well, whatever 'tis," commented another worker. "Oi don't like it. Oi can tell ee that."

The only one of them who had not said anything, as yet, did so now. "Some say – it be John – come back." He was straight faced, but those close at hand would have detected some concern in his voice. The effect was to silence any further conversation. The same man recalled something that had happened earlier in the summer. It had been about midday, and he had been working near the church. A disturbing noise had come from an area to the east of the forest: the unmistakable sound of a grown man's scream. As there had been no further disturbance, he had not gone to investigate. However – it did bother him now.

The men rose to their feet to trudge back to their homes and families, brushing the white sawdust sediment from their clothing as they went.

Two days later, Suzanne was spending a quiet evening with Dalmar at his cottage. Fly was asleep in his basket in the kitchen. The popular musical duo, The Carpenters, could be heard on the music system. Coffee and a shared glass of brandy were on the table by the fireplace.

Suzanne had read all of Dalmar's poetry, some of it several times. She liked the dramatic lyrical pieces and the prose work, but she tended to avoid the romantic verse. She was quite frank about it, having told Christine that she did not wish to read a love poem written by Dalmar, unless it was about her. Christine suggested – that no doubt her day would come.

All the windows in the house were open wide, and both the front and back doors were ajar in a vain attempt to attract a wandering breeze. Dalmar had not bothered to put on a shirt after having taken a bath, just a pair of well-worn jeans. Suzanne was dressed in shorts and a white blouse.

Her head lay on her man's shoulder, and he had his arm around her. Something in the lyrics of Karen Carpenter's singing of the song, 'Close to You', stirred her emotions, and Dalmar lightly brushed away a tear that had fallen halfway down her cheek. In response, she had turned her head up to him. There was love in her eyes. He felt protectiveness for her, sensing emotional fragility in the girl: a melancholic mood. He drew her more to him by clenching the muscles in his right arm.

Later, perhaps it was their lack of attire that made their embrace become more urgent, or perhaps it was the heat, or a combination of both. Dalmar had not made any attempt to change the last record, which had finished ten minutes ago, and Suzanne could not have cared less. It was about this time that Dalmar took her head from his shoulder and kissed her passionately. The kiss held firm until his intention became obvious, and Suzanne's response was equal to his. She made a sound, the sound that is the sign of the human female's physical love note the world over: she moaned. He undid the two buttons that still held her blouse together, and slowly slid it off her shoulders. She was not wearing a brassier. His right hand caressed her waist, and then moving more onto her, the palm of that hand, ever so lightly, touched a nipple. The effect on Suzanne was electric, and she arched her back towards him, as though to make the two them, as one.

Over the road in Beech Cottage, Christine lay on the settee with her head on Tim's shoulder. Both were sharing that feeling of happiness and satisfaction that comes from matters having worked out well: the enjoyment of the life they were leading, their love for each other and good health. They belonged completely to one another. They were each other's property, and such precious property must be protected. If one of them were to lose the other ... the thought was unthinkable.

For the time being, there was not much more they could do to improve the cottage. Now they needed to save up funds in order to purchase furniture and appliances. They had both decided that the next item should be of entertainment value and had agreed on a stereo music system.

While the romance between Dalmar and Suzanne continued, neither of them supposed that Suzanne would be leaving them just yet. She might even elect to get a job in the area. Despite the gloom of large-scale unemployment in the country, there seemed to be plenty of secretarial vacancies in the local towns. Her brother made it clear that she was very welcome to stay on if she wished.

"Fancy going over to the Claymans for a quick drink darling?" asked Tim. "I could do with something long and cold."

Christine made up her mind quickly. "Okay – I'll just go and put a comb through my hair."

In ten minutes, they were seated in their favourite table booth in the long bar. They were not talking much. Christine cradled her drink for a moment feeling the cold moisture on the sides of the glass. She looked out of the window watching the coming and goings in the car park. Tim was studying her face and wondering in his good fortune to have such a wife. This was not a new emotion for him; he often did wonder at it. She turned her head to look at him. "You're staring at me?" There was a smile on her lips.

"That is because I love you," he said.

Christine spoke no further. She looked kindly and fondly upon him and reached out with both hands to lay them on his.

Later, in their bed, following making love, neither of them would have been able to explain a strange marital happening. She had communicated something to her husband without saying anything. Namely, she did not wish to take the pill that prevented conceiving. He had reacted to the wordless message by merely nodding in acquiescence.

Soon, Christine fell asleep with her head partly on her husband's shoulder, and partly on his chest. Tim lay there thinking and enjoying the moment.

Unexpectedly, the peaceful reverie was broken by a noise: an awesome, loud hissing accompanied by a hideous deep note: like nothing on Earth. Tim's body went stiff. Normally he would have risen to investigate, but he did not wish to disturb his wife who continued to sleep. The sound had lasted for a few seconds and came from the back of the cottage, off in the woods. He remembered then the noise they had heard on the evening of their first day here. The odd sound left him with a feeling of dread. Then he remembered something else, and it did not help. He recalled Dalmar's question about unusual noises when they had briefly discussed John the Red, and then he remembered Suzanne's similar query, with Allen Haddle in the Claymans bar.

Not far away, Suzanne lay in her lover's bed, in a similar position to that of her sister-in-law with her brother. She was also asleep.

Dalmar heard the same sound, which, although further away, was still distinct. At first, he felt disbelief, followed by a deep emotional fear lasting several moments. This was replaced by a determined anger; an old anger that lay dormant within him. "So," he said in an ominously quiet tone, "it is time …"

From the sleepy head on his chest came a small, "Mmm."

CHAPTER THIRTEEN

THE SECRET POND

The first Monday in August dawned with a heat haze over the New Forest; however, it was completely filtered by the sun quite early in the day. From then on, the heat increased in intensity to reach ninety-six degrees in the shade. Holidaymakers lay sprawled along the beaches and visited the seawater frequently. People at work carried out their duties at a much slower pace. For the school children, during the summer holiday, it was a magical time.

Julia Thornton had now been officially declared 'a missing person'. All those that knew her were completely mystified. A lot of them feared the worst. Some – even considered that she had been murdered. But – what was the motive? None of her personal possessions appeared to have been touched, and there was no sign of any attempt at a break in at her home.

In the afternoon, Christine and Suzanne Westward were enjoying the sunshine in the back garden of Beech Cottage. They had taken to looking after Fly during the day, and he was stretched out contentedly in the shade under Christine's lounger. The girls had just finished exhaustively discussing the Julia Thornton mystery, having read the latest information in the local newspaper.

Suzanne was in a dreamy world now she was in love. Christine was not able to get much sense out of her. She frequently gently teased her sister-in-law during their in-depth discussions.

"Phew – it's so hot! I wish we had a swimming pool," said Christine.

"Ooh yes," agreed Suzanne. After a pause she carried on. "Hey! – Did I tell you Dalmar knows a pond in the woods, not too far from here, where you can have a super swim. He reckoned very few people knew about it."

"Did he tell you how to get there?"

"Actually, he wrote it down. I've got it upstairs – somewhere."

"I expect it would have dried up in this drought," considered Christine. "Or else it's become stagnant and smelly."

"No – apparently, an underground spring rises there, So, it is always fresh and sparkling clear … I think." She wrinkled her brow, trying to recall exactly what Dalmar had told her.

Christine thought for a moment. "Let's try and find it," she said suddenly.

Suzanne looked worried. "Isn't it rather hot to go for a walk?" she said looking at her sister-in-law doubtfully. "And Dalmar will be here soon." She had not completely lost her apprehensive feelings about the forest.

Christine, for the time being, had forgotten the incident with Ma Hessil and her dog. She now had no concerns at all. "Oh, we'll leave a note on the door. He won't get back for at least an hour or so, will he? Surely you can bear to be parted for a *few* minutes?" Christine teased. "Come on, it will be fabulous searching. How far?"

"About half a mile ... I think."

"It will be fun trying to find it. What do you say?"

"Yes, all right," said Suzanne warming to the idea. "We can take Fly with us: it will be good exercise for him." The collie sensed something was up and jumped to his feet expectantly.

They went upstairs to the bedrooms and put on jeans and blouses over their bikinis, exchanging flip-flops for sandals. Suzanne found the written directions in her bedroom. Locating a scrap of paper in the kitchen, she wrote:

DALMAR   We have gone to find the Secret Pond.
Fly is with us.
Back soon. S xxx

She pinned it on the back door.

They set off without towels: Christine insisted that they would be dry by the time they got halfway home. Proceeding at a slow pace, they took the path through the beech trees, until they met the firebreak that ran north to south. A strong walk took them over the brow of a small hill, and about half a mile further on, they met another firebreak forming a crossroads.

"That's right," said Suzanne. "He says you go over two crossovers before turning off." The deeply rutted clearway from numerous tractor tires was as hard as rock underfoot and made walking a bit uncomfortable. Fly, uncharacteristically, stayed by their sides instead of bounding on ahead. Now, he preferred to walk slowly with the two women, and his panting seemed to get more and more urgent: his thick coat was not made for this climate.

Long lines of conifers stretched away endlessly on the right-hand boundary of the clearway, and tall green bracken lined both sides. The little stream that normally tumbled down the left was non-existent, its course being completely dry. At intervals, clumps of silver birch took over from the fir trees: the sun filtering through their abundant small leaves causing pale streaky highlights on the pale bark.

They passed the second junction of paths and both of them began to scan the right-hand aspect. "We have to look for a much narrower track." Dalmar told me that it is normally quite lush," said Susanne wiping perspiration from her brow with her left arm. "Ah – that is probably it." She pointed at an obvious break in the trees a little way ahead. They started down. It was cooler and more verdant than the firebreaks had been. "Now we want another pathway, again going off to the right. Oh Lord! I hope I've got this right. Remember the way back Chris."

Having progressed about a couple of hundred yards, Christine, leading the way, announced, "Is this it?" She pointed down a dark tunnel of small hazel trees, which disappeared round a bend.

"Let's give it a try," said Suzanne.

The undergrowth was so dense that very little could be seen. They would certainly have missed the pond altogether had something very strange not happened. They came to a little dip in the path where the hazel tree branches did not meet overhead, allowing the light to shine through. Fly, in front, suddenly froze and refused to move. When Christine tried to pull him, holding his collar, he stubbornly stood his ground and started to bark. Two or three large birds, being startled by the din took to flight with a clatter of wings, making the girls jump.

"What's that?" exclaimed Suzanne.

Christine looked up. "Ducks. That's it! ... That's where the pond is." She gave an extra tug on Fly's collar. He just would not budge. and no amount of coaxing would persuade him. "Let's leave him: I bet he will follow in his own time."

Reluctantly, Suzanne started to make her way off the track, alongside some brambles, gingerly picking at the briars with her fingertips. Christine followed, but Fly stayed put and started whining. Before very long, with much cursing at the undergrowth, the girls came upon the pond. It was as well that they had worn jeans, but even so they picked up the odd scratch on their arms from numerous blackberry bramble briars. Suzanne parted some tall grasses between a few larch trees, and there in front of her glistened the waters of a natural sanctuary. The pond was fairly large, about seventy feet long and twenty-five wide. Her first comment was a loud "Wow!"

Christine joined her and they scrambled through the lower larch branches onto a grey and white rocky bank, covered in the crevices by bluebell greenery. Neither of them said anything for a moment or two, because before them was a beautiful sight. Apart from anything else the existence of a crystal-clear pool, around here, was a geological freak. The surrounding rocks looked like granite. This was extremely unusual for the area. The conifers, which in some places came right to the water's edge, did not have it all their own way. Here and there, thick rhododendron bushes and a couple of birch trees had crept in as well. The reflection of all this in the water – was stunning. Sunshine found its way into the central area of the pond and its rays penetrated some of the larches on the far bank.

"It must be a fantastic sight in the spring," commented Christine. "Just imagine it, with the bluebells and rhododendron in full bloom!"

"Hmm," was all Suzanne could say.

After a while Christine stood up. "I'm going in. Come on Suz!"

Suzanne was in the process of studying a large Sweet Chestnut tree that rose up out of the rhododendron bushes over to her left. Its branches overhung the water's edge: a superlative cameo picture. "I hope Fly will be okay?" she said with concern.

"He'll be waiting for us on the path. Don't worry. Probably finds it all a bit strange: picked up a scent he doesn't like, I guess." She stepped out of her shoes, pulled down her jeans and released her blouse buttons. Then in her pink bikini, she gingerly put half a foot in the water. "Ouch! It feels cold." She lowered herself in and was surprised to find herself up to her waist before her feet touched a slippery bed. It felt firm however, so she straightened her body to its full height, uttering little gasping noises. Making up her mind, she took a deep breath and launched herself towards the centre of the pool. She was a good swimmer and was soon cleaving her way through the water to the far bank. Following this she splashed about a bit and shouted across to Suzanne. "It's fantastic!"

Suzanne stood up and shed her clothes down to her bikini, and surprisingly, without hesitation, executed a neat dive with hardly a splash. She was soon alongside Christine making excited sounds at the sudden refreshing chill. They giggled and splashed at each other for some time. Christine pointed to the rocks where their clothes were. A timid looking Fly was stretching his head and sniffing eagerly at them. Suzanne felt great relief to see him.

After a while they rested; Christine by floating on her back, with Suzanne gently treading water. It was then that Suzanne noticed something she thought peculiar. Apart from the sound of the ripples made by them and Fly's soft panting, everything seemed eerily silent. The air was especially still. All the noise they had recently made, she presumed, was the cause – having frightened away not only the ducks, but other birds as well. Nevertheless, she began to feel uneasy and looked around, studying the water's edge.

Christine started to slowly roll over and over in the water. When she stopped and looked up, she was surprised to see Suzanne clambering up the bank. "Hey! ... you're not getting out already are you Suz?"

Suzanne called over her shoulder. "You carry on. Goin' to keep Fly company."

"It's so refreshing. I feel *fantastic* now!" shouted Christine and started to breaststroke over towards the far bank, under the chestnut tree.

Suzanne got dressed and while petting Fly she became acutely aware of the dog's body stiffening under her hand. Then came an exclamation of surprise from the direction of her sister-in-law. Suddenly – there was a very loud scream! The ear-piercing scream of a terrified woman! Suzanne spun around. Illuminated by the periphery of the sun's rays under the chestnut tree, Christine stood waist deep in the water with a look of sheer horror on her face. Twisted round her neck was the coil of a vile looking snake. The evil, deadly looking head, larger in proportion to its body, was raised parallel to Christine's head. Suzanne stared, in disbelief. Set in bold silhouette against the dark backdrop of the shadows, her sister-in-law's sun-tanned body had become revoltingly tarnished by the coils of a large serpent like creature, tightly wrapped around her and coloured a vivid, dark pulsating red. Christine started to flail her arms across its head in panic.

At this point Fly barked loudly. Due to the echo effect across the pond, it seemed very loud. In a movement faster than the human eye could follow the snake struck! Christine let out another scream; only this time it was one of agonizing pain. Then came a shrieking hiss. It was a dreadful – vandalising, shattering noise.

But Fly's barking must have distracted the snake. Like a released spring, it uncoiled itself from the distraught girl and swam towards the nearest bank in a fast-meandering motion. To Suzanne, it looked astoundingly long before it wriggled out of the water and disappeared into the undergrowth. Christine screamed again and desperately started splashing through the water towards Suzanne, who jumped in to assist her. By the time Suzanne had struggled to get the traumatised woman to the edge of the pond, Christine went still – leaving the only sounds – the settling of disturbed water and a collie's anxious whining.

CHAPTER FOURTEEN

"WHERE IS IT NOW?"

Dalmar cut the engine of his Triumph and parked outside Beech Cottage. He glanced at his watch. It was twenty minutes past five. Looking at the house he could not see any sign of life, so he went around the back. He saw the note pinned to the door.

A cry, in the air, like a very distant call for help, made him falter in his steps. He read the note. Then he heard a definite but far away scream coming from the direction of the deeper forest. It triggered him into urgent action. He vaulted the gate and practically fell in the Triumph's open top. Grappling with the glove box compartment, he opened it and felt inside. His fingers closed over a coil of thin grade rope. Straightening himself up, he threw his suit jacket onto the passenger seat of the car, together with his tie, which he had hurriedly un-knotted from his neck. All the while he kept hearing faint, far-off horrific screams and he began to develop a desperate sense of urgency, almost despair. He quickly tied the small length of rope around his waist and tore off in the direction of the church.

He could hear a dog's distant bark. 'That's Fly,' he thought. His chest, very soon, felt as though it was on fire, and he cursed his smoking habit. Crashing through the fence near the church, not bothering with the stile, he started down the main fire clearance path.

The Forestry Commission did not have any staff working in this area of the woodland today. If there had been, one of them might have witnessed the sight of a man, jacket and tie-less perhaps, but nevertheless dressed in unsuitable clothing running as fast as he could into the depths of the forest. This would have appeared somewhat unusual.

As Dalmar approached the first crossover of paths, he saw Fly. The collie came bounding up to him and stopped. He did not make his usual leap and cuddle greeting with wagging tail. Jerking his head, the dog took off again, in the direction from which he had come. Dalmar followed, not stopping in his charge. He had already run for approximately a third of a mile as fast as he could. By the time he arrived at the hazel tree tunnel he was seriously short of breath. But he brazenly ignored it, and literally fought his way by sheer power of physique over exhaustion, along the tunnel and through the bramble until he found them.

Suzanne, sobbing, held Christine's head in her arms. The poor girl had made one attempt to get her sister-in-law out of the water so that she could go and get help, but over the last ten minutes she had been shocked into a dreadful state of hopelessness, believing – it was already too late. Images of her brother – distraught, tightened around her brain.

Dalmar tried to take everything in. Worryingly obvious was the wound showing on Christine's left shoulder.

"What's ... happened!" he urgently asked, his words separated with a pressing pause for breath. Without hesitation, he jumped into the water to assist Suzanne. He managed to get both his arms under Christine's body, before lifting her out and placing her more securely onto the rocky bank. "Chris – can you hear me!" She showed no sign of consciousness. Dalmar looked into Suzanne's face, all the while still breathing hard. The lights had dimmed in her eyes. She was in a state of shock. "Now – Suzanne – listen to me." He took her head in his hands imploring her.

"Yes," came a weak reply.

"Has Christine been bitten?"

Another barely audible, "Yes."

"Was it a big snake?"

"Yes." Raising her head to show a tear-lined face, she added – a little louder – "*Very*. Under that tree over there," and she raised a shaking hand to point across the pond.

"Where is it now?"

"Don't know." She shook her head frantically. "It swam over to that bank. Gone."

"Darling ... you must do something very important. Go to Beech Cottage and phone for an ambulance – 999 ... you understand? Go my darling. Go like the wind."

Suzanne, even in shock, at last grasped the urgency and snapped out of her forlorn state. She climbed out of the water and got to her feet. They found the cottage door key in Christine's jeans and then without a word she put on her shoes and, glancing anxiously over her shoulder, stumbled across the long grasses and hidden briars, ignoring fresh scratches. Once on the path – she ran.

Fly made a sudden movement attracting his master's attention. "Fly – away!" said Dalmar in a raised voice. Given permission, the collie ran off after Suzanne, who drew courage when she saw the dog come bounding up to her side.

Dalmar looked at Christine. Strands of dank hair lay across her pallid face. A purple area showed violently around what was probably a fang incision mark on her shoulder. Dark blue tentacles were spreading away from it. He did not lose any more time. Rising to his feet, he tossed her blouse and jeans over his shoulder: he would need these very soon. Then he bent at the knees to allow him to raise her to a cradled position in his arms.

"Now for the difficult bit," he said aloud. "Come on Chris. Let's get you to a hospital."

Meanwhile, Suzanne, with Fly a little way ahead, thought she would drop from exhaustion as she ran and ran. Gone was the refreshing feeling of the swim. In its place had come the atmosphere of dread, and a feeling of nausea. As her running began to slow, Fly kept stopping to try and encourage her. After a long-haul uphill, and an absolute age, it seemed to the poor girl, they came to the path by the main road. For one panicky moment she thought about hailing a passing motorist but dismissed it and ran on to Beech Cottage. On arrival, she fought frantically with the back-door key and rushed into the hallway. Within seconds, she had dialled the emergency services.

"Which service do you require?" said a cool, metallic female voice.

"Ambulance." And after a couple of deep gulps of air. "Quick please!" Suzanne, although breathless, was able to provide the information required before she was put through to Winchester Hospital, Accident and Emergency department. When asked the nature of the trauma she blurted out – "John the Red," before realising that would mean nothing to them. "Snakebite," she said simply.

There was a pause before a man's voice came on the line. "What sort of snake?"

"The Red Adder," replied Suzanne.

"Could you bring the injured person into us? An adder bite is not that serious. There should be no immediate danger."

Suzanne lost reason. "No danger! She is probably already dead! This was *no* ordinary adder!" The male voice relented not asking for any further explanation. An ambulance was on its way.

Suzanne did not leave it at that. Even in her distressed state she had sufficient presence of mind to realise that this emergency called for specialist attention. Her next call was to Dr David Andrews. Luckily the doctor had just finished a late surgery when she rang. It took him a moment to place whom he was talking to. "How can I be of help?" he asked.

"I think Christine has been bitten by John the Red. Please come – we need you!"

David Andrews was staggered. He went silent for a while – trying to take it in – listening to the frightened girl's breathing. 'It can't be,' he thought to himself. 'Not the Red Adder!' The urgency of the situation galvanized him into action. "Yes." A pause. "Are you at the cottage?"

"Yes ... Dalmar – I mean my boyfriend is with her ... She was attacked while having a swim in the Secret Pond."

David could discern the dreadful distress in the girl on the other end of the telephone. Not bothering to question what he did not understand, such as the Secret Pond, he just said, "I'll be with you as soon as possible."

There followed a nail-biting wait of about twenty, very long minutes with a panting collie for company, before David Andrew's Jaguar screeched to a halt outside Beech Cottage, spraying a small amount of debris against Dalmar's car. At the same time, a flashing blue light heralded the arrival of the ambulance approaching from the opposite direction. After raising a hand in 'hello' to Suzanne, David introduced himself to the two paramedics and explained the situation. One of them retrieved a stretcher from the rear of the vehicle, and David got hold of his medical bag.

With Fly leading the way, they all set off. They had not walked more than twenty-five yards before the doctor stopped. "Hold on – how far is this pond? And where exactly?" He turned to Suzanne. She briefly explained the pond's whereabouts. "In that case, why don't we try to drive…?" He stopped speaking for coming around the bend in front of them, under a beech tree, was a tall man carrying a girl on his back. Fly rushed forward to greet them.

Dalmar felt intense relief to see the ambulance. Remarkably, he had managed to avoid giving Christine any serious scratches, but the hazel tunnel had proved to be a backbreaking ordeal. Somehow, using a crab like walk he had carried the injured woman, still in the cradled position, back to the path. Once there he hoisted her into a fireman's lift and started walking as fast as he could. He was aware that if he were to lose his balance and fall; the effect on Christine might have been fatal, so he did not attempt to run. It is doubtful, considering the high temperature and uphill gradient that he would have been able to keep up a strong pace for long. This is where Christine's clothing, draped across his shoulder, had come in useful, cushioning her body against the continuous up and down movement.

"Doctor Andrews is here with the ambulance crew. How is she?" Suzanne said as she met him.

"You've – done well!" He said looked into her eyes through his perspiration moisture. And to her other question he mouthed, 'a don't know.'

David Andrews took charge from that moment on. Under his direction the ambulance men opened the stretcher and placed it on the ground in a plant free patch. The doctor, with a powerful feeling of apprehension, assisted Dalmar in lowering Christine onto it. Instantly, he was relieved, because she let out a faint moan.

The doctor studied the wound on her shoulder while feeling her pulse. Then he turned a puzzled look in the direction of Dalmar's exhausted features.

"Only one fang incision?" Dalmar looked at the doctor for confirmation. David gave a curt nod in reply.

"Right. I shall go with her to the hospital. Do you want to come?" The question was directed at Suzanne.

"Yes … yes please," she answered. She took Dalmar's hand and looked into his face.

"I'll stay here and wait for Tim." He anticipated her request. "Does he know?"

"I'm afraid not – no time," she said over her shoulder while running off to join the rest in the ambulance. The truth was that she had not been able to face calling her brother.

Dalmar watched, as the vehicle's blue light commenced flashing, and the driver drove cautiously across the rough ground. Once on the road, the siren started and the ambulance accelerated away at an ever-increasing speed, attracting attention from people outside the Claymans Heron.

Dalmar untied the end of the rope from around his waist and put it in on one of the back seats of his car. The intended purpose for its use – a tourniquet – had not been appropriate to the area of the wound. It occurred to him, obliquely, that he could have used his tie. He turned and went through the gate into the cottage garden, with Fly trailing behind.

Inside the cottage, he hung Christine's jeans and top over the staircase banister.

There was a new item in the hallway. Dalmar found himself looking at a natural wood framed mirror: oak by the look of it. But it was not the finery of the mirror that caught his attention. It was the odd apparition that looked back at him. His hair had lost most of its normal curl and hung lankily over his forehead. His face was streaked with sweat and dark spots from the traces of vegetable matter that had been in his way. His once white shirt was liberally smeared with various shades of green, and spots of blood were evident on his arms. The grey suit trousers, following their immersion in the pond, looked awful.

Fly nuzzled against his right leg. He reached down and patted his head reassuringly. "Well done boy. Well done." He knelt down and cuddled the animal, who showed his pleasure with snorts and grunts and much tail wagging.

Dalmar was brought back to reality by a sudden thought. He realised that certainly Christine, and, maybe Suzanne, had actually seen the infamous reptile. The significance of this, as far as he knew, was that no other reliable living person had.

It rather looked as though the old lady, known as Ma Hessil, had been telling the truth. It was possible that there would now be an accurate description to refer to. Breaking off from these thoughts, he went into the cloakroom and doused his face with cold water.

As the ambulance sped towards Winchester, Suzanne studied her sister-in-law's ashen face. The crew had radioed through to the hospital to ask them to stand by with anti-venom to treat what was presumed to be a dangerous viper. This was at the request of David Andrews.

"Suzanne," said David turning from his attention to Christine, "That man of yours. How far away was this pond?"

"Over half a mile, I should think. Why?"

"Well – what he did – carrying Christine all that way – so quickly, could be crucial. However, we have a long way to go yet. Driver – sorry about this, but I'm afraid time is of the essence." With that the ambulance stepped up a notch in its speed. It was probably as fast as it could go. As the vehicle pitched and yawed around the bends, Suzanne and the doctor had to hold onto grab rails in order to stop themselves being flung about. Looking out of the back window, Suzanne grimaced; they seemed to push other traffic aside going through the village of Crowsley. The noise of the siren was deafening, and, she thought, frightening.

Christine appeared to be falling into a coma brought on by extreme shock and pain. Her body not only had to fight the awful intrusion of this deadly venom, but also, her brain could not have stood the agony inflicted on her nerve tissue without going into some form of protective unconsciousness. Still in her bikini, she lay under a stark white sheet, with the snakebite wound clearly visible on her left shoulder. Red and bruised all over, it looked horrible.

They were now approaching the top of the hill above the village of Pitt, and the hospital was only a mile and a half away. The driver, with siren wailing, went over two red traffic lights before turning right into the emergency entrance of Winchester Hospital. The ambulance stopped outside some large glass doors, which were swung open by waiting nurses. The paramedics opened the vehicle's rear doors letting bright sunlight stream in on the patient.

Christine was taken straight up to a ward where a cannula was connected to a vein above her left wrist. The anti-venom serum was then given intravenously.

Suzanne was permitted to stay with her. A consultant would soon be in attendance. David Andrews reassured Suzanne explaining to her that Christine's condition, regarding the serum's progress, would be closely monitored. She was connected to a machine that measured her heart rate. The rhythmic beat sounded immediately. Suzanne found it scary because it was obvious what the nurses would be listening for, yet the sound was soon quelled and a visual signal with alarm point was put through to the nurse's station outside the ward.

Satisfied, David left the hospital having done all he could. Suzanne thanked him profusely. She decided to await the arrival of her brother in the allocated area outside the ward. Thankfully, the dreadful feeling of nausea, brought on by the original shock had subsided.

CHAPTER FIFTEEN

"WE MAY BE VERY GRATEFUL TO HIM."

Tim Westward was driving home via Salisbury, this being the quickest way to return after his field trip. He now wished he had telephoned his wife before starting the journey. It was later than he thought, and he knew she might worry. At a quarter to seven he finally drove into the drive by Beech Cottage. 'What's all this?' he thought to himself. 'Not only was Dalmar's car there, but that black saloon had to be Dr Andrews' Jaguar.' Tim was immediately worried. Just then, Fly and Dalmar came out to see him.

Tim looked at Dalmar's appearance. "Blimey – what have you been doing? Fighting a war?" He smiled – then something in Dalmar's face – made him stop.

"Tim … Christine has been taken to hospital. Snake bite." Then he told him what had happened.

Tim's face paled. "What sort of snake?" He looked at Dalmar – dread in his eyes.

"I don't know for sure. It could be … a Red Adder."

"Not John the Red surely?"

"Not sure Tim. I didn't see it. Would you like me to drive you to the hospital? Suzanne is still with her."

Tim hesitated. "Yes. Thank you," he said, dazed with the shock of the terrible news.

"Can I leave Fly in the cottage?"

"Yes, of course," came a quiet reply. Dalmar took the reluctant dog inside and locked the back door.

Both men climbed into the T.R.6 and Dalmar drove off. "How bad is it?" Tim shouted over the wind noise. "Where did it get her?"

"On her left shoulder." Dalmar glanced over to Tim so as to make himself heard. "Apparently it attacked her from a tree she was swimming under."

"Was she conscious afterwards?"

Dalmar couldn't lie. "No – but maybe that is for the best."

"Why – was she in a lot of pain?"

"She probably was, but I hope that is very much in the past now."

"Because she will have been given anti-snakebite serum?"

"Yes."

Tim thought for a moment, before making a little nod. Neither man said much after that. The important matter, for both of them, was to get to the hospital quickly.

On arrival, they walked hastily into the accident and emergency entrance. Dalmar asked the receptionist if a Mrs Christine Westward had been admitted. She looked at his dishevelled state, and then at some papers for what seemed like a long time. Eventually she said, "Christine Westward – Victoria Ward." Both men looked blank, so she gave them directions. What neither of them knew – was that part of the Victoria Ward was currently being used for intensive care. The two men had to go up a couple of flights of stairs, and then along a long corridor before they found it.

When Suzanne spotted them enter the visitor's area, she rushed over to her brother and embraced him. "Oh Tim! – I'm so glad you're here." She let go and looked into his anxious face. "So far so good," she said deliberately "There is a consultant with her now. We have to wait."

"I want to see her?" implored her brother.

"You will soon ... We just have to hang on until he has finished." Her voice had a heavy tone of pleading. She gave her boyfriend a big hug and then indicated an area where there were some vacant seats. Dalmar offered to get hot drinks from the vending machines he had spotted nearby. Suzanne said she would like a coffee. Tim declined.

In Dalmar's absence the consultant came up to them. Suzanne introduced her brother explaining that he was the casualty's husband.

"How is she doctor?"

"Your wife is in a critical condition. We are doing everything we can to make her comfortable." Tim went ashen. The consultant whose name was Lombard had been asked a direct question, and he had no hesitation in giving a direct answer. "However, there is a chance, if she can survive the night. She seems a very strong-willed young woman." Mr Lombard paused here as if trying to decide whether to say anything else. Instead, he asked a question. "Tell me, your G.P. has said something about a freak adder. Do you know anything else that may help us?"

"Have you heard of John the Red?" Suzanne blurted out without really thinking about it. Her brother gasped in horror. Mr Lombard looked puzzled.

"Dalmar said it was a red adder." Tim looked into his sister's eyes.

"THE Red Adder, Tim I know – I saw it."

Her brother sat down. "Oh my God!" He had not wanted to believe it up to now. "

"I'm afraid I need enlightening – who or what is the Red Adder?" asked the confused consultant.

"A strange snake that lives in Yewhurst wood. Dr David Andrews will give you more information than we can," Suzanne suggested.

"But ... how come she is still alive ... I mean the Red Adder!" exclaimed Tim; his faced masked in a mixture of sheer concern and horror.

"I don't know," answered his sister.

"Apparently a man carried your injured wife;" the consultant looked at Tim, "with some rapidity from the depths of a forest?"

"My friend – over there." Suzanne pointed a finger at Dalmar, who was waiting for the vending machine to do its stuff.

"We may be very grateful to him," said Lombard. "Mr Westward, your wife has been given twice the dose of anti-venom usually provided for the common adder bite. We considered this the best treatment in the light of what information we have."

Tim, on hearing all this was very quiet. He was sensible enough to know that if this treatment were wrong, his wife would die. Mr Lombard carried on. "As a precaution, we are having sent down from London some anti-venom for the treatment of a puff adder bite, probably one of the world's most toxic vipers. If necessary – we will use it." He made a compassionate gesture with both hands held out and low. "You must excuse me ... further duties. The ward sister will look after you."

Suzanne thanked him and he left. For a consultant, he looked the part; silver hair, oval face, a little portly and wearing a smart dark grey suit.

When Dalmar returned carrying a cup of coffee for Suzanne, he found her leaning over her distraught brother who was sobbing with his head bowed. The scene looked so distressing that Dalmar thought the worst. Suzanne looked up on his approach and seeing the expression on his face mouthed a 'No'. Additionally. she shook her head.

It was Tim who broke up this situation. The way was now clear for him to see his wife. He stood to his feet dabbing at his eyes with a tissue Suzanne had given him. "Where is she? – I'll go to her." Suzanne took him to the ward entrance and pointed to a screened area over in the left-hand corner.

There were only six beds in intensive care, all screened off with curtaining. Most of the other patients were elderly, but there was one other young person receiving treatment for a collapsed lung.

Christine looked pale. Her shoulder was now bandaged. She lay on her back breathing slowly as though in blissful sleep. Her long blonde hair, still crinkly from the pond water, cascaded down onto the bed linen. Tim bent over and kissed her lips. To him, they felt colder than usual. He sat down in a chair by her bedside and gently held her right hand in his. He was obviously shocked at seeing his wife in this state and remained silent for a long while.

Only a short time remained before the end of the visiting period for the hospital, but because Christine's condition was critical, Tim was allowed to stay. He told the other two to go on, saying he would call if there were any problems. Suzanne did not want to, but her brother insisted. "Go and get some rest." She understood and gave him a fond embrace.

Dalmar and Suzanne drove straight back to Beech Cottage. Conversation was sparse mostly because the car's hood was still down. Dr Andrew's car was no longer there. He must have got a lift, somehow, from the hospital. Fly greeted them with an inordinate amount of licking. He was most definitely very pleased to see them. What Suzanne wanted most was a hot bath. Dalmar said he would go to his cottage, do the same, and then return. He realised that his girlfriend would have to remain by the telephone.

He was back within the hour, scrubbed and changed, with a can of food and some biscuits for his dog. Suzanne, her dark hair still wet from a shampoo and rinse, wore a satin navy-blue dressing gown with her bare toes protruding from its lower folds. She gave her lover a reticent smile.

"Any news?" he enquired, suspecting the smile meant no news was good news. She shook her head. They ate a snack meal while Fly, after his supper, went into a deep sleep by their side.

"Must be absolutely bushed," said Suzanne. And then the telephone rang. Dalmar made a move of his head suggesting he take the call. She nodded.

He left the kitchen table making his chair leg groan as he dragged it back. The noise sounded rudely intrusive over the telephone bell. Suzanne's face seemed to lose its deep tan in seconds. Dalmar crossed the hall and picked up the receiver. "The Westward's residence," he announced.

"Oh hello. Doctor Andrews. Just calling to enquire about Christine?"

"Hello Doctor. No news yet."

"Is that Dalmar?"

"Yes."

"Thanks for what you did this afternoon?"

"And thank *you*!" Dalmar from his emphasis on the 'you' made it clear where he thought the most important help had come from."

There was a pause. "Right – well let me know if I can do anything?" Dalmar felt that the statement was genuine and had not been made out of politeness.

"Okay. I'll probably run Suzanne into the hospital in the morning – before I go to work. Her husband is there now, and no doubt will remain by her side all night."

"Right – let's hope the anti-venom works quickly… Bye"

"Bye and thanks for ringing." Dalmar replaced the receiver. What had not escaped both men's thoughts, was that if Christine survived, she would be the first bite victim of a Red Adder variety snake to do so. This prompted the question. Why should this snake be the same type as the one that existed in the 1940's?

Suzanne guessed, during the telephone conversation, who the caller was. She was very relieved, and it showed in her face: the colour returning at once. They discussed the night's plans together. Suzanne did not want to be alone, but she felt she could not invite her lover to stay. Dalmar felt the same, so they decided to leave Fly where he was. He did not take much persuading and flopped down on Suzanne's bed as though it was his anyway. After getting a promise that he would be telephoned if anything happened, Dalmar departed. Their kiss to each other was short, but full of love.

CHAPTER SIXTEEN

"IF YOU NOTICE ANY CHANGE…"

During that evening Tim made several trips to various vending machines for bars of chocolate and hot drinks. It was not because he needed them. It was because he had to do something to relieve his desperate anxiety.

Christine was alive, but the consultant had said her condition was critical. Many thoughts were criss-crossing his mind. 'How could some odd, freak snake reappear after twenty-seven years? Surely, prolonged hot weather could not cause it. Should he telephone Christine's parents?' This was another thought that kept nagging him. He decided to leave it until the morning when there might be less traumatic news. 'Why give them a sleepless night?'

The ward was in half-light now; the clock said two-twenty a.m. Tim had taken up a permanent position, with his head slightly bowed, while holding Christine's limp hand in his. A staff nurse came into view, "Everything okay?" A thoughtful, kind face appeared in front of him. The question had been asked in a whisper. He noticed that her eyes twinkled under her uniform cap, and her lips were naturally full and rosy red. 'It suited her,' he thought, but this was just observation – his emotional thoughts were centred elsewhere.

"Yes." As he replied Tim raised his head and stretched his shoulder muscles.

He was brought back to his responsibility when she said before leaving him. "If you notice any change, please come and get me. I'm at the desk, just through the doors to the left."

"Don't worry, I will," he said. "Thank you." She smiled at him again.

At some stage, he started to find it difficult to stay awake. He stayed in the same position for a long time, before deciding to pay a call of nature. After using the toilet, he could not resist dowsing his face with cold water, leaving it wet.

Back at Christine's bedside, about an hour passed before Tim came out of a long reverie, rather than sleep, to become aware that some things were different. He looked at his wife's face. She was breathing in short gasps. Tim rose to his feet, trying to subdue a feeling of panic. At the same time the front curtain was pulled back, urgently, and a new staff nurse came in followed by a white-coated doctor. "We need to give your wife some more anti-venom." The nurse spoke to him quickly. "Please could you wait in the visitor's area? I will come and get you when we have finished." She placed a hand under Tim's upper arm and guided him out, really, before he could say anything at all. He cast an anxious look over his shoulder as he left. The sight of his wife's pale, somnolent face did not help him.

Tim went out and stood in the waiting area, in an extremely agitated manner. He received sympathetic looks from two other nurses on duty. After a while, he noticed that one of them was intently studying the visual pulses from a machine. He immediately realised that this was connected to Christine: the cardiac monitor. Even Tim knew those pulses of light were too fast. Perhaps, fortunately, he had not been aware that the alarm had sounded earlier before the doctor was summoned.

Tim Westward did not move, intently watching – watching. Suddenly there was an increase in the rapidity of the blinking light. The two nurses were aware that Tim was looking at the monitor behind and to one side of them across the half-circular counter. The nurse monitoring it rose to her feet. Tim's world stopped and stayed in abeyance. How long he stood rooted to the same spot, both feet firmly planted on the tiled flooring with his arms hanging down, slightly bent, his fists clenched, and his face set in an expression of rigid apprehension, he would never know. Then – slowly, the rapidity of the flashing light ebbed until it went back to how it had been before: still too fast, at the speed which had originally set off the alarm.

Some more time past, during which Tim relaxed his fists, but that was all. After this the first thing that happened was that the nurse, on some unseen signal, sat down and immediately the light pulse went back to what it had been before the doctor had been called. Normal. As she turned and looked at the patient's husband, she slowly let out a sigh. Then the doctor and the staff nurse came out to him. Both looked mightily relieved. "Mr Westward, we have given your wife some anti-venom which has been especially sent down from London. I believe Mr Lombard, the consultant, explained…?"

Tim held up his right hand. "Yes," he said weakly.

"Hopefully, she will now sleep comfortably for some hours," said the doctor. "That is what we want to happen. An immediate crisis has just passed, but it will be some while before the new serum fully takes effect."

"Right …   thank *you*, Doctor," said Tim, feeling unsure, relieved, but still frightened.   'There must, surely, be a risk of overdose,' he thought. The doctor smiled unaware of the question in Tim's mind. He had been told exactly what to do if this patient faltered. It was very new ground for him.

The staff nurse took Tim back to Christine's bedside. He thanked her while being acutely aware that his entire body seemed to be coated in moisture – the result of extreme nervous perspiration.

Left alone again, he began to feel the dreadful reality of his situation. It had now completely dawned on him that he might lose his wife. A black brooding feeling covered his head, like the presence of some gigantic problem, only far more acute. He looked at Christine's face. Her closed eyelids, with their lashes laid down on her cheeks, were so peaceful in their beauty. But he could not help but feel a rising panic with the thought that those eyes might never open again. He gripped the chair leg with his free arm and tried to calm himself. His own eyes became filled with liquid, and he said, "Come on girl – keep fighting. I love you – too much."

Suzanne stirred as Fly woke her up by lying across her stomach and giving her face a wet lick. It was just after six in the morning. She had slept much better than she thought she would, probably from sheer exhaustion. She was aware – Christine must have survived the night, and the consultant had said that would be the crucial time. Going down to the kitchen, she gave the hungry collie his breakfast. Then she took a cup of coffee up to the bathroom and prepared herself for Dalmar's arrival. The roadster's deep note announced him at just after seven a.m. Leaving Fly in charge, they wasted no time in driving to Winchester.

When they arrived outside the hospital ward, they were told Christine was in, what appeared to be, a no-change situation, until Tim told them what had happened during the night. He looked drawn and very tired. A small ginger shadow lay across the lower part of his face. The duty staff nurse informed them that Mr Lombard would be making his rounds in about two hours. She said that they should all go home. They would be called if there was any change in the patient's condition. Tim wanted to stay, but his sister had a better idea. She suggested that she remain while Dalmar dropped him off. Tim eventually agreed to this. After all, as Suzanne pointed out, he must get together something for his wife to wear: a nightdress, her more important cosmetics, a toothbrush and paste. Unfortunately, she had not thought to bring anything herself. This, of course, was entirely due to the drama of the situation.

At nine forty-five, Suzanne was shaken from her vigil at Christine's bedside by the arrival of the consultant, a senior nurse and another doctor. Mr Lombard read the reports, noting what had happened during the night. He said to Suzanne that in his opinion the worst might be over, but it was too early to be certain. Later, providing there was no repeat of last night's relapse, they would commence a saline drip to give the patient some liquid sustenance. He smiled at Suzanne, sensing her fearful state, and inquired as to her brother's whereabouts. She explained that he had been here all night. She hoped he was now sleeping.

After Mr Lombard's entourage left, Suzanne pondered whether she should ring Tim and let him have a progress report but decided against it. If he were asleep, it would be better to leave him. She did, however, go and use the pay phone to talk to Dalmar at his office, and let him know the latest. They agreed that he would see her sometime that evening, either at the hospital or Beech Cottage. Before Suzanne was able to put the telephone down, he said something he had not said to her before; "I love you, bright eyes." Those last words made her feel much better. If it had not been for the seriousness of the situation with her sister-in-law's well-being, she would have danced with joy. When he had addressed her as 'darling' at the Secret Pond, she wondered whether he had really meant it, or had it been just because of the drama of the moment. Now she knew. "Come on Chris, get better," she said to herself, "I want to share my good news with you."

Tim awoke with a stiff neck at just before eleven o'clock. He literally rolled out of the armchair where he was snoozing. On coming around, his first act was to call the hospital. A nurse gave him the news that there was no change in his wife's condition. He made a call to his employers, explaining the situation, before he paused to clean his teeth, wash his face and change into casual clothes. Then he strode out to the Morris and drove away, still unshaven.

He had trouble finding a place to park his car when he got to the hospital. It seemed to be a busy time. At length, a kind person came up and spoke to him. "Looking for a space? I'm just leaving – over there." The man pointed to a Vauxhall saloon.

Tim said, "Thank you," and drove over to await the vacancy.

Once in the ward, Suzanne saw him coming and went to meet him. A nurse told them that they were going to transfer Christine to a private room.

"I thought you had to pay for a private room?" Tim said to no one in particular.

"You do," said the nurse. "The person making the payment wishes to remain anonymous." Tim and his sister looked at each other, mouths slightly apart.

"Oh well, thank you to whoever," Tim said matter-of-factly. "At least she is out of intensive care. That must be good."

They had to disconnect the cardiac monitor and the drip, temporarily, while they moved the patient. It was not far away and only took a few minutes. Inside, there was a small window that looked out over the hospital lawns.

"The National Health Service surely can't have provided those flowers?" Suzanne pointed to a vase with a beautiful bouquet on a side table. It was well away from the bed in order to give room for medical equipment. There was no card attached, but Suzanne was right, a florist had delivered them. The staff nurse confirmed it. This oblique happening reminded Tim that it was time he went to telephone Christine's parents!

After placing some coins in the box, Tim hesitated before dialling. How on earth was he going to explain all this to his in-laws? He might have some smattering of knowledge about the Red Adder, but to anyone else it would be sheer science fiction. He decided to play it down. Christine's mother came on the telephone. "Why, hello Tim dear," she greeted him. He asked her if her husband was there, but no, he was at his office. Nowadays Christine's father was more of a consultant at the firm, and only went to work on the odd day; unfortunately, this was one of them. "Our daughter has been bitten by a snake, dear. What sort of snake?" Tim explained that it was an adder which had nasty venom. He went on to tell her that she was still ill, but, hopefully, the worst was over. Quite naturally, she became very concerned, and said she would contact her husband and telephone him back. Tim told her that there was no need for them to come to Winchester. He would keep them fully informed, but he had the distinct impression that this advice would go unheeded. He returned to Christine's bedside.

One and a half hours after the move from intensive care, Suzanne thought she could see an improvement in Christine's pallor. She mentioned this to her brother, to try and cheer him up, as much as anything else.

A nurse came into the room and informed Tim that he was wanted on the public telephone. It was Christine's father. "How is she?" was his immediate question. Tim told him. "Right! Her mother and I have booked into the Claymans Heron hotel. We will ring you when we get there. Bye." Then he rang off, leaving Tim with a telephone receiver held to his ear, stunned and temporarily immobilised. He was worried that, in their eyes, he had done something wrong. He shrugged it off. 'There were more urgent matters and why should they not come and see their daughter?'

Tim took advantage of the next hour to grill his sister about yesterday afternoon's happenings. After she told him for the first time what had led up to the incident, Tim asked her, "Where is this Secret Pond?" Suzanne explained and told him not to blame her man. She pointed out that it had been on Christine's insistence that they had gone.

"Yes – it would be," he agreed. Then they went on to talk about the attack and Tim was particularly interested in the description of the snake itself. He expressed surprise at Suzanne's estimation of its length. "Six feet! Are you sure?"

"Well ... yes ... pretty sure. It was *very* long."

"That is a big snake: especially for this country. Probably getting on for python size. Hardly a blooming adder!"

Suzanne shrugged her shoulders." I'll tell you something else;" she looked up into her brother's face.

"What's that?"

"Well – Dalmar just appeared with Fly at the scene. Okay, we left a note on the back door of the cottage to tell him where we were – but – well – not only must Fly have known that Dalmar had arrived at Beech Cottage. God knows how – presumably he left us to go to him. And then – somehow or other…"

"He persuaded his master to follow him back," Tim interrupted her.

"Yes – and the speed ... well – it seemed no time at all…" She left the thought hanging in the air, because something happened that made them both forget all about it.

"Hello," said a familiar voice from across the room … Tim and Suzanne jerked their heads in Christine's direction. Two, fully open, slightly bloodshot, but nevertheless pale blue-green eyes were looking straight at them. Tim could not remember the last time he had openly wept. Unbounded tears of relief and joy flowed, unabashed, down his fair cheeks. Crossing the few short paces to her bed, he held out his hands to place them over hers.

CHAPTER SEVENTEEN

"ARE YOU ABSOLUTELY SURE ABOUT THAT?"

Christine did not stay awake for long; however, she had regained consciousness and subsequently fallen asleep naturally. She was no longer on the critical list, but because she had suffered severe blood poisoning, and had a lot of anti-bodies in her system from the extensive dosage of anti-venom serum, recovery might be slow due to some possible side effects. Nevertheless, the doctors thought that she should be eating properly within a day or so. Her mother and father visited that evening, and although they were not able to converse with their daughter, clearly, relief showed on their faces.

In all the confusion, Tim had completely forgotten to bring her personal possessions, including a much-needed nightdress and toiletries. It was Suzanne who finally packed up a suitcase and asked Christine's mother to take it with her.

During the evening, Tim, Dalmar and Suzanne were all at Beech Cottage when the telephone rang. Tim answered the call and David Andrews announced himself. "Tim – I have to say that my wife and I are delighted at the good news. So relieved for you. Please pass on my best wishes to your good lady and tell her I look forward to treating her during her convalescence."

"Thank you, David – I will. Oh and … it was good of you to come to her aid so quickly after the accident."

"Not at all. Least one could do. Now then, I'm sorry about this, but I've been asked if I could arrange a meeting with your sister. Got some top brass with loads of questions. At the moment, it is restricted to a Forestry Commission executive and a police inspector. Could you both come to my house? I had in mind tomorrow evening?"

Tim thought for a short while. "Look … would you mind if it was here? I feel I should be near our telephone."

David could see the point. "All right – unless you hear to the contrary, we will be at your house around seven-thirtyish. All right?"

"Okay – don't you think Dalmar Hunter should be present?"

"Ah yes … agreed. See you all tomorrow."

"Bye." Tim put down the receiver. When he told his sister, she was not happy but, nevertheless, understood the reasoning. Someone's life could be taken next.

"You do realise that when it comes to a description of the snake, Christine is going to have the best information. For heaven's sake the horrid thing was on top of her!"

"Yes Suz, but leave her out of it for as long as poss' … okay?"

"Okay," she said.

The person who looked the most apprehensive about tomorrow's meeting was, without a doubt, Dalmar. When Tim advised him that his presence would be required, he lowered his eyes and stroked his dog's back, more in comfort for himself than to please Fly.

The next day saw Tim again excused work and he went with his sister to visit Christine, after having shared breakfast with her parents at the Claymans Heron. During that meal some rather searching questions were directed at him.

Christine's father, quite understandably, could not fathom what sort of snake had bitten his daughter. He extracted a promise from Tim and Suzanne that they would stay away from the area of the attack until something had been done. "Probably some foreign reptile that a lunatic collector has set free. I should like to catch it and shove it up..."

"Now that's enough Bruce!" his wife admonished him. "What do your mother and father think about this business, Tim?"

Brother and sister looked at each other. In the drama of it all, they had totally forgotten to telephone them. "Err – not sure yet," stammered Tim. "We are having a longer – chat tonight." He got off lightly with the lie.

At Winchester Hospital, Tim and his sister arrived to see Christine in a drowsy state but awake. She had just had something to eat. The cardiac monitor and cannula had been disconnected the evening before on Mr Lombard's instructions.

"Tim – what has happened?" his wife mumbled. "I remember some awful dream. They say an adder bit me."

Sensing her confusion, Tim was tactful. "Darling, you have had a bad time, but you are on the mend. How do you feel?"

"Very weak ... this awful headache, I wish it would go away."

"Have they given you anything for it?" Suzanne asked her, coming closer at the same time, so that she could be more easily heard.

"Just gone to get some painkillers..." She drifted. "I – I feel ... so sleepy."

"That's all right, sweetheart," said Tim quickly. "That's the best thing. Don't fight it." And with that, she closed her eyes.

A nurse came with some tablets and a glass of water. Seeing that Christine was asleep, she left the drink and took the tablets away after exchanging whispered greetings with her visitors.

"Do you think Christine will remember it all later?" Suzanne asked her brother.

"To be honest, I hope not Suz. That little lot is enough to give anyone nightmares for life." Suzanne nodded; the long-term effects of the trauma had been something that worried her as well. They stayed for nearly two hours before Christine awoke again. Her headache had all but gone, and she felt a lot better – dramatically so: there was colour in her cheeks. Soon, she asked to go to the bathroom. With Suzanne's help she managed the short distance to and from without any mishap. While there she had a very refreshing wash.

Back in bed, and for the first time propped up so that her back was straight, she again asked what had happened? Tim decided to tell her. He referred to the snake as a red adder in much the same way that Dalmar had done.

"Do you know Tim I really can't remember much. I do remember you being there Suz, and ... yes ... Fly: he was scared of something – I remember that." Suzanne nodded and placed her left hand on Christine's arm. "When I was washing, I noticed that I had a bruised shoulder. It's ever so tender. Did I have a fall?" The dressing had been removed in order to allow the wound to be exposed and facilitate healing.

"No, that is where the snake bit you," answered Tim with a little smile.

"Oh!" Christine looked much more like her normal self suddenly, "I feel a bit famey," she said.

"Would it be possible to ask a few questions?" A voice came out of nowhere, as though in answer to Christine's remark. It belonged to a lady in her early thirties, wearing a mid-green suit and carrying a thin briefcase under her left arm. She looked very fit. Her figure showed signs of being muscular, but not over so. She wore silver-framed spectacles on a determined face of good complexion. Her hair was cut in the style of an American television actress of the time: long, blonde and curled under at the back and sides. "Mary Taylor of the Winchester Chronicle," she carried on, not waiting for an answer to her request. "Saw the report on your snakebite. Thought it sounded unusual. High toxin snake poison apparently? May I?" And she pointed to a chair, off to one side. Again, she did not wait for a reply and went to push the chair towards Christine's bed.

Suzanne and Tim gaped at her. Tim was in an inward panic. He cursed himself for leaving the door open. His thoughts immediately sprang to the meeting taking place at Beech Cottage later. He knew that any details must not be divulged yet, at least, not from their lips. Christine looked at the reporter totally nonplussed.

Rescue came quickly and efficiently from the nursing staff. Two of them came striding in. "Mary – this is a private room – have you been invited?" one of them asked, glancing at Suzanne and her brother at the same time. Tim held both hands open in front of him, making it obvious that she had not. With that, the disappointed Mary Taylor was ushered out of the room.

"They've stolen my one and only chance of fame," joked Christine. Mary Taylor would not have got much information out of her though, because not only was her memory of the incident very cloudy, but she soon subsided back into sleep. Tim and his sister left a message on a piece of paper by her bedside, which told her that her mother and father would be visiting this evening, and Tim would be back tomorrow. Then they left. On the way home they stopped at a local shop. Suzanne wanted to get some bits, as she referred to them, for tonight's gathering.

Christine's parents went over to Beech Cottage during the afternoon and Tim showed them around. They both seemed pleased with the property, but, of course, missed their daughter not being present for their first visit.

Dr Andrews was interrupted in his surgery by a telephone call from a reporter on the Winchester Chronicle. He was a little annoyed that the information about him being the attending general practitioner, at the snakebite incident, had got out. Later, he calmed down, when administration staff at the hospital informed him that the reporter must have read confidential information, without the knowledge of hospital staff. Due to the reporter's persistence, the doctor could only get away by making an appointment for a further telephone conversation, the next day.

At seven-thirty that evening, David Andrews parked his car outside Beech Cottage. Almost immediately a small saloon pulled up alongside. A middle-aged gentleman got out. He was dressed in lightweight trousers with a thin cotton shirt sporting a Police Federation tie. The two men greeted each other with familiarity. A brief discussion followed, before the doctor opened the gate and, leading the way, went to knock on the front door.

Suzanne opened it. "Good evening, Doctor," she said, her usual radiant smile on her face. Her complexion had returned to normal: the dusky tan setting off those fabulous eyes. They looked like dark topaz circles glittering in bright ocean spray.

"Hello again, Suzanne," David said stepping inside. "May I introduce Chief Inspector Wilkins?" Suzanne smiled at him, while opening the door wider.

The inspector offered his hand and shook hers lightly. "Actually, Chief Inspector retired, to be correct." He spoke in a soft, mature voice. There was some perspiration on his forehead, and he looked as though he might have had to rush to get here on time. They went through to the sitting room and David introduced the inspector to Dalmar and Tim.

"The Chief Inspector is here more as an observer. We don't think, at this stage, that the local police force need be involved. Our next guests are going to be the prime movers; two gentlemen from the Forestry Commission." David then went on to explain to Tim, Dalmar and Suzanne that any search for the snake would be conducted by forestry personnel, but, obviously, they will need as much information as possible.

Suzanne let them settle in a seat. Earlier, they had brought some of the dining room chairs through, to provide enough. "Now – perhaps I can get you two gentleman some refreshment?" she asked.

David noticed Tim and Dalmar were both drinking beers. He asked if he could have one as well, while the inspector requested a cup of tea, adding, "If it isn't too much trouble?"

Before Suzanne could get to the kitchen, a Land Rover, complete with Forestry Commission livery, pulled up outside. She answered the door to two serious looking men. David suddenly appeared behind her. Butting in he said, "Good evening. We spoke on the telephone – David Andrews." They shook hands and before they could announce themselves, the doctor suggested that they come into the front room, where he would introduce everyone at the same time.

Once they were altogether, he named everybody in turn before announcing who the newcomers were. "Charles Brewster is an executive officer with the Forestry Commission based at Lyndhurst – I believe?" He looked at this gentleman for confirmation. He received a nod from the elder of the two men. "And you, Sir, are the Forest Officer?" asked the doctor addressing the younger man.

"Stephen Knopner – I'm the local bod." Tim and Dalmar studied him. This was the boss of Yewhurst Wood, in other words. He was possibly in his mid-thirties, possessing prominent cheekbones with a square jaw and a big mouth, which, when caught smiling seemed to enlarge his eyes. His blond hair was untidy, particularly on the front of his head: too much of it. He wore a forest ranger's uniform and carried it off in style, being superbly fit with a sport labelled physique. Sleepless nights showed in the fatigue on his face, probably the result of being a parent with young children.

Everyone shook hands and Tim came to Suzanne's assistance, so that he could attend to the drinks while she made the tea. When this was done and all were seated in the front room, with Suzanne perched on the settee-arm next to Dalmar; David raised his voice slightly to attract attention. "Well – I suggest we get this meeting under way. I will just mention again that the Chief Inspector is here as an observer. He will report back to the Hampshire Constabulary at Winchester, but it will probably not be necessary for them to take any action at this time." David paused and looked at Charles Brewster. "May I suggest you kick off?"

Brewster was middle-aged, balding a little, and looked too hot in his dark grey suit. "Yes – excuse me, would you?" He took off his jacket and placed it over the back of the chair. This exertion caused one of the lenses in his spectacles to mist up slightly. "Right – it seems to me that we need those people," here he looked at his hosts, "who were on the spot, to tell their story. Who would like to go first?"

Tim interjected at this point. He had to raise his voice to be heard above the exaggerated crunching noises emanating from Stephen's mouth. He had helped himself to a liberal quantity of roasted peanuts from a small bowl on the table in front of him. "My sister is the main witness. My wife is the other, but as you probably know she is still in hospital recovering from the incident. I take it you know about the snakebite?"

David butted in. "I have told them all I know Tim, so the answer is yes."

"Okay," said Brewster. "I am going to suggest that there are no interruptions while this young lady relates the events." Nobody appeared to disagree. "Right; Suzanne, the floor is yours."

She looked nervous. Dalmar put an arm around her waist. "Okay then. Obviously, it was Christine who saw the snake close up, but I'll do my best." To her great credit she left nothing out, except tree names, preferring simple descriptions like tall or large. When she reached the point where Dalmar arrived at the pond and she, subsequently, left the scene of the attack to get help, she stopped. "Do you want Dalmar to carry on?"

Curiously, for a hot evening, while the tale was told, hardly anyone touched their drinks. Those present who knew little about the incident showed their amazement in the expressions on their faces. Brewster spoke. "Right; I think that will do for now. Thank you ... Stephen, any questions?" he said turning to his colleague.

The forestry officer had a look on his face of sheer incredulity. He stared at Suzanne with his mouth slightly open, before he said anything. He wanted to say, 'You must be joking?' but knew that would be unwise. "What the blazes is this 'John the Red'?"

"Oh dear," David cut in. "This is not going to make a great deal of sense, unless you are in the know about something that happened quite a long time ago." He glanced at Charles Brewster. "May I? I'll be brief."

"Please do," said the forestry executive politely.

When he had finished, Stephen expressed surprise that he had never heard anything about it. "You are surely not suggesting that Mr John the Red is alive and well – now?" The slight Cumbrian burr to his voice gave him an enquiring style of speech.

"Maybe." The voice was Dalmar's. He said nothing else. Tim glanced at him with a searching look, but his face remained impassive.

Stephen Knopner jerked his shoulders, in disbelief. "No matter," he said. "Six feet! Are you quite sure about that? The adder is unlikely to reach a length of more than four feet at the outside."

"My brother queried that as well," Suzanne answered. "I told him that it was very long and – it was!" she said, giving Stephen a disapproving glance. She did not like his tone.

"When you say bright red?"

"Not a post office red. More of a cherry red." Suzanne interrupted him.

"Really." Stephen opened his eyes wide in mock astonishment before shaking his head. "This Secret Pond." Here, he hesitated, choosing his words. "As far as I am aware, there is no pond in Yewhurst Wood. True, you sometimes get a temporary one after a period of prolonged rain. That is hardly likely at this time." The sarcasm in his voice was evident to all.

Suzanne did not ignore the man's disbelief. She sought confirmation. "Dalmar?"

"It exists all right," was his comment. He turned in his seat to give the forestry man a firm look.

Stephen came right back at him. "Then perhaps you could show us?"

"Certainly," replied Dalmar succinctly. "When do you want me to make myself available?"

Once the rather toxic atmosphere had been calmed by David Andrews, a general discussion about time and place followed. Dalmar; David if he could make it, Stephen Knopner and two or three forestry workers would meet at the church car park at ten o'clock on Saturday morning.

Before finishing, Dalmar was asked to conclude. He kept it brief, because it was of little interest concerning the existence of the Red Adder. He explained that when he saw that Christine had been bitten on her shoulder, he was extremely apprehensive about her chances of survival. He could hardly apply a tourniquet to her shoulder. So, having sent Suzanne on ahead to call an ambulance, he concentrated on getting the unconscious girl to Beech Cottage, as quickly as he could. He was very much aware that this was the urgent necessity, so that she could be treated with anti-venom.

After this, they all stood up to leave. Dalmar made a point of getting close to Stephen before he climbed into the Forestry Commission Land Rover. "You are somewhat doubtful about this aren't you?"

Stephen was taken aback at the directness. In a softer tone than he had used earlier, and without sarcasm, he said, "Do you blame me?"

"Not altogether – but I can assure you that my girlfriend is perfectly sane, and the proof is in Winchester Hospital. She did not suffer a normal adder bite, and she very nearly didn't make it."

Stephen thought for a moment. "Okay. We'll get to the bottom of the matter." He held out his hand. Dalmar shook it and they both smiled pointedly at each other.

They all left soon after this.

Back inside Dalmar assisted in helping the other two clear-up. "Glad they didn't insist that you come along on Saturday, Suzanne," he said.

"I wouldn't have gone if they had," she replied in a no-nonsense tone. "I'm not too happy about you going either. Can you imagine Christine letting Tim go?"

"I don't know where this Secret Pond is." Tim joined in. "Thank goodness."

"Well – I am committed now," said Dalmar with a shrug of the shoulders. "It shouldn't take long."

CHAPTER EIGHTEEN

SHE SENSED SOMETHING IN THAT SIGH.

At eleven-thirty the next morning, after the fifth attempt, Mary Taylor finally got through on the telephone to Dr Andrews. "Doctor," she breathed at him, "can we carry on where we left off yesterday?" Without waiting for a reply, she asked, "What's all this about an adder with a nasty bite?"

"I take it you are referring to a patient who was admitted to a ward at Winchester Hospital?"

"Yes," came a quick reply.

"How did you get to see this report?" The doctor was becoming suspicious.

"Communications," Mary bluffed. "You mean this lady stumbled on ... How did it happen anyway?"

David paused. He did not want to get into all this with the press. "Not sure, presumably she trod on it, or something similar."

"Doctor, I may be blonde, but I'm not that stupid. The report states that she was bitten on the shoulder. How?"

"Ah yes, sorry, I wasn't thinking properly. That's right; she must have fallen onto it: tripped up or..."

"So – this young lady went for a walk. Where did it happen?"

"I believe ..." There was a long pause, "umm – somewhere around the village of Yewhurst."

"Excuse me, Dr Andrews, but I was under the impression that you actually attended to the lady...?"

"Ye-es."

"Well – where was that!"

"In Yewhurst."

"Okay, but Yewhurst is quite a big village. So – this snake looks like any other adder, but its bite is rather nasty?"

"It may not look exactly like the adder." As soon as David said these words, he knew he would rue the day. He let out a sigh of regret.

Mary Taylor was a reporter of a few years' experience. She sensed something in that sigh. Something that told her – there might be a bigger story here. 'Also, had there not been another matter in the news recently concerning Yewhurst?' She cleared her mind of the thought to concentrate on the current conversation. "How do you mean?" she asked in a soft, measured tone.

"We are looking into it. The Forestry Commission is involved. Can I let you know? Have you a number where I can reach you?"

"The Forestry Commission at Lyndhurst – why? Oh, I see – Yewhurst's woodland is one of their domains, is it?"

"Yes." Once again David wished he had kept his mouth under a tighter censorship. Mary then gave him her office number, thanked him and rang off. Five minutes later, she was onto the Forestry Commission at Lyndhurst, who told her how to contact the Yewhurst office. One more telephone call and Mary found herself talking to Stephen Knopner. She was lucky to get connected directly to him.

"Sorry – who?"

"Mary Taylor of the Winchester Chronicle." She spoke slowly, enunciating every syllable.

"How can I help?"

"I understand you are looking into the matter of this fierce adder that attacked a lady and nearly killed her."

Stephen had to think for a moment. His mind was on other matters. Then yesterday evening's episode came back to him. "You are a little premature."

"How do you mean?"

"Well – the search is planned for Saturday. Why don't you ring my secretary after the weekend? Should be able to put the matter into this world by then."

"Sorry – this world – not with you?"

"Think it's a load of exaggerated cobblers myself, but don't quote me on that. Ring me on Monday – as I say."

"Okay ... you are going to search for this snake on Saturday. Forgive me, but how are you going to find an adder in the Yewhurst forests?   I mean this one we are talking about, which presumably looks like any other..."

She did not get any further. An exasperated Stephen Knopner interrupted her. "I hardly think, a six-foot long, bright red serpent with deadly venom that attacks people from trees, bears much resemblance to any of the normal snake occupants in Yewhurst Wood. Goodbye!" Mary sat with her mouth slightly apart and the telephone still connected to her right ear. The dialling tone purred. Then she put down the receiver, rose to her feet, and went to see her editor.

Meanwhile, things were going well at Winchester hospital for the Westwards. Christine was stable and looked to be making a rapid recovery. She had held a long conversation with her parents the evening before. They were now on their way home, having been promised a telephone call as soon as their daughter was discharged from hospital.

"Tim – the doctor says I can leave tomorrow – all being well," Christine flung the words at her husband as soon as he walked into her room.

They kissed. "That is the best news I've had in a long while."

"They say I'll need a bit of a convalescence period: lots of sleep. Apparently, my blood is almost back to normal, but my brain needs the rest. Don't really understand it."

"Well, it isn't any kind of problem while Suz is with us. I'll go back to work on Monday, and we'll see how we go."

"Fine. Tell me what's been happening?" Tim brought her up to date and told her about the meeting at Beech Cottage with the forestry men.

"Poor Dalmar. Mind you, I wouldn't be any help – this Secret Pond is just a very vague memory with me. Not sure I want to remember it anyway."

"Hear, hear. Don't you worry one iota. It will all be sorted out, I'm sure." The dismal truth, to Tim, was that if this snake was not accounted for very soon, and with absolute finality, their dream home would be seriously tarnished. This was a thought that had started to preoccupy his mind. At first, he tried to dismiss the feeling, but it would not go away.

He had brought some more toiletries with him; which Suzanne had gathered together and a couple of magazines. Surreptitiously, he pushed a large bar of chocolate under her pillow. Christine laughed. "What are you doing that for?"

"Wasn't sure if it was allowed," he said in a whisper.

Christine retrieved the chocolate and placed it on the bedside table. "Tim – it isn't whisky!"

Tim's face broke back into that marvellous playful grin of his. Something he had not done for a while. He stayed all morning, because he did not intend to return until the next day, and then it would be with her clothes – ready for her to come home following the consultant's authorised discharge. At just after twelve o'clock, he kissed her with some passion, saying that he loved her far too much, and she was never to scare him like that again.

She smiled, "Tomorrow can't come soon enough," she said.

During the middle of the afternoon, Stephen Knopner replaced the handset on the radio in the Land Rover. He looked extremely disgruntled. His secretary had just told him that the editor of the Winchester Chronicle had asked her what time the search for the *serpent* was scheduled to start, this coming Saturday, and could a reporter and photographer attend. He could not believe that this fairy tale, as he now described it, had got to this stage and he was very annoyed that it should be allowed to cause him so much trouble. He had to admit, privately to himself, that if he had not made that colourful remark to the reporter, he would not now be in this position.

He knew that Yewhurst Wood must be closed to the general public as soon as possible, causing him to have to work late to prepare the notices, which would need to be displayed at all the public entrance areas some time the following morning.

He called his secretary back, after thinking everything through carefully, and instructed her to telephone the editor and inform him that by order of the Forestry Commission, Yewhurst Wood would be closed to the public – including the press – until further notice. He would personally call when he had more information, next week. In his own mind, he was quite sure that it would be the end of the matter, when they had found absolutely nothing.

Meanwhile, he had other serious concerns to attend to, like the idiot walkers he had admonished earlier for casually wandering along smoking cigars. Due to the long dry spell, this was something that constantly worried him. Fire in the forest could ruin years of work and destroy the harvest of the future. Then it suddenly dawned on him that no public access could mean – no fires. He smiled inwardly to himself. Perhaps, it might be a distinct advantage to keep this little lot going for as long as possible, until that is, it started to rain.

That evening Suzanne cooked Tim and Dalmar a light meal at her lover's house. Tim left fairly early saying he wanted to be by the telephone, just in case, and to get things ready for his wife's homecoming. "Going to put the vacuum cleaner round," his sister had teased him, for she knew that was not what he meant.

Alone together, Suzanne expressed concern to Dalmar over the day after tomorrow. "You will be careful?" she pleaded. Second only to Christine, she knew what he might come up against. "And I hope you will leave Fly with me?"

"Doubt that I would be allowed to take him anyway." he satisfied her. Fly looked at him – well aware that he was being talked about. "I still cannot believe that those forestry guys didn't know about that pond. It is so unique. Mind you, I plead guilty to not telling anyone, apart from you, of its existence. Wanted to keep it to myself. I'll never forget the day I first stumbled across it. At the time, I was regretting having decided to explore that narrow pathway, it was so overgrown, and then I heard ducks squabbling.

When I climbed over those rocks and laid eyes on it, I thought I was dreaming. I mean it's like taking a spec out of, I don't know – the Scottish Highlands – and dropping it in Yewhurst Wood. It was before I had Fly, and I was on my own. Stayed there for an hour or more: such a tranquil spot." He paused for a moment to alter the position of embrace around Suzanne. "However, I never imagined that I was one of just a few who knew about it. Presumably, I'm not the only one."

"What puzzles me," said Suzanne, "is surely you would think they couldn't have missed it when they planted the young trees? Some of them are right by the water!"

Dalmar turned his head towards hers. "*That* – is a very good point. I'll mention it when I see Stephen on Saturday."

"Good luck. Mr Sarcasm with a capital S. '*As far as I am aware.*' Supercilious so and so." She took him off very well, even getting the dialect to perfection.

"He's all right really, just under stress." Dalmar then went on to enlighten her about the problem of forest fires during the current dry weather. One mistake by one careless person could cause disaster.

Her mind registered this, realising the enormity of the problem. "Mind you, I still don't like him." It would take an awful lot to change her opinion. The man had doubted her word.

When Tim drove the estate car into the hospital car park on Friday morning, he thought the place had more bustle about it than the other times he had visited. And when he walked into the main building and started negotiating the long corridors, there certainly seemed to be more activity. It worried him because he thought this would delay the consultant's rounds. He need not have been bothered, for, if anything, Mr Lombard was early.

He looked even more impressive today dressed in a dark blue pin-stripe suit that set off his silver-grey hair. He was in good humour, and it made his excellent news about Christine more evocative. "Well, you have proved them all wrong ... err ... Mrs Westward," he said as he glanced at her notes. "That includes me – thought we would be having the pleasure of your company for a few days. No – the place for you – now – is at home. Plenty of rest and something you won't get here ... peace." Christine and Tim almost whooped with joy. "Your blood is nearly back to normal," Lombard continued. "I suggest you go and see your G.P. in about three weeks. He will probably need you to have another blood test. Should be able to give the all clear after that." There were smiles all round as they shook hands before leaving.

Tim sat down on the bed and for a while the two of them held hands chatting. Before long, a nursing sister came in. "Well, you can go home as soon as you are ready," she announced.

Christine went off to the facility area to have a wash and get changed into the clothes that Tim had brought with him. He waited for her outside her room, having gathered up her personal belongings and the case Suzanne had packed. It now included the bikini she had been wearing when the Red Adder attacked her: an item of clothing she would not be wearing again.

When she was ready, Tim went to get the car and parked it near the entrance, so that his wife would not have to walk further than necessary. Meanwhile, she said goodbye to the staff and thanked them all profusely. They had been very good to her and the professional care was of the highest quality. She walked slowly along the corridors. "Feels like I have just played a double hockey match," she complained, referring to the stiffness in her limbs.

About half an hour later, Suzanne opened the door to them with a gigantic smile on her face. She had been giving the cottage a quick spruce up. In his excitement Tim had neglected to telephone to say that Christine was definitely coming home, even though Suzanne had asked him to. She showed surprise and joy at the same time at the sight of her sister-in-law.

The three of them spent a pleasant day. Christine was fussed over a great deal, but she knew that it was not all about helping her convalesce. She knew it was because she was loved. When she telephoned her parents later, they were thrilled to hear that their daughter was back home. She had a long conversation with her mother.

Good wishes and words of endearment were passed on from her brothers and other members of her family. Some get-well-soon cards had already arrived with the morning post.

When eventually, Christine and Tim found themselves lying side by side in their bed, they cuddled tightly at the sheer joy of being close again.

A little later, Tim could feel his wife drifting off to sleep. The blissful moment was abruptly shattered. Behind them, in the forest – he heard it – and he felt Christine stiffen alongside him. That horrendous sound: the strident hiss with its malevolent low tremble. Tim said nothing, hoping his wife was asleep. But she was not, and her soft whispered words were a death note to his dreams. "Tim … I don't want to live here ... anymore."

He said nothing for a while, and then in the same hushed tone replied, "I hear you my darling." He stayed awake for a long time after that. There had been no movement from his sister's room, so he presumed she had not heard the noise. Knowing her, she would not have been able to remain alone if she had. He knew what his wife's words had been about. It was the statement from a woman, who, having made up her mind that now was the time to start a family, did not consider this a safe place to do so.

CHAPTER NINETEEN

"SORRY - MUST HAVE MISSED IT."

The main vehicle entrance to Yewhurst Wood is at the far end of the Chapp hamlet, and at half past eight on the Saturday morning, Mary Taylor and a photographer were leaning up against their car, enjoying the early morning sunshine. Following discussions with her editor they had decided on a course of action. Initially, it was to just sit and wait for something to happen.

During the next hour several people came along, mostly on foot, but others parked their cars before extricating their canine pets. Mary asked some of them if they knew anything about a search for a large snake taking place this morning. The surprise on the face of those questioned was evident and, obviously, curious. Apart from this a notice was on display banning entry to non-forestry personnel until further notice. During one resulting discussion other dog walkers joined in; some of them expressing annoyance at having their usual routes barred. None of them knew anything about a search, and not one had the slightest knowledge concerning a young woman who had suffered a bad snakebite.

At a quarter to ten, the photographer noticed some activity in the drive of one of the houses belonging to the Forestry Commission. Three men were loading a few items into the back of a four-wheel drive vehicle; one of these looked like a shotgun in a carrying sleeve. Then, all three climbed in and drove out of the drive going right past them, fairly fast. Mary noticed that the driver looked pointedly in their direction. On impulse, she motioned to the photographer to board their car and they followed. The Land Rover turned left, very soon ... she did likewise. The vehicle went down a steep dip by the side of the church before coming up to a junction with the main road through the village. It again turned left passed the pedestrian entrance to the church, and, afterwards, immediately left by a white-ringed tree. Mary followed. She found herself in a small car park that was intended for the use of churchgoers and people attending to graves. The Land Rover parked next to a black Jaguar, by the side of which two men stood talking.

One of these was Dalmar, dressed in his usual blue jeans with an open-necked, navy blue, short sleeve shirt. Today he opted for a pair of stout shoes instead of his usual moccasins. He had just strolled up from Beech Cottage, where he had been pleased to see Christine smiling and looking relaxed. The other man was Dr David Andrews. He looked as though he had just been kitted out for a jungle safari, with khaki shirt and trousers and black leather boots. Even his spectacles were now dark brown, instead of his usual silver variety. Over his shoulders he wore a small rucksack containing his medical items.

Stephen Knopner went over to say hello to Dalmar and David. Motioning his two colleagues to join him, he made introductions. "Jim Pearce," he said pointing out a medium height, slightly overweight, dark-haired man, "and Ginger Styles." His finger moved to a thin, wiry-looking individual with a long nose and stubbly chin. Both men were dressed similarly to their boss, in forestry ranger uniforms. They greeted the doctor and Dalmar, both of whom shook hands giving out their first names as they did so.

"Are you the gentlemen carrying out the search?" an audacious female voice shouted from across the car park. At the same time, the click of a camera could be heard. Mary strode boldly up to the five men and held out a hand to Stephen Knopner. "We spoke on the telephone." She blazed emerald, green eyes at him. "Mary Taylor, Winchester Chronicle."

Stephen shook her hand lightly. "Ah – yes." He paused before saying, "Not sure what you are doing here? I'm afraid we have no information for you yet. Monday will be the earliest..."

"That's all right. Just thought we would catch you before you start. Tell me, what do you hope to find?" Without waiting for a reply, she turned to address David, "Are you Dr Andrews?" She was guessing.

David decided to cool all this down if he could. He shook Mary's proffered hand but stated quite bluntly. "No comment is available at the moment."

The reporter suddenly switched off the charm and hardened her tone. "Mr Knopner – why has the public been banned from using the established right of way through these woods?"

David replied for him. "As we have said, no comment at this time. Mr Knopner will issue a statement on Monday morning, so I suggest your editor contact his office then." This was experience talking. A single mention of public safety would incite a barrage of questions.

Mary relented. She pursed her lips and gave an exaggerated shrug of her shoulders. "Okay, but we *are* entitled to hang around here!" she raised her voice after them as they walked away.

"We may be some time!" Stephen advised her over his shoulder. "Dalmar, I believe you are leading the way?" And he made a movement with his right hand to beckon him on.

Our reporter's astuteness picked this up and she hurriedly wrote down the name wondering about the correct spelling. 'Why was *he* leading the way?' she thought. The five men soon disappeared entering the woods at the other side of the graveyard. They made their way onto the main firebreak. It was the same hard-baked, deep-rutted surface that Dalmar remembered running over a few days ago. The sun, after its steady climb into the cloudless sky from the east, was just over the highest of the conifers.

They walked five abreast down the wide track. On the right, David in his safari gear with the rucksack firmly anchored around his waist; then came Dalmar in his denim. Stephen walked in the centre with a pack on his back housing a short-wave radio; alongside him was Jim with a canvas gun sleeve slung over his left shoulder containing a twelve-bore shotgun, and on his belt could be seen at least ten cartridges inserted into loops. Finally, on the left, strode Ginger with a hand axe attached to his belt by a leather head-guard.

After about twenty-five minutes, they reached the first path crossing where the firebreaks for north-south met east-west. They carried straight on, progressing swiftly along a narrowing, but more verdant way. At the next crossing Dalmar again pointed straight ahead. They were now well into the forest and any traffic noise from the road had lost itself among the countless trees a while ago.

"Well, here we are," Dalmar showed them a pathway overgrown by hazel growth on both sides.

"Ginger?" said Stephen looking at the appropriately named man with his thick crop of red hair and extensively freckled face.

Ginger peered down the track and rubbed his chin. "Don't go to no pond. Goes over to Handley's farm look." After more thoughtful chin rubbing, he added: "About six-seven hundred yards to fields look."

"Yes, I know," said Dalmar. "The pond is over to the right, about three hundred yards up this path."

"Good ... lead on." Stephen beckoned to Dalmar. He followed behind, bending low to stop his backpack from snagging the branches above him. Then came the two rangers with David in the rear. After a while Dalmar started peering through the hazel trees on his right-hand side. He kept doing this for a further hundred yards or more. However, he noticed nothing familiar appertaining to his last visit. He went some way further, but it all seemed strange to him. While the others looked on, he made them start by suddenly clapping his hands loudly, two or three times. But nothing happened. He began to look very uncomfortable and continued for another fifty yards or so, often hesitating. Eventually, Stephen could not contain himself. "We've come rather more than three hundred yards. Will shortly be in the fields – out of the woodland..."

"Sorry, must have missed it. We'll have to go back," said Dalmar trying to hide his concern. When they had retraced their steps some of the way, he asked Stephen if he could go into the undergrowth on the left-hand side of the track.

"Be my guest," Stephen said. Dalmar had no suitable knife or stout stick to help him, and he found it very hard going given the dense growth, both from the hazel trees and the thick grasses and brambles below. With much effort, he managed to get about twenty feet or so away from the path. He was looking for the tall sweet chestnut. But although he looked in all directions, he still could not recognize anything to tell him the pond was nearby. Then he began to think. 'There must be another track off the main one. Perhaps just a bit farther.' He struggled back and broke the news.

When they had clambered free and reached the wider path, David said to Dalmar in an undertone. "Having a spot of bother?"

"Think I know where I went wrong. We need to find another trail, like this, not far, I should think." He wiped the sweat beads forming on his brow. It was very hot.

They found another track going off to the right a little way further along the main path. Dalmar breathed a sigh of relief. Using the same formation, they went off again down a similar tunnel of hazel trees. They had not gone more than three hundred yards before they came to a small wooden gate. It looked out over scrubland towards a large field, with a farmhouse chimney poking out of a copse area on the other side.

"Was going to say. This where this'un come out," said Ginger. "Handley's Farm look."

"And now what?" accused Stephen, glancing at Dalmar in a sceptical way.

"I don't understand it," said the abashed man. "It doesn't make any sense. Admittedly, I have only been to the pond a few times, but ... I'm sorry ... I've let you down."

"Which path did you go down the other day?" David asked, trying to be helpful.

"Well, I thought it was the first one because those ... bushes – next to it looked familiar. But now – I am not sure. Tell you what, so that I don't waste any more of your time, let me look on my own for a while. You see the pond had some larches around it, and I haven't seen any."

"There are no larches in this part of the plantation," commented Stephen in an exasperated manner.

That answered another question for Dalmar, so he did not bother with it. "Well – trees which look like larches." He felt confused and incompetent.

Stephen looked at Dalmar. 'Wouldn't have thought this man would tell lies,' he considered. Something is wrong here.' "I've got a better idea. Back by the main path, you may have noticed a very tall pine. The reason that Ginger is here is because he is very good at climbing trees. Why don't we let him shin up and have a look?"

"Brilliant!" exclaimed David. If there was a pond, he would be bound to see it from up there. Dalmar was much relieved at this suggestion and made an appreciative movement with his right hand. On the way back to the main path, he felt low. 'Where could he have gone wrong? Suzanne had found the pond straight away, having received very basic directions.' He felt as though he was in the middle of a nightmare, where no reason existed. He had been looking forward to showing Stephen the pond. It would have given him great satisfaction. Now – it was difficult for him to keep his head up.

CHAPTER TWENTY

"HAVE YOU EVER SEEN ANYTHING LIKE THAT?"

When they arrived at the tree referred to; instinctively they all cast their eyes up its massive trunk. It was a Scots pine, with the familiar soft rouge branchless area running up the better part of its height. Dalmar thought that it must be over a hundred feet high, and if Ginger could scale it to the highest branches, a few feet from the top; he would certainly have a good view. Stephen gave him the go-ahead with a curt nod. What followed was extraordinary.

Ginger removed the belt holding the axe and left it on the ground. From experience, he knew that the fewer things about him that might get snagged, the better. Then he took off his watch and placed it next to the axe. He stood for a while studying the tree from a small distance away; so that he could see as far up as possible, obviously working out a route. He held a hand above his eyes to shield them from the sunlight. In a sudden move, he dropped his arm and approached the base of the trunk purposefully. There were no branches for at least the first thirty feet, and Dalmar thought that he would use some sort of aid to scale this. But no, he literally went virtually straight up. A ranger's boot is strong but supple. Ginger seemed to anchor a toe onto a strip of bark, and then move up without hesitation. Raised formations of it grew vertically about eight inches in length, whilst varying into masses of different shapes. It appeared that the trick, or perhaps necessity, was to not linger, thus putting the least strain on the bark formations as possible.

Ginger's hand would reach up and with his finger ends, grasp a knob of bark and then haul himself up, it seemed, effortlessly. The same routine followed with his other foot and hand accordingly. What amazed David and Dalmar was the speed with which he climbed. The layman would think that he would wish to test the strength of each handhold before trusting his weight to it, but he assessed them by feel, instantly. Sometimes he rejected a hold moving onto another. Soon he arrived at the first group of branches and hoisted himself onto a huge arm like structure, before lifting a leg in one movement. The result left him standing on it. The man's agility and small limb strength was mesmerizing. He continued up another long stretch of bare trunk in the same manner as he had before. As the height got more dangerous, his speed, if anything, increased.

"Have you ever seen anything like that?" David commented with his face masked in admiration.

"Wouldn't have thought it possible," said Dalmar.

"I know," concurred Stephen. "I asked him why he was so fearless at climbing, and he told me that as a child, his parents had to stop him from taking on cliffs at the seaside at a very young age. He probably scales something in the region of a dozen trees a month. He is very useful to us; I can tell you."

They all moved back at this stage, so that they could monitor Ginger's progress as he got higher and higher. At one point, he stopped and scanned the forest in the area of the sought-after pond. He did not yell down to announce any observation, and therefore carried on with the ascent. When he had gained some more height, he suddenly leaned out to peer pointedly over his shoulder in the direction that the allusive pond should have been. He seemed to be astounded at something making some sort of inaudible exclamation; then as though seeking further clarification continued climbing.

Jim, who knew Ginger better than his boss commented, "It'll be about now that he has to be careful. He once told me that at anything over fifty feet he must fight a crazy feeling that – if necessary – he could fly." Unlike Ginger, Jim appeared to have little local dialect.

The climber was nearing the last growth of branches before the summit. There would be no point in going any higher. They were waiting for him to stop and make another scan when Jim said, "Aye, aye, something's up!"

Ginger had indeed halted. His head had come level with the lowest of the highest branches, and he was just about to haul himself onto it, when a movement on the branch on the other side of the trunk, caught his eye. Expecting to see a bird, he turned his head to look. He was used to a startled rook or another type of high-perching bird suddenly flying off. Such an occurrence did not worry him. But what he saw made the marrow in his bones go icy cold. The broad head of a large viper was looking at him. Ginger was shocked. The head was raised in a low striking position with its body coiled around the branch. Thoughts raced through his mind. Among them, he knew he must start down immediately before it changed its position. Then he noticed something very strange, which kept his attention. From the neck, working towards the tail, rapidly, it was changing from a dull brown colour to a vivid deep red. A black zigzag stood out on its back and the yellow eyes with dark vertical black pupils stared at him menacingly. Ginger was just about to make his first step downwards, when the snake raised its head a little more.

'I must get out of here,' his mind raced. But he was too late; the viper opened its mouth showing two large fangs right at the front of a dark cave-like aperture. There came a strong thrusting sound... 'STUTT!' Ginger took his hands from the tree-trunk and clasped them to his eyes. He experienced a dreadful pain. The pain got worse. Great tongues of agony coursed inside his head. Flailing his arms wildly, he lost both footholds, and fell backwards.

The Shy Avenger   Scardthomas

The watchers on the ground all gasped in horror as Ginger's body crashed down to the next set off branches. Stephen, who like every-one else supposed he had fallen, hoped that the branches would break his fall, and, at best, he might even get a hold to stop the plunge.

"Oh no!" shouted Jim in alarm, as Ginger appeared to cannon off a large branch halfway down and bounce with audible bone crushing off another. Then, he let out a gurgled scream and plummeted, unchecked, to fall into the undergrowth just off the path, with a pronounced double thud! This was followed by complete silence. No cries of pain – not even a moan.

"My God!" shouted Stephen rushing over with David close behind.

"Hold it!" came a shout from Dalmar. "Sorry… David you carry on! Stephen! – is Jim any good with that!?" Dalmar was pointing at the man's shoulder indicating the gun.

Stephen sensed a real urgency in Dalmar's tone. "He's the local clay pigeon shoot champion. Why?" He stopped his headlong rush to Ginger and let the doctor through.

"Jim," Dalmar approached the shocked ranger. "The growth near the top of that pine, from where Ginger fell. Can you get on that and wait for my signal?"

The ranger glanced at his boss for permission. Stephen nodded. In one movement, Jim let the zip go on the gun sleeve with one hand, extracting the twelve-bore shotgun with the other, breaking it for loading single handed. He took two cartridges from his belt and inserted them in their chambers, closed the barrels, released the safety catch, and said to Dalmar without looking at him, "I'm on it."

For a short while, all three men strained their eyes towards the top of the pine. Stephen was about to ask what they were waiting for, when Dalmar said firmly. "Now! – Do you see it!?" The snake had launched itself from the pine and appeared suspended in a static double 'S', with what looked like fins extended in two positions along the body. Jim found himself faced with a very difficult shot. He raised the gun to his shoulder; the blue-black over-under barrels glinting in the mid-morning sunlight. He sighted on the flying object; went ahead in its descent and pulled the trigger – once and almost immediately – twice. Two loud reports rang out through the forest. The snake's head suddenly struck back on its own body and plummeted towards the ground.

"Look out Doctor!" shouted Dalmar. David, who had found Ginger's inert body, and was exploring his considerable injuries, jumped to his feet, looking around him. He need not have worried; the creature landed some yards away.

Dalmar and Stephen went in search. The snake lay still: apparently quite dead. Neither man spoke for a while, before Stephen made the observation, "Hardly six feet. I would say – more like four. And that rusty brown is certainly not a *cherry* red – would you agree?" Dalmar made no answer. Stephen continued, "However, that is no ordinary adder, I grant you. It is too wide in its girth and what are those loose folds of skin?

Probably some bloody twit's pet. It's either escaped, or more likely, the owner couldn't handle it. So, the thing's been dumped on us! Damn good shot Jim," said Stephen. "Very difficult … under pressure. Well done." Dalmar also gave him a congratulatory nod. All three men urgently went to see the extent of Ginger's injuries. They received a terrible shock. David looked around when they approached.

"How is he? We'll need an ambulance I guess?" Stephen asked.

"Yes," the doctor replied … "but there's no hurry." That statement meant only one thing, and they all knew what it was. Considering the height, the man fell from, this was not surprising. But due to his climbing ability, none of them had expected it.

After a long, hushed pause, Stephen said, "How? … Did he break his neck?"

David with head bowed, but still in a kneeling position by the body, pointed to Ginger's closed eyes. They looked like swollen, rotten mushrooms: both of them. "What the?" Stephen said, screwing up his face in disgust.

"Certainly, he will have suffered a few broken bones," said the doctor. "Several ribs, but … no. I'll bet – *this* is what has killed him." Again, he gestured towards the awful mess that a few minutes ago had been Ginger's bright, cheery blue eyes.

"How do you mean?" asked Jim in a depressed tone.

"I don't know," replied David, "but I think that thing lying over there..."

"You mean he has been bitten in the eyes: not possible," interrupted Stephen while in the act of getting the radio set up.

"Not bitten," said a voice from behind them. It was Dalmar.

"Go on," encouraged the doctor.

"Spat at?" Dalmar's intonation suggested a question.

"That is the only explanation I can come up with," agreed David. "But we shall have to see what a post-mortem tells us. Anyway … there is nothing I can do."

"Must be some sort of devil snake – the one they talk about in the village," said Jim, traumatised.

This remark was not lost on his boss, but he kept his queries to himself, for the time being. He cranked the battery to life on the transmitter and hoisted the short aerial. "FO to base – FO to base – over."

There was only a short wait before a girl's voice answered. "Hello – base to FO. Over" There followed urgent instructions from Stephen to get an ambulance to meet them at Yewhurst Church car park.

With one leg kneeling and the other in the crouched position, the forestry boss looked at his dead employee. It dawned on him that the welfare of the man had been his responsibility. He had never had a fatality in his work force up till now, or, for that matter a serious accident, some near scrapes, but thankfully, nothing serious. He attributed a lot of this to his quality of management. The truth was that he never expected anything as serious as this to happen in his entire career. Quickly he came to his senses. A freak occurrence such as this was exactly what it was. Dalmar was standing next to him asking if he would like him to carry Ginger's body?

This was not as strange as it might look. Dalmar, in his capacity as an assistant purser had been close to tragedy before. On one occasion, he had to deal with a suicide passenger who had cut his throat with a razor blade.

Jim and Stephen helped get the dead man into an upright position, and then Dalmar bent down and put his head between Ginger's legs, hoisting him into a fireman's lift. He winced as he straightened up. 'For a slight man, Ginger's body felt very heavy – much heavier than Christine,' he thought bizarrely.

The doctor put his medical bag back onto his back and Stephen gathered the radio up by its straps, carrying it in his right hand. Jim placed the twelve-bore back in its' carrying case, collected Ginger's belt, watch and axe and they set off. Stephen suggested that the snake's body remain where it was. Arrangements would be made to collect it later.

All four of them were deeply shocked at the tragedy. The atmosphere was heavy, with a distressing feeling of morbid-ness. After a long silence, eventually, Stephen spoke. "Apart from finding out exactly what that reptile is, I guess that is that. I shall be able to give the all clear and have the 'no admittance' notices taken down – even though…" His voice trailed off: it was clear that he was referring to the loss of a life.

"Yes," agreed David.

Puffing somewhat while he spoke, Dalmar said. "Personally – that is the last thing – I would advise doing."

"And what makes *you* say that?" came Stephen's brusque response.

"That snake, as you rightly observed, was about four feet long. The one that attacked Christine – was, apparently, half as long again."

Stephen came back. "No disrespect, but we have only one witness's description for that, and I would remind you that it took place in a terrain that has yet to be verified."

The words stung Dalmar. "Granted, but as I have said before, Suzanne would not exaggerate by that much, in my admittedly biased opinion." The forest officer's mind began to waver. Some fifteen minutes earlier, he had been full of scorn for the whole Red Adder business. But now, a strange snake had been encountered and he had a dead employee on his hands. Stephen and David stopped walking. Jim went on a couple of steps before turning to look back in their direction, questioningly. Dalmar paused.

David was the first to speak. "Are you saying – there are – or rather were – two of them – Red Adders that is?"

"Two – or more." Dalmar carried on walking; the load was easier that way.

"Hell's teeth!" exclaimed Stephen, although in a subdued manner, as though out of respect for Ginger. Nobody said anything for some considerable time, until they reached the brow of the low incline, where the wide clearway dropped down for a few hundred yards near the car park.

"I suppose – the lady from the press – is still there?" Dalmar asked between heavy pants. "We had better decide what to say?"

"Damn woman!" Stephen said in an exasperated tone. He hesitated, wondering what to do. They could hardly hide Ginger's body.

"May I – talk to her?" volunteered David.

"Be my guest," Stephen jumped in quickly, so as not to let him change his mind. "I know Ginger wasn't married, mercifully. He has a mother, I believe?" His question was directed at Jim.

"Yes – lives in the village," he replied.

When they got within sight of the church parking area down near the road, they could clearly see Mary Taylor leap from her car, closely followed by the photographer with his equipment. Stephen cursed again. "Don't worry, I'll cover you," David reminded him.

They could not get to the other side of the gate before Mary was on them; the photographer's camera clicking persistently. Even from a distance, the atmosphere given off by the four men, one of whom was carrying the fifth member of the expedition, told the waiting press duo that something tragic had occurred.

"What happened?" asked Mary, as she closed on them. She looked concerned and excited at the same time. Dalmar tried to keep at the back of the group. He had perspired excessively from perspiration through the exertion of carrying Ginger, and he considered that taking pictures of dead bodies unethical.

"Been an accident," said the doctor. "Poor chap fell from a high tree. Regretfully, he did not survive the fall."

"What! Do you mean he is dead!?" Mary looked aghast. However, this did not seem to deter the photographer, who if anything, stepped up the rate of his camera shutter.

"Yes, *very* distressing," said David. "That's all we can say right now. You understand that we must inform his family immediately."

"How did it happen? Did you find anything? What about the snake?" Mary persisted but was pushed aside as she continued to barrage them with questions. The group made their way through the gate to the car park. She did not get any more information because all of them were distracted by the arrival of an ambulance turning in off the road. There was no siren or flashing lights. Dalmar immediately skirted around with Ginger's body and made his way towards it. David followed him.

Mary redirected her questions at Stephen, who held up his hand in negation. "Doctor Andrews will answer all your queries. I have to go; talk to you later." With that he grabbed hold of Jim and they bundled their gear into the Land Rover, shouted goodbye to David and drove off without saying anything at all to Dalmar.

As soon as the ambulance had left, Mary demanded more answers. Dalmar wondered whether he should depart. He did not have to. David caught his eye and by clever facial language, without giving anything away, made it obvious to him that he should quietly make his escape. While the photographer and Mary's back were turned, Dalmar left. He needed no further prompting. He went through a small gap in some rhododendron bushes and weaved his way between two yew trees, before joining the path leading to Beech Cottage. He walked the rest of the way at a fast pace, all the while rotating the muscles in his shoulders by swinging his upper arms backwards and forwards, to relieve the aches caused by his recent burden.

Meanwhile, David was left to pacify Mary. "A snake has been found which *is* larger than the normal adder. More on that later when we have the necessary information. Try Mr Knopner's office on Monday."

Mary was about to ask where the snake was, when she suddenly realised that was probably the reason for the rapid departure of the forest officer, who no doubt had it with him. Then she thought to herself that he could hardly have hidden a large snake about his person. "Where is it?" she asked immediately.

"Had to kill it, I'm afraid. Got too close."

"Who did that?" she immediately countered, remembering two gunshots they had heard.

"Not sure," lied the doctor. "Too much going on."

"Back to the deceased, who was he?" Here David gave those details he knew: Ginger's last name and the fact that there was only one immediate family relative, his mother. One thing completely left him in ignorance. Ginger was obviously a nickname, and he had no idea as to what the poor man's proper first name was.

Something had just released a detail from Mary's brain. She made a sudden intake of breath and looked at the doctor with a wide-eyed expression. "I don't suppose that snake could have bitten the lady who is missing?"

Dr Andrews stopped in his tracks. The thought had not occurred to him. But as his mind raced, he shook his head. "As far as I know, Julia Thornton used to spend a lot of time in here – in the church grounds. I don't think she went into the depths of the forest."

"If you say so," said Mary. "Just a thought." Satisfied for now, she walked off with the photographer to her car. She looked as though she was going to drive away but changed her mind and wound down the window. David thought she was going to wave. Instead, she fired another question at him. "Who is – Dalmar?"

This took the doctor aback. He openly stammered in his answer. "Err – just a friend helper – I – I think. Better ask him yourself." Mary decided to leave it and drove off towards Winchester. The photographer would have to get busy in the developing laboratory, and she had to contact her editor. This story- was about to go national.

Meanwhile, Stephen and Jim's rapid departure had not been just to escape from the local press. The main intent was the recovery of the snake's body. They drove back to the Chapp area of the village and stopped off at a forestry shed to pick up a large canvas bag and some tough gloves. Then, they went into the woodland from another entrance, and by means of a sharp right turn took the four-wheel drive vehicle right along a firebreak, until it joined the far end of the one where Ginger's tragic death had taken place. Soon they came up to the big Scots pine. Everything looked to be back to its usual peace. They climbed out of the vehicle and went to the position where they had left the dead snake. There was nothing there except some disturbed grasses in the area where it had landed, and what looked like dried blood, but nothing else. Their immediate reaction was that they had been wrong in presuming it had been killed by gunshot. After gaping at the empty space momentarily, Stephen said, "It was dead, wasn't it?"

"I would have bet big money on it," commented Jim.

"It is hardly likely that there would be any predators about. The badger and fox wouldn't be hunting at this time, and, anyway, your shooting should have kept anything away from here for ages. So, what the heck...?" asked a perplexed Stephen.

Jim scratched his head.

"Well – if it is still alive – where is it? Couldn't possibly have gone far. Better get your gun, Jim." He did as he was told and ran over to the Land Rover, collected the shotgun, made it ready and loaded, but left the barrels broken as a safety measure. For the next quarter of an hour, they looked all around within a fifty-yard radius. There was not the slightest sign of it. As well as the snake itself, they also concentrated on seeking further blood deposits, but there appeared to be no trace whatsoever.

"It hasn't gone up that bloody tree again?" Stephen said searching for an explanation. They both went out onto the track to scan the pine. Stephen kept a pair of binoculars in a compartment in his vehicle. With these he made a long search of the tree from top to bottom but could not see anything that gave him concern.

After that, they gave up and drove back. Stephen explained to Jim that he would drop him at his home and then go and break the tragic news to Ginger's mother.

The sad loss of a colleague had not completely gripped Jim. It did now. "Can I come with you?" he asked. And when Stephen gave him an enquiring look, he said, "Well – we were mates see – Ginger and me. He was godfather to my eldest nipper. So, I know his mum – pretty well."

Stephen just said, "Of course. Thanks. Anyhow – you know where she lives."

They parked the Land Rover at the forest officer's home. Mrs Styles lived a few hundred yards along the road in a small, thatched cottage. They walked down a hill and passed through the gate that heralded a very steep narrow path, bounded by lavender plants in full bloom on each side. At the top was the front door, badly in need of some paint repair. The two men made their way towards it and Stephen gripped the large black doorknocker. He used it, carefully, three times. Despite his caution, it sounded far too loud, sending a disturbing echo into the interior of the house as though heralding the awful message. It made Jim visibly shudder, as he stood holding the deceased man's wristwatch in his right hand.

CHAPTER TWENTY-ONE

"WELL, THAT ANSWERS THAT."

Dalmar would have preferred to have gone straight home and have a wash, but he could hardly pass Beech Cottage without calling in. He found Suzanne with her brother and Christine in the back garden.

For Tim and his sister, picture hanging had been the order of the morning, while Christine rested. They only had seven items to put up, so it had not taken very long, despite Tim's insistence that accurate measurements must be taken to get each one at the right height. It took three attempts to get the bluebell scene landscape plum in the centre, above the mantelpiece.

Fly heard his master coming long before anyone else. Suzanne jumped up and ran towards him. One look at his face and she could tell something awful had happened. They had all been waiting with some curiosity, after hearing the gunshots an hour earlier. "What's happened?" Suzanne demanded.

Dalmar sat down on a canvas chair and removed his shirt.

"Well go on!" Suzanne said impatiently.

"I have made a complete fool of myself," he announced. "Despite several attempts, I just could not find that pond: it has disappeared into thin air! You can imagine the looks I got from Stephen Knopner."

"Dalmar ... that's impossible. Christine and I went straight to it following your directions," Suzanne said looking confused.

"Let him continue," said Tim. Dalmar related most of the details concerning the search for the pond, up until the time it was suggested that Ginger climb the tree.

"Who is Ginger?" asked Tim.

"Ah ... or was," he replied in a barely audible manner.

"What are you saying?" asked Christine entering the conversation for the first time. Suzanne had an extremely worried look on her face.

Dalmar first explained about Ginger and Jim's part in the morning's affair, and then went on to tell them about the tragedy. He did not mention that he had carried the dead man's body.

On hearing of the fatality, Tim stood up and went to his wife's side, laying a hand on her right shoulder. She was the first to speak. "Was he married ... this Ginger?"

"No ... lived with his mother in the village – I believe."

Christine sighed and looked at her sister-in-law, whose face had gone pale. "Well ... at least the snake has gone," she said. Dalmar made no comment. He thought it prudent, at this stage, not to mention that it was highly unlikely to be the same reptile that had attacked her.

"I'll make a sandwich for you darling," said Suzanne. "Would you like a drink?"

"Thanks. Actually, I would really like a glass of water."

About half an hour later, after Dalmar had enjoyed his refreshment, and they had all talked in a somewhat subdued fashion following the morning's sad occurrence, Suzanne suggested to her man that they leave Tim and Christine to relax together for the afternoon. No doubt Christine would need an afternoon nap anyway.

While having a quick bath and a change of clothes at his home, Dalmar asked Suzanne if she would like to go out somewhere for the rest of the day. He felt he needed to. "How about a walk around Southsea Castle? Get some sea air."

"How long will it take us to get there?" she asked.

"About an hour."

"Okay."

They decided to leave Fly at home and gave him plenty of food and water to keep him going.

Despite the aggravation of getting there, the tonic of the sea breeze worked. Dalmar parked the Six just off the Ladies Mile at Southsea, and they walked out onto the promenade looking over the channel that runs between southern England and the Isle of Wight. It is a busy seaway because of the adjacent naval base at Portsmouth, and the large merchant shipping docks at Southampton. With Southsea Castle on their left, they strolled east taking in the exhilarating maritime scenery.

Following the walk, they treated themselves to an ice-cream, the soft Italian type with a milk chocolate flake stuck in the top. Dalmar had to take his handkerchief to the tip of Suzanne's nose. She seemed oblivious to the dab of ice-cream displayed prominently at its end.

Instead of going back to the car straight away, they went down to a fun-fair park and played children for a couple of hours. Suzanne mercilessly punished Dalmar's courteousness on the bumper cars, but he got his self-respect back at a shooting gallery, when he won a large cuddly teddy bear and teased Suzanne by threatening to keep it for himself.

They finished off the visit with hot-dogs, before making their way home as dusk was descending. Dalmar took a different route, so that they could stop on top of Portsdown Hill to enjoy one of the best night views in the United Kingdom. Below them, stretching away into the middle distance were the lights of Portsmouth and Southsea: two miles of twinkling gold and amber tones, finishing with the colours of the decorative seaside illuminations, and then the navy blue of the Solent Sea. Below the horizon they could clearly make out the pinprick lights of the town of Ryde in the Isle of Wight, and, behind those, the island's dark silhouetted landscape climbing into the deep ultramarine sky.

Such was the attraction of the panoramic forward view that neither of them looked into the black heavens above their heads. If they had, they would have seen another wonderful sight: the tumult of twinkling stars spread across a cloudless sky.

Dalmar held Suzanne close on the edge of the precipitous grass slope. As they glanced at each other during the romantic spell of the new night, she turned her head to his. He kissed her raised lips firmly and they melted into one another ... in love.

"How do you feel – after your awful morning?" she asked, almost whispering into his ear.

"Lousy ... can't help thinking what Ginger's mum must be going through. Poor woman."

When they arrived home, after an exuberant welcome from Fly, Suzanne phoned Tim to enquire after Christine's well-being. To her surprise she was told that after a long afternoon sleep, she was much refreshed and now – bored – already.

So, as a result, the four of them spent the remainder of the evening at Dalmar's cottage. It was while they were seated, relaxing, that Suzanne asked her lover if she could have one of his cigarettes?

"Sorry. No," he replied.

"What do you mean? Have you run out?" She countered showing a crinkle on her brow.

He looked at her for a short while and said with a soft smile. "Not very observant - are you?"

Christine made a calculated guess and asked; "Have you given up?"

"What!?" said Suzanne all wide eyed.

"Packed it in the day of your injury. It was the running: my chest was on fire."

"Congratulations," said Tim, looking pleased.

"Funny really. I have always enjoyed smoking, but – well – the trauma of it all." Dalmar gave a short shrug of his shoulders.

"Doesn't help me," said Suzanne with a pout. "Surely you must have one somewhere?" She started glancing around at likely places.

"Nope, threw the last packet away. Oh – wait a minute." He opened a drawer in the built-in dresser by the chimneybreast. "Yup. How about this?" And he tossed an aluminium cigar case at her.

To her credit Suzanne caught it, and then grimaced. "No thanks – you horrid man. I don't smoke cigars. Urgh." She handed it back. Her brother laughed.

A little later and very late for a call, the telephone rang. Dalmar muttered and went to answer it. David Andrew's voice came over the instrument. "Ah, tracked you down at last. Look – I am very sorry to call at such a late hour, but I thought you should know something."

"Go on," said Dalmar. He closed the earpiece of the telephone closer to his head on hearing the identity of the caller.

"Stephen called me this afternoon. Apparently, the body of the snake Jim shot has completely disappeared."

"What ..." Dalmar had to stop himself and then lower his voice. "How long after we left did, they go to retrieve it?"

"Straight away. Stephen is of the opinion that it can't have been dead and must have gone into cover. They say they searched the immediate area thoroughly and drew a blank."

"Could something have taken it? A predator?"

"Again, Stephen reckons that there isn't much that would ... in daylight. It was hidden from hawks and the recent shooting would have frightened anything else off."

"What about some*body*?"

"Similar thought occurred to me – but who?"

"Search me," Dalmar replied, unhelpfully. "Anything you want me to do?"

"No, no – just keeping you informed. Better tell Tim and the ladies. They will want to keep away from the woodland. Oh, and by the way, you were right, that was very nasty venom in Ginger's eyes. One other thing. When you – so astutely – got Jim Pearce to shoot the snake – was it headed in my direction?"

Caught by surprise with the question, Dalmar had to think before giving an answer. "Possibly."

"Oh, I see – well anyway, thank you. You – you may have saved my life."

"Ah," said Dalmar – feebly.

After this both men said, "Goodnight."

"Who was that?" Suzanne was the first to ask when he came back into the sitting room.

"David Andrews, asking after your health, Christine."

"What – at this time of night? He's keen." Raising her eyebrows, she said, "I have an appointment to see him on Thursday."

The windows were wide open in the bay area and Suzanne had put some music on the stereo system: the album 'Days of Future Passed' by the Moody Blues. Dalmar caught Tim's eye and made a movement with his head towards the kitchen. The two men left the girls chatting. Dalmar carried on through the kitchen, opening the stable door, and went out into the garden. Here, they could not be heard from the inside, especially as their voices would be further drowned by the music. The night was dark and still, although the lights from the Claymans Heron softened the blackness a little. Dalmar spoke. "You remember, I told you that a forestry chap shot the Red Adder?"

"Ye-es." Tim replied.

"Well, they can't find the body; apparently it has disappeared." He then went on to tell Tim in more detail about the arguments as to whether it was alive or dead.

"What do *you* think?" Tim looked into Dalmar's eyes as he asked the question.

"I am sure it was dead. As sure as one can be."

"Well – that sounds pretty definite, which leaves the only solution that somebody has taken it."

"Looks like..." But Dalmar could add nothing to that.

"If that *is* the case, we won't be seeing anymore Red Adders."

"Sorry to disappoint you Tim, but I don't think it is as simple as that." He explained to him about the difference in the sizes between the one that attacked his wife, and the snake that killed the forester.

Tim took this in and kept his thoughts to himself. He changed the subject. "You wouldn't happen to know who paid for Christine's private room at the hospital? They won't tell me, and it was arranged before my parents-in-law knew about her hospitalisation – so it wasn't them."

"It certainly wasn't me, if that is your drift. If I could afford it – which is doubtful – I would ask your consent before arranging anything like that."

"Right – okay. Hope you didn't mind me asking?"

"Not at all. Another mystery it seems."

Tim sighed before saying, "Yes. Shall we go back and break the news." Then, he hesitated. "No ... I see why you have not told them yet. No point in causing unnecessary alarm."

As if in answer to that remark, from far away, they heard a sound. It stood out above the babble of voices coming from people leaving the pub. It was that loathsome sound they had all come to dread. "Well – that answers that," said Tim in a hushed and very disappointing tone. Before they entered under the glass overhang by the stable door, he said, "Some time ago you asked us about strange noises. Was that what you meant?"

"Yes."

"You knew it was the Red Adder ... or – or John the Red?"

"Yes," and then reading another question on Tim's face. "That is, I suspected it was." Tim didn't say anything; he thought the reply strange, somehow, but he was not sure why.

"You know – there were several factors that helped Christine's eventual recovery after she had been bitten. Not the least of which was the speed with which you managed to get her back to Beech Cottage." Dalmar suddenly looked acutely embarrassed. "Well – I would like to say a big thank you." Tim held out his right hand.

Dalmar shook it, coyly. "Thing is ... if I hadn't mentioned the damned pond in the first place..."

"Come on!" said Tim emphatically. "It would have happened anyway, sooner or later with this continuous hot weather – perhaps we might all have gone. Who knows?" Dalmar saw the point – not a little relieved.

Lyrics from the Moody Blues record wafted out to greet them. 'Nights in white satin, never reaching the end. Letters I've written...'

It was clear, when they re-entered the sitting room that the girls had not heard the snake. They didn't even enquire as to where their men had been, for they were engaged in an earnest conversation about something else, having to talk loudly above the music.

CHAPTER TWENTY-TWO

HEADLINE NEWS.

At half past eight on the Sunday morning, Tim Westward received a telephone call from a reporter working for a well-known popular newspaper. The reporter asked him if he could have a statement from his wife about the snake that attacked her. Tim felt angry at the intrusion. He thought fast and told the caller that his wife was staying with her parents. She was not to be disturbed. The reporter then switched his questions to Tim, asking how much he knew about the attack. Tim avoided giving too much detail concerning the snake itself, pleading ignorance, and suggested that he contact the Forestry Commission for further details. The newspaperman rang off.

Christine called down from the bedroom. "Who was that on the phone?"

"A reporter from the Daily what- you -mecallit."

"What?"

"Hold on – I'll make you a cup of tea and bring it up. Tell you then."

Christine was in the kitchen in her nightdress in seconds. "*Who* did you say?" she asked. Her husband told her and followed it up with the details of the conversation.

"Did you tell them it had been killed?" Christine innocently asked. Tim had no choice but to inform his wife of the latest developments in that regard. "So – there is still something out there," Christine said, looking badly shaken. Although her memory was still cloudy about her nasty experience, she was clearly very affected by it. A vivid scene from the attack would stay with her forever. This was the sight of the utterly revolting head of the snake looking at her, close to; followed by the indescribable pain she suffered during and after the bite. Anyhow, matters were much more serious now. A man had been killed.

Tim took note of the expression on her face. "Chris, would you like to spend a few days with your parents, until the press lose interest?"

Christine thought about it for a little while, but not for long. "No. Let's get it over with Tim. The next time they call, I'll speak to them – okay?"

"Good idea. Better warn Dalmar and Suz. I'll give them a ring in about half an hour. They'll be up by then – surely?"

Christine glanced at a clock. "I should leave it a bit longer if I were you." She had a subtle smile on her face.

Stephen Knopner was really upset at being called to the telephone on a Sunday morning, at home. He had been interrupted whilst enjoying some family time with his two young sons and one-year-old daughter. Unfortunately, the man on duty at the Forestry Commission office thought that the call from a national daily newspaper was important enough to warrant disturbing him. Stephen cursed himself for not leaving appropriate instructions. The reporter broached the subject of the snake. Instantly, the forest officer decided to tell the man everything he knew. He related the facts about Ginger Style's death and gave a brief description of the snake. When prompted he gave out details about Christine Westward's involvement, and, finally, he emphasized that the public were not permitted to set foot in any part of Yewhurst Wood, until the matter was resolved. That action would now be getting police assistance.

The reporter could hardly believe his ears. The Winchester Chronicle had supplied a draft of the story in case their parent company's 'daily' was interested, and he had decided to follow it up on his Sunday morning shift. Attached to the draft was a cutting from the Chronicle relating to an item of news that had taken place earlier in the year. The cutting reported the disappearance of Julia Thornton. The reporter asked Stephen if he thought there might be a connection. The forestry man was dumbfounded. The notion had never occurred to him, so he said so.

Tim and Christine spent most of Sunday at Dalmar's cottage. There was one main topic of conversation. It concerned who was going to say what to the press and whether there was anything that anyone did not wish to be mentioned. This was where Dalmar spoke up. "May I suggest that we stick to the basics? If you don't mind, I would very much appreciate it if we could leave out my involvement. Let's just keep to the obvious points."

"Don't you want any glory?" Suzanne looked up at him, while sunning herself on the parched lawn. Dalmar had not had to mow it for weeks: the lack of rain had stunted growth.

"No thanks," he replied.

"Well, I'll certainly back you," supported Tim. "Let's try and leave your name out altogether. Should be possible" And so it was agreed. Christine would tell her story, which would be a vague memory of the truth, and Suzanne would embellish it, if required.

However, before any of this took place, Dalmar got quite a shock after he arrived at work the following day. He saw the front page of a tabloid newspaper, with its massive headline, being held up by somebody reading the middle pages in the staff canteen. He passed it by at first and went back for another look, hardly believing what he thought he had seen. 'DEVIL SNAKES – AT LARGE – IN THE NEW FOREST,' on three bold lines. He went over to the seated man whose face was hidden.

"Excuse me?" he asked. He waited while the reader lowered the paper.

"Sorry mate?" said a surprised, round-faced head wearing tiny spectacles.

"Could I take a quick look at the front page?" asked Dalmar as politely as possible.

"Be my guest," was the reply. "Supposed to be taking the kids to the Forest next Saturday. No bloody way I'm going near the place!" (*Forest* in this case referred to The New Forest, the many square miles of woodland near the coast in southern Hampshire.)

Dalmar glanced at the newspaper owner, with acknowledgement, and then read the front-page story. 'Young housewife attacked and nearly killed by giant red serpent.' Then later, 'Forestry man falls to his death from two-hundred-foot-high tree following attack by spitting snake!' There was a picture of him carrying the dead man. Fortunately, Ginger's body occluded his own features and there was no mention of the identity of the bearer. He made a quick scan and could see two or three names listed, but not his. Christine's was, together with Stephen Knopner, Dr David Andrews and the late Gordon (Ginger) Styles. Thanking the newspaper owner, Dalmar rushed off in the direction of his office. Once there he put a call through to Beech Cottage. It was engaged because Tim was talking to his wife on the same subject from his place of work.

"Have you heard from anyone yet?" Tim asked.

"Yes," his wife answered him. "My mum has just been on the phone; apparently we are headline news." Tim then read out the gist of the article on page one and four of the newspaper. "There! told you I'd be famous, she chortled."

Tim chuckled; "Maybe they'll leave it at that, probably won't bother you now." Christine replied that she hoped so and agreed to keep him informed if any reporters made contact.

Dalmar did not get through to Suzanne. Each time he called the line was busy. He tried every half-hour for two hours, until finally, he realised their telephone had been disconnected, and he had a fairly good idea as to why.

Christine and Suzanne received calls from different newspapers, until they got utterly fed up, and, after letting Tim know, left the telephone off for the time being. It had not occurred to Suzanne, caught up in the pressure of it all, that Dalmar might be trying to make a call.

It did not end there. At about one o'clock, a Ford Capri pulled up outside Beech Cottage's gate. Suzanne spotted it from an upstairs window. The man who got out was a stranger, and, she considered, probably had something to do with the press, although he looked vaguely familiar.

She rushed downstairs and whispered to Christine urgently. They decided to hide and not answer the door. They ignored the ringing bell and crept upstairs knowing that they would not be spotted from there. Fly did his duty wonderfully. He barked loudly and growled right by the base of the door; so that the man was under no illusions that it would not be a good idea to nose around. After a while, a small white card was poked through the letterbox. Fly snapped at it. The girls heard the car start and watched as it was driven away. They went downstairs to look. Suzanne calmed the excited collie and picked up what was clearly a business card from the doormat. A neat black script read, 'Jonathon Shure', with some qualification initials alongside and underneath, 'The Zoological Society.' A London address and telephone number followed.

"Oh dear," said Christine, looking over her sister-in-law's right shoulder. "We should have let that one in. Never mind, Tim can contact him. I don't like talking to experts about this."

"I know what you mean. I have felt the sword of sarcasm already." Suzanne went on to tell Christine about Stephen Knopner's disbelieving tone.

Because their telephone had been taken 'off the hook,' various parties from the media had not been able to get through. Most of the daily newspapers, local television and radio had driven Stephen's office mad, demanding interviews. He fled into the forest on a pretend mission and left his unfortunate secretary to face it all. The result was that nobody from the media had managed to secure an appointment.

David Andrews had engineered a similar escape by permanently being out on call. The conclusion of all this was that the press decided the most likely avenue to add more meat to their stories, was to take up position outside the Westward's residence and wait. So it was that three cars from the popular press pulled up outside Beech Cottage, almost at the same time, complete with reporters and photographers. Petrified, the girls feigned being out and avoided showing any signs of life in the house. Much to their chagrin, no one moved on. All three car occupants hung around outside chatting, smoking and lounging on their vehicle's bonnet. Within an hour a television crew had joined them.

Christine pushed the buttons down on the main part of the telephone to get the dialling tone back and called her husband.

"Good God!" exclaimed Tim, when he heard of the recent events. "I'll be home as soon as I can." Christine crept upstairs to join Suzanne, who was peering through a slit between the curtain and window frame, in the main bedroom.

"There's another TV crew now, and what looks like some more press in a big car."

"Probably a broadsheet," said a grinning Christine, beginning to lose her fear. She was starting to become amused by the whole thing. "Tim's on his way. I'm fed up with this! How do you fancy making this lot some tea? Let's get it over with."

'Typical Chris.' Suzanne thought. 'Concerned one minute and bold the next.' "All right," she said.

With that, they went downstairs, and, after Suzanne had ushered a very dejected Fly into the rear garden, Christine opened the front door and said in a loud voice, "Good afternoon gentleman!" Twelve men and two ladies stopped their idle chat and stared in her direction. Then, almost as one, galvanized into action. The reporters commenced shouting, and the cameras started clicking. Christine held up her hand. She was a striking figure with her eye-catching blonde hair; dressed in denim shorts and a white top. Her pale, blue-green eyes flashed at them all. "Rule number one. No one is allowed in the house or garden. Rule number two; no questions will be answered until my husband gets home. In the meantime, who would like a cup of tea?"

CHAPTER TWENTY-THREE

ONE GUEST WAS DIRECTLY INVOLVED.

While the media were getting information from the Westwards, the Reverend Paul Sanders and Jack Path were discussing the presence of the policemen near the church car park. Paul was explaining to Jack that because there was an access to the forest at the end of the graveyard, and the gate by the road, the authorities felt they must both be covered. At all other points of entry to Yewhurst Wood, six in all, police were on duty backing up the notices forbidding entry.

"How be that gal who got bitten? Do'ee know?" Jack asked the clergyman, scratching at the hair just off his forehead.

"Recovering well, I'm told." That reminds me; I really must go and see them at Beech Cottage. To be honest I wanted the dust to settle first, if you know what I mean?"

"Oh, I does Vicar, I'm sure you'm be right. They'll have had a lot of unwelcome attention. An' what-about poor Nora Styles?"

"Funeral's on Friday. Not looking forward to that one bit. Dear lady, her son was all she had." He hesitated a moment before continuing. "I have to say that I am more than a little worried that this will fuel the local folk stories?"

"She be a friend o' Ma Hessil's, that's for sure?"

"Exactly," added Paul. Looking in the direction of the policemen, he said, "I think perhaps I should go and say hello." He brushed a fallen twig from his left arm. "Good afternoon, Jack. You are doing a grand job – as always."

"Thank you, Vicar. Bye now." Jack Path smiled at the vicar's departing back and resumed his task of sweeping cut grass out of the path verges. He glanced at the empty seat by the Wellingtonia, stopping in a sweep at mid-push, and stayed like that for some time. It was not just the empty seat that troubled him. He was also thinking a great deal about the odd flying object he had seen leap from one tree to another, not so long ago. He had not mentioned it to another living soul, fearing derision.

Sometime later, after the vicar had finished talking to the policemen and left the scene, Jack's attention was distracted by the arrival of some agitated forestry workers. They were shouting, trying to summon the attention of the police.

As Tim Westward drove up to Beech Cottage in his convertible car, his head and shoulders clearly visible to all, he felt very conspicuous as he parked on the verge. A mass of curious eyes turned on him. His wife came running so as to get there first. "Sorry darling. You are about to get a barrage of questions."

Tim shrugged his shoulders and clambered out of the car. Christine introduced her husband to the media gathering. He was rather amused to see them all lounging about in their shirtsleeves; some of them holding a cup and saucer, which, he noticed, came from their kitchen. Indeed – there was a barrage of questions. Up to now the reporters had granted Christine Westward's wish and waited until her husband's arrival. She immediately regretted introducing him quite so quickly.

After a time of incomprehensible shouting, one of the reporters suggested that perhaps they could have a photography session. After which, the television people would get their turn. Tim agreed. So followed an extraordinary few minutes in which Christine, Suzanne at some length, particularly when it came to the snake's description, answered many questions while the cameras clicked away.

Beam, the cat, who lived with his owners across the road, appeared on the scene. She was made a fuss of by some of the reporters, going from group to group with tail raised high, purring to order whenever she got a response.

The most obvious omission in the line of questioning was any reference to John the Red. Stephen had not let that one slip out. The reporters simply referred to it as a 'large snake' or 'serpent'. Tim and Christine were asked about their home. Were they not worried because of its proximity to the woods in question? Christine agreed that she certainly was. But no, Tim said they were not planning to do anything about it yet, keeping any private thoughts to themselves. They took some personal details, ages, and occupation in Tim's case, and how they had come to be living here. It seemed to Tim that the television recordings, which had to be done by two different crews at the same time took even longer, however, it was wrapped up in half the time.

When they finally left, the three Westwards relaxed in the back garden with a well-earned cold drink. Poor Fly had been left on his own while all this had been going on. Due to the constant noise and babble of voices from the front of the house, it had nearly driven his canine curiosity mad, and now they had gone. He lay down under a bush, sulking.

Tim suddenly leapt to his feet. "Is the telephone still switched off?"

"Yes," answered Christine. "I should leave it like that as well."

"In a minute – must go and call Mum. Bet she has been trying to get through."

"Oh Lord! Yes – please do Tim," said Suzanne. As luck would have it, their parents did not take the newspaper, which had published the story. They had been out on a day trip to Glastonbury. A neighbour had seen the paper and wondered if there was a connection but had only just informed them when they arrived home a few minutes before. His mother reminded him that they were supposed to be coming to visit them soon. Tim promised to call her back after he had discussed it with Christine. Having been assured that her daughter-in-law had now fully recovered from her awful experience, she let her son go with strict instructions to keep away from the woodland where the snake lived. Tim made no comment, thinking to himself that might be a little difficult as they were right on top of it.

When Dalmar arrived to collect Fly, he was practically knocked over by the dog before being told that if he wanted a beer, he would have to help himself because no one was moving. He returned with a bottle in his hand and sat down with it on the grass. Suzanne told him of their amazing day.

He was not surprised. "Just a thought," he said, "but you are very welcome to camp at my place until this all dies down?"

Tim looked at Christine before saying. "Thanks ... could we sleep on it?"

"Sure," Dalmar responded.

"I'll come over with you this evening if I may?" suggested Suzanne.

"Of course," was the quick reply.

"Incidentally Dalmar," said Tim, "couldn't help notice that you carried the unfortunate forest ranger who got killed on Saturday. Saw it in the newspaper, although they didn't mention you by name. That must have taken some doing?"

"What!?" exclaimed Suzanne.

"Yes – well – you know. Needed doing," replied an embarrassed Dalmar. "Not pleasant – I assure you."

"I'll bet it wasn't," joined in Christine. She thought to herself that he must be getting fed up with having to carry people about in that forest, dead or alive!

They all chatted for a little while longer before Dalmar and Suzanne left combining a walk for Fly in the woodland near their home first.

Every late news broadcast on the television that evening gave detailed information about the Red Adders among their minor items. A lot of it featured the tragedy of the death of Ginger Styles and showed the house where his mother lived. The newspapers, the following morning, did not have the story as front-page news, but all of them included photographs with the appropriate columns on the inside pages. The only person who was at all photogenic was Christine and the popular press showed her in a larger format than anyone else.

The following day, the police carried on with their guard duties at the various entrances to Yewhurst Wood. It seemed that no one was quite sure just what was going to happen. But something was stirring in official corridors. David Andrews had become involved and, obviously, Stephen Knopner. There were rumours among some of the Claymans Heron staff that a meeting room had been booked in a week's time.

The hotel was starting to pick-up extra trade. Sometimes it was just a curious passer-by, but one guest was directly involved: his name was Jonathon Shure. For a zoologist, he was a dapper man; preferring fairly smart attire, which was not the usual practice for most of his profession. He was in his late forties, married with two children in their early teens. That evening, he was not happy because so far, all the people he wanted to see to arrange the forthcoming conference had not been available. This meant that he had to make several appointments for the next day. Arrangements had been made to hold the meeting next Monday, 18th August. The hotel's second largest reception room had been reserved, and members of the press were to be invited to a conference on conclusion of the main event. This was scheduled for six o'clock in the late afternoon.

On the guest list for this conference were himself, Sir Michael Ensford, Mr T. Chang, Stephen Knopner, Dr David Andrews and Mr Wilfred Blyte, science officer with the Forestry Commission. Chairing the event would be Sir Michael, who was very well known as a reptilian expert. Mr Chang, by invitation of the British Government, would be coming all the way from Malaysia. Also, after local enquiries, Allen Haddle had been asked, due to his involvement with a similar snake in the nineteen-forties. All six had acknowledged acceptance of their invitations, but Jonathon needed to see some of them individually before the meeting, so that time would not be wasted on superfluous facts. He was determined to give Sir Michael a steadfast agenda. He sat back in the chair by a desk in the hotel room, and, raising his arms, ran his fingers through the prematurely greying hair. His eyes were blue with tempers of grey-green and the high cheekbones gave him handsome features. Both head profiles showed off well when he made his frequent appearances on wildlife television documentaries.

Meanwhile at Beech Cottage, apart from friends and family and a quick visit from the Reverend Paul Sanders, the only local person to constantly enquire after Christine Westward's well-being was Jean Haddle. Due to her cheerful personality the attention was not irksome. She visited once and telephoned a couple of times, always starting her approach with the words, "I don't want to be a nuisance - but…" She gave the first part of the word 'nuisance' a strong accentuation.

CHAPTER TWENTY-FOUR

"SAME SUBJECT – I'M AFRAID."

The day after the press activity, Suzanne was passing the telephone in Beech Cottage, when it made her start with its unexpected strident ringing. "Can you get it," shouted Tim from an armchair in the sitting room. He was enjoying a refreshing cup of tea after his working day. His wife was in the kitchen preparing supper.

For the girls, a couple of telephone calls enquiring after the progress of Christine's recovery, and a short visit from Paul Sanders had been the day's bounty. The peace had been very welcome. Even the weather was slightly cooler, although there was still no sign of any rain.

"Tim – it's for you – David Andrews." Suzanne held out the telephone. She looked annoyed and muttered something. Tim gave her an enquiring look and then shrugged his shoulders, making his way into the hall.

"Tim – sorry to bother you. Thought you should know something." The doctor's voice came loud and clear through the earpiece.

"Hello – what's that David? Hear there is some sort of conference being planned about the Red Adders?"

"That's right, on Monday at the Claymans. Got a few experts attending: should be interesting. They are going to follow it with a press gathering, so that the media will know the conclusions immediately. I'll give you a call afterwards, if you like. I am one of the invited guests, so I'll be able to give you the inside story."

"Thanks, that'll be useful. What's this other matter about?"

"Same subject – I'm afraid. They've found the body of another victim. Sorry to be gruesome. It was badly decomposed, probably happened about eight to nine weeks ago..."

"Not Julia Thornton?" interrupted Tim.

"No – no. Thankfully. Don't know the identity yet: a middle-aged man. Early indications point to a vagrant. That's all I have, except that his death was definitely caused by a Red Adder. No doubt about it."

"Where did they find him?"

"You're not going to like this. It's the main reason why I am letting you know. Not far from the back of your garden."

Tim was shocked. "My God! We haven't heard anything. When was it discovered?"

"Yesterday. Some forestry guys came across it. If you look out of a rear first floor window, I expect you will be able to see a big oak about three or four hundred yards from your boundary. It's the only tall tree there. The body was found lying at its base. Because all the press boys were gathered at your place, nobody noticed the goings on at the church end. It was quicker for them to carry the deceased along the path than to try and break through at the back of your home."

"I see," said Tim. "Well thanks for telling me." Then thinking of nothing he could add. "We will hear from you on Monday?"

"All right. Sorry and all that but felt you should know."

"Absolutely." The telephone conversation then ended. Tim went upstairs, ignoring the inquiring requests from the ladies. Both had heard Julia's name mentioned and other sides of the one-way conversation had alerted their curiosity. From Suzanne's bedroom Tim could clearly see the oak tree referred to. He stared at its broad leafy top and wondered whether there was anything lurking there. 'Now what to do?' he said to himself. Dalmar was due over to share a light supper with them. He decided to have a quiet word with him first.

When he eventually came down, Christine was standing in the hall with her hands on her hips, looking cross. "What's the matter with you?" asked Tim, "Suz has got some sort of cob on as well." In confirmation of that last statement, his sister appeared at the entrance to the sitting room, still wearing a peeved expression on her face.

"Well?" said his wife.

"Well what?"

"What did our doctor want you for?"

"Private." If Tim wanted to start a fight, he certainly knew how to do it.

"Oh, *private* is it! No supper for you then." Christine still had her hands on her hips.

"Oh, come on, I'm starving!" he pleaded.

"Then spill the goods," she insisted.

"After supper."

"No – now!" Christine's face was beginning to flush.

"You know what darling?" Tim had a slight grin on his face. This annoyed her even more. She did not answer him, returning his question with a cold look. "I think you have fully recovered." As he said this Tim bolted. He ducked under his wife's arm and ran out of the back door straight into a welcoming collie at full pounce. Both dog and man ended up on the ground, although Fly instantly jumped back onto his four feet looking playful. Christine and Suzanne burst out laughing, forgetting their annoyance.

"Serves you right!" said his sister, between strings of giggles.

Dalmar, having arrived a little behind Fly, looked a bit unsure of it all. He helped Tim to his feet, at the same time calming down the ebullient dog.

"David Andrews has been on the phone," said Suzanne quickly. "He wouldn't speak to me, and Tim won't tell us what it was about." She went to give her man a welcoming kiss.

"I'm waiting," said Christine, with her hands on her hips again.

Tim regained his composure and gave in. He asked them all to join him in the sitting room, pouring Dalmar a drink before enlightening them.

There was a silence afterwards, before Suzanne said, "I need a drink now."

"A suggestion." Dalmar held up his right hand with an opened cupped palm. They all looked at him. "Just 'til this all blows over. You are welcome to stay at my place." He looked at Christine.

Tim looked in Christine's direction. It looked as though his immediate problem had been solved. "It's up to you. But – it does sound like a good idea." He added with a slight chuckle, "If Dalmar can bear it?"

"Absolutely. No problem come whenever you like," Dalmar confirmed.

Suzanne stood up and came over to his side. She kissed him on the top of his head while he remained seated, with a thankful look in her eyes.

"By the way, wifey," said Tim, "Who is Jonathon Shure?" He brandished a business card he had found on the mantelpiece.

"Her lover," said Suzanne with a cheeky grin.

Christine chortled. "Actually – don't know. Suzanne and I hid from him and didn't answer the door. Thought he was another reporter. We found the card on the doormat."

Tim studied it before handing it to Dalmar. "Wonder if we should give him a ring?"

"Probably got something to do with this conference they are talking about in the Claymans. I should let him contact you, if I were you." Dalmar commented.

Another side to the Red Adder drama was taking place. Curious onlookers – having seen the stories in the press and on television, both locally and further afield, were beginning to make a nuisance of themselves. The police had to stop many a so-called walker, often turning out to be a professional reporter, complete with photographic equipment hidden in a rucksack. The two-hundred-millimetre lens, virtually impossible to hide effectively, due to its length, was quite a common sight. By the end of the week, the police were reasonably confident that no one had managed to trespass inside the designated boundaries of the banned area.

Christine finally made up her mind to take up Dalmar's offer. Tim supported her, and it was agreed that as from Saturday evening, they would stay at his cottage, Suzanne as well, naturally. There was not much discussion between her and her loved one about it. Because of Tim and Christine's predicament, it just happened that she would stay with him on a more permanent basis. Dalmar had to get some spare keys cut in a hurry.

It was, however, emotionally depressing for Tim and Christine. This was hardly what their dream home was about. Over the past weeks, Tim had privately expressed anger and frustration at the existence of the Red Adders, and he regretted the experience of this abnormal heat wave. A typical English summer would probably not have resulted in these freak reptiles re-appearing.

The most likely reason for the unusual curiosity from the general public was due to some newspaper's preponderance for overstatement. A six-foot long snake, in the world's encyclopaedia, was of no great significance. In existence, were several dangerous snakes whose overall length far exceeded that. Referring to the pine that Ginger Styles had climbed, as a two-hundred-foot-high tree was an exaggeration. Also, Yewhurst Wood was not within the boundaries of The New Forest, National Park.

Stephen Knopner and Charles Brewster could not leave matters until the conference, or, for that matter, rely on its conclusions. Discussing the scientific reasons for the existence of the snakes was all very well and might lead to assistance as to what action to take, but some immediate plans, in the opinion of the Forestry Commission, ought to be made. They had put to Chief Inspector Wilkins the idea of organizing a large shoot. This would involve inviting several game shoot syndicates to take part in a systematic sweep of the entire Yewhurst Wood area. Following a meeting with some of these syndicates, forestry representatives and the police, it was decided that the shoot would be organised for the following Wednesday, 21st August.

In all, three shooting syndicates were to be involved, plus three clay pigeon shooting clubs. The operation would commence from three points: the gate adjacent to the church, Chapp and Gardeners Lane. They would sweep north and then back south, all the while edging east to arrive a mile or so away from where they started. The time agreed on to commence the operation would be eight o'clock. Because the shooting organizations would be providing their own refreshments, there was not a lot in the way of back up facilities to arrange. The most important seemed to be medical. The St John Ambulance organization was contacted, and they agreed to install first aid stations at all three points. David Andrews would base himself at the Forestry Commission office, in order to be able to drive to the aid of a snakebite victim with anti-venom serum, as soon as alerted. A supply was to be made available from Winchester Hospital, and David himself would collect it the day before.

Ginger Style's funeral was not well attended. From his family, there was only the sad figure of his mother supported by Ma Hessil. Most of the mourners were made up of forestry workers and management. The village churchyard was, at least, being used for its proper use.

During the organised shoot the police would have to arrange the control of sightseers and endeavour to sort out any traffic problems arising. Hauled out of retirement to organise it, Chief Inspector Wilkins found himself doing a great deal more work than he had bargained for. The worst duty of all was controlling the needs of the press. He knew he could not just ban them, because they had a public duty, but he had to ensure their safety and everybody else's. It seemed to him that they needed a central communication point away from the forestry office. That was how he came to be speaking to the manager of the Claymans Heron, Floyd Hemming, on Saturday morning.

First, he had to establish whether a commercial business would provide a facility at no cost. Floyd was very aware of the extra profits the whole matter was providing in his quest to meet his company's budget, but he also felt a community need as well. He did not contact his head office for permission but went ahead and decided to turn the entire hotel lobby area into a press communications and information base. The media were told that there would be direct radio links to each of the shooting parties.

Christine got the green light from David Andrews. All that remained for her was to have a further blood test later in the month and, if it were clear, that would be that. In other words, her blood having been severely poisoned by the snake's venom was, in all probability, now completely free of it.

At Dalmar's cottage, the two couples all got on well and tried to make the best of the situation.

The four of them had a lazy weekend spending most of it lounging about on the garden lawn. So as to provide some relief from the serious situation they were in, Tim suggested that they book a tennis court in Winchester for Sunday afternoon. Tim and Christine had the full kit but the other two had to hire tennis rackets and dress for the game as best they could. Suzanne borrowed some white shorts from her sister-in-law. They were a little too tight and promised to restrict her movement somewhat. She did have a pair of tennis shoes, which she had packed as an afterthought. Dalmar put on some dark blue shorts, which together with a white sports shirt looked perfectly alright. They played mixed couples and Dalmar and Suzanne got soundly beaten by three games to love in the first set but managed to win one game in the second.

Afterwards, Suzanne was a bit depressed. She felt she had let her partner down, even though it was only a friendly game. While discussing the afternoon's exertions on the way back to Yewhurst, Dalmar cheered her up by stating that if he were to play Christine in a singles match, he very much doubted that he would be the victor. He commented on her ability.

All at once Suzanne noticed a broadening smirk on her brother's face, reflected in the driving mirror. "Just a minute, didn't you win something big when you were in your teens, Chris?" she asked.

Tim got in first. "She was a finalist in the Surrey Junior County Championship, at the age of sixteen."

"Ooh – Tim!   Right!   – next time you can play with me," expostulated Suzanne, at the same time developing a sulky pout. Dalmar though, had to chortle.

CHAPTER TWENTY-FIVE

"THERE IS NOTHING REMOTELY LIKE THEM..."

Early on Monday morning, Jonathon Shure braced himself outside the Claymans Heron waiting for the arrival of the conference delegates. He was pleased to see the media were not yet in evidence. He looked very smart wearing neatly pressed pale beige trousers, soft-leather brown shoes, an expertly tailored single-breasted navy-blue blazer, and an ivory-coloured shirt sporting the Zoological Society's tie. Jonathan, certainly, stood out in a crowd. He was good-looking possessing an air of distinction that can come with advancing maturity.

At a quarter to nine Sir Michael Ensford's chauffeur driven car, a black Rover 2000, entered the car park. The driver pulled up by the main entrance to the hotel, climbed quickly out and opened the rear door wide. A neatly dressed Malaysian gentleman disembarked. He was petite and elegant with the air of an aristocrat. Jonathon had expected an Asian twang to his voice. There was none. He spoke with a slightly clipped English Oxford accent.

"Good morning. Mr Shure?"

"Hello ... Mr Chang?" greeted Jonathon smiling.

"That's him!" said a booming voice from the other side of the car. Sir Michael, who was well known to Jonathon, appeared round the back of the Rover with a broad grin illuminated by a large silver moustache. They all shook hands and exchanged small talk before going into the hotel.

Mr T. Chang had a small case of papers with him, but Sir Michael was empty-handed. He was obviously used to having such things provided for him. Jonathon took them through to a conference room off to the left. As they passed by the reception counter Floyd Hemming introduced himself. He was fairly short in stature but carried it off with an air of authority and a certain engaging friendliness produced by his pleasant face, which was dominated by jet-black eyes and frequent enquiring grins. He was well groomed with neatly trimmed dark hair. "If you find you need anything we have not laid on, please let me know," he appealed to them.

They thanked him and Sir Michael gave an extra broad smile to the two lady receptionists behind the counter. He was easily recognizable from countless television appearances. Today he had chosen formal attire to compliment his chairmanship of the conference; a dark grey suit with white shirt and the same society tie that Jonathon was wearing.

The conference room was normally naturally light because facing onto the entrance was a wall of windows. It looked out onto wooded scenery and a couple of old farm cottages. Today, large drapes covered the entire expanse to stop prying eyes. The room was therefore rather sombre; however, the fine ten-foot long beechwood table added the right contemporary atmosphere. Around the table were eight tubular chrome chairs with sand-coloured padded seats. The three gentlemen took their places, as indicated by name plaques, with Sir Michael at its head and Jonathon immediately to his left.

"Coffee is on its way gentleman," said Jonathon. "Mr Chang, would you prefer tea?"

"I would ... thank you," came a stiff reply. Jonathon picked up a small telephone from a side-table and ordered the drinks.

Before anyone could say anything else, there was a light tap on the door. Jonathon opened it and three men entered, Stephen Knopner carrying a notebook and pen, Dr David Andrews with a large briefcase and finally Allen Haddle carrying nothing. Following introductions, Stephen immediately took off his jacket, a Forestry Commission badged blazer, and hung it over the back of his chair. A little while later came another knock on the door, once again Jonathon opened it. A slight, middle-aged man with wispy light brown hair, a hooked nose and enormous ears came in. He hung onto a faded leather briefcase and walked with a slight stoop. "My apologies," he squeaked in a strange but aggressive voice. "Damned car would not start! Had to get a neighbour to give me a lift." Sir Michael could not believe his eyes; the man was wearing sandals which showed off a pair of bright red socks. Stephen recognized him as Wilfred Blyte, the senior science officer with the Forestry Commission based at Lyndhurst.

At this point a waiter entered carrying a tray of hot drink apparatus and crockery.

Before Sir Michael was formally invited to take the chair and commence the proceedings; on cue, Jonathon's secretary came in carrying a bunch of papers. He introduced her as Joan as she handed each person a copy of the agenda. She possessed a freckled face with dark Gallic hair, and her eyes were quite green; added to this she had a solid figure, which gave her a sound presence.

The agenda read as follows:

Introduction: Sir Michael Ensford, O.B.E.
Item 1: The History of the Red Adder, 1947/48: Mr. Allen Haddle.
Item 2: Recent events: Dr. David Andrews.
Coffee.
Item 3: What is the Red Adder? Mr. T Chang and Mr. Jonathon Shure.
Lunch.
Item 4: Action required: Group discussion.
Tea.
Item 5: Conclusions and Recommendations.
Final draft: Press release.
Press Conference: approx. 6 p.m.

While they all studied this, a waiter entered carrying the hot drinks. At this point, Jonathon switched on a large complicated looking Ferrograph tape-recorder, and the twin spools started their slow revolving motion.

Sir Michael commenced his introduction from a seated position. After thanking everyone present for attending, he gave a special welcome to Mr Chang who had come all the way from the other side of the world. He then addressed the conference delegates as follows. "The prime target for today's gathering is to come up with helpful assistance in order that these snakes, habiting, virtually, a stone's throw from here, may be eliminated, however much some of us would like to capture a specimen alive. In other words, the zoological or scientific interest must take second place to public safety." He emphasized one other important point. "One factor, from the evidence gathered so far, is this. There does not appear to be a similarity to another species of snake elsewhere in the world. There is nothing remotely like them anywhere on our planet. Having said that, I feel it most important to clear up a couple of things.

The snakes in question have become known as The Red Adders. Now there is a snake referred to as a red adder or red viper. It is a dwarf snake living on the Western Cape of South Africa. Its colouring is copper so as to blend with the sandy soil it inhabits. Also, a juvenile female snake, from our own European or northern adder which may take on a deep copper hue, is sometimes called a red adder. Neither of these reptiles should be confused with The Red Adder of Yewhurst."

With that he concluded his introduction and invited Mr Allen Haddle to begin. He asked him to start by explaining who he was, and how he came to be involved in the early years of this strange phenomenon.

Allen rose. He looked surprisingly at home when it came to public speaking. He related the facts and the facts only, from that day in 1947 when he was called to the house on the Great Mile to attend to a dog that had collapsed in adjacent woodland, and on to the fatality that occurred to a man followed by further deaths in 1948. He did not embellish the matter with estimates on the potency of the venom, or the differences between vipers and other poisonous snakes. He thought this would be insulting the experts gathered around him.

After he finished, Jonathon asked him several questions on the quality of the venom found in the dog, particularly referring to the sample that had been sent to a laboratory at Southampton University, and their subsequent report confirming that it was the most poisonous venom ever attributed to a viper. Jonathon tried to establish a link between this reptile and the common adder. An attempt had been made to contact the widow of the man who died on the Great Mile, but without success. She had apparently remarried and emigrated, and it was not known where she finally domiciled. A lot of the evidence had become the subject of folklore among the farming community in the village and therefore unreliable. However, from the descriptions and medical evidence they did have, they could be sure that there was a definite link with the viper family, if not exclusively, the adder.

Dr David Andrews, with the overhead lighting causing flecks of gold to dance on the lenses of his grand spectacles, spoke next. He opened his black briefcase and took out five sheets of foolscap paper liberally hand-written in large letters. He started from when the rumours first began in early June this year with the death of an old lady's spaniel, and gradually took them through the most recent attacks.

Because he knew his audience expected it, he spent some time on the description of the snake provided by Suzanne Westward. Also, he did not spare any detail when it came to the snake's ability to spit venom and its apparent aerial capabilities. Having, although briefly, seen the prone body of this Red Adder on the ground, he tried to be thorough with the physical description.

The first question again came from Jonathon. "Referring to the snake that you actually saw. Did you happen to notice the shape of its head?"

David thought for a while and then answered, "Wide and triangular." Before Jonathon could ask another question, he said, "Actually I have a sketch. It was done from memory, after I heard that the body of the snake had gone missing. Can't guarantee accuracy I'm afraid." Rummaging further in his briefcase, he brought it out. Jonathon and Sir Michael practically fell upon it as David slid the piece of paper across the table. The drawing was of the snake as-a-whole, so details of its head were a little vague, but still Jonathon expressed his appreciation and asked if he might borrow it. David waved a hand indicating agreement.

Before Jonathon put the sketch with his own papers, it was passed around for the other delegates to look at. Meanwhile Jonathon continued with his questions. "Are you certain that the markings on the snake's back were a zigzag and not inverted triangles?"

"Oh, definitely. The zigzag was *very* striking."

"I see," Jonathon looked disappointed.

"I know where you were heading," said Sir Michael, "Bad luck." Jonathon smiled knowingly.

Mr Chang raised his right hand. "May I?" he said.

"Of course." Sir Michael waved an acknowledgement.

"Dr Andrews," Mr Chang began and out came the almost impeccable English. "I would like to discuss the aerial ability of the snake you described in more detail if I may?" David nodded in acquiescence. "Would you describe the descent as flying or gliding?"

"I suggest you ask Stephen here about that, because I did not see the event you are referring to. I was attending to the late Mr Styles at the time."

"Oh, I see, then perhaps Mr … Knopner," he said, glancing at his copy of the guest list, "Would you be so good?"

"Sure," Stephen answered shifting slightly in his seat. "It was a glide. The snake stayed in the formation of a…" He made a wavy motion with his right hand.

"Like the letter S?" suggested Mr Chang.

"Yes – but possibly with an extra bend."

"Thank you? Did you notice any finlike protuberances on the body?"

"Yes – sort of like those on a flying fish – I would say."

Mr Chang finished with another polite, "Thank you." That concluded this part of the agenda.

However, David Andrews quickly rose to his feet. "Gentlemen ... I feel it may rest upon my shoulders to mention something else?" Noticing the chairman's quick nod, he carried on. "It has to do with the amount of venom known to have entered Mrs Westward's bloodstream. You see – it was a very small amount." He hesitated briefly, trying to think of the best way to illustrate the matter. "Actually – you would have difficulty in writing a few words supposing it were ink on a fountain-pen's nib. I must further add that if the discharge of venom from the snake's fangs had been fractionally larger ... Christine Westward – would certainly have died." While he had their undivided attention, he went on. "Put bluntly, following a proper bite from one of these snakes, if an anti-venom injection, applicable for a very poisonous viper, was not administered – within two to three minutes ... it might be too late."

Following this sobering revelation, they broke for morning coffee and biscuits.

The break was allowed to last for a good half-an-hour so that the delegates could mingle and chat to each other in an informal way. David Andrews found himself with Allen Haddle and the two forestry men. He asked Stephen how he was coping with all the press attention? "Absolute bloody nightmare!" he replied. "In fact, today is a blessing, in a way."

"I sympathize. Been getting a bit myself, but so far I've managed to fend them off by leaving messages that I was out on a call."

"Wilfred – have your boffins come up with anything on these snakes?" Stephen lowered his head to ask the question, Wilfred being short in stature.

"Sorry, no, just rather vague theories, I'm afraid." From his tone, it was clear Wilfred Blyte was not apologising.

"Wish I could exist on theories," said Stephen, the sarcasm in his voice all too evident.

Wilfred came straight back at him. "We do our bit! You field boy's think you know it all." And then quieter although still aggressive. "Come and see me at Lyndhurst, I'll show you." There was really nothing strange about this inter-departmental rivalry.

Dr Andrews quickly changed the subject. The other group were busy discussing the latest events in Malaysia, and Mr Chang was enlightening them about certain political matters.

CHAPTER TWENTY-SIX

"WE HAVE A MYSTERY."

When they returned to their seats Sir Michael reminded them of the next item on the agenda, which solely hinged on the opinions of Jonathon Shure and Mr Chang. 'What is the Red Adder?' He invited Jonathon to lead off.

The conference organiser stood up. Although only in his late forties, in the room's strange light he looked almost totally grey. He had a good head of hair which was currently, perhaps, a little too long. His olive-blue eyes glanced around the room. Just in time, he remembered the tape recorder and asked Joan to switch it on. "Gentleman," he began. "I am going to start by making a confession. It was my intention to interview the surviving victim of one of these extraordinary snake attacks. But Dr Andrews has informed me that her memory of the event is vague, so I decided not to take doubtful evidence. However, we do have reliable information from the sightings made by Dr Andrews and Mr Knopner. Therefore, I am going to base my thoughts on these and what Miss Westward witnessed when her sister-in-law was attacked. The events of 1947 and 1948 seem to have a bearing on the matter, simply because of the similarities concerned, albeit some twenty-seven years apart."

Jonathon then launched into a lengthy speech concerning some of the world's most dangerous snakes, and any similarity they might have with the Red Adders of Yewhurst Wood. These included the red spitting cobra, Gabon viper and many others. What became obvious to all of his audience was that none of them were even close. Broadly, they were either not vipers, or their venom attacked the respiratory system instead of the blood vessels, and they simply did not have anything like the same potency of poison. He mentioned that when he first heard about the Red Adder, he thought it was probably a Burmese bushmaster that can reach *twelve* feet in length and possess very dangerous venom, almost on a par with The Red Adder. However, it does not glide, can't spit, does not have the same markings and although it can be reddish, definitely not to the same degree as described by some witnesses."

The sheer depth of Jonathon's speech, which carried on for some time left the other delegates in no doubt as to his comprehensive knowledge in the reptilian world.

He finished off by saying, "The most consistent difference between the Red Adders and any of the world's population of snakes is this. Snakebites on a human being are the occasion of accident or defence. Okay, some snakes are more aggressive than others. We all know about the King Cobra, and there is a viper, the Fer-de-lance from

South America. Both these snakes cause numerous fatalities to humans. But, not even these two deliberately attack, as in the incident with Christine Westward."

"Gentleman, I am now going to hand over to Mr Chang and, if I may," here he glanced at Sir Michael adding, "I would like to come back briefly when he has finished." The chairman nodded and asked the Malaysian to proceed.

He rose to his feet while Jonathon poured himself a glass of water from a squat shaped glass jug. "My connection to this matter may seem obvious in that my native country does possess some flying snakes." The best known of these is called the Golden Tree snake. It just so happens that a record exists, which clearly shows that just such a snake went missing, fairly near here, in 1945." Suddenly there were raised heads from several members of the audience who were not aware of this. "It disappeared while in the custody of Southampton Zoo." One man who did know about it was David Andrews and he nodded vigorously.

"The golden tree snake does not actually fly; it glides by flattening out its body. There is a lot of loose skin, which may give the appearance of fins as the air currents inflate prominent parts. It can glide for some distance from a lofty position, and this practice is used for attack on its food source: rodents, lizard's, etc and, also, to get away from predators." As he spoke, the Oxford accent was almost very refined. "It only reaches about three feet in length, has a narrow body being a tree dweller and its venom is not strong. It would not be fatal to mankind."

"Apart from the gliding ability, the only other real factor that it has in common with this Red Adder, I believe, is that it is not nocturnal and hunts during the day. I mention this because of the Red Adder's recent aggressive activities. However, even that doesn't conclusively prove this point. Where the golden tree snake differs the greatest, or for that matter, any tree snake, is that they are not vipers." Without giving any kind of warning Mr Chang suddenly sat down. Sir Michael had to affirm with him that he had indeed finished for the time being. He got a smile in confirmation.

Jonathon was asked to complete the morning's session. "Gentlemen, we have been asked the question, what is the Red Adder? It is an unknown species of snake possessing the characteristics of a viper, of the most potent venom variety. When I say unknown, I wish to make it clear that nothing like them exists on Earth. They are the most-deadly snakes ever encountered by mankind. Allen Haddle coughed. Knowing where he lived, David Andrews was not surprised. Only a road separated his house from the forest where the Red Adders habited. High branches on the tall trees which grew, in places, on either side of that road interconnected.

"We know," continued Jonathon, "that they can reach approximately six feet in length and, maybe, given time, considerably more. I personally expect one could grow to double that size." This comment attracted some raised eyebrows. "I would like to conclude by asking a question. Has anyone any evidence that the Red Adder makes any kind of noise?"

"What – you mean, like a hiss?" asked Wilfred.

"Not necessarily."

"I completely forgot," David blurted out looking hastily at Stephen for confirmation. "Suzanne Westward who witnessed the attack on her sister-in-law said something about a loud ... a *very* loud – hiss ... with an accompanying growl. But I'm not sure if that happened at the time of the attack on Mrs Westward, or whether others have heard it."

Stephen looked up from his doodling. "She only mentioned a loud hiss. I cannot recall anything about another noise. Must ask my lads if they have heard anything."

"I see," said Jonathon. "How odd."

"Has anyone else heard it?" The question came from Sir Michael. "Mr Haddle, you live within earshot of these woods, I believe?"

"Yes, I do. But I can't say I have heard anything unusual," he replied. "But to be honest, I am a little deaf. I must ask my wife if she has heard any strange noises."

After that, they broke for lunch and in order that any prying eyes from the media were avoided, the meal of cold meats and salad was brought in and laid out on a side table. While they were eating, Stephen Knopner, out of the blue, said, "One thing surprises me a bit," and he looked at Jonathon, "Why didn't you ask that bloke Dalmar to this meeting?"

Jonathon looked confused. "Sorry, Dal? ... I don't know about this."

"Miss Westward's other half. David here will tell you. Seems to know a lot about this snake."

"What makes you say that?" asked Jonathon. Most of the others were all curious now.

"Well, after Ginger fell from the Scot's Pine, he knew the thing ... *our snake* ... was about to fly when we didn't even know it was there." If Stephen had wanted to stage a period of complete silence, he got it; for nobody, apart from the doctor, understood.

Sir Michael eventually broke the hush. "Please – could you explain in more detail?"   So, Stephen told them about the shooting incident.

 Later, they went through a side door up to the hotel bedroom area, which took them to some private toilet facilities. Allen Haddle approached David on the way back. "Who is this Dalmar?" he said.

"Oh, have you not met him? Suzanne Westward's young man; lives just down the road. Dalmar Hunter is his full name – I believe." Allen held the door open for the doctor to re-enter the conference room. Joan was waiting for them. She restarted the recorder.

The group discussion that followed, which was about what action needed to be taken, generally went along with plans that had already been made, namely, the organised shoot, which was taking place on Wednesday. Official requests were made that if the gunmen were lucky enough to get a specimen, dead or alive, then it should be placed in the care of Jonathon's office for the necessary examinations to be carried out. Yewhurst Wood would remain out of bounds, enforced by the police. After they had this sorted into areas of priority, Jonathon sparked an unexpected firework. "There is one possibility we have not yet discussed. I feel we should be failing in our duty if we did not mention it."

"You are going backwards Jonathon," said Sir Michael with slight exasperation, "But carry on."

"Thank you, Mr Chairman." Then he asked everybody the following question. "Could man have anything to do with the existence of these snakes?"

Sir Michael looked straight at the speaker. "Are you suggesting accidentally – or on purpose?"

The reply was definite. "On purpose."

"Oh, here we go!" Everyone spun around and looked in the direction of Wilfred Blyte. His face was thunderous. "The TV prima donnas just had to get their bloody stupid science fiction crap in – eh?"

"I beg your pardon?" said Sir Michael with a disciplinary tone to his voice.

"For God's sake! How can a man, or for that matter an army, create a brand-new species in five minutes?" Wilfred raised his eyes to the ceiling.

Stephen nudged David and whispered up close, "Oh dear, someone's got scorpions in his pants." The doctor had to stifle a sudden urge to laugh.

"Hardly five minutes." Jonathon defended himself. "We are talking about at least twenty-five years and probably more!"

"In evolutionary terms that is milli-seconds!" countered Wilfred. He was going very red in the face. "Absolute rubbish!   Romantic tosh!"

There was an embarrassing silence for a while. "I am sorry you take that view," said Jonathon, clearly taken aback at the ferocity of the verbal attack. None of them would have expected it from Wilfred. "For instance – mongrel dogs. It has probably taken less than twenty years in some cases…"

"Dogs are not reptiles – I assure you!" continued Wilfred.

Sir Michael stepped in hurriedly. "All right – all right. Any mention of man's interference in the manner indicated, for the time being, will be deleted. Joan, could you?" He glanced across at her.

"But it is on the tape?" She pointed at the whirling recorder. Stephen giggled – audibly.

"No – it is no matter." Wilfred suddenly calmed down and added. "As long as we can leave it there?"

Sir Michael nodded in agreement and held out a hand to fend off a repost by Jonathon. The verbally wounded man shook his head in disbelief. The chairman, temporarily, had difficulty in getting things back to where they should be after that. "What is to be done about the Red Adders?" he reminded them.

"The question arises;" Jonathon refused to allow Wilfred's outburst to cloud his professional thoroughness, "What do we do if the shoot is unsuccessful?"

"Good one." Sir Michael made a point of saying, "Any suggestions?"

There was a very long silence while brains were thinking hard, before Jonathon suggested that it might be a good idea to arrange a meeting with the Hampshire Constabulary, the local health authority and, of course, the Forestry Commission.

"Anyone else – suggestions?" Sir Michael requested. There was no further comment from the others, so he asked for it to be recorded in the minutes that in the event of the shoot being a failure, Jonathon's proposed meeting would be put into effect. Following this there was a great deal of conversation about the small facets and implications of this type of reptile's arrival in the English countryside – of which by far the most important was a question raised by Mr Chang.

"I don't suppose anyone knows what sex these two snakes are?" I mean there are two that may exist, isn't that so?" There was general confirmation of this. "Should we consider the matter of procreation then? After all, you may well have a male and a female out there, and if you don't get one of them soon…" He let his voice trail off. This alarming thought gripped most of them.

"That's interesting," chipped in Wilfred. "We don't know if these reptiles are full-bloodied vipers, tree snakes or what? Also, we don't know if they're egg-laying or live-bearing?" He looked expectantly at Jonathon and Sir Michael together.

Jonathon kept quiet and it was left to Sir Michael to say; "In cold climates snakes are live-bearing. In temperate and tropical zones, they are egg-laying: this is a temperate zone. So even if they are a previously undiscovered species, one would assume that they are egg-laying. Having said that, though, our female adder is live bearing, an exception to the rule. I'm afraid, we have another – don't know."

Jonathon decided to join in. "Tree snakes presumably nest in trees?" He put this to Mr Chang.

"Some do," he replied. "Somehow, I doubt that these fellows will. Too big."

Sir Michael and Jonathon both nodded in agreement. "So," Sir Michael summed up, "if there is nil result in trying to capture or kill one of them before hibernation takes place, we may have a nest of eggs or a pregnant mother to face next spring, and if not discovered – well I wouldn't like to be in your shoes." This took the smile off Stephen's face. The remark was addressed to him, and the implications were obvious.

"Next," the chairman went on. "Why are they so aggressive? And, I am going to lump the two together, why have they only appeared in very hot climatic years? We know about 1947 and 1948. 1959 is suspected, and now we have 1975."

"I am afraid I am completely at a loss," cut in Jonathon Shure.

The Shy Avenger   Scardthomas

"Also, this business about red colouring – when attacking perhaps?"

Sir Michael looked round the table. David Andrews raised his hand a little. "Dr Andrews – please do," said Sir Michael.

"Well, this is a layman's suggestion." He looked very unsure of himself. "The attacks always seem to occur, under or near the tree that our Red Adder is…"

"Go on," Sir Michael encouraged.

"So, if we are looking for a natural reason. It must be territorial."

"Oh well done Doctor," David looked proud like a praised schoolboy. "You may have something there," added the chairman.

Jonathon carried it further, "What about the veterinary profession. Got any comments Mr Haddle?"

Allen thought for a long while before replying. Stephen lent forward to give him a look, thinking he might have fallen asleep. "I'm afraid not," he said finally.

"Gentlemen, may I offer a solution to your dilemma?" Mr Chang did not wait for an answer. "If you mention to the press – all this negativity – you will *hang* yourselves." The clever use of 'you,' exonerated him from all responsibility. "I suggest that you declare the scientific reason for the existence of these reptiles will be the subject of an on-going investigation. Perhaps you could provide helpful advice, for instance, what to do if someone else gets bitten. I should also like to make the final observation that after the second snake had been shot and presumed dead; it might have been feigning death. Some snakes can do this very effectively."

Sir Michael decided that this would be a good time to break for tea. Following that, they would prepare their conclusions for the press. Floyd Hemming's wife, Jan, appeared, to show them a back way out to the hotel garden and lawns, so that they could have some fresh air away from the gathering media entourage. Tea was served on the terrace. Jan was a tall slender woman with a clever trait about her personality: she could smile when she did not feel like doing so, and yet look genuine.

Following the break, they decided to adopt Mr Chang's suggestion and prepare a list of recommendations for public advice. The first was to emphasize the need to obey the 'keep out' notices at the various entrances to Yewhurst Wood. Secondly, in the event of attending a bite victim: first calm the patient and lay them flat, if possible, without moving the injured part of the body. Try to immobilize the limb by use of a splint and position the damaged area below heart level. Third; get the patient to hospital as soon as possible, informing staff there that a Red Adder has bitten the victim, so that the correct anti-venom may be prepared. Other points were not to cut open the wound and suck. Do not apply an arterial tourniquet or cool the area of the bite. And finally, don't administer alcohol.

After this, they all concentrated on the draft for the press announcement.

It was now late afternoon. The media had already taken their places in the largest conference room at the hotel. A constant buzz was evident, caused by the tension of urgent expectation. Present were reporters and broadcasters, photographers and television camera crews. Facing them was a small top table with two seats and a curved barrier of microphones. At last, Sir Michael Ensford and Jonathon Shure entered. A hush fell.

The rest of the conference delegates made a dignified retreat to the hotel bar. David and Allen decided to have a quick drink and then leave before the press hoards descended. However, they did not get away quite as quickly as they intended because they met Thomas Hurn, the actor, who was full of curiosity.

Sir Michael made a short speech. He made it clear that they could come to no firm conclusion on the matter, further announcing an ongoing investigation. They supported the planned shoot for the coming Wednesday and stated that, depending on the results of this, there would be a follow up meeting with Hampshire Police, Hampshire County Council and the Forestry Commission. He then read out their short list of recommendations.

The British Broadcasting Corporation's correspondent was the first allowed to ask a question. He was blunt and to the point and seemed to echo other feelings among the audience. "Is that it, Sir Michael? So far – we have had a serious injury and two fatalities caused by a, so-called, fierce serpent inhabiting the area. Is that it? There is great public interest in this matter – you know."

"Yes Mr Raine." Sir Michael Ensford paused; making sure everyone could hear him. "We have a MYSTERY in capital letters." This was Sir Michael at his best. There was nothing that fascinated the public more than an unsolved mystery.

Andrew Raine was about to say something, when he saw the point, and stood with his mouth slightly open. Then he remembered to ask one other question. "Do you think that there might be a connection concerning the elderly lady, who went missing from this village in June this year?"

Sir Michael urgently glanced at Jonathon. He knew nothing of this.

Jonathon moved his head closer to the microphones. "Up to now, there is no evidence that Miss Thornton has been attacked by one of these snakes."

Quite a few of the reporters would like to have left there and then to telephone their newspapers. However, there followed numerous questions concerning the origin of the reptiles from other interested parties among the media, and how dangerous they might be? With the help of Jonathon, Sir Michael gave them the details and to both their credit they carefully avoided stating possibilities. The conference finished with a request that the media use the parking facilities at this hotel on Wednesday, so as not to clog up the vitally important vehicle movement that would take place at the forest entrances, especially in the event of an ambulance being required. There would be a press conference at the hotel after the hunt when a senior officer from the Hampshire Constabulary would make a statement.

Today, the media were from the British press. The only international interest concerned one reporter employed by an Australian newspaper.

Tim Westward was not terribly surprised at the conference's outcome. He, Dalmar and the two girls were watching a live news programme. At the end Dalmar switched off the television. "All the more reason for you good folk to carry on staying here, I feel," he commented.

"Thanks, Dalmar," Christine gave him an affectionate smile which, although genuine, did not reflect how she felt inside. She was getting really fed up. The novelty had worn off and she wanted her own home back. There seemed very little chance of that happening in the near future.

Her husband read the signs. 'Something would have to be done – soon,' he thought to himself. 'Decisions would have to be made.' Not for the first time, he inwardly cursed these snakes in very strong language. "If you want to stay on for a while at your parents after next weekend, I will understand," he said. Christine looked at him and gave him a reassuring hug.

At least Suzanne was blissfully happy.

True to his promise David Andrews tracked them down and telephoned at seven-thirty. He spoke at length to Tim and enquired after his patient. Before he hung up, he asked if any of them had heard any strange noises coming from the woods. Tim was able to give the first reliable information on this matter. Before the doctor rang off, he made a suggestion. "Why don't you put a tape recorder in the woods – at night? Reel to reel – with a long-playing capacity."

"What a good idea," said David.

CHAPTER TWENTY-SEVEN

THIS WAS SOMETHING NEW.

On Monday evening Dalmar received two telephone calls. He found the first the most harrowing. "Hello, sorry to disturb your well-earned rest from the daily graft," said a pleasant voice. "My name is Jonathon Shure. I am a member of the panel investigating the Red Adder phenomenon. Am I speaking to Mr Dalmar Hunter?"

"You are, how can I help?"

"Look – I wondered if you could spare me a few moments – some time when it is convenient? You may have some information that could be useful to us."

"Can't think what it might be. Try me now. If you like." The last thing Dalmar wanted was an official meeting.

"All right – let me take you back to your expedition into the forest with Stephen Knopner. We were wondering how you knew there was a snake in the pine after Mr Styles fell. And, how you knew it would – shall we say – take off at any moment?"

After a short pause, Dalmar replied, "Seen it before while walking my dog. Sorry – but there is nothing of scientific value in this. I am just a guy who frequently walks his dog in Yewhurst Wood… Or did."

"I see… so at some point, you saw one of these snakes and witnessed it glide?"

"Yes."

"Where was that exactly?"

"I was heading away from the churchyard on the footpath between the Claymans crossing and the church. What I saw was a long way off – so I didn't have a clue as to what it might be. Out of the corner of my eye, I noticed a movement near the top of a tall tree. It was a long thin object that appeared to be gliding." Dalmar stopped briefly, before carrying on. "Just after Ginger Styles fell – I saw something red at about the point near the top of the tree from where he had fallen. It suddenly occurred to me what that might be – and what it might do."

"I wonder why no one else saw this?"

"Sorry – can't answer that one – but they were probably too preoccupied with Ginger's plight."

"Could I ask you something else – to do with the attack on Mrs Westward?"

"Go ahead."

"Well – you seemed, by all accounts, to know what you were dealing with?"

Dalmar was taken aback. "Really … no more than anyone else who lives around here, surely?"

After a long pause, Jonathon spoke. "I see. You have been most helpful. May I call you again if anything needs clarifying?"

"If you think I can be of any help, of course, but I am afraid I'm very much the layman."

"Ah – I was thinking more in the witness mode."

"Okay." And they said their goodbyes.

Before the second call occurred, Suzanne and Fly arrived. They had been for a walk in the early evening light, off Brook Road, and missed Dalmar's homecoming. Suzanne was about to prepare the evening meal. Christine and Tim would be joining them later. After a kiss or two, he mentioned sketchy details of his telephone conversation with Jonathon Shure. "Told you they would catch up with you," she said.

"Yes, but he isn't press, thank goodness."

At the bottom of the spiral staircase the telephone rang again. It had its own little shelf to stand on, so that the user could sit on one of the stair steps in comfort. Dalmar took up his position and picked up the receiver causing a sudden halt to its tringing. "Hello again," said a now familiar voice, "Who have I got there?"

"Dalmar … Doctor Andrews?"

"Hello. Thought you all might be interested in the findings of the post-mortem on the body of the vagrant they found the other day?"

"Certainly would, go on."

"They have got an identity. Lord knows how, but there you go: amazing what they can do nowadays. Apparently, he was a soldier of some repute many years ago. Helped win an important beachhead for us in the D-Day invasion. Must have fallen on hard times – poor soul. However, fatality was definitely caused by a dose of very powerful venom. There isn't much doubt as to where that came from."

"Sounds like a sad story," commented Dalmar. "Any close relatives? Someone who can explain things?"

"No. Well – no one's come to light as yet. Anyhow, thought you would all like to know. Be seeing you soon, no doubt."

"Thanks David – thanks very much."

Christine and Tim walked through the open back door as Dalmar put down the receiver. They were brought up to date.

Early on Wednesday morning ninety people met at the three setting off points for the shoot. Yet another day with an endless cloudless sky greeted them. There was a contrasting array of clothing between the game shooting syndicates and the clay pigeon clubs. The syndicates tended to be fairly sophisticated wearing moleskin shirts and trousers, and despite the hot weather many of them sported the proverbial green wellies. Several men wore waxed hats purely to keep the sun off their heads.

The clay shooters, however, looked like a collection of mercenaries. Some, with their cartridge belts, could have been taken for the best Mexican banditti of the Wild West. But when it came to the kind of shotgun shooting skill needed today, their fine-tuned technique would probably be the better suited.

If they were lucky enough to catch sight of one of the Red Adders stationary in a tree, then it would not matter who was taking aim. It should not be missed. But if the snake got into a gliding attack, not all of them would be as reliable as Jim Pearce. It would be more a question of the number of guns aiming at the same target, rather than individual accuracy.

The press kept to their word and congregated at the Claymans Heron hotel. In the lobby, reporters were sitting around playing cards or finding other ways of relieving the boredom.

Unaware motorists passing by the starting points for the shoot would probably not turn their heads. The number of vehicles had been kept to a minimum by using every available seat, rather than turning up singly or in pairs, and the shooting participants themselves were soon in the cover of the woods. That only left the St John's Ambulance uniformed personnel visible.

By eight-thirty all three teams had made a start. Those lucky enough to be on pathways could carry a shotgun in the break position, but only some of them were able to stick exclusively to these routes, simply because there were not enough such paths. Others, frequently, had to make parallel sorties into the dense undergrowth. In those circumstances, they could not carry a gun, so they had to leave it in its sheath, slung over a shoulder. This had to be the worst time of year to undergo this exercise. The growth had reached its thickest and highest points. Some of the bracken was over six feet tall, and the bramble briars were incredibly strong. Those that possessed bush or sheath knives were usually asked to go off the tracks. This was a dubious pleasure, because in no time many a person was suffering from skin abrasions and. or, torn clothing. Progress was very slow and if you were one of those not involved in negotiating the undergrowth, there was a lot of waiting around. It did however give ample sighting time. The whole object was to scan the tops and leafy areas of the tall trees encountered. All participants had been forewarned to bring along a pair of binoculars. For safety reasons, they were also advised not to go too close to any of these lofty giants. As the heat of the day grew, it became more and more uncomfortable, especially for those dressed in traditional shooting attire. There was much complaining, but most of it was of a good nature and erred on the humorous side.

Yewhurst Wood was not just planted with conifer. There was a great deal of deciduous woodland left intact from times past. From the point of view of the onlooker, rather than the forester, it presented a varied and striking beauty all of its own. At any one time, you could be on a grassy path lined on one side by forty to sixty-foot tall pines, and, on the other, by a varied mixture of ash, beech and chestnut with light coloured leaves; oak in the medium and holly and yew trees with dark foliage. Also, there were considerable changes in light density as the pines let little through, and the floor under them had virtually no growth causing the existence of a spongy carpet of dead needles.

Conversely, beneath the deciduous trees plenty of sunshine filtered in giving a second layer of vegetation with grasses, bramble and bracken which this time formed pastel greens, while rhododendron provided the deeper tones. In the patches of ground in between were rich rugs of red and copper from last season's fallen leaves. The whole provided close line views of magical appeal, which quelled the mind of other matters allowing admiration that could be taken in and stored in the brain's memory cells.

Stephen Knopner and Charles Brewster had arranged an operational communications system. Stephen and David Andrews were in the forest flitting about from one shooting party to the other in a Land Rover. David had changed his plan, preferring to be in the field, rather than at a base. Each group was allotted short-wave radio sets and, with these, were able to communicate directly to Brewster at the Chapp forestry office, who, in turn, could talk to Stephen. They tested everything before starting the drives, and by lunchtime had had no cause to use it.

All three shooting parties, in their respective areas, spread themselves out on the forest floor to eat their sandwiches, quench their thirst, and for those that desired it, there was ample coffee available from large vacuum flasks. So far, no one had spotted anything unusual. There had, of course, been sightings of lizards and even one of the common adder basking in the sun, but nothing unusual.

The afternoon progressed in much the same way, except that they were now going back towards the roads bordering the forest, having reached the end of the wood on the northern boundary. It became rather obvious to many of the participants, and certainly to Stephen, that it would not be possible to cover every part of the forest. They therefore stuck to those areas possessing tall trees.

Not one shotgun report was heard in the entire day. Not even due to a mistake, such as a startled bird, or something in a tree that they were not sure of. Absolutely nothing. Many of the volunteers felt cheated because of their scratched arms, legs and even faces; never mind ruined clothing. Disappointed, they all went home without a single sighting.

What none of them knew was that there had been a sighting during the late afternoon, but not by a human being. Beam, the female cat, while waiting patiently in an attacking position, hidden from view near a promising rodent's lair, was seriously disturbed by the sound of one of the shooting parties heading her way. This was something new. Frequently she happened upon forestry workers. They did not bother her and more than likely never even noticed the quiet animal. But this was different: the numbers, and the noise. She bolted and headed for home. To make her passage considerably shorter she took a tough but attainable route through a part of the plantation. While scrabbling over a bank of built up fallen conifer leaves, she came to an abrupt halt. All the hairs along her back reached for an unseen sky. Her tail went straight up and stayed like that. Sheer fear was written all over her face. Straight in front of her was the broad head of a large viper. The cat was virtually motionless. But so was the snake who regarded this intrusion with complete disdain. Suddenly Beam came to her senses and shot off in the other direction, floundering all over the place until she burst free of the plantation onto, thankfully, a familiar path. She did not stop running until she reached the road, and, once safely on the other side, she never, ever, went back again.

The media, who had been waiting all day, either in the Claymans Heron reception lounge or by their motor cars in the parking area, could not believe it, when the chief inspector finally entered the lobby and made his short announcement. It was an enormous anti-climax. All of them had expected something; certainly not a great big zero.

Tim and Christine listened to the results of the day's events at Yewhurst Wood on an early evening news broadcast at Beech Cottage. They were in the process of getting items of clothing together before going over to join Suzanne and Dalmar.

"Can't say it makes things any better," said Christine. "There are at least two of the damned things still out there. I mean… they can't have gone anywhere. They just missed them."

"If you ask me, you would need thousands of men to properly comb those woods." Tim's comment sounded a little bitter. "Never mind, we will get a break over the weekend. I am quite looking forward to staying with your mother and father."

"Good," she said.

They found Dalmar and Suzanne enjoying the fleets of departing reporters and TV crews. "It will be nice to have things back to normal," said Suzanne. She looked slightly flushed for some reason. "Perhaps we could go for a drink at the Claymans tomorrow evening?" She looked at her brother and his wife in turn, seeking agreement.

"Ever wondered why it is called the Claymans Heron?" Dalmar asked them. He had one eyebrow slightly raised in a knowing sort of way.

"Oh, here we go," cajoled Suzanne. "Not another one of your strange theories." She had spent enough time with him now to doubt some of his reasoning. He meant well himself, but often could not see the flaws in his ideas, simply because he was too one-tracked about them. Tim and Christine chortled at his expense.

"No," Dalmar smiled bashfully. "Listen; there is something in this. Can't be certain – but I believe it has nothing to do with the bird. They say there used to be a heronry around here, whatever that might have been. It doesn't make any sense. What has the heron, feathered variety, got to do with clay-men?"

"But – there is a huge great sign out by the road with a bird on it, and an even larger model of one by the hotel entrance," said Christine. Suzanne was about to put the tip of her index finger to her temple when something stopped her.

"Yes, but you must agree that it is very good commercially. The heron is an attractive and much-admired bird. You know – it's a darn good image," continued Dalmar determinedly.

"Right – agreed," said Tim, and Christine nodded.

"There is another meaning for the word 'heron'," Dalmar explained. "It is a type of clay. Roughly two feet down all round here is a seam of clay. A year and a half ago, I had it analysed by a laboratory that specializes in that kind of thing. Not sure where they sent the sample, but I don't think it was local."

"Probably Edinburgh," interrupted Tim.

"Ah yes, of course, you would know. Anyway, it turns out that it *is* suitable for pottery. Not perfect – but suitable." He finished at that.

"Potters clay!" exclaimed Christine, as though making an extraordinary discovery.

"Well, the area was known for it," said Tim. "There used to be quite an industry, in craft terms, around this part of Hampshire. And that must mean that the clay was mined, if you like, somewhere nearby."

"Precisely," said Dalmar.

"If that is the case, why don't the owners of the Claymans make a thing of it – rather than portray the bird?" said Christine

"Presumably, because they don't know," her brother wagged a finger at her. "Why don't you tell them?"

She was let off the hook. "Already done that," said Dalmar. "Weren't interested, probably a case of why upset the apple cart?"

"Seems a shame," Suzanne carried on. "They could have a kiln and real potters making and selling Claymans Heron jugs and things.

"What a lovely idea," Christine agreed.

After this, Suzanne declared that supper was ready and then added. "No – I think a Mr Clayman probably had a heron as a pet." Dalmar rewarded her with an exasperated look.

CHAPTER TWENTY-EIGHT

THE LAST TOUCH WITH HER WORLD.

At two-thirty in the morning a small black sports car entered the car park at Yewhurst churchyard. It was Friday the 29th August. Mary Taylor, the reporter with the Winchester paper had been right, there were no policemen keeping a vigil. She parked alongside one of the hedges screening the car park from the graveyard area and switched off the lights. As the noise of the vehicle's engine ceased it became very quiet, quite suddenly. She wound down her window. A cool breeze brushed her right cheek. Taking a camera off the back seat, together with a black canvas bag containing a vacuum flask of coffee and a bar of fruit and nut chocolate, she looked longingly at a torch in a recessed shelf but shrugged off the temptation. Closing the window, she stepped out of the car. The door-catch went click on a very still night. She looked up. The black heavens above her twinkled all over with tiny pinpricks of light.

For about the tenth time that day, she developed a trembling fear. Here she was about to go into the forest inhabited by one or two, maybe more, of the world's most deadly snakes, who, it seemed, went out of their way to attack people. She stood by the car one hand lying comfortably against a wing mirror: the last touch with her world.

Having talked to an acquaintance who had walked along some of the paths in this forest, Mary knew that if she went through the gate and veered off to the right and then fought her way through some tall bracken for about fifty yards or so, she would come to a wide path.

Mary was not miffed at having her baby swept into the realms of the national press. She understood all that, but she was disappointed that the story had gone cold. Also, she saw a chance to progress from where she stood. It had done her career a great deal of good so far, but one more step of significance would catapult her into the celebrity world of media reporting. That is what she craved, and this was her chance: her only chance. She had a plan which she was quite confident she could execute. Up to now, during-the-course of this story she had been lucky and hoped that it would hold. Mary believed that it was her time.

Opening the gate, she walked a little way into the woods and then stopped to further accustom her eyes to the darkness. Her good fortune was indeed holding for it was a great deal lighter than she had expected due to the cloudless sky. Although the moon was halfway through its cycle, it made all the difference. The great pale semi-circle shone its pearlescent light for her.

She was dressed in a body-hugging black outfit. The top was a soft woollen long-sleeved polo necked jumper. Although she was not used to this sort of thing, she had seen the scratches on some of the shooting party members. Black jeans made up her lower garment and her footwear comprised of a pair of dark tennis shoes. Mary had especially dyed the later for tonight's expedition. The significant things that interfered with the all black look were her long blonde hair, which took on a startling greyish white tone in the moonlight, and her silver-rimmed spectacles glistening like out of place jewellery.

When the party returned after the Ginger Styles tragedy, she recalled them appearing from the depth of bracken and blackberry bramble about fifty yards from the gate on the right-hand side. After a short while, she found signs of a sort of path that looked rarely used. From what she had gathered she would have to get through this densely grown patch before she found a larger pathway going off to her left. That track went down to a heavy five bar gate by the road. The trouble was there were all these frightening dark areas in the shadows that could hide anything. She was deliberately entering the woods without using the gate to help avoid detection. With luck, she would have left the forest before the policemen took up their duties later.

The bracken, although moist from the dew, did not present any difficulty. She just brushed it aside. It was spotting the brambles in the grey light that was tricky, as she discovered painfully. Within seconds, a great tentacle had wrapped itself around a leg and pierced her ankle badly. She winced and as soon as she attempted, gingerly, to handle the briar – got her thumb punctured. She wished she had worn gloves. Placing the wounded limb into her mouth, she sucked at it thoughtfully. There was only one way to do this – very carefully. Mary hooked the bag over her shoulder so that it fell halfway down her back on its straps, and then she put her head through the camera carrying cord so that it lay just under her breasts. This freed both hands to give her better balance. She worked her way forward like a dancer, half-pirouetting between the clumps of growth that might contain the bramble thorns. Suffering a few more wounds, she eventually came to the clearing she was hoping to find. "Good – so far so good," she muttered to herself.

Out in the clear, she walked right in the middle of the firebreak, which varied in width from ten to twelve yards. To start with it gave her a sense of security. The first part went uphill and bent round to the right and in no time her sight connection with the gate by the road vanished. It was then that she got her first feelings of real fear. Now, she was deep in the forest, alone with its night stillness. An owl hooted: the long mournful notes of the tawny owl. It seemed so eerie. The trees on the right-hand side were very black and made it impossible to see among them. The whole border, stretching up some fifteen yards in height, was like an enormous dark curtain. The left-hand aspect of the path was a great deal friendlier, for although there were many deep shadows, the moonlight penetrated in lots of places. True, there were ghostly shapes that would worry many a person, but Mary found the opposite boundary awful, and she started to walk away from it.

The grass around her feet was strong and thick in places especially with the addition of abundant thistle, but that was not the main problem. She suddenly stumbled when her left foot caught the hard crust of a deep trough ploughed by a heavy vehicle during the previous winter. Then, the rains caused the heavy clay to sink under even the lightest foot, so when a large, wheeled logging truck passed over; here was the result as though carved in stone.

Pausing for a while made the fear worse. 'Should she turn around and go home?' After all, no one knew she was here. She felt so utterly alone. And now she started to see things: unexplained shapes in the gloom. Apart from the owl, there had been no sound except that of her own exertions and the disturbance she made on the flora. So, when she stopped the silence was absolute. There had not even been the noise of the odd vehicle travelling along the now distant road. Nothing – nothing at all.

At a time when Mary leased needed it, an uncomfortable thought came into her mind. Did snakes hunt at night? She seemed to recall someone talking about that. Was she, in fact, placing herself at enormous risk? The Red Adder's attacked people. They would not be hiding from her – quite the opposite. Mary Taylor turned around and started to head back to the car park. Then she spoke to herself aloud. "Mary! Mary! This won't do. Come on. Pull yourself together." She stopped and did something that she had not done in years. Yesterday afternoon, on impulse, she had bought a packet of cigarettes and a box of matches. She found them in her pockets. The cellophane wrapping on the cigarettes proved a frustrating hazard, but her fingernails finally did the job. Both the cellophane and the silver paper at the top of the pack were discarded, impatiently. She struck a match and lit the end of the cigarette. This act, with its blaze of noisy light immediately cheered her. She had been a non-smoker for the last six years, so she had no intention of inhaling. Taking a long draught of smoke, she tasted the acrid tobacco and then blew it out loudly with a soft whistling sound. The task, thankfully, got her over the panic attack. She turned back and continued walking deeper into the forest for some time.

After a while she came to a crossing of ways. The path she was on continued, she noticed, but in a narrower vein. Coming from the left was a wider and, it seemed, more important way. This, she decided, was as far as she needed to go. What she required now was somewhere to sit so that she could await the arrival of the first light of dawn.

One of the precautions she intended to take was not to pass under a tall tree. So, her resting place must be below something of modest height. Just around the bend, going west, she came across such a location: an old fallen tree stump lying near some birches. She sat down on it. 'Good,' she thought, it seemed dry having been sheltered from any forming dew. Mary pulled back the sleeve on her left wrist and looked at her watch. She could not make out the time, so again she struck a match and noticed that it was half past three. "Good heavens!" she said aloud. A whole hour had gone already. It would be getting light in another two hours. Next on the list was a cup of coffee. Disentangling her shoulder bag. she took the top off the vacuum flask, which was to serve as the cup, unscrewed the sealed cap and sniffed the hot coffee aroma before pouring herself a generous amount.

Her mind wandered to her office and the obvious attention that an admiring male reporter had been paying her recently. 'Funny,' she mused; 'He never showed any interest before this Red Adder business: must have got him going somehow.' She was not interested. Her career was what mattered, and she was quite happy to get on with it. She worked at least six days a week, often on Sundays as well. Not being an office person most of her extra hours were spent out and about interviewing people.

Her father had outlived her mother even though he was eight years her senior. A tragic riding accident had been the cause. Being only sixteen at the time, it had left Mary with a huge hole in her life.

Now, being such a long way from the family home she missed her father a great deal, but there was another – much more important reason why she frequently made the long trip to the northwest of England. Mary Taylor had a secret; or, at least, a secret from people around here. She had a six-year-old daughter. The father, an ex-boyfriend had emigrated to Australia without having any knowledge of the pregnancy.

Mary regularly sent funds to her father to assist with her daughters keep. Surprisingly, he did not seem to mind this encumbrance. He seemed to treat it as an extended fatherhood. Father and granddaughter got on extremely well.

Casting off these thoughts she took her mind back to her plan for this morning.

Getting a photograph of the Red Adder would be amazing, but she did not expect to manage that. She intended to commit a flagrant act of trespass in order to get several pictures of the snake's habitat. There had been some images published purporting to be just that, but they had all proved to be false. Hers would be the real thing. She had progressed far enough into the woodland for them to be genuine. As for her trespassing misdemeanour, well that would be up to the Forestry Commission, and no doubt they would prosecute. If they did not, then all sorts of violations might take place. But she was quite convinced that the resulting publicity would be more than worth it. Getting away undetected was paramount so that the photographs could be published. She was pretty sure that the police would not be on duty at the gate until at least seven o'clock. That would give her plenty of time to get back to the car – and away.

Later, she did not realise it, but she began to doze in the sitting position, her head bent forward. She awoke suddenly. Everything seemed as it was. The same grey view. Over to her right was the junction with the dark conifers on its boundary. In front of her there were more fir trees, which were not as tall as the others: possibly a younger planting. And to her left, a long, long path, joining on its own horizon in a misty distance obstructed by the night.

She had another look at her wristwatch. On this occasion she managed to read the time without striking a match. It was just after four-thirty. 'Great,' she thought, 'Only another hour or so until dawn.' She guessed that the first light would appear somewhere over to her right.

A part of her plan had been to experience night-time in the Red Adder's lair. She could exaggerate a bit and say that she had been here since midnight. No one would know. The shadowy sights were firmly imprinted on her mind. It was the lack of sounds that surprised her. There had been one distant owl hoot and she thought she had heard a fox or badger earlier on, but that was all. Her right hand crumbled away some bark on the tree stump and made her aware of her uncomfortable seat.

'Time for some of that chocolate,' she decided. While reaching in her canvas bag, she glanced up, her attention caught by a movement in the grass on the track. Then she went very still – her left hand remaining inside the bag. Something very long was moving through that tall grass, and it was coming towards her. It seemed to be meandering while keeping to the centre of the path. Mary was thankful that she was seated near the edge, and in the darkest shadows. As it got nearer, she suddenly realised, with an icy horror, that it was an enormous snake. It was considerably longer than the estimates given by recent witnesses: absolutely nothing like her perception of an adder. She became aware of her heartbeat that seemed to have become a thudding drum. It was difficult in the gloom to make out the size of the reptile's girth, but she was sure it was larger than some of the more exotic snakes, which inhabited other continents. If it had not been for the moonlight, she would probably not have seen it in time, and her movements might have attracted attention. For a moment she thought about reaching for her camera. 'A photograph of the Red Adder would be fantastic!' She also knew that to take a photograph would mean certain death. It would have to be flash photography. She would not be able to defend herself in the resulting attack; neither would she be able to run away. The snake would outstrip her in seconds. Self-preservation won over foolhardy ambition.

There was no sign of the redness talked about. The snake was nearly level with her position, and she could just make out the black zigzag markings on its back. Once or twice, she caught sight of an amber tinged eye, almost shining in the dull gloom. Mary had never been so terrified in her entire life. Drawing level, it had just started to pass her, when unaccountably, at that moment, it stopped. Slowly, very slowly, a large triangular head raised itself upwards, and kept on going until it was at least two and half feet above the ground. The snake was not looking in her direction. Mary was desperately frightened. Muscles all over her body started to tremble uncontrollably. She became aware that she was wetting herself and tried to clench her groin to stop the flow. At that moment the snake's head started to sway from left to right in a rhythmic motion. Left ... right, left ... right, left ... right, backwards and forwards, left

... right, left ... right. Then Mary saw something else. Visible, only a few feet from the snake, was the outline of a rabbit sitting up on its hind-legs. It was looking directly at the reptile, and seemed to be transfixed, long ears pointing straight up. 'Of course,' comprehended the immobile girl; 'the snake was hypnotizing the small animal. What was it doing out of its burrow?' The next event happened so quickly that Mary hardly saw it. The snake's head stopped swaying and a fraction of a second later the rabbit was in its mouth. There was a fleeting flicker from the unfortunate animal's back legs, and then it was still. Holding the body in its jaw, the serpent continued on its journey, although with a quickened movement which emitted a cold, fearsome slithering sound until it reached the path junction. It went straight over and entered the dark pines.

Slowly... Mary's limbs came back to normal. Feeling the dampness between her legs, she was glad she was wearing black and when she thought about it, those dark clothes had probably saved her life. Her head, especially her pale hair, had been shielded by overhanging leaves from the tree behind. What she could not know, was that normally the snake would have registered the powerful odour of her urine, but, fortunately, because its attention was elsewhere, it had not done so.

Some moments later, while she extricated a shaking hand from her bag, which was still holding the bar of chocolate, she broke off four squared sections and ate quickly. She knew it would help to get her blood sugar up. She sat there for a long time with her head bowed before she realised that the foreground near her was getting lighter. She looked up; dawn light was starting to show in the east. In another half an hour she could take photographs, and then it would be time to get away from here as fast as she possibly could. All her being was crying out for her to get out of there now. It was not that far to the car park. She would be there in forty minutes.

'But no – she had done really well, and her luck must hold, just another half an hour.' It was then that the birds began their dawn chorus. The very first was the robin with its lone, heraldic notes, closely followed by a thrush. Within ten minutes just a few calls had grown into a loud harmony of sound. The contrast between that and the silence of the night was stark. It helped abate the deep fear she felt within her.

Therefore, she waited. Another cigarette was smoked and this time she remembered to put it out properly. After that she risked standing up for a while. It was good to stretch her limbs and she swung her arms up and down to get stiffened muscles toned. Some colour came back into her fair cheeks. For a busy person she ate sensibly and took regular exercise by carrying out a generous session at Winchester's public swimming pool, usually, twice a week. However, for now, Mary finished off the coffee and chocolate.

Another thought came into her mind. She must have a go at tracking down that Dalmar fellow. She still had a feeling that there was something mysterious about him. 'Anyway,' she smiled to herself, 'he was really handsome.'

175

At last, it was time to go and get those photographs taken. There were only a few shadows left in some of the more obscure areas. She extricated the camera from its case. It was a good one. She had treated herself to it last year: a single lens reflex type with a really fine quality lens, which enabled her to take low light pictures without the use of a flash attachment. This facility, with the arrival of dawn, was appropriate now. After switching on the meter, she checked that it was working and started by taking photographs of all the views in the immediate vicinity. Every time she pressed the button which operated the shutter, it made a satisfying distinctive clunk.

When she finished, she took a long look in the direction she had to go. 'Was that awful snake still about?' The question kept nagging at her as she walked slowly, staying right in the middle of the wide path and casting constant glances, particularly towards the pine forest on her left. It was still very difficult to see anything under those trees. There was very little light which was not surprising. The mature pines cascaded down from a thirty-five to fifty-foot height, pyramiding out as they went. As there was only the minimal distance between them virtually no light passed through to the ground. The pines themselves were a striking variety displaying huge needle leaf shape chandeliers at the end of each bough.

Mary stopped to take some photographs for detail illustrations. Gradually, she reached the top of the hill where the path bent round to the left leading down to the gate by the road. She felt a surge of joy when she first sighted this. Soon, it would be all over, and she would be heading home for a shower and change of clothes. She took some shots of the scenery on her way down to join the cut through to the churchyard burial ground.

The results of all the hot dry weather were clear to the on-looking eye. Normally, at this time of year, everything would be at full growth. However, the evidence could be seen in the colouring of the grasses and weeds on the paths. A lot of them were parched brown from lack of water, and, as a result, dwarfed in height. But the usual stalwart wildflowers were in abundance. They were just starting to open their blooms to the new day. The yellow golden rod, the blue speedwell and showing starkly against the fresh green bracken the purple foxglove. Low down and just visible in places grew the small white flowers of the pignut, and the keen botanist would be able to spot many more varieties.

She could now see why she had trouble keeping her balance earlier in the night. The rutted surface was baked almost as hard as man-made concrete and everywhere there was dust. Her tennis shoes were covered in beige sediment and had lost their black look. The lower parts of her jeans were also liberally spattered with the powdery deposit. In the east the sun had now risen just above some of the lower trees which gave her full vision on the scenery.

With daylight coming upon the woodland, she had to adjust her light settings on the camera. She decided to save the rest of the film, so that she could take some pictures of the ornamental trees by the church, especially the tall ones. There had been some photographs in the newspapers and film used on television, but she would be capturing the view from this side – from the inside.

Mary was starting to feel elated. It was creeping upon her in anticipation of the attention she would inevitably receive. Not only had all her plans for her expedition been fulfilled, but a happening of immense importance had occurred. She had seen the snake. It had been only a few feet from her, in the centre of its territory, at a time most people would consider terrifying: the middle of the night.

Something on the ground, in an area of shorter grass up against some bracken stalks, caught her eye. It was the gentle movement of a large, striking looking butterfly's wings opening and closing. Treading softly, she edged closer, until she was almost on top of it. Mary had never seen such a beautiful butterfly, but she had no idea as to what it was. Its flashing blue and purple colours were a sheer delight. Unbeknown to her, she was very fortunate to witness a rare visit to the ground by a Purple Emperor. There were only a few colonies of this butterfly still in existence in the British Isles, and Yewhurst Wood was the habitat of one of those colonies; but their preferred environment was high up in the big oaks. They were not often seen by lowly man. Having her camera at the ready, she quickly adjusted the lens focus to near subjects, and took a shot. She was only just in time before it flew off. Mary watched as it disappeared heading towards a lofty oak.

It had been dark when she last passed this way, but now she could make out a possible path, which meandered through the tall bracken partly obscured by this season's growth. Anyway, it looked as though it went in the right direction. So, she hung the camera around her neck, together with her black bag, and started through.

Almost at once she snagged her trousers on a bramble stem, which went right through into her skin. She let out a muted cry before, gingerly, disentangled herself. After five minutes she thought she was doing well as she managed to avoid any more wounds. She paused for a while puzzled by something. It took a few seconds for her to understand what it was. The birds had stopped singing. True, the dawn chorus had faded out sometime ago, but their intermittent chatter had kept her company all the way back ...until now. Mary shrugged her shoulders. Maybe the noise of her disturbing the undergrowth had frightened them. All at once she came to an area where there was some immensely high bracken. It was extremely thick. She could not make out the line of the path at all. Perhaps she had gone the wrong way? No – somehow, she was sure this was the route she had taken, although coming from the other direction.

"TSSSSSSCH-WUMPP!"   Straight in front of her the bracken parted in all directions and a thick briar slashed across her face! It stung badly and she felt the blood running down her cheek. Mary did not have time to cry out, for there thrashing about not five yards away was an enormous, vivid red snake. Shocked, she stood with her face frozen in a terrified mask. Her eyes looked upon the reptile in acute alarm. The blood red colour of the immensely hostile, nightmarish being stood out in massive contrast against the stark crisp green vegetation. Abruptly, it stopped beating the undergrowth with its considerable body, bringing a leaden silence that seemed just as frightening ... Slowly – it raised its head. That head was fearsome. Its eyes fixed on hers with an air of malevolence that leapt at her mind in a horrid wave. This was the ultimate servant of evil that barred her path. Before Mary could move, it opened a great black cave of a mouth and let forth an astounding noise. The high pitch of the hiss instantly deafened the poor girl. It threatened to destroy the walls of her eardrums. She clasped her hands over both sides of her head. A simultaneous roaring trembled down her legs reverberating through the very soles of her feet. The whole was a shattering, raucous horror. The long forked-tongue vibrated at an un-see-able rate, and oversized fangs were clearly visible at the front of its mouth. The large head, now only a few feet away from the petrified girl with deep channelled scales etched over the top, looked utterly threatening ... It was too much. Mary Taylor – collapsed to the ground, uttering a loud, gargled cry.

One of the policemen on duty that day arrived at the car park early. He had volunteered to switch off and retrieve the recording equipment that had been set up by Jonathon Shure yesterday evening. As he dismounted from his patrol motorcycle, he heard the most extraordinary horrendous noise coming from the woods. He had absolutely no idea what it was. He had never heard anything like it before. This was soon followed by what sounded like a women's strangled scream.

The police constable made his way through the gate and ran, with some trepidation, in the direction from which he had heard the cry. He thought that the noises had come from over to the right, so he took a narrow winding path through some high ferns. The brambles slowed him up but when he had negotiated a particularly tall clump of bracken, he came to a sudden halt. There, before him, lay what appeared to be, an unconscious young woman. He bent down and took hold of her wrist. There was no pulse.

The Red Adder had not touched Mary Taylor ... Her heart had stopped.

A short distance away, a professional standard tape recorder was whirring away at a slow pace, being switched to an extended play mode. It was under a plastic cloche. Two leads were joined to it. One, a very long cable, was taking electric power from the rear of the church: the other was connected to a microphone that dangled a few feet in the air from the lower branches of a young ash. The whole ghastly happening – had been captured in stereo hi-fidelity sound.

CHAPTER TWENTY-NINE

"THERE IS ONLY ONE THING THEY CAN DO."

Early on Friday evening, Tim and Christine could be seen loading rather more suitcases into their car, than would normally be needed for a weekend's visit to parents. Following this, they negotiated the unusual amount of activity on the road by the hotel, and headed east, still ignorant of the cause for this sudden resurgence of interest.

The death of Mary Taylor brought the media circus back to Yewhurst. The Claymans Heron was crammed with reporters, photographers, film crews plus administrators and broadcast presenters from other nationalities. Floyd Hemming, the hotel manager, was in a state of utter exhaustion. Since the discovery of Mary's body by the policeman that morning, and subsequent confirmation that it had something to do with the Red Adder, his life had been made up of tentacles of extreme pressure. As soon as he released one, another would twist itself around him. When he turned down someone for accommodation, he would often receive a demand from his senior management, and even directors of the company, to sort something out. By eight o'clock that evening he had staff sleeping in the most unusual places having given up their own quarters. How he was going to feed all his patrons, he did not know. Fortunately, he need not have worried. Many of the reporting contingents got out of the crush and reserved tables at nearby restaurants and public houses.

A hasty press conference had been arranged for ten o'clock the following morning at the hotel. Meanwhile, police security at Yewhurst Wood had been increased to cover the night. Reporters were all over the place. It did not take long for a couple of them to discover a way into the forest at the back of the church, and police officers had to make a dash to put a stop to it.

Suzanne could not fail to notice the huge amount of activity by the hotel, as she walked over to her lover's house late in the afternoon. As soon as Dalmar arrived home, he and Suzanne literally hid in their little cottage. They had the place to themselves for the first time in quite a while. The two of them had decided not to watch any television or to switch on a radio, and so cocoon themselves from whatever the drama appertaining to the press activity might be. In truth, they did not want anything to disturb their privacy, even important news.

The last week's weather had been blissful – dry, sunny, but not too hot. There always seemed to be a cool breeze, which was not too invasive but during the day it had become hot and very humid. Poor Fly did not like it and he spent most of the time flopped in some corner, panting. This climate was not suitable for his heavy coat. Dalmar and

Suzanne found themselves back to the nights of lying naked on the bed with no bedclothes on top of them, and although they cuddled a great deal there were frequent breaks lying apart. Body proximity only exacerbated the problem of keeping cool. But it all had a romanticism of its own: tropical love in an English country setting.

It was this strangeness that produced an atmosphere of stark surrealism. Silly instances would make them go into fits of giggles as though partially intoxicated. After making love Dalmar lay flat on his back trying to invite coolness to the nerve ends of his body. A large moth came fluttering through the open window, bashed itself against the ceiling light lampshade, and fell straight down into his pubic hairs. Mr 'Casual' suddenly shrieked and came upright like a sprung mousetrap, before leaping off the bed to disentangle the fluttering moth from its excursion into a wiry jungle. Suzanne had witnessed all and started a bout of uncontrollable hysterics, which, after he had recovered from the shock, eventually, set Dalmar going.

The next morning, they were brought back to reality. Dalmar forgot their pact and switched on the Roberts radio, which was housed on a shelf near the window in the bathroom. They had risen late because the early morning brought a little relief from the humidity, so they had lain together enjoying their closeness. It was now just after ten o'clock and Dalmar had just applied shaving foam to the lower half of his face. He was about to take a safety razor to one cheek, the other hand positioned under his chin as a support, when he heard the following. "We interrupt this broadcast to bring you a special news announcement. A press conference has just been held at the village of Yewhurst in the county of Hampshire. The police have issued the following Statement. *"The young female reporter who died yesterday, apparently as a result of a so called 'Red Adder' attack, has been identified as Mary Taylor, a journalist who had been employed by a local newspaper. She leaves a six-year-old daughter who is being cared for by her father. Death was caused by cardiac arrest, possibly brought on by fright. The evidence for this is supported by a tape-recording scientists obtained near the scene of her death, quite by chance."* There was a short pause. *"The father of the deceased woman has given consent for us to broadcast part of this recording, in order that residents near Yewhurst Wood may evaluate whether they have heard anything similar. Consent has also been obtained from the Zoological Society of London, to whom the recording belongs."*

Suzanne heard the announcer's resonant male voice from the kitchen. She came into view at the bathroom's open doorway. Dalmar's razor was still suspended in mid-air. The recording started with a sound like plant life being violently disturbed. This was followed immediately by a startled female cry. What came next made Suzanne drop a, fortunately, nearly empty mug of coffee on the carpet, and Dalmar to nick himself on his lower right chin. The most appalling sound invaded their eardrums: a similar sound to that which they had both come to loathe, but only heard before at some distance. Suzanne thought her eyes had gone funny. She could have sworn the four toothbrushes, hanging in a rack around the base of a mug, vibrated.

All over the country thousands of listeners stopped what they were doing and froze into a trance that seemed to come from an age – long ago; of a deep fear that belonged with their ancestors, as though momentarily reborn.

Suzanne was the first to speak while fumbling for the mug on the bathroom floor. "Poor woman! – and oh – her little girl."

Dalmar was dabbing at his wound with a tissue trying to stop the blood flow. "You realise," he said above the voice on the radio; "this does not help Christine and Tim's predicament?"

"No," Suzanne agreed with a sigh. "It is such a shame. What do you think they will do?" This was the first time that either of them acknowledged that the couple might not want to stay at Beech Cottage. Suzanne turned off the radio silencing the announcer's voice in mid-sentence.

"There is only one thing they can do." Dalmar said with finality.

"Sell?" came a soft girl's voice.

"Unfortunately – yes. Trouble is – who is going to buy the place now?"

Another sigh escaped from Suzanne's mouth. She puckered her eyebrows with a deep frown. "Perhaps a snake expert: the Mr Shure who telephoned you. You never know."

"That, my darling is wishful thinking. But I agree with you. It is a terrible shame. The place was Tim's dream house, and I'll wager – for Christine it was going to be their family nest."

"Do you know, I reckon they *are* thinking about starting a family. What made you think it?" The female mind suddenly got very interested.

"Nothing anybody said. It is ... well ... nature," and he shrugged his shoulders while reapplying the razor to finish his shave.

"Oh," said Suzanne, obviously disappointed. She went to get a cloth. Dalmar allowed himself a secret smile.

Suzanne found Fly hiding under the kitchen table. He did not normally go there: must have been the hideous noise on the radio.

Progressively, throughout the day the humidity level increased, until it became so energy sapping that Suzanne flumped down on the settee and declared that she did not know what to cook for supper. They had only consumed a couple of biscuits with fruit drinks during the day, so something was needed. Dalmar thought for a while. "Cauliflower cheese," he said. "I'll make it." Fortunately for Suzanne, her palate liked the idea, so she kept quiet. It turned out to be a good choice, tasty and light.

They spent the evening in a lover's cuddle listening to music; Pink Floyd's Dark Side of The Moon followed by Mike Oldfield's Tubular Bells. At about eleven o'clock they went to bed and were soon asleep.

Around one in the morning, both of them woke, when a

tremendous clap of thunder brought Fly up from the kitchen yelping. Suzanne drowsily climbed off the bed to calm the terrified animal. Dalmar stirred. Blinding flashes kept coming and going before his eyes. Crash! – another enormous bang! Only this time it was directly overhead. It peeled away in a series of loud explosions as though the sky was being torn apart. It took a few moments helped by the sound of torrential rain before Dalmar could grasp exactly what was happening. This was not a normal summer thunderstorm. It was a full-blown tropical electrical storm. He went to the bedroom window and looked out. Virtually continuous lightning flashes illuminated the horizon. The last time he had seen anything like this, he had been serving as an assistant purser on an ocean-going liner, while anchored off Rio de Janeiro.

"Suzanne – come with me!" he demanded.

"Where!?" she exclaimed, not particularly wanting to go anywhere.

"Trust me," he looked at her, his eyes sparkling.

"What about Fly?"

"Don't worry." With that he practically ran down the spiral staircase and opened the front door on its rarely used creaking hinges.

When she realised, he was going outside, Suzanne shouted at him above another clap of thunder. "You aren't going out in this!"

"Yes, don't be scared. It will be alright."

Suzanne became even more alarmed when she understood that he intended her to accompany him. "But we haven't got any clothes on!"

Dalmar stopped with the door half-open. "Oh, what the hell!" he shouted. "Come on – follow me!" He ran across the lawn splashing in the surface water that lay on the hard ground. Suzanne followed waving behind her for Fly to remain where he was. She need not have worried; nothing would possess the dog to go outside in a thunderstorm! She flinched all over at the sudden impact of the driving, chilling rain. It was falling like a cascade from a powerful showerhead and made it difficult to see. Dalmar held the wire down on the fence by the field, so that Suzanne could climb over it. After she had safely done so, he took her hand. She looked up into his eyes trying to make out if he had gone raving mad. He pulled her along at a fast walk, until they reached the middle of the field. "Now – get down!" he said urgently.

As she did – crying out when her bare bottom hit a thistle, she finally got to say. "What are we doing? This is lunacy! What about the lightning?"

Her man's ridiculous reply was to say, "That is why I asked you to sit down." Then he put his arm around her shoulder. They were obviously both very wet. The rain ran down their bodies in a continuous band of rivulets. Their hair lay flat against their faces, black against the lightning light on their skin. "Now, my darling," he whispered loudly in her ear. "Watch!"

It did not take long for her to begin to comprehend what this was all about. She altered her position to one of kneeling on her haunches, which was marginally more comfortable.

She looked at the extremities of the field, their house and garden and the one next door; the hedge running by the road on the left and over fields going away to the distance. Straight in front, about three hundred yards further, lay another hedge leading to a farmhouse and outbuildings. Over to their right were more fields finishing in the corner behind them with the dark forest. These boundaries formed the outlines of their world, but there was another field of vision, up, up, towards the continuous flashes caused by the electric storm's lightning, illuminating the whole circular arena. Varying in visibility, sheets of rain slanting across the sky kept falling to the earth. The brilliant discharges caused curtains of silver, reflected off the rain, to travel in undulating waves over the landscape. Suzanne glanced at Dalmar's face and saw the glint of excitement in his eyes. There they were – two human beings alone amongst this mighty power. Nature in dramatic mood. Nature as an inferno of danger. They were cheating death because they were at their most vulnerable, naked and out in the open. The adrenalin started to build up in Suzanne's body and made her feel wonderful. A massive clap of thunder rolled over their heads which temporarily startled her. Suzanne became aware of distant rumbling reverberating all the while, like gunfire in some awful battle. A great tongue of fork lightning danced down and struck something a couple of miles away.

"It's fantastic!" she shouted in Dalmar's ear.

"Yes – I know!" he said in raised voice and playfully cuffed her with his left hand. She gave him a broad grin. Her beautiful eyes giving off sparkles of bright light imitating the storm in miniature, which set against her black wet hair made her look sensuous as well as lovely.

Suddenly they were brought back to reality. A great fork of dazzling whiteness came from almost straight overhead and shot down so fast that they could not follow it with their vision. A large oak tree caught fire straight ahead of them, not far from the farmhouse, sending giant sparks cascading a hundred or so feet into the air before falling to earth. The next moment the tree, from the very heart of its massive trunk, burst into flames. They both jumped to their feet. Dalmar reached out a hand to Suzanne and shouted, "Run!" She did not need any second prompting. They did Olympian speeds across the field as the most enormous crash of thunder enveloped the immediate area, repeating itself in a loud staccato, causing them to duck their heads involuntary. When Dalmar arrived at the fence, which bounded the back-lawn area of the cottage, he faltered in his charge so as to help Suzanne over the wire, but she waved him aside and, by placing both hands on the top of a wooden upright, executed a perfect vault. He followed suit, dangly bits waving in the wind.

Fly was standing in the open doorway barking his complete disapproval of these goings on. Once inside, Dalmar grabbed two towels from the bathroom and they entered the kitchen for some room to move. He handed a towel to Suzanne so that they could give themselves a good rub down, while laughing and gesticulating like school children in a boisterous playground. Fly seemed to understand and jumped up and down with the odd muffled bark. He was experiencing great relief at the sudden reduction in the level of humidity.

"Oh! I can't wait to tell Christine about that," said Suzanne with an excited air.

"Yes, and I shall tell her it was all your idea – she will think you have gone bonkers." As he said this, her lover tried to make a quick exit through the nearest doorway. Suzanne picked up a wooden serving spoon from the sink draining board. It was still wet – and she used it to great effect.

CHAPTER THIRTY

"YOU COULD SAY THAT."

Tim Westward did not return to Dalmar's cottage until Tuesday evening, having gone straight to work in the morning from Surrey. Monday had been a public holiday. He found Dalmar and Suzanne waiting. They both greeted him as though they had not seen him for ages.

"What have you done with your wife?" Suzanne asked, suddenly realising he was alone. She had wondered all day why Christine had not been dropped off earlier. "Is she staying on for a while with her parents?" she queried, looking disappointed.

Tim sighed; "Yes – you could say that." He looked dreadfully lost and sad.

"Tim – whatever's happened?" she asked anxiously. Dalmar looked very concerned too. Even Fly caught the mood and whined at him.

"I'm afraid Christine will never be coming back to Yewhurst.... not to stay anyway. That reporter's demise was the last straw. I have put Beech Cottage on the market," he said conclusively.

"Oh – no." Suzanne went to her brother and gave him a big hug. After a while she pulled back and said, "Can't say I am all that surprised." Inside she was hurting as well. She was going to miss her sister-in-law. Christine had become her confidant. Hence the next question. "But where will you go? What about your job?"

"When we have sold the cottage, we plan to move out Alresford way: the other side of Winchester. You know – near the Bush where we had lunch after the auction?"

"Well – that will be nice." She wanted to add that they would not be too far away. But felt she could not presume to be still living with Dalmar in a few months' time.

Her lover said it for her: "At least it won't be that distant from here."

"No," Tim agreed. Pausing briefly, he added, "Tell you what, let me buy you both a drink. Let's go to Crowsley for a change; looks as though there is still a big media contingent at the Claymans." Dalmar and Suzanne both liked the idea.

Over a beverage or two at the Queen's Head, Dalmar made sure that Tim knew he would be welcome to stay whenever he wished. Tim accepted gratefully – mentioning that he would be going to Guildford at the weekends, although they did plan to spend some time at his mother and father's home in Taunton. "My parents never did get to see Beech Cottage," he added sorrowfully.

During the next few days, a meeting between representatives of the Forestry Commission, Hampshire Constabulary, plus delegates from the county health department was hurriedly arranged. It took place at Winchester to avoid the media. The result was announced in a press release early on Wednesday morning. As soon as possible, probably within four weeks, daytime observation teams were to be established in key areas in Yewhurst Wood. These teams would be equipped with the necessary nets and specialist poles for catching, just to be on the safe side, python sized snakes. Additionally, there would also be an expert rifleman attached to each group.

Heading the operation would be Jonathon Shure, the zoologist. This satisfied the press, whose vast assemblage immediately dispersed from the village leaving a mere handful of journalists loitering about at the Claymans Heron.

At half past seven the following morning Dalmar was giving Fly his breakfast when the telephone ringing interrupted him. As he answered it, he was surprised to hear the voice of an elderly lady with a local dialect. "Sorry ter trouble yer. Could Oi speak te Mr Timotie Westwaard? Beggin' yer parden."

"Hold on, I'll get him. Won't be long," answered Dalmar. He held his hand over the mouthpiece and called upstairs to Tim who was getting dressed. "Tim – it's for you."

A sleepy and dishevelled sandy-haired young man awkwardly negotiated the spiral staircase. He mouthed, 'Who is it?' Dalmar shook his head and handed him the telephone. "Hello, Tim Westward," he cautiously announced.

"This be Mrs. 'essil. Could Oi 'av a werd like?"

"Of course," Tim did not really know what to say; he was so surprised.

"Could ee come an' see us, sort of urgent like?"

Tim hesitated. "I'm afraid I am off to work – shortly."

"Don't matter. How's about this evenin'?"

"At your house?"

"Yes. Do yer remember where'n tis?"

"Yes. Supposing I come straight after work ... about six-thirty?"

"Thaat-a-be foine. Ta." And the line went dead. Tim looked questioningly at the receiver. He tapped the instrument a few times and pursed his lips.

"Dalmar?" he called into the kitchen.

"Ye-s," a hidden face replied.

"Are you working late tonight?"

"No – should be home about the usual time. Why?"

"That was the infamous Ma Hessil. She has asked me to go and see her – for some urgent reason. I have just made an arrangement to go over to her home at Chapp, at half past six this evening. Don't suppose I could persuade you to come?"

"Why? Do you want someone to hold your hand?" Dalmar half joked.

"You could say that."

Dalmar poked his head around the kitchen door to look at Tim's face. Almost immediately he understood. Tim and Christine were selling their dream home because of those snakes, and while he was not above helping an old lady, he must dread any further involvement. "Okay – as long as you think she won't mind?"

The relief showed in Tim's face. "Na ... she'll probably be delighted to see your dark good looks."

"What's all this about someone's dark good looks?" A sleepy looking Suzanne appeared, descending the stairs.

"Looking at you Suz – right at this minute ... dark yes – good looking ... no." Her brother turned his head away in mock horror.

Suzanne pushed him aside at the bottom of the stairs. "Well, if you don't want to tell me." She tossed her black mane as if in defiance. Eventually, Tim explained, at the same time informing his sister that they were leaving her alone for a while this evening. When she heard about Ma Hessil, her female curiosity was intense, and she was desperate to find out more. "Can I come?" she asked.

"No," said her brother.

"Why not?" There was petulance written all over her face.

"Because you weren't asked." He dare not mention that Dalmar's presence had not been requested either.

"I expect she would love me to come. What's her telephone number?"

"I have no idea. No – I am not looking it up and N. O. you are not coming! Just forget it. Wait for us here. Will tell you all about it afterwards – there's a good little girl."

"Don't you 'good little girl' me!" Suzanne biffed her brother on his upper arm and went straight into the bathroom, shutting the door firmly to emphasise her annoyance. Tim grinned with pleasure and did a silent 'Oh' with his mouth for Dalmar's attention, who was tactfully keeping very quiet.

During the day, Dalmar telephoned Suzanne at his home and suggested to her that rather than rush a meal when he and Tim got home, they could all go over to the Claymans for something to eat after they returned from visiting Ma Hessil, as whatever it was, she wanted to talk to them about probably would not take very long. Suzanne was pleased to be finally included.

The days spent at the cottage while the men were at work were joyful when Christine was around, but Suzanne knew that from now on – even if she kept herself busy with housework or gardening, she would get lonely. However, there were all the wonderful positive sides to her romance with Dalmar, which she so enjoyed, for instance, one in particular – living with him.

One small matter irritated her whenever she thought about it. Three days ago, while hanging a pair of Dalmar's trousers in his wardrobe, she noticed a strange article in the bottom left-hand corner partially covered by a pair of shoes. She picked it up. It was a bright yellow lady's handbag with a long shoulder strap. After he arrived home late in the afternoon, she brought up the matter in a roundabout way, asking him whether he had ever had any other girlfriends staying here. The answer was an embarrassed, "Nothing serious."

Later, during the day, Christine rang and explained more to her about their decisions. Suzanne completely understood. There were many times herself when she felt the original magic of the area had been severely tarnished. But she was also quite sure that the magic would one day return. They had a long chat and agreed to call each other at least once a week. Suzanne told her all about their summer madness during the electric storm. Her sister-in-law was amazed.

About four o'clock, three children, two young boys and a girl called to see if they could take Fly for a walk. Suzanne had met them. Their parents lived in a larger house farther down the gravel lane. Even so, she thought she ought to check with Dalmar first. She explained this to them, and they were happy to come back the next day. Suzanne thought they seemed really nice children, obviously fond of animals. She wondered why they had not got any of their own. The younger of the two boys told her that their mother suffered from bad asthma attacks and having any kind of hairy animal sharing their home would cause her great distress.

Dalmar and Tim knocked on Ma Hessil's door just after six-thirty that evening. She was not long in answering. "Aah," she said as she looked at Dalmar. "Oi t'aut yer moight bring ee." Both men looked surprised at this.

"I hope you don't mind," said Tim. "This is my sister's gentleman." He thought that was the best way to introduce Dalmar, who looked somewhat amused.

"Is ee na– well good for ee," and she stood back and waved them in. Dalmar found the low ceiling most uncomfortable. He was glad when eventually they got seated. Ma Hessil sat in a wooden rocking chair which seemed to have lost its rocking ability. The room had a strange smell about it: a mixture of musty clothes and last winter's burnt ashes. Otherwise, it was what you would expect in an old lady's country cottage – sparse, although comfortable to her standards. Tim was taken with an old bakelite cased valve radio, which looked to be in working order. There was no television.

This was the first time that Dalmar had been introduced to the notorious Ma Hessil, although he had often seen her out and about, usually walking her dog before it had died earlier in the year. Close to, he was fascinated by her appearance. How she could bear all those clothes, even during a normal summer's temperatures, he did not know. What she wore, under what appeared to be a heavy grey pullover, was anyone's guess, but her lower half definitely consisted of at least two layers of skirts. Too much full grey hair was swept back from her crown, probably by a brush, where she had made a recent attempt to make herself presentable. Her dark eyes kept glancing from one to the other of the two men. The many crease lines on the extremities of her cheeks and under the shadows below her eyes, told of a lifetime of great emotion, not all of which was sad. Dalmar found himself trying not to stare at the one solitary tooth she still seemed to possess. Even when seated she kept her walking stick by her side held tightly in her right hand. It looked as though it had been used for far more than a support judging by its many gouges and imperfections. The handle sported the most delicate silver covering with an engraved crest. The constant contact with the palm of her hand kept it in a brilliant state of polish. She wore slippers but they were not what one would expect to see on a woman. These were quite definitely – masculine.

The two men were placed in an old two-seater leather settee which squeaked against their trousers. She did not offer them any refreshment and got straight down to the reason for asking Tim to call. While rearranging her skirts she looked at them, from one to the other, straight in their eyes. She pointed at Tim. "Yaan Oi knows Oi can trust ... and as for ee," her finger changed direction towards Dalmar. "Well, if'n yer caan't trust ee, in this'n maatter – then who can ee?" Dalmar and Tim looked at each other, and then Tim nodded at the old lady in a reassuring way. Dalmar appeared a little perplexed. She carried on. "Oi reckons that yer'd be only folks likely te believe un, and you likely think Oi be talkin' a load of rubbish at te'end, t'eny rate. Still – Oi must troi to cen- cenvince yer." She then went on to tell them about the ultimate tragedy concerning the bond of friendship. Neither man interrupted her from start to finish.

The story began towards the end of World War Two, during the D-Day invasion by the Allied forces on the beaches of Normandy. Her husband Robert and his best friend, John Head, were in the same landing craft. However, they were not infantrymen. Due to their knowledge of explosives gained as gravel pit blasters, they had been drafted into the Royal Engineers, 28th Regiment and further trained in demolition practices. Their task, during the landing, was to eliminate hostile obstructions, such as an enemy machine gun post with concrete reinforcement.

The Royal Marine Commandos they were attached to became pinned down in the sands by just such a heavily armoured machine gun emplacement. To get close enough to lay the explosive charges, one of the sapper engineers had to run some four hundred yards out ahead of the advance positions held by the British force. John Head volunteered for the task.

The brave soldier almost made it unscathed by running in a haphazard fashion, all the while bailing out the detonating reel of wire, but he was hit by gunfire at the last minute which shattered part of one of his legs. While suffering excruciating pain, he crawled the last few yards and managed to set the charges. Unfortunately, he did not have the strength, or mobility, to return. He may have passed out; nobody will ever know.

Bob Hessil wanted to go to him, but his commanding officer gave the order to press the detonating plunger. It was not known if Robert pushed down that plunger, because, later, he could not recall. It *is* known that he pleaded with the officer to change his mind. John was blown to pieces, literally. The machine gun emplacement was destroyed, and the beachhead was taken for the Allied forces.

John Head received the Victoria Cross posthumously, and the commanding officer involved confirmed that he had given the order to detonate on the grounds that time was running out: he could not risk any more of his men to attempt a rescue. Despite this, Doris Head, John's estranged wife, could not accept that it was not Bob's fault, nor did she realise the torment the poor man went through, daily living with the knowledge that he may have killed his best friend.

Doris lived next door to the Hessil's, and, where-as in the past they had all been the closest of neighbours, she now turned against them. She openly slandered their names all over the village, continually threatening revenge. So much so, that at one time the Hessil's seriously considered moving away. But then, suddenly, Doris changed, and instead of haranguing them at every opportunity, she went into what appeared to be a permanent sulk. She now rarely spoke and began to behave in an odd way: almost witch-like. Considering there was a history, long ago, of practising witchcraft in her family, it did not take much to start tongues wagging.

She had a brother who lived not too far away. As a boy he had studied hard at school and done well. In his late teens, he took elocution lessons and lost his dialect, something that his friends refused to recognise. "Yer dun need ter taalk posh to be understood," declared Ma Hessil, "Ee were daarn good ter 'er – ee was."

One evening in mid-summer 1947 a small shoddy red envelope was placed through the letterbox of the Hessil's home. Ma Hessil herself picked it up off the doormat. Inside was a similarly coloured piece of notepaper scorched all-round the edges.

The old lady fumbled inside a pocket hidden somewhere in her upper skirt layer and produced a piece of paper. She handed it to Tim. On her invitation, he read out what was written on it. The writing was barely legible.

"Your House is Henceforth Accursed
Revenge from another World shall arrive
In a time soon to come to pass
John shall return in a place not far from here
There he shall practice his art
With weapons provided within himself
To form a being more deadly
To man than any that hath so far existed
'Till he be that proficient

To come and avenge all.
Nothing may prevent Nothing save fire."

The note had browned with age and the crease around the folds made it almost impossible to decipher in some areas. Tim guessed, where necessary, and the old lady did not correct him. "'Ceurse Doris ne'er wrote it," she said. "Couldn't spell haalf them werds could 'er? 'An' it weren't her 'and – Oi can tell ee."

With an almost imperceptible nodding head, she went on to relate the events the two men already knew about in 1947 and 1948, but from her point of view. How John came back as *John the Red,* and the gleam that developed in Doris's eyes as those terrible days unfolded. She told them how terrified she and her husband had been, and when they lost their only son due to snakebite, she wanted to murder Doris, or 'the witch' as she termed her.

After Big Harry killed the snake, she and her husband felt a little better. She paused and inhaled before making a heavy sigh. "We wes allays froightened ee'd come baack cause ee were not destroied be foire see. As t'e note says – only fire'll kill'un." She paused again, sighing even more. "'Course ee come back didn't ee. First ee killed me ol' man, in fifty-nine. Doctor says it were a stroke. Loikely was, but it were froight that killed 'im fer sure. Ee were out waalkin' – see, in ter woods o'er there." She moved her head in a vague direction. "Must have seen Jaahn. T'was a hot year that'un. Ee all'ays appears in hot summers loike. Course Doris had passed away some years before but made no diff''rence. Na look what's ben happening. Yer poor woife." She looked at Tim. "My friend Nora Styles has lost her son, and den there's thaat reeporter girl. Which brings un' to one o' the reasons fer askin' yer here tonight. They give out te name of that army off'cer who lost his loife this year in the forest look. It were on the woirless. Did yer hear?"

Both Tim and Dalmar shook their heads not knowing where this was leading. She straightened her back before saying, "'Is name were Capin Harold Young." She looked at both men in turn searching their eyes for something. After a while Tim thought, perhaps, he was expected to make some comment, but the name meant nothing to him. "Te very same Capt'in Young thet gave the order ter blow Doris's ol' man to king'om-com." She got the reaction she had been hoping for. Tim's face stretched into the biggest imitation of a gasping fish imaginable. Dalmar sat bolt upright and stared at the old lady. Up to now both men were going along with the story, with great sympathy yes, but not with any conviction. Suddenly, the entire matter had been changed. Could she be right? Was this witchcraft? "You see, Oi be'n roight all aleng." Her face was impassive.

Dalmar was the first to speak. "Does anyone else know of this ... connection?"

"Na ... possibly Nora, Ginge's mum – bet Oi doubt it. An don't yer go tellin' any o' those know-it-all toffs! You hear. Oi been tellin' you in confid – in confi…"

"Confidence?" suggested Tim.

"Yer – thaat be it."

Tim and Dalmar both made gesticulations swearing obedience. 'This needed thinking about anyway,' thought Tim.

Ma Hessil carried on. "Na what Oi really wan'ed to see yer abaat, an impress on yer– is this. Yer knows ee must be destroied by foire?" She did not wait for any acknowledgement. "Well, Oi want yerr to promise me that if you have anyt'ing ter - ter do with … Jaahn's death … an Oi expect yer will, make sure ter body be burnt. And when Oi say burnt, Oi mean – ter ashes!"

Tim heard his voice come straight in. "What makes you think one of us will have anything to do with this – John the Red's – demise?"

"Just do," was the simple answer.

Tim looked at Dalmar before saying. "Well, if as you say, we have something to do with its dead body, then yes, I for one will certainly burn it." He said this without any real hope that the matter would end as Ma Hessil seemed to think. She immediately looked at Dalmar. Being in the path of those piercing eyes would make anyone nod in agreement – and he did.

"Of course, you realise that there are two or more of them at least?" Dalmar asked the question of her directly.

A smile grew on her face. It was not very cheerful. "There be only two … ter two haalves … remember … after Big Harry kill'un." And then the smile got even less endearing. "Or ter be truthfull – tere used ter be … Na … tere only un'."

"How do you know that?" asked Tim.

"Cause Oi burnt ee, that's 'ow." She burst into cackles of loud laughter. "Oi was tere see," she pointed at Dalmar. "Oi were watchin' yer from te woods. Thet haalf of Jaahn's body did never cum back ter life. Oi took in." More laughter. "Oi 'ad a bloody gert bonfoire thaat aaft'noon."

Shortly after this, Dalmar and Tim were able to get to their feet and make the necessary conversation to get them out of the front door. Ma Hessil pleaded with them not to tell a soul about the evening's revelations and reminded them of their promise. On their way down the garden path, she said good night to Tim. He acknowledged her. Then she said, "Goodnoight – Jaahn." Dalmar stopped in his stride, and without turning around waved an arm over his shoulder, before continuing on his way.

Once out of the lady's garden Tim apologised to his companion. "Sorry, I completely forgot to tell her your name."

"It isn't important," said Dalmar.

"Funny how people around here always refer to a bloke as John when they don't know what to call them," commented Tim. Dalmar smiled ruefully.

They went back to the cottage to collect Suzanne and very soon all three were enjoying their meal in the Claymans Heron.

Suzanne extracted a version of Ma Hessil's story from both men in turn; in the process they swore her to secrecy. When Tim mentioned the identity of the tramp that had been found dead a couple of weeks ago, as Captain Harold Young, it did not mean anything to her. But when she was told of the connection to Ma Hessil's husband and their next-door neighbour, she exclaimed "What!" The diners, near to their table, turned and stared. This did not put her off and she probably was not aware of their curiosity, for she said it again, almost as loudly. Tim and Dalmar looked embarrassed, and her brother asked her to keep her voice down. She continued to ply them with innumerable questions while demolishing a plate of gammon, egg and chips. Her brother was just about to ask her to leave off when she suddenly said, "What a dreadfully sad story," and ceased any further enquiries.

"When you are having one of your long chats with my wife over the telephone," and then as an afterthought Tim commented, "God knows what this is costing you Dalmar?"

"Actually – nothing brother dear," interrupted Suzanne. "Christine phones me. You were saying?"

"Oh. – Good. Well, the thing is, please don't mention about Ma Hessil being convinced that one of us is going to be present at the death of this – John the Red."

"Surely you don't believe that?" she asked him with a worried look.

"No, but I would rather Christine didn't know about it."

"Yes – okay," Suzanne said seriously.

"Sounds like one of us is going to do a Saint George," Dalmar said with a wry smile. "Anyhow, at least we are back to a single snake – I hope. Rather feel the authorities should know they now only have one to beware of."

"Couldn't we drop a hint to someone – like Stephen Knopner? David Andrews would get too inquisitive, but Stephen…" Tim let the thought hang in the air. They all considered this for a while.

"An anonymous note," said Suzanne. "That's it."

"I think you may be right," affirmed her brother. "Shall we sleep on it?"

"Good idea," agreed Dalmar. "I'm bushed."

Outside the rain was falling steadily. It looked set-in. England's normal summer had arrived – late, but enough to make everyone aware that the long dry sunny days, experienced in recent months, were a rare event.

CHAPTER THIRTY-ONE

"MUST ASK HIM ABOUT IT."

Suzanne was given the responsibility over the anonymous letter. She was the least likely to be recognised delivering it, and she had the most time in which to execute the task. She sat herself down on Friday morning after the men had gone to work. Tim had taken his suitcase and they would not be seeing him again until Monday evening, although Christine would be making an early morning trip with him to collect her car and have lunch with her sister-in-law.

Carefully, Suzanne set up Dalmar's typewriter on the table in the sitting room window alcove. Fly came and settled himself down between her legs, supplying a warm comforting feeling with his body pressed up against her. She typed the text on some plain writing paper and placed it in an envelope with Stephen Knopner's name, also typed, on the face.

The note read:

1st September 1975.

To whom it may concern.

Thought you should know that the body of the snake shot by an employee of The Forestry Commission, last summer, has been burnt.

Anonym.

She sealed the envelope and let Fly stay where he was for a while, before disturbing him in the name of a walk, which he was more than happy to do. As a considerable part of the way necessitated going along pavements by the road, she put him on a lead. He would be getting a good run, no doubt, when the three children came for him that afternoon. Dalmar had given his consent. He knew them all and was quite happy about it, asking Suzanne to make sure to tell them not to enter Yewhurst Wood. Going near these same woods was preying on her mind right now, for in order to drop the letter at the Forestry Commission office, she had to do just that. Her best route was to go along the road to the church and then turn up a side road to Chapp. She was very glad of Fly's company.

After crossing over the road by the Claymans Heron, she noticed that a young man was watching her from the hotel's patio area. She became bothered because he started to run in their direction, then crossed the road and came up behind them.

"Ecuse me Miss – may I have a word?" Suzanne held Fly back on the lead and turned to face him. "Jack Tuppence – Daily Crusader," he puffed at her. Suzanne could not help the appearance of a smirk on her face. "I know, I know," said the young man. "Not my fault. My ancestor's ... Are you a local resident?"

'Ah,' thought Suzanne, this gave her a way out of the predicament. "Aah, Oi be," she said in her best imitation of the local dialect.

"Great!" Exclaimed Jack with enthusiasm. "What do you reckon to these large snakes then?"

"What doo's Oi t'ink." Suzanne surprised herself. She was dressed in blue denim and her blouse had seen better days. It was clean but a little faded from its original dark blue colour. "You'm be married?" she asked.

Jack smiled broadly. "I am as a matter of fact; wife's just had a baby – a boy."

"T'en if Oi' were ee – Oi 'ud get moiself 'ome."

"Oh, and why is that?" Jack looked suddenly serious.

"Cause if'n you don't..." Suzanne nearly dropped an enormous clanger by mentioning John the Red. She stopped herself just in time. "T'en them Red Adders will be cumin to get you – you mark me words."

"But why?" persisted Jack.

"Cause t'ey dun loike reeporters." She nodded her head vigorously.

"Pardon ... don't like – reporters – you say – why?" He thrust his head forward and squinted with one eye as though emphasising his query.

"Dunno. Jus' don't. Killed that young lady – did'n they?"

"I see," the young newspaperman decided that this was not going to lead to much of a story. "Sorry to have troubled you ... M'aam." With that he turned on his heel and started to walk back to the hotel, shoulders slouching. Suzanne allowed herself a smile.

This encounter got her past the church without thinking about dangerous snakes once. She gave a tug on Fly's lead and they turned left off the main road to go around the bend towards Chapp. She was pleased to see the vicar, Paul Sanders, coming the other way. He recognised her and gave her a grin and a "Hello". During their chat, he was really upset to find out that her brother and his wife were leaving the village. "What a shame." He looked searchingly at Suzanne. "I suppose it has a lot to do with a certain reptile, and the proximity of their cottage to these woods?" He received a nod in confirmation. After they had concluded a short conversation, he watched them continue on their way before heading towards his church.

When Suzanne and Fly came level with the Forestry Commission office, she glanced behind her to make sure no one was about and then quickly walked up the short drive. There were no windows overlooking the immediate entrance. She had been worried about that. Taking the envelope out of her pocket she hurriedly flipped it through the letterbox and, in haste, went back to the road. She had to give Fly a tug: the dog was disappointed, thinking he was about to visit someone.

The walk back was uneventful, but she still found it frightening. She wished there was a footpath on the other side of the road, so that they could get further away from some of the tall trees. However, Fly showed no signs of being perturbed, and this reassured her.

Beech Cottage looked lonely, but she went into the garden, checked the doors by hand and peered into the windows to make sure all was secure. She wondered if there were any would-be buyers yet. The estate agent's 'For Sale' sign was prominently displayed just off the entrance to the drive. To date, she had not heard of anyone making enquiries. Passing by the Claymans she was relieved to see that the reporter who had chased after her was nowhere to be seen.

Fly had a wonderful time with the two young boys and girl who came, as promised, to take him for a walk in the afternoon. They went into the wooded area down Brook Road, and he ran with them while they played their imaginary games. When they handed him back to Suzanne, he went inside and flopped down on the sitting room hearthrug.

During the weekend, Suzanne and Dalmar made some tentative plans. He had not taken any holiday for the current year. All the suggestions came from Suzanne. Her eyes twinkled as she put two thoughts to him. One was to visit the Lake District where she had an aunt and uncle living. They had already invited them, including Fly, for a few days, and secondly; she broached the subject of visiting her mother and father in Somerset. Dalmar thought a trip to Cumbria and the Lake District was an excellent idea. He proposed that they spend two days with her relatives and the rest of the week at a self-catering cottage, which he had heard of by recommendation from a work colleague. They could plan another break later in the year, perhaps visiting her parents, before going on to the deep southwest as well. Suzanne liked the itinerary, and they made plans to travel in a few weeks' time.

Christine walked up the gravel path of Dalmar's garden at eight-thirty on Monday morning. Despite having risen early to make the journey from Guildford, she looked radiant. It was a dull morning and the air-hung stale after a night of rain, but this did not affect her mood. Tim had dropped her off before going to his office in Winchester. The top half of the stable door was ajar. She called out. "Wakey wakey! It's your early morning call!"

Suzanne came charging from the direction of the sitting room. "Chris!" She unbolted the bottom half of the door and embraced her sister-in-law. Then she stood back. "You look stunning. You are even more beautiful than you were before. How?" And she shook her head admiringly.

"Still the same ol' me. Make us a coffee – I'm gasping for one. Dalmar already gone to work?" Suzanne confirmed that he had. Christine had a handful of letters she found by the milk bottle holders just outside the back door. The postman had got into the habit of leaving the post here due to the cover provided by the glass pelmet. It saved him having to traipse around to the front door with its awkward tiny letterbox. She handed them to Suzanne and pointed to the official looking brown envelope on the top. "Someone has given Dalmar an extra initial," she said. Suzanne took the bundle. The addressee read: 'J.D. Hunter., Esq.'

"You know – I've seen that before," commented Suzanne. "Must ask him about it. Right – coffee it is." She placed the letters on the kitchen dresser.

The morning sped by for them as they indulged in lengthy conversation.

About eleven-thirty the telephone rang. Suzanne was surprised to find Tim on the other end. "Is Chris with you?"

"Yes, I'll get her. How are you?"

"Okay."

"I'm okay as well. But you obviously couldn't care less." She took the receiver away from her ear before a chagrined Tim could reply and gave it to her sister-in-law.

"Hello darling – what's up?" Christine spoke into the mouthpiece.

"Nothing – on the contrary – brilliant news. Someone has accepted our asking price for Beech Cottage. What's more it's a cash buyer. He will complete as soon as we are ready."

"Good heavens!" Christine was genuinely dumbfounded. They had expected the sale to take much longer.

"So – we have got some serious house hunting to do," continued her husband. "I have asked our agent to let us have details of anything for sale in our price bracket around Alresford. They are sending them to you at Guildford. I am going to ring a few other agents later. Okay?"

"How exciting! We will be able to ponder next weekend."

"Yes, anyhow, must get back to the grind. Bye love."

"Bye darling. Wonderful news! Thanks for letting me know." When she came off the telephone, Suzanne was standing next to her, curiosity written all over her face. Christine enlightened her.

Later, Christine asked Suzanne if she would come with her to Beech Cottage to collect the Ford. They took Fly who had not stopped fussing around Christine all morning. Unusually for him, he had missed her arrival being asleep upstairs, but not for long. Dalmar had given the station wagon a run over the weekend, so it started first time. Most of Christine's clothes and shoes had already been taken out of the cottage, there were just a few items remaining. They bundled them into the back of the estate and Christine said urgently, "Quick – let's get out of here, I can see some curious bods stirring by the Claymans. They'll be over here in no time." They found space for Fly and set off towards Crowsley. As they passed the hotel, three men looked intently at the car. One of them was Jack Twopence. Suzanne related the story of her encounter with him.

"He looks sweet. Where shall we go for lunch? It's my treat," said Christine.

"Oh, one of the pubs in Crowsley: we don't want to go too far because you have to come back to drop us off."

They both chose soft drinks and a plate of scampi and chips. Fly behaved himself after getting a small bowl of water from the landlady and they were able to talk animatedly about the future home that Christine hoped to acquire. When she said goodbye in the middle of the afternoon, she cheered Suzanne up by saying, "Of course, you realise I shall probably be back next week, or the week after to look at properties. You will help me – won't you?"

"Yes please!" A glorious smile illuminated Suzanne's face.

In the evening Tim explained to Dalmar how the offer for Beech Cottage had come about. "The guy who is buying it is some sort of developer and, apparently, he wants to obtain planning permission to extend. Not just a lean-to, but almost double the size."

"Wow!" exclaimed Suzanne. "Won't that take up most of the garden?"

"Seems to think he can buy a bit more land from the forestry people. He wasn't in the least bit bothered about John the Red. Reckons that by the time he has finished what he wants to achieve it will all have blown over. Probably right as well."

"Oh well, good house hunting," Dalmar raised his glass as he spoke. They were all enjoying a gin and tonic for a change. Tim was trying to find some cheer in what they were doing. He knew his wife was a great deal happier, and that was what really mattered. There was no doubt that some of the villages in the Itchen and Meon river valleys were very picturesque, and this was the area in which they hoped to find a house.

Dalmar reserved the self-catering accommodation for the second part of their holiday successfully. It was in the Langdale Valley, surrounded by mountains on all sides. Fly would love it. After all, it was more his sort of country than where they lived now. Dalmar found himself looking forward to it immensely. He started behaving like a teenager, investigating whether he had the proper gear for fell walking. Finally, he took his girlfriend's advice. "Wait until we get there. I'll take you to some shops on our first day. You will see what I mean. They have got the right stuff. A lot of what you will find around here is not suitable." Suzanne was already well equipped for fell walking. She kept it all at her aunt and uncle's home, where she had stayed for a few weeks every year since she was fifteen.

She adored the Lake District; it was where she would really like to live one day. Her aunt was her mother's elder sister; a little bossy, but otherwise amiable. She was known as Maggie, short for Margaret, and Tim often enjoyed huge amusement over the way his sister became annoyed because Aunt Maggie had told her off for something quite unexpected.

Nothing got back to them concerning the results of their anonymous note to Stephen Knopner, and they dare not make enquiries.

Dalmar began to get panicky, worrying that the police might check his typewriter. Tim tried to make him feel better by saying that it did not merit that level of investigation. But Dalmar was not so sure. Those snakes had killed, and the police might carry out house-to-house questioning if it were a murder investigation. He seriously thought about getting rid of the typewriter. However, as the days passed and not a thing was heard, it bothered him less.

House details began to arrive at Christine's parents' home later that week. By the time Tim arrived on Friday evening, she had already earmarked two of them for a visit. A few days later, the list had increased to five. Christine, therefore, agreed to go and stay at Dalmar's house from the beginning of the following week. She and Suzanne would have an initial look at the properties, and if there were anything she really liked, a second visit would be made with her husband.

The very first house that the two girls called on in the afternoon of the Monday was in the village of Cheriton. It was ideal, not thatched, but delightful and it even had a brook running across the bottom of the garden. Tim fell in love with it as well, when he was dragged out late that very afternoon. For him, it made things far more positive because it had considerably more internal space, generally, than Beech Cottage. They decided not to bother to go and see the others. Tim made an offer on Tuesday morning, below the asking price. It was refused.

He telephoned Christine and gave her the news. "Can't say I am really surprised. Can we afford to pay the whole whack?" she asked of him.

"Yes, but it would mean we would have nothing spare. We wouldn't be able to carry out any alterations. Just the odd bit of painting."

"Well, Chris and Suz, your local team of decorators are at your service."

"That's my girl," said Tim smiling to himself, "I'll up the offer." And so it was that Christine and Tim found themselves due to move house for the second time that year. The reality was that the move would take place in about a month's time, shortly after Dalmar and Suzanne returned from their vacation.

"Guess what we are coming home to after our holiday?" Suzanne greeted her man with when he got in from work. Christine was standing nearby, and Dalmar recognised the sultry look that she had given him the night she cajoled him into helping at the furniture auction.

"Oh no – suddenly I have a bad back," he said.

"Uh, huh-huh. None of that. And no falling down mountains either; we want you fit and well, understand?" admonished Christine. Dalmar held up his hands.

The conveyance was all arranged very quickly with only the legal matters to be dealt with. Christine and Suzanne renewed their daytime life, which revolved around Fly and shopping trips, plus a bit of gardening. Tim and Christine were off to Taunton that coming weekend, but, after that, they would start packing up at Beech Cottage. Even though Suzanne would be there to help Christine admitted she was dreading it. The thought of being near those woods filled her with renewed fear and gave her a dry, acrid taste in the mouth.

CHAPTER THIRTY-TWO

"UNLESS – THAT SOMEONE WAS KNOWN TO HIM."

Meanwhile, Jonathon Shure had arranged a meeting. There were only two other participants, Wilfred Blyte, the science officer and Stephen Knopner. On Wednesday evening, at the Forestry Commission's regional offices at Lyndhurst, the three men joined up: Wilfred's office was the venue, so he stayed on after his day's work. Jonathon collected Stephen from Yewhurst and drove over with him. The forest officer forewarned him about the state of Wilfred's office. "You will be lucky if you can find anywhere to sit down. I have never seen so many books in such a small place." When they arrived, Jonathon could see what he meant. There was no sign of any scientific instruments, just masses of reference books.

Jonathon's task, that evening, was to see if he could keep the public out of Yewhurst Wood, at least until November, and to inform the two forestry men of the systematic opinion concerning the Red Adder recorded sound. He had consulted with Sir Michael Ensford, and, also, two eminent zoologists based at the London Zoo.

By now, Stephen had been given carte blanche on the subject of public access. This was mainly due to his immediate superior's illness. Charles Brewster had been suffering recently with glandular fever.

Wilfred's keenness to find out about the latest information on the Red Adder was only too evident. "Come on – what's the latest on the snake itself?" he asked impatiently.

Jonathon had been dreading this, remembering the man's outburst at the conference. He braced himself. "Would it surprise you to know that our conclusion is that the Red Adder of Yewhurst ... " he paused, "that is what this reptile is officially known as, by the way – is an evolutionary freak."

"Ah ... at last," Wifred was beaming at him. Jonathon was amazed and he knew he must have shown it in his facial expression. "And I'll tell you something else; this is just the first of many in my opinion."

"What do you mean?" asked the zoologist.

"Granted, it may take unusual weather to help it along, but it is man's interference with nature that is the cause. I say this, as opposed to man's deliberate meddling if you get my drift." There then followed a long discussion about the use of pesticides and fertilisers, which, Wilfred was quite convinced, had brought about the existence of the extraordinary Red Adders. Stephen kept quiet most of the time. He was content, on this occasion, just to listen.

"Is it accepted," Stephen finally asked, "that there is now only one of the bastards?"

"You mean, with reference to the anonymous note?" said Jonathon.

"What's all this?" Wilfred knew nothing about it. Stephen explained briefly before Jonathon answered.

"We are of the opinion that if someone says they burnt the Red Adder that your man shot, then they probably did." Jonathon looked confident in this judgment.

"But who the blazes was watching us? They must have been pretty close, otherwise they wouldn't have had a clue where the body of the snake was. You would have thought Ginger would have spotted them from the tree he was climbing. He would have called out." Stephen remarked.

"Unless – that someone was known to him," Jonathon said quietly.

Stephen's eyebrows went up and he raised the first finger of his right hand. "Ah," he said. After a pause, he added, "If I had considered the matter properly, I should have left Jim Pearce with Ginger's body and brought the Land Rover to them. That would have avoided some distasteful press photographs, and you probably would have had a snake's remains to study. But – that man, Dalmar Hunter volunteered to carry Ginger, which, I am sure was damned hard work. It is almost as though; by taking him up on his offer, I was punishing him for leading us into all this. Perhaps I made a mistake."

Wilfred had thought that for some time, but, uncharacteristically, he elected to change the subject. "Got any theories about that extraordinary racket you have on tape – following the reporter's death? I mean – it was the snake – yes?"

"Well," Jonathon started, "there is a problem with that. Granted – it is a unique sound." Here he suddenly hunched his shoulders as though there might be an alarming implication. "You see a noise of that decibel rating, in most people's opinion, especially our lot, could not have come from a six-foot long snake. It would have to be a *great* deal larger. Probably double the size. Not only in length but girth as well. It is easy to see why. I won't bore you with the technicalities."

Neither Wilfred nor Stephen had any comment to add. They both remained silent; their minds occupied with thoughts on the implications.

At this point they officially closed the meeting and drove around the corner to a hotel for a drink in the bar. It was there that Stephen enlightened them both about the old local name for the Red Adder, 'John the Red.' He suggested to Jonathon that he talk to Dr David Andrews about it. Listening to him, Jonathon was amazed that the press had not got hold of this angle at all. They agreed, between them, that they would not tell the media. It could not possibly help matters.

A week later, after Tim and Christine returned from Taunton, hustle and bustle at the Claymans Heron suggested that the observation teams were getting things together. The overseas visitors (specialists in snake catching) were not staying at the Claymans, but at the White Horse in Romsey, in order that the few reporters still in the vicinity would not bother them.

Equipment, in the shape of large nets and special poles with loops on the end, among other items, were being delivered to the Forestry Commission's office at Chapp. There were to be three teams made up of two snake specialists, an army sniper and a medical person, who would have about them some anti-venom serum taken from a refrigerated source each morning. The eldest reptile expert would be the team leader in each case. One team was to be based a mile into the forest, another further down in an area not yet researched, and the last team would be over towards Chapp and the woodland near the centre of the village. Nothing was to be announced, but the authorities intended to get them in place a week ahead of schedule. The date set was the following Monday.

David Andrews called at Dalmar's house early in the evening on Thursday before Tim and Christine went away to Guildford: he had a difficult request to make. Facing up to Christine he came right out with it. "A television production company, Capital River T.V., wants to make what they term a 'sensible documentary' about the Red Adder. Would you agree to be interviewed as the only survivor following an attack?"

"David – what is the point? I can't remember anything about it," answered Christine straight away.

"What – nothing?" Dr Andrews looked taken aback. He fully expected that by now all of her memory of the incident would have returned.

"Absolutely nothing. Well – I remember setting out with Suzanne to find the Secret Pond ... and I remember waking up in hospital with a splitting headache. That any good?"

"No – hardly." He studied her face. It was impassive: beautiful, stubborn, but impassive. "Perhaps I should have another look at you? How have you been feeling?"

"You *are* looking at me David. I am fine – okay?"

He laughed, "All right – I'll leave you alone for now." He turned his attention to her sister-in-law. "In that case, Suzanne, I must ask if you could repeat the details you gave to the Forestry Commission at Beech Cottage?"

"When?" was her immediate reply.

"Oh, not for ages, sometime in the late autumn apparently."

"Sure, I'll be around." She said this without really thinking. She had not discussed things long-term with Dalmar. But, anyway, her brother and sister-in-law would need some help in their new house. While the doctor was there, Tim informed him of their impending move. He had heard that they were trying to sell Beech Cottage and was surprised at the quick result.

"Oh dear, I shall be losing two patients. Cheriton eh? Mind you – it is a very pretty village." He wished them well before grabbing the attention of Dalmar. "And what about you? Will you talk to the television people when I can arrange it?"

Dalmar was getting himself and Tim a beer at the time. He turned around and looking David straight in the eye said, "No."

"Oh," David looked shocked at the frankness. "Oh ... all right ... understood and all that." He was clearly embarrassed. "Right – well I must be on my way."

"David?" interrupted Dalmar. "Not my scene – okay? Going to have a beer?" He held up a bottle of cold Dutch lager.

"Uh – right – oh, no thank you – got a couple of calls to make ... cheerio for now." He waved to them all before turning to walk up the long path to the end of the garden.

"Dalmar – you are not leaving me to face the television crew, alone are you?" Suzanne looked worried.

"Didn't say I wouldn't hold your hand. Just not going to spout myself," he answered her. "Anyway, what the hell is he getting involved for? Fame hunting if you ask me."

"Oh, come on – that's not fair. That man has given up a lot of his time over that darn snake," Suzanne scolded him.

"Suppose," Dalmar acquiesced.

Tim came up and whispered in Dalmar's ear. "Been a naughty boy then?" Dalmar gave him a scowl and the two men retreated into the sitting room leaving the ladies to chat alone.

"Can you really not remember anything?" Suzanne almost stuck her head under Christine's face, while she was preparing runner beans at the kitchen sink. Christine raised her head a shade, and her face transposed to an enormous grin from ear to ear. Suzanne had never seen her do that before. Then Christine gave her a quick but obvious wink. Suzanne nearly dropped her drink. "You!" she spluttered. "You..." She was prevented from saying anything else by the wet palm of a hand placed over her mouth.

"Actually, it is a good way to handle it – I've decided." Christine explained. "The whole thing becomes like a bad nightmare and let's face it; we all have those from time to time." She looked at her sister-in-law, who instantly calmed down, but, nevertheless, smirked repeatedly for the next half an hour or so.

The two ladies were getting on well with the laborious business of packing. It was especially irksome given that Christine had already been through the exercise earlier on in the year, and Beech Cottage was meant to have been a family home for the foreseeable future. What did motivate them both was that they felt very uncomfortable being so near to Red Adder territory. Although there had never been any recorded attacks on human property, there was always a first time.

Tim had done some of the difficult jobs in the evenings, light shades and lamps that needed disconnecting and the original ceiling roses put back in their place: that kind of thing. It was especially galling to him. After all, this was supposed to have been their dream home. It had lasted approximately four months, and when you had to dismantle items such a short time after having put them in place, he would hardly have enjoyed it. By the time the pair left for Taunton on Friday evening, quite a lot had been achieved.

Early in the morning, on a dampish October day, the observation teams assembled at the church car park. The press were totally unaware, although it would not take them long to realise what was happening. Jonathon Shure had a sort of roving command of all the teams, simply because he had arranged the whole operation. He looked very different today. Casual cotton trousers, in a stone tint, and a corduroy brown shirt with two breast pockets replaced his normal smart suit. The manicure, however, was still immaculate and his dark silvery hair was neatly combed. His soft olive eyes darted everywhere.

The teams were made up of a mixed bunch, he considered. They included the various men experienced in reptile handling: two from Africa, one from Australia, one from North America and two from the United Kingdom. What intrigued Jonathon was the fact that some of them seemed to be attired in their country of origin's trekking style of clothing. Also, there was a quite frightening array of knife handles sticking out of sheaths attached to their belts. These belts portrayed an assortment of animal leathers.

The medical men all had the same black shoulder bag, which, among other things, contained the possible life saving anti-venom serum, individually cased in the latest small vacuum frozen containers. Then there were the British army riflemen in their operational uniforms of camouflage cotton. Needless to say, they looked the most professional of the lot.

When he thought it was the appropriate moment, Jonathon asked all the team members to gather around him. It took a little while for this to be successfully accomplished. Before starting his address, Jonathon thought it prudent to remind everyone present that they were on Church of England property. The vicar of Yewhurst had given his consent to its use, and the zoologist made them aware, although to most it was obvious, that they were on consecrated ground, therefore noise levels should be kept to a minimum.

"Gentlemen, in a moment I am going to ask the team leaders to introduce each member of their group so that we all know who is who, and with whom you are going to work, possibly, for the next week or so. But before I do, there are one or two things that you should all know.

Now, I apologize to those of you who are herpetologists and already have knowledge of some of the matters that I am going to mention. But I am quite sure that it is right that everybody taking part should hear this. Firstly, it is most important for you to know that the snake that is habiting these woods, behind me, is extremely dangerous. It has already taken the lives of three people, and very nearly killed a fourth. Furthermore, to our knowledge, it appears to be some sort of evolutionary freak in that nothing like it has existed before. It can attack from the air by gliding from trees. It can spit venom into your eyes with great accuracy. Finally, it can strike in the normal manner and possesses the deadliest of venom, probably in great quantity. In other words, once bitten the poison is not only very potent, but the dose will be massive due to the force of the injection, making a truly awful combination, hitherto, unknown in the world."

Some of the snake experts looked at Jonathon and raised their eyes. This was something none of them had expected. "However," he went on, "we don't think we are talking about a particularly large snake. One witness has talked about 'six feet', so let us say a maximum of seven." He kept his own thoughts on this to himself, fearing that some of the participants might pull out if they knew of his fears. "There are some basic facts I should like to make you aware of. If a person has the odour of a snake's diet on them, and we are talking principally of rodents, lizards etc, then that person will become prey. It might, therefore, be prudent to be aware of this ... yes – even rabbit droppings." Jonathon quickly threw this in. He knew that some of the men here might well question the snake's size if he dwelt too much on the possibility of rabbits themselves as prey. "Snakes are very aware of their surroundings and have the ability to detect nervousness in an individual person. Normally, it would then go on the defence. However, the Red Adder, up to now has shown nothing but aggression. This makes it all the more dangerous. Assume, therefore, that it is out to get you and watch your back!" He paused to allow the last words to sink in.

"All right – that's it from me. We shall be in constant communication with each other as your team leaders will explain. The day's observation will finish at five-thirty this afternoon and we will all meet here afterwards, so please make your way back to this car park in good time. That is, presuming that nothing dramatic has happened in the meantime. In the event of an encounter by a team other than your own, your team radio will keep you informed. Thank you – and good luck."

Jonathon then introduced the three-team leaders to everyone, and they, in turn, read out which personnel were attached to them. It was a full half an hour before all three groups were ready to move off. Only the reptile experts knew each other already. Familiarising the medical staff and the army riflemen was something that could not be done in a few minutes.

A week later, Dalmar and Suzanne were loading up the T.R.6, with an excited Fly looking on during the early hours of Monday morning. They would not see Tim and Christine for seven days as Tim would be dropping his wife off at Dalmar's cottage a good hour after they had left. Fly was not the only one who was excited. Dalmar had his car serviced during the week and had given it a good valet the day before. He was like a child looking forward to his first cycle trip away from home, and Suzanne bustled about with her wonderful bright eyes showing vibrant anticipation of what was to come.

The only trouble with using a two-seater sports car to go on vacation is the lack of luggage space. It was fortunate that Suzanne kept her mountain clothes at her aunt and uncle's house, because there was only room for the one suitcase. Fly took up all the space in the small storage area behind the front seats. After finishing a final cup of coffee, they set off on the first stage of their journey, heading for the Savernake Forest and Marlborough.

The journey went well. They joined the south-north motorway route just past Cheltenham, to take them to the other side of Birmingham before stopping for some refreshments. Apart from a halt to let Fly have a run at Savernake earlier, they made very good time. "At this rate," said Dalmar, "we will be in the Lakes by four." And they were.

CHAPTER THIRTY-THREE

NEVER BEFORE WITNESSED BY MANKIND.

The observation teams failed to sight anything out of the ordinary in the first week. Jonathon Shure was extremely disappointed. 'How come,' he thought to himself, 'a girl takes an early morning walk in these woods – gets herself killed, and *we* have not seen anything in six days!'

Now well into October, the first autumnal colours were beginning to appear on some of the deciduous trees. The gentle tints of gold and sienna, especially in sunlight, looked pleasing.

By the following Tuesday some members of the various teams were beginning to doubt that the creature they sought still inhabited the area.

After the usual lunch of soup, sandwiches and some fruit, Private Brian Dace, the sniper attached to the team keeping watch in the furthest extremes of the forest, announced that he was going for a short stroll to stretch his legs. The other three members of the team assumed he was going to relieve himself. This was not the soldier's intention, at least not the prime intention. There was a strict rule in force that smoking was not permitted due to the fire risk. Although there had been some rain recently, it was still abnormally dry, and Stephen Knopner was taking no chances. Private Dace had sneaked a quick roll-up cigarette yesterday, and he intended to do the same today. It was just too long to go without tobacco as far as he was concerned.

For his group, the morning had been uneventful. The routine of getting the equipment to their station, and then to spread out, while keeping sight of at least one member of the team, had gone according to plan. They spent their time scanning tall trees – but not exclusively. For all anyone knew, Mary Taylor might have had her encounter from the ground, so a wary eye was kept in all directions. Brian Dace often changed his routine to practice un-slinging his sniper rifle, loading and taking aim at a point on a distant tree. As he always did this from a standing position, he would twist his left arm through the sling before raising the butt of the rifle to his shoulder to give extra steadiness to his aim. Quite often, he would incorporate a range set on the telescopic sight and refocus the lens accordingly.

Before setting out for his smoke, he adjusted the beret on his head, which bore the badge of the Royal Hampshire Regiment with its emblem of a tiger, super scribed 'India' and a double red rose fringed in gold. All three of the snipers taking part were from this regiment. They were barracked some twenty odd miles away.

Continuing on the path until its natural bend took him out of sight; he extricated his tin of tobacco and papers from one of his uniform trouser pockets. In the last hour the wind had gone around to the northwest. As well as having a distinctive chill, it also brought strong gusty conditions. Brian had to tuck himself a little into the trees to get shelter. He propped the rifle up against a trunk and made himself a cigarette, struck a match, and drew to ignite the end. The first draught of smoke was blissful and gave him a very pleasant feeling in his head: a feeling of exotic calmness. He was not a powerfully built man and had veered on the slighter frame all through his childhood. Under tight blond curly hair, peeking out from his beret on a low forehead, two large pale blue eyes looked out into the forest.

His mind went to his family; his wife who had seemingly unknown limits to her cheerfulness, and to his two young daughters. He adored them, and so found himself looking forward to leave due to him at the end of next week.

While on a combined cadet force summer camp at the age of sixteen he had discovered his accuracy at shooting. Then it was target practice with a .22 rifle. Two years later he came top for his county with the standard .303 army rifle and was third in his class at the Bisley shooting ranges in 1972. Obviously, these skills were put to good use when he joined the Royal Hampshire's a year later.

When he had finished smoking, he carefully extinguished the butt of the cigarette by crushing it under one of his army boots, until he was sure that it was. Then he rose to his feet and did what the others had supposed he had gone away to do. Zipping up his trousers, he walked back onto the path and re-slung the L42 Enfield rifle over his right shoulder. Alerted by distant voices, he turned to look in that direction. No doubt, they belonged to the observation team nearest to his own, and when he thought about it, they were not that far away. His team were currently searching in the southern extremity of their area, and, quite possibly, this other team were looking in the most northern part of their patch.

Beyond – he found himself studying a very tall tree. He did not know what variety, but he was pretty sure it was not native to southern England. It reminded him of the giant sequoia, which he had seen often when visiting relatives on the west coast of America a few years ago.

Incredibly for that distance, something held his attention. It looked like a small, elongated flash of red very close to the top of the tree: so far away, it was miniscule, but because it was odd, caught the eye. That is to say, it caught his eye, for ninety-five out of a hundred of us would not have the long-range vision to be able to see it. He turned to go back to join the rest of the team. Then he stopped and turned around. It was still there – stationary – a speck of deep red lying amongst the branches high in the fir. Taking his camouflaged coloured monocular from a narrow trouser pocket, he held it up to his right eye, and focused on the summit of the tree in question. With the monocular's twenty-five times magnification, he could clearly make out something very peculiar. A wild thought occurred to him, and he started to retrace his steps back to his group, but came to a halt, almost immediately. 'It might be gone if he was not really sharp,' he thought, his mind racing. He turned around again and started running, tightly holding on to the squat telescope. He knew he was way out of range to try a shot; he needed to get considerably closer as quickly as possible. The other observation team must be about five hundred yards away, somewhere around a bend in the path, up ahead. 'Perhaps he could make contact with them,' he thought hopefully.

After running about half that distance an awkward lying stone caught him out as his left foot came down hard. He lost balance, winced as his ankle turned a little, stumbled, but did not fall. He recovered himself and was about to start running again when he glanced up to peer into the distance at that tree. The red speck had gone. He cursed, and, raising the monocular to his eye, studied the higher most regions of the giant tree. Unexpectedly, into his view came dots of red appearing very close to the top: they were moving. He was still far too far away to execute a shot, and, anyway, he was breathing too hard to make a sniper's effort.

Private Dace placed the small telescope back in its special pocket and started to run towards the still distant tree once more. He was certain, now, that he was doing the right thing. If he could make up five hundred yards or even less, he might have a chance, if whatever it was stayed there long enough for his breathing to return to normal. With this, in mind he tried to go at a fast trot, rather than a sprint. The rifle bounced uncomfortably on his shoulder so he un-slung it and carried it in his right hand. He would have time enough to load when he got within range.

With the naked eye, after a while, he could make out that the red dots had reached the summit of the sequoia, and then something happened that caused him to stop dead in his stride, gasping and standing in a crabbed position, head craning towards the tree, as though in disbelief. A strange object appeared to have launched itself from the treetop. It was moving through the air: a ribbon like shape, holding its height in the strong wind, like a kite. For what seemed ages, it hung suspended. But it was not stationary: one thing gave away the fact that it was moving. The ribbon, forming a static triple S, started to get larger – because it was getting nearer, until it became obvious that it was not ribbon-like, but possessed a body form, while not completely round, nevertheless a form: an animal form. Brian Dace became aware of an unusual feeling that rapidly enveloped his brain. It was the feeling that he was watching something unique: a happening never before witnessed by mankind.

After what seemed like some time, but probably occurring in a mere second or two, the flying object disappeared behind a bank of conifers on the bend in front of him, some three hundred and seventy-five yards away.

The soldier straightened up. 'Well – that was that – but should he continue?' He thought the other team should be right about where it landed. Unexpectedly, he had no time to think about this. First, there were some distant shouts. And then coming around that bend – heading straight towards him, lower, but still at thirty to forty feet off the ground was that formation of stark, deep red. It was now considerably bigger, and a fear grew upon the soldier. An atmosphere of such intensity enveloped him. Whatever it was seemed to have an aura of immense power about it. He stood with his mouth open, until the awful truth dawned. It could easily reach him and would probably land just about where he was standing. He brought the rifle to waist height and snapped back the bolt of the loading chamber. His left hand streaked to the flap pocket of his khaki trousers. Blessedly, the button released quickly, and his hand closed over a shell. All the time he kept glancing toward the flying object. It was no longer an object. Quite clearly, it was now visible as a very large snake: a serpent. Suddenly, its head seemed to drop and with it came a rapid descent that brought its approach much faster than he had anticipated. He dropped the live shell on the ground. Straight in front of him, ten to twelve feet in the air was a monstrous snake, with its head raised above the line of the body. Due to the distended skin that body looked enormous. Its mouth was wide open. Brian could clearly make out the awesome looking fangs. A momentary feeling, placing him in a prehistoric age, flashed through his mind. He let out an exclamation, and raised the rifle up horizontally, at arm's length, in an effort to ward it off. This should have worked, but just before impact the giant snake's head dipped, impossibly, under the rifle, and its jaws closed over Brian's right shoulder. He screamed as a massive injection of pain hit the nerves all through the base of his neck and down one side of his body. The force of the impact hurled the soldier to the ground with such power that his head went back hard against the solid clay soil. His rifle fell with a clatter beside him. Fortunately, … the soldier felt no further pain.

CHAPTER THIRTY-FOUR

UNUSUAL – FOR A PINE.

Private Dace's scream caused not only members of his own team to run in his direction, but, also, the team that he had just been trying to contact. It was not just the scream that brought this team heading towards him. Two of them, although in utter disbelief, had seen the snake fly over their heads.

First to arrive at the scene was the medical man from this group. Other team members were following with equipment. Because he had had farther to come, the Australian leader of Brian Dace's squad took a little while to arrive. Breathless, he went up to the medic attending to the soldier. "Any – chance – of him – talkin'?"

"I'm afraid not." There was a long pause. "This man is dead." The speaker was a young doctor from Winchester Hospital. He had already loosened the buttons on the top part of the soldier's uniform, having been alerted by serious skin discolouration on the man's neck. The bite wound was obvious. There was no point in using the anti-venom serum. He did not even bother to take his medical bag from his shoulder.

"You've got to be kiddin'?" said the Australian in a strong Outback dialect.

"See for yourself," the doctor offered, standing up with an outstretched arm pointing at the body.

The Australian, whose name was Jack Kanton, did so. He bent down and investigated the face of the prostrate soldier. Soon, he said, "This guy have a weak heart – eh?"

He looked at everybody, and everybody looked at him, until the leader of the other team, an American said, "Can't say that's all that likely." He spoke in a southern state drawl.

"How do you mean?" questioned Jack.

"Weell – they wouldn't choose a guy with a weak heart to serve in the British Army – would they?"

Jack took this in before making a curt nod. "Anyone see anythin'?" he asked. This was when the other team members told him about the large, red reptilian like creature that had literally sailed over their heads.

One of them mentioned that it was very big and he added the observation, "Awesome!" Jack took this in and immediately looked toward the interior of the conifer plantation next to them, as did the other snake experts almost in unison. No one heeded the farther side of the path, there seemed little doubt from anyone as to which way the big reptile had gone. They all assumed it would head for maximum cover.

After a while, Jack Kanton and the American went into a quick discussion. "The nets will be next to useless in there," Jack pointed at the confined dark mass of trees in front of them.

"Agreed – so it's the rods?"

"You with one and me with the other." Jack said 'other' with the tone higher than the rest of the sentence, as though asking a question. They then explained what they planned to do to the rest of them. Jack and the American would enter the conifer area immediately adjacent to where the body of the soldier lay. They would both carry a long pole with a grab hook on the end. This was a contraption that had a pulley leaver; so that once you had ensnared the snake's head with the loop, a quick pull on the lever by your hand, at the other end of the pole, would trap its head – hopefully. The two other snake experts were to take up positions with the nets on the edge of the path, and the medics would stand by.

First, Jack Kanton got on the field telephone and informed Jonathon Shure, in what was his normal brusque manner, of the disastrous encounter. Jonathon, sounding horrified, said he would be with them as soon as possible, but to carry on with their plan.

Jack was a big man, standing six foot four inches tall with a powerful physique to go with it. Now approaching his fiftieth year, the grey shaggy hairstyle gave him a wild appearance. He had hollow looking cheeks that rose to encompass a large mouth with a generous supply of teeth. His cold grey eyes could be transformed when he smiled, but he rarely did so. The years spent in the Australian Outback had given him a leathery skin. To some he had an imposing appearance.

"Right, let's get on with it," he barked. "Could your army man stand ready loaded?" He threw this suggestion at the other team leader, the American, known as Rattlesnake Ben. Between the two of them there was a massive wealth of knowledge about poisonous snakes. Ben looked at the sitting figure of his army sniper. He was staring fixedly at the body of Brian Dace. They had not been close friends but would have known each other well. No doubt he was shocked, but it must have crossed his mind that this would be one of the last places he would expect to witness a colleague's death.

The two team leaders, agreeing to return after fifteen minutes if their search was negative, entered under the low overhanging branches of the fir plantation, about twenty-five yards apart, so as to be in hearing distance of one another. This was not going to be easy. Although there was no ground growth to negotiate the trees were only about eight feet apart and, consequently, the bottom branches caused considerable obstruction for a human being trying to make his way between them. Jack, with his extra height, had to stoop most of the time and Rattlesnake Ben who was nearly six-foot tall had similar problems. They used the grab poles to assist in fending off light growth, and there were a few grunts from both of them. Then, after a while, the necessity to keep quiet took over, especially when they lost the light from the pathway behind them.

It became very dark with the abundant growth of the pines above shutting out most daylight. Only a little filtered through here and there.

Ben stopped his advance for a while to wait until his eyes became accustomed to the gloom. He had a slightly bulbous nose, more on one side than the other. There was a tight dimple in the middle of his large chin instead of a cleft, and he had lots of wispy grey hair on the back of his broad neck. He extracted a compass from his mountain jacket pocket and checked the bearing. The luminous north spot glowed enough for him to do this successfully. It would be easy to get lost in this lot, he knew only too well, having made an idiot of himself on two occasions when he was a young man. Now, he was a very experienced woodsman used by the United States government to assist them in wilderness knowledge all over their country. He could still hear Jack moving through the woods, a short distance away. He cursed as his bald head snagged against a low branch. Reaching up with one of his massive, calloused hands he felt the tender spot. He could easily make out the blood on his fingers as he pulled his hand away. He wiped it against his deep green heavy fabric shirt and then ignored the wound.

About now, Ben decided to concentrate a little more on looking for a large venomous snake. His deep brown eyes peered into the heavy growth. His knowledge was extensive, especially when it came to all types of rattlesnake. They gave him no fear whatsoever, for he knew how to prevent a strike in the unlikely event of accidentally getting too close.

He was quite sure, what he was likely to come across, was something like the eastern diamond rattlesnake, which can reach eight feet in length. It inhabited the coastal plains of Louisiana and North Carolina and was considered a dangerous snake. It did not, however, glide from treetops, and it would have to be severely provoked before going on the attack, also, possessing the ability to spit venom was not part of its arsenal. Ben, therefore, refrained from keeping his eyes only on the ground, which he would have done when looking out for a rattler. He now had to frequently peer above him, with prolonged studying of the lower branches of the trees. He guessed that, right now, his target was probably coloured in tones of deep brown, which would blend in very well with the surroundings. It was now presumed, by most of the experts, that the Red Adder only became red when attacking.

Satisfied that he was, himself, in tune with these surroundings, he bent down and crawled under a particularly low set of branches, and entered some new scenery, except that it was very much the same as that which he had already come through. Ben headed further directly into the plantation. He was not sure how much farther he went, but he noticed that the sounds emanating from Jack had ceased. Everything seemed eerily quiet. Either the Australian had stopped his advance, or they had drifted apart. Ben placed the catchpole down on the ground and moved forward a little, before standing to his full height by putting his head between two branches. The release of discomfort to his back was blissful. He looked around him: just the usual dark boughs and twigs. The mass of small dead conifer leaves at his feet formed a sort of

The Shy Avenger

spongy carpet. 'A guy could sleep soundly on that,' he thought to himself. He glanced along the branches immediately by his head. They were thick and tangled, almost interwoven, unusual – for a pine.

Suddenly, his mind went blind numb. That was not a branch interwoven with another. It was a large brown snake coiled around a bough, about two feet away from his head! Hardly breathing, he let his eyes follow along the body, until, there, just in front of him, appearing from the other side of the branch, came a broad triangular head about seven to eight inches across. At first, Ben wanted to cry out, but the sound became a gargle of dryness in his throat. Two, vivid amber eyes, with a vertical diamond rust and black coloured pupil stared straight at him. Ben knew that this was a viper from the shape of the head, but in all his years he had never seen anything quite so ugly. The corrugated flutes, disappearing under the base of the head, seemed extra-large in the dull light. Being as their two heads were, by now, only about two feet apart, Ben was surprised that the snake's mouth had not come open for a strike. At the same time the top of the reptile's head started to change colour. In the deep gloom, a brazen red tone progressively made its way down the body, disappearing on the other side of the branch with the snake's coil, until the full colour change reached nearly to the tail. Now, even more prominent, were the black zigzag markings on its back. This, without a doubt, was the largest reptile he had ever seen. Ben wanted to duck his head down and run, but his nerves went taught in determination.

Although Ben had no direct experience of the spitting cobras, he knew what was going on. As the Red Adder's eyes locked onto his, Ben started to sway his head gently backwards and forwards – very, very slowly. The snake tried to follow, and Ben immediately alternated the sway, faltering the return move every now and then, so that the reptile got confused and unable to line up a trajectory. All the while this was going on, Ben's right hand slowly extracted his carbon steel hunting knife from its sheaf. This was his pride and joy. An Idaho craftsman had especially made it. The U.S. government presented it to him after twenty-five years' service. Keeping up the faltering sway, Ben gradually brought the long blade up to waist height. Now – he was ready. One quick jab upward and the Red Adder would be ready for the Natural History Museum. But he had forgotten something, and all his knowledge could not have armed his defences for what took place next. The snake's mouth gushed open and let forth a hideous noise that left Ben desperately trying to keep hold of the knife. All he wanted to do – was cover his ears!

Nearby, Jack Kanton stopped his advance as though paralysed when he heard the dreadful shrieking hiss. As soon as it ceased, after at least twenty seconds or so, he shouted and began crashing his way through the dense firs in the direction from which the awful noise had come.

On the pathway, everyone else acted in alarm at the racket.

Jonathon Shure who had arrived, and, just that second, switched off the engine on the Land Rover, was just in time to witness it, for the first time, close at hand. Then they heard Jack shout as he tried to make his way towards Rattlesnake Ben. All of them, two herpetologists, two medics, a single rifleman and Jonathon went to the very edge of the plantation and started to edge into it. "Hold it!" yelled Jonathon. "One doctor and myself!" He crouched down and started fending off the small twigs and branches in his way.

Jack came across a manic, charging Ben, trying to run through the plantation. He kept crashing into trees and branches all the while holding his hands over his face. "Here mate! Take my hand – for god's sake!" yelled Jack. He grabbed Ben's right arm and started pulling him in the direction of the pathway.

Shortly, Jonathon and a medic joined them. Nobody asked any questions. They pushed and pulled and pressed down on Ben's head at the right moments until they were in the light near the edge of the rows of pines. Then they saw Ben's face. It was a sickly blue except for a dreadfully swollen purple and black smeared nose. His eyes were blood red, and his mouth and hand movements were of a man in terrible pain. He stumbled out onto the pathway and grotesquely stood in front of the body of the soldier, before jerking his thumb back over his head toward the plantation – once … twice. Then he let out a desperate – hard toned scream – before falling face down with a loud thud – onto the unforgiving clay. Perhaps one or two of those standing near him should have been in support, but the sheer horror of Ben's facial appearance, held them all in rigid shock.

The remaining army sniper who had loaded up and was holding his rifle at the ready, turned urgently back to the forest as though expecting something terrible to follow the men out.

The first man to go to Ben's aid was the young doctor who had been waiting outside the plantation. The other one came up right behind him, after extracting his medical bag that had got caught up in some briars at the last minute. Between them, they turned the big man over. His face now seemed to be almost totally dark blue and purple, with some redness around the nose. Immediately, one of them started to prepare anti-venom serum. The other doctor carried out a check on the injured man's condition. Jonathon and the rest crowded round, looking on with anxiety spread over all their faces. Very soon the medic carrying out the examination held out a hand to stop the other from filling the syringe any further. There was no pulse. Rattlesnake Ben - had died. Attempts at resuscitation would be pointless. His brain had been fatally poisoned.

Reading the situation from the body language of the doctors, one of the snake experts grabbed Jack's catching pole and started to head toward the conifers. "Hold it!" shouted Jonathon after him, in a very direct way. "That will do. I am not risking any more lives. We are wrapping this up – right now!"

"I'll get the bastard!" The man with the pole pleaded.

"No – Kris," Jonathon ordered. "I'm sorry, but two men dead within half an hour. We have to leave it! There are acres of plantation that the snake could have moved to by now." Nobody else disagreed. Most of them wanted to get away – far away, as quickly as possible.

"Where'd it get him?" Jack asked the doctors.

"It looks like – right on the end of his nose from what I can see," replied the one near the body in a hushed and revered tone. "But we will have to await a post-mortem. There might be other bites, you see."

"I doubt it. One strike – then away," came the Australian drawl. "Must 'ave caught him at head height, from a branch." Here he paused and sighed. "Bloody shame. Good man – Ben." At this, the herpetologist who had tried to re-enter the plantation, a sensitive black man from Kenya, broke down and started sobbing. The other snake expert went over to comfort him.

One by one, Rattlesnake Ben and Brian Dace's bodies were placed, side-by-side, in the four-wheel drive vehicle. A catcher pole was still in the plantation where Ben had left it. Jonathon decreed that it could stay there. One or two items of clothing and equipment were still at the base site of Jack's observation team, so a doctor and one of the snake experts went to retrieve them, with strict instructions to watch out for themselves and to run for it at the slightest sign of anything untoward. Jack and Jonathon drove off in the vehicle with the nets, leaving the rest to return to the car park on foot.

On the way Jonathon radioed ahead to organise an ambulance. Both casualties might be dead, but the correct routines had to be carried out. He also called up the leader of the remaining observation team and instructed him to pack up. Naturally, he wanted to know why, and was extremely shocked to hear of the tragedies. They had already been alerted that something was wrong, having overheard the earlier conversation when Jonathon was originally contacted.

Christine and Tim spent Monday night on their own at Dalmar's cottage. They brought back some much-needed items from Suzanne's wardrobe at her parent's home. Although a few garments had been sent by post, courteously dispatched by her mother over the last couple of months, she was going to need some of her winter clothes very soon. Late on Tuesday afternoon, Christine heard a great deal of activity going on by the Claymans Heron. She decided to postpone a visit to Beech Cottage and listen to a radio news broadcast at six o'clock, to see if something had happened. Tim got home in time to hear it as well. Obviously, the main news item was about the deaths of the young army man and the American. Rattlesnake Ben's body was to be flown to the United States immediately.

"Tim," I'm not asking *you* to do this, because I know you are busy at work. But I should like to try and bring forward our completion date. The sooner we leave Beech Cottage – the better." She looked at her husband in a demanding, rather than a pleading way. "I'll contact our solicitor in the morning – okay?" Tim went to his wife and kissed her.

CHAPTER THIRTY-FIVE

SHE WOULD NEVER HAVE ENVISAGED.

Dalmar and Suzanne had decided to boycott television during their holiday, not because of John the Red, but just as a change. Suzanne's aunt and uncle hardly ever used it anyway. Maggie said that her husband only watched major sporting events, most particularly the university boat race, and she, herself, was a book person. She fussed about over Dalmar and even more so over Fly, who seemed to be enjoying himself in the strange surroundings. There was so much new sniffing to be done.

Because of the recent newspaper stories, Maggie asked Suzanne for information about the Red Adders, but she left it alone when she sensed that it was distressing for the girl. They were rewarded with one of her aunt's noted Lancashire hot-pot dishes. Dalmar ate rather too much and his tummy hurt afterwards. Suzanne's uncle, Reginald, told him that he had felt like that on numerous occasions following some of his wife's dishes. Judging by his rather rotund appearance, Dalmar was not surprised. They were a childless couple, which explained why Reginald got spoilt, and Margaret tended to fuss over Suzanne as if she were her own daughter.

The holiday couple went to bed early. They were both tired after the long journey, even though the traffic levels had been sparse.

As promised, Suzanne took Dalmar into Grasmere village on the Tuesday morning, and he spent far too much money on mountain apparel for himself. Although Suzanne was already well equipped with the right clothes, he insisted on buying her a large, cuddly woollen sweater. When she tried it on, she looked adorable, her bright eyes twinkling over the big roll neck collar of navy blue. He bought it because he liked looking at her wearing it. She did not complain. The knitting had been done, with some skill, using very good quality Scottish wool.

Displayed in the window of a shop selling posters and framed prints was a large study of a butterfly. It caught Dalmar's eye. Suzanne saw the picture almost at the same time, and she instantly recognised it. The Hampshire Constabulary had returned all Mary Taylor's personal effects to her father. He had the film in her camera processed and released the pictures to the media. Newspaper supplements and magazines used the coloured photographs of the woodland. Great emphasis was placed on their actual location: it being part of the likely habitat of the Red Adders. The study of the Purple Emperor butterfly had been shown on television. It was a remarkably good shot of this rare insect. Being curious, they entered the shop and made enquiries. The proprietor told them it was, currently, the best-selling poster print, and sales were breaking all records. Mary Taylor, posthumously, had achieved the fame she had craved, and in a direction that she would never have envisaged. Due to royalties, her daughter's future private education funding was virtually secure.

In the afternoon a steady drizzle was falling, but that did not stop them motoring over to Buttermere lake via Honister pass. They executed a short climb up the lower slopes of a mountain, traversing over to their right to come all the way down by a tumbling stream. At times, it was possible to carry out a great deal of the descent in the beck, jumping from rock to rock. It was such good fun that they arrived back at the car flushed with exuberance.

It had been sheer joy to watch Fly, in the kind of country that was his birth-right, making constant dashes hither and thither. Dalmar kept him away from the higher areas as there were sheep grazing. As an untrained sheep dog, he would be an unknown quantity. When they took him on an actual mountain walk later in the week, it would be necessary to have him on a reign until he learnt to obey his master's commands. The dog's antics coming down the stream were sometimes comical and often downright noisy as he barked in utter enjoyment.

And so it was that they left Maggie and Reg on Wednesday morning to go to their self-catering cottage in Langdale. They stopped in the town of Ambleside, on the way, to get supplies. While Suzanne looked for their requirements in a small supermarket, Dalmar sat outside a cafe with his dog, enjoying a cup of coffee and watching the passers-by. Some of them were local people going about their daily tasks, but the majority, like him, were tourists.

His tranquillity was suddenly dashed. A folded daily newspaper displayed on a stand caught his eye. The headline read: 'RED ADDER CLAIMS TWO MORE VICTIMS.'

"Are you going to buy it?" Dalmar turned around in his seat at the sound of his loved one's voice. Then he nodded and went to do just that. Suzanne placed her shopping bags under the table and stroked Fly's soft hair around the underside of his neck, her man returned with the newspaper and a coffee in a plastic container for her. In some trepidation, they read the front page together. After a while, Suzanne spoke. "I think I had better find a telephone and give Christine a ring; see if she is all right. Those poor men and their families. Honestly darling, it is just too awful!"

"There's a telephone kiosk just around the corner," Dalmar told her. He stood up and gathered a handful of loose change from his trouser pocket. "Here, take these coins. That should do." Fly made a move to go with her. "No. Stay boy," his master commanded. The collie gave a light whine and then lay down again.

She had to wait for a few minutes as there was someone else using the call box, but fortunately, Christine was at Dalmar's house when she got through. "Chris, we have only just heard the news. How terrible! Are you and Tim okay?"

"Hello Suz. Yes, we are both fine." She paused to gather herself. "I know – it's horrid. I won't go to Beech Cottage without Tim. Just can't do it. The Claymans is absolutely crawling with press people. We never walk over – always use a car – and while we are there, we never answer the door to anyone unless they're familiar. How are you both getting on – enjoying it?"

"Immensely! We're just going on to our self-catering cottage. I was buying some food when we saw the headline in a newspaper. We were worried about you – on your own there." She tactfully did not mention her original panicky concern on seeing the headline, although, she realised almost at once that Aunt Maggie would have heard if a family member was involved.

"Actually, it is Tim who will be on his own. I'm going to mum and dad's tomorrow. He will be joining me at the weekend and then it's frantic last-minute packing, early next week. I have managed to bring forward the move date. Beech Cottage will cease to be ours as from next Thursday, all being well. Stand by with your muscles: we need you."

"Oh ... have you got the removal men coming?"

"Yes, don't worry. I was teasing you! You can help me with our lighter clobber."

"Of course." Susanne had a light chuckle to her voice. "Look, the money is going to run out soon. I will talk with you next Monday – okay?"

"Look forward to it Suz. Now go and drag that man of yours up a mountain or two. Bye ... and thanks for calling."

"Look after yourselves. Lots of love." Suzanne put down the receiver and went back to Dalmar and Fly.

Their accommodation in the Langdale Valley was sparse, but it had all they needed. Its strongest attribute was a glorious view of the Langdale Pikes, and when evening came, the light showed off the two lumpy peaks to their best effect. Sometimes they took on the appearance of crouching lions.

Fly was itching to get out there and they had to take him for a long walk, but neither of them objected. Suzanne loved this part of the world. The mountain air suited her.

They enjoyed each other's company to the full over the next few days. As the weather was fair, they decided to climb the Pikes on their first day.

Poor Fly had to stay on a lead all the time. Dalmar used the situation to train him not to chase after the sheep. Whenever he tried to pull away with an obvious intention, he would get a short sharp, "No!" thrown at him and whenever he did as he was told he would get words of praise – not to mention the odd treat. The important matter was to ensure that when, finally, he would be allowed off the lead, he must obey the commands, "Stay" and "Heel" immediately.

Suzanne was rather surprised at her boyfriend's fitness on the mountain. After he got over the initial breathlessness and aching upper leg muscles, he seemed to settle into a natural fell walker's gait.

Inexperienced mountain trekkers tend to rush at the steep slopes. This results in numerous pauses being required to regain their strength. Seasoned walkers will take their time, and use the full soles of their feet, rather than putting all the weight on the ball of the foot. After an hour or two, this makes a great deal of difference to a walker's overall stamina. They both shared the same ideal when it came to the enjoyment of the terrain. Neither of them were that motivated about attaining summits. The most important recreation was to find the best viewpoint, sometimes not the highest, and then to spend long periods of silence gazing at the panoramas.

This recreation was a great deal more enjoyable when the precipitation habits of the Lakeland were in abeyance. Regretfully, this was a rare event, but the abundant lakes and tumbling gills had to be filled by something. It was not so much pouring rain that obscured the view, but mist. Mist from dampness: mist from low clouds. Therefore, if you had a good day on the fells, it was generally because of finding one with a kind climate. Dalmar and Suzanne had two such days. They were lucky.

On Friday, they visited a particularly beautiful area called Tarn Hows, near Coniston. The scenery consisted of a series of picturesque lakes balanced with forest backdrops and the surrounding fells. The full, rich autumnal colours on the trees were beautiful in their own right, but when doubled up by their reflections in the water, the effect was mind stilling. Dalmar and Suzanne could appreciate the area's appeal, even though they witnessed it in a steady fall of light rain. Fly ... well he charged all over the place, unperturbed.

Thoroughly invigorated in physical health and well-being they made the long car journey back to Hampshire on the Sunday, to a quiet cottage. At such times, it was extra special to have a dog as companion. The animal instantly gave the home a sense of being lived in.

Early that evening, after they had enjoyed a meal of scrambled eggs, cooked a la Suzanne style with Dijon mustard, a thought suddenly occurred to the girl. It was a thought she found troubling. She confided it to Dalmar. "Tell me, in the original story of John the Red – and I don't think anyone is arguing about this – didn't the snake get scared off from the Great Mile and move? I mean with all this activity going on, mightn't the same thing happen?" Her man put down the book he was reading and pondered her question. He thought for rather too long. "Hello!" she said impatiently, "Anyone at home?"

He looked up. His mind could see a lot more than she was bargaining for. Finally, he said, "That – Suzanne, is a very good point. In fact, I don't think we can leave it there. Somebody else may have thought of it, but I don't think we can take that for granted."

"Are you going to talk to David Andrews?" she asked him, surprise showing in the furrow on her brow.

"No," – he hesitated before saying, "This man – Jonathon Shure. He is in charge, I believe. And he said to phone him if we came up with anything useful. My darling – I think you have."

Dalmar did not delay, but when he telephoned the Claymans Heron hotel, he was told that Mr Shure would not be returning until the following day. "I'll call him from my office," he told Suzanne. She was a trifle surprised at his keenness. After all, usually, he tried to avoid any involvement. But she left it at that and did not enquire further.

The next morning, at Beech Cottage, Christine and Suzanne enjoyed a major catch up, all the while carrying on with the loathsome task of packing china, glass and cooking vessels in several cardboard boxes. In such a short time, it was amazing how much had been added to their general possessions since arriving at Beech Cottage.

By the time Jonathon Shure had driven down from London, he was still uncertain as to what to do concerning the Red Adder. Unsurprisingly to him, there had been some unsuitable criticism of his handling of things so far, particularly from the press. There was, however, one undertaking, which he had arranged to take place on Wednesday morning. He had chartered an aerial photography company to carry out a thorough sweep of Yewhurst Wood, subject to satisfactory visibility. The long-range weather forecast was good, overcast, but that was an advantage. Too much sunshine caused glare that could hide the vital information.

Any further use of the observation teams would have to involve considerably more manpower. This would almost certainly mean the use of troops. His instinct mistrusted this: an army to kill one snake. It seemed ridiculous. He could imagine the press slaughtering him with their criticism. During the afternoon, he received two telephone calls, which radically assisted him in making up his mind.

The first was from Dalmar Hunter. When his secretary called him, while he was in the bathroom in his suite at the Claymans Heron, he had to think about the name for a second or two before it registered. He went to the little study area of the room and took the call. "Hello – nice to hear from you," he said sincerely.

"Good afternoon – do you have a minute?" Dalmar asked.

"Yes, by all means."

"This fact may have already occurred to you and your advisors, so stop me if it has."

"All right."

"Are you familiar with the 1947- 48 Red Adder?"

"Yes, Allen Haddle gave us a run down at the conference."

"Right, do you recall that the snake moved to a different territory in 1948?"

"Ye-s." Jonathon wondered where this was leading.

"Do you know why it moved, or why it is presumed that it moved? And bear in mind that it didn't just go next door, so to speak."

"Didn't they carry out a large sweep of the area? Of course, it was a much smaller patch; couldn't do the same thing in Yewhurst Wood, well not practically. It would take thousands..." He stopped as his brain grasped what this was all about. "Are you suggesting that if we interfere too much, our Red Adder of today will up sticks and move?"

"Yes."

The simple answer took Jonathon aback. "I see." There was a small period of silence. "Mr Hunter – you have been very helpful – very helpful indeed. Thank you."

"Not at all. It was my girl-friend's suggestion, actually."

"Well, thank her for me, would you?"

CHAPTER THIRTY-SIX

"SHAME HE NEVER MADE IT."

Later that afternoon Jack Kanton called Jonathon Shure from his hotel in Romsey. He was getting impatient hanging around waiting for instructions. Over the weekend, in London, he visited a few old friends and did some sightseeing, but right now he was tired of being cooped up in a hotel. It did not suit his lifestyle at all. "Come to any decisions yet, mate?"

Jonathon had been expecting this. Although Jack was under his command, he was nevertheless a volunteer. A paid volunteer, but he had a certain amount of independence attached to his responsibilities. "Almost," replied Jonathon. Will have something by the end of the day – certainly."

"Okay, will you call me back?"

Jonathon knew that meant today. "Of course."

"Wan'na know what I think?"

"Yes, please," said Jonathon with respect. He could hear Jack was drawing on a pipe. Every now and then the tell-tale phup, phup, could clearly be heard. Jonathon wondered what style of pipe it might be. He could imagine him smoking a curved type, with a large bowl.

"That bugger that calls itself a snake and thinks it's a jet bloody aircraft, will be goin' into hibernation shortly, yep?"

"A matter of weeks probably."

"Then I should let the bugger. And pray to our Sadie's glass arse that it never wakes up." Jonathon was left holding the telephone as Jack rang off. He stayed in that position for some time, until a smile started to spread over his face. That, he thought, might be the best advice he had heard yet.

Before he let the media know his immediate plans, he had a duty to advise Stephen Knopner. It was late in the afternoon when he got him in his office. After the pleasantries, Jonathon told Stephen that the observation teams would not be going back, and that hibernation would be allowed to take its natural course. He advised that the safety 'No Admittance,' notices could come down, subject to Stephen's own approval, in late November, but they would have to monitor the situation next year. He had in mind a large team of single sights-men as he called them, to watch for the snake's reappearance. However, that would very much depend on sufficient funding. It would not surprise him if the authorities, after an inactive winter, might be a little unforthcoming. Stephen understood all this and said he would have to consult with his superiors about the access to the footpaths. "There is one other matter," said Jonathon.

"Go on."

"Ben Nicholson, otherwise known as Rattlesnake Ben, had a knife. It was a very special knife apparently, made of carboned steel. Said to be worth about five hundred US dollars."

"What!" interrupted Stephen with his usual candour. "A carbon steel knife is never worth that much! Must have a fourteen carat, solid gold handle."

"Well – anyway, it is very special and was missing from the sheath attached to his belt. The family has asked us to try and recover it. Don't suppose your people could have a look?"

"With all due respects: tell the family if they want it, they can come and get it. None of my men are going anywhere near that part of the forest for about a month."

"I see," said Jonathon. "Would you mind if I did?"

"Be my guest." ...   Stephen thought for a while. "Better let me know when though. You will need an escort."

"I know where it is."

"Maybe – but I insist."

"All right – will call you back. Have to see when I can arrange it."

"Right – speak to you later."

After he put the telephone down, Jonathon made up his mind to take Jack Kanton along. Without him, the exact route that Rattlesnake Ben took to enter the plantation would be in question. Also, he might have some idea as to how far Ben had gone. A crazy thought occurred to him. If the knife was missing – had he used it? Was the Red Adder wounded, or perhaps – even dead? He called Jack to advise of his decision to drop the observation team operation, and, also, to ask him to delay his return to Australia for a day or two. Jack agreed.

Two telephone calls later and the small expedition was arranged for the following afternoon. Jonathon would collect Jack from his hotel and drive the two of them to Stephen's office at Chapp.

In the morning, Christine, Suzanne and Fly were making their way by the least obvious route to Beech Cottage, when they came across Allen Haddle and his little white terrier. Fly gave a superb imitation of class snobbery by disdainfully ignoring the terrier's persistent barking. Eventually, after a good deal of lead tugging and shouts of "Quiet Jupiter!" from Allen, the terrier settled for a subdued growl. "Long time no see," greeted Allen.

"How are you and Jean?" immediately answered Christine. "You are looking perky."

"Thank you – yes," he chuckled. "My wife is her usual cheerful self. But what is this disturbing news I have been hearing ... you are moving?"

Christine grimaced. "Afraid so." She did not try to explain. Allen looked uncomfortable. Then he said, "You know – when we met in the hotel bar all those months ago ... I – little dreamt..."

"Oh – we know that," Suzanne interrupted him reaching out her hand to touch his arm. "Nobody could have known about the horrid events which have taken place." Christine nodded in agreement.

"By the way, your young man, Dalmar is it? Dalmar Hunter?" Jupiter had stopped growling and now pointedly presented his back to the collie.

"Yes," said Suzanne puzzled.

"Haven't met him, but – but has he," here he hesitated before repeating himself, "Has he lived in this area before?"

Suzanne thought briefly, "Not to my knowledge ... No, I'm sure he hasn't – but – wait a minute, I think he said something about being born not far from here. Yes – yes. I remember now – he did."

"Right. His name seemed familiar – that's all. Probably got confused with someone else I expect. Not important." Here he looked at Christine. "The very best of luck with your new home. I do hope it turns out to be less dramatic than here. Well – I'm sure it will be. I won't say a final goodbye because we hope to see something of you." He waved a low arm in Suzanne's direction as an explanation.

"Of course," granted Christine, "I expect you will."

"Oh good. Say hello to your husband for me."

"I will – thank you," and they both smiled a farewell expression to him as he and the terrier continued with their walk. "Well," commented Christine, "*He* isn't frightened of any snakes." She said this because Allen ignored the 'No Admittance' notices by the woodland entrance at Beech Cottage and took a route between the path and the road.

"Probably thinks Jupiter will see them off," said Suzanne. Both girls giggled.

When Jack and Jonathon arrived at Stephen's office at Chapp, good to his word, Stephen was ready and waiting for them, together with Jim Pearce who was carrying a sleeved shotgun over his left shoulder. They transferred to the forestry officer's Land Rover and headed off into the woods. The fire-break routes were still very hard, even though they had had a good fall of rain overnight, so they made good time to the site of the recent tragedy.

"Just here," said Jack in a definite tone. He recognized the point where the soldier had fallen.

They did not waste any time and got straight on with the task. Stephen stayed with the Land Rover and sent Jim into the pines with the other two. It was very difficult for him to manoeuvre the gun at the same time as having to bend down, so he took it off his shoulder. It was Jonathon who suggested it might be an idea if he got loaded up, because although he did not expect the snake to still be in the area, it was better to be prepared. Jim left the gun cover behind and carried the shotgun, in the broken position for safety reasons, but with cartridges ready in the barrels. Jack led the way. He had to make a calculated guess as to the route Ben had taken. There were one or two signs of

The Shy Avenger

broken twigs which helped him. He guessed that Ben would not have gone more than two hundred yards. It was slow going, fending off the small branches and briars. Jonathon switched on a powerful torch. It made a difference to the clarity of visibility but cast too many shadows – so he quickly switched it off.

Shortly, the zoologist raised the question, "Do you reckon he went any further than this?"

"Nope," answered Jack. "I'll try returning on a different tack." All three men felt ill at ease. Jack and Jonathon kept casting quick glances at the branches nearest to them. Jim was just plain terrified, and repetitively made exaggerated grunts.

It was Jack who spotted it. In fact, his right foot struck something hard. It was not the knife, but the snake catching pole that had been left behind. At first, Jack and Jonathon were fooled, thinking that Ben probably dropped it when he was attacked. They started scuffing up the pine needles with their boots, where it lay. Then it occurred to Jonathon that he may have laid the pole down for some reason. So, they started to scan the ground in the immediate area. Almost directly below one of the conifers there it was. Even in the gloom, the sheen of the blade was only partly hidden by dead needles. Before Jack picked it up he had a very, very long look at the tree it was lying under. Jonathon, although pleased at the find, did the same and he gave Jim a glance. Jim read the suggestion and clicked the barrels home. He went down on one knee and watched sharp eyed. There was a purpose now, so he was not frightened any more. Jack picked up the knife He admired the work in the hardwood handle and noted that not a spot of rust lay on the blade's surface, despite the recent rain, some of which would be bound to have dripped down through the conifer above. This was attributable to the quality of the steel from which it had been forged.

Before moving off, he laid a hand on the branch just above the knife's lie. He tried to figure out what had happened. 'Right here, Ben could have stood to his full height. He was probably enjoying the feeling of relief in doing so – when – what?' Remembering the reptile's shrieking din sent quite a shudder through Jack's frame. 'Ben had been bitten in the face, which meant that the snake's head must have been just about …' He sensed Jonathon by his side.

"Do you think the Red Adder was lying on this branch?" Jonathon whispered.

"Likely … yeah," came the short reply. The hard man was feeling the negative atmosphere.

"There is an outside chance…" Jonathon stopped what he was saying, at the same time finding a deep trouser pocket to contain the torch. "May I have a look at that knife please?" One glance gave him the necessary information. "No – perhaps not," was all he said. If Ben had wounded the snake, there would possibly have been some feint sign on the knife. It was clean, very clean. "I was going to suggest that we look around a bit in case the snake had been injured, but that hardly seems necessary. Let's go." He glanced at Jim who rose to his feet breaking the gun barrels once more.

The three men found Stephen peering into the black plantation. "Any luck?" he quizzed. Jonathon raised the knife for him to see. "May I?" Stephen held out a hand. Jonathon obliged and Stephen held it up to the sunlight, which had just made an appearance. "Je'es," he said.

"Aye," said Jack. "Didn't save the man though – did it?" He tossed the catching pole into the back of the Land Rover.

When they got back to the forestry office, Stephen fished in his pocket and pulled something out. "Here's another souvenir for you," and he handed Jonathon a live .303 shell.

It was Jack who answered Jonathon's quizzical expression. "The soldier must have tried to load up before the snake got him. There was nothin' in the magazine of his rifle. Shame he never made it."

The next day Jack Kanton returned to his country on the far side of the world.

Thursday soon arrived. Tim had obviously taken the day off. Also, he had Friday as part of his holiday, therefore he could devote from now until Monday morning to the move. Suzanne had packed a small suitcase so that she could stay for a few days. Dalmar would be able to give them some assistance over the weekend, but Fly had to be left with the people next door before Dalmar went to work in the morning. The removal van was on time and they were all loaded and ready by eleven o'clock. David Andrews stopped to wish them well. He was out on a call and saw the big lorry outside Beech Cottage.

When the estate agent telephoned to give the all clear, Tim went to the gate and told the removal men to head for Cheriton. Then he stood looking at the cottage and said simply, "Bye." He had now ceased to feel disappointed and just wanted to get on with life in general. Christine and Suzanne got into the station wagon, which was absolutely loaded to the roof with last minute items of clothing, shoes, coat hangers and other domestic articles. The Morris seemed to be overflowing as well. However, a brand-new stereo system lay on the back seat, still in its packaging.

As they drove off, Christine let out a dramatic sigh. She received an affectionate tap on her arm from Suzanne, and an understanding smile.

Getting the Westward's functional in their new home over the next few days turned out to be a lot of fun. The couple seemed to be back to their happy demeanour of several weeks before. Although it was a bit heavy on the pocket, they had lots of pub food to leave themselves free from cooking and dirty dishes, while they unpacked the numerous boxes all over again. It was a good opportunity to try out some of the nearby inns. They went to their local in Cheriton itself, one high up on the chalk downs and also a famous hostelry referred to as The Pub with No Name.

After the weekend, Suzanne stayed on with Christine for a few days to help, and Dalmar's next-door neighbours carried on with their daytime dog sitting. Fly did not mind this. Familiar scents always pleased him.

And so Dalmar found himself without human company on his return from the office. It was on one of these evenings that he received yet another visit from David Andrews. "On your own? Where's young Suzanne?"

Dalmar explained.

The doctor handed him a large envelope. "Stephen thought you might be interested in these, or rather ... to peruse. He wants them back when you have finished. No hurry though. They are the results of a recent aerial photo-shoot of Yewhurst Wood."

"Oh ... I presume reference the pond?" Dalmar raised an eyebrow as he looked at David.

"Spot on. Anyhow, I'll leave them with you. Perhaps you could drop them back at his office some time?"

"Okay." He offered David some refreshment, but he declined and departed with his usual reassuring smile.

Dalmar noted that the photographs had been taken on a cloudy day. He peered at the one where he thought the pond should have been. There was no sign of any water.

He was surprised to discover how much he missed Suzanne, and, consequently, was very pleased to go and collect her on Thursday evening.

When they drove back, he took her into the Claymans. She was amazed to find the car park back to normal. The media caravan had gone.

They ordered a couple of drinks and stood at the bar. By Dalmar's side, three men in suits were conversing with one another. A casual observer could easily deduce that all three worked for a large concern. The younger of them, apparently, lived in the neighbourhood. One, a very short, stout man was telling a story about a meeting he had with a high-powered business executive, and how he had not been impressed with him, and *he* wouldn't have offered him a job, and so on.

Just then, a casually dressed young man, noticing an acquaintance, came up and said, "Hello" to the local man, making it obvious he wished to be sociable. Although a little embarrassed by the intrusion, he nevertheless introduced him to what he termed his operations manager and managing director; the latter being the one short in stature. Dalmar noticed that an overhanging belly hid the front of the belt holding up his trousers.

The managing director asked the newcomer what his line of work was? He explained that he was an artist trying to scratch a living, and being an engaging person returned the question. "Oh – we're in the rat race," the managing director replied with a light smile on his face. The other two businessmen smiled with him, nodding in agreement.

Dalmar could not resist it. He turned slightly and made eye contact

229

with the orator. "You are saying – that you are a rat?" Suzanne was dumbfounded. She had been distracted watching some people saying goodbyes to each other. She turned in alarm to see what was going on.

The short man was quick. "I wasn't aware – that you had been invited to join this conversation?" He spoke with a slight Scottish burr, which gave him sharpness of diction.

"Well," Dalmar turned the palm of his left hand open, "If you are in a race for rats – then in order to take part – you must be a rat." Suzanne was surprised at the sarcasm in his voice. So fast that it caught everyone by surprise, the short man's right arm, holding a nearly full pint of beer, jerked upwards. The next moment, Dalmar's face felt the shock of the cold liquid splash into him forcing him to close his eyes and splutter. The beer ran down into his shirt, partially soaking the top half of his body. A considerable amount sank into his now blackened locks, causing them to hang lankly over his forehead. He blinked and opened his eyes trying to find somewhere to rest his glass. The managing director had gone. Suzanne grabbed Dalmar's arm and rescued his drink. The two remaining businessmen were staring, open-mouthed.

"I say," said the artist. "That'll teach you." At first, Dalmar glared at him, then he saw the understanding look in his benign face.

"Yes – you are right," he said, and allowed Suzanne to pull him away, as she directed a suitably apologetic expression at the businessmen at the same time. She practically dragged him out of the pub. A lot of people were looking at them, curiously.

"Why on earth did you speak to them like that?" she admonished him when they were outside.

"Sorry – couldn't stop myself. Just something about that guy's cock sure attitude."

"Pooh – look who's talking?" was her judgment on that. Dalmar turned his lips inward. It was time for him to shut up.

While he was taking a bath, following the incident, Dalmar felt the full force of his chagrin. How inconsiderate he had just been. For some reason he simply could not understand, he had completely disregarded the effect his interference on someone else's conversation would have on Suzanne. Why? Surely such prejudices he might have about some people, could not over-ride his feelings for the most important person in his life. But they just had. He became saddened at his guilt. Dalmar detested the modern equivalent of cut and thrust in business. However, he was the first to admit that it might have something to do with his lack of talent in that direction.

"Suzanne?" he called out, straightening up, having just immersed his head, covered in shampoo, under a cascading shower rose. She came to the bathroom doorway looking demure and very attractive. In the half-light, her shoulder-length dark hair fell down the still dusky cheeks of her face, and out of them shone those deeply emotive eyes. "I'm sorry," he said, and again huskily, "I'm really sorry."

"Any room in there for another one?" she smirked.

Later, cuddled together squatting on the floor in the sitting room, Suzanne asked Dalmar if he thought she needed to lose any weight. She often felt that she might be a little too rotund for his tastes. His reply pleased her. "Sweetheart – it isn't the geography. It's the person."

Two smartly dressed men were standing near an expensive looking powerful sports car in the Claymans Heron car park on Friday morning. It was Jonathon's new, much prized possession, "I hope you will be back to visit us, but not under the circumstances of recent times," said Floyd Hemming.

Jonathon Shure shut the rather sparse boot of the vehicle where he had just placed his suitcase. He shook Floyd's hand. "Let us hope," he said. "Although I shall not return this winter, that's for sure. I shall be writing to your head office expressing my sincere appreciation for all you have done." Jonathon gave him a strong smile. "I mean it," he added; "A big thanks. Tell Jan I am very grateful." Floyd thanked him and stood back to watch as the new car motored off in the direction of the London road.

The hotel was now back to normal, but soon he would have the busy season to contend with. Winter approached. By the time the New Year celebrations were over, he and his staff would be exhausted. And who knows what problems might ensue in the meantime. He sighed and lowered his head. Before he entered the thatched building, he turned and glanced at the woodland on the other side of the road. "What a summer!" he said.

CHAPTER THIRTY-SEVEN

THE UNEXPETED VISITOR.

Two weekends later, after Christine and Tim had begun to settle themselves in their new home, Suzanne decided to go and visit her parents for five days, before she and Dalmar went to Taunton in a few weeks' time. She told her man that she intended to catch a train on Wednesday and asked him to drop her at the station on his way to work.

Although they had been parted while Suzanne was staying at her brother's new house; this time, she felt a pang of deep sadness. They kissed and cuddled meaningfully before she went onto the platform, and as Dalmar walked back to the car a feeling of emptiness came upon him. He was starting to think about wanting her in his life on a more permanent basis. Fly seemed to sense something that morning and gave Suzanne an extra licking, which she did not particularly want, but had born it, so as not to hurt the animal's feelings.

In Suzanne's absence, Dalmar decided to do some interior decorating himself. Although Christine had invited him over for Sunday lunch, he had declined explaining that he intended to live in old clothes for the weekend and paint some walls. This is where a dog is at its least useful. They simply do not understand the difference between wet and dry paint; except that one smells more than the other, and therefore should be investigated. Dalmar did not wish to shut him out of the room he was attending to, but after twice cleaning liberal amounts of paint from the collie's coat, he was forced to do just that, and consequently put up with the resultant whining.

He was working on the middle bedroom. If an odour of paint was still in evidence when Suzanne returned, he was sure she would cope with it. After all her efforts at Beech Cottage, she must be used to it by now. A year ago, there had been a major water leak in this room, when the cold tank in the roof had overflowed while he was at work one day. He had returned home to find water cascading through the ceiling onto the bedroom floor - and the bed. Fortunately, it had not started to soak through to the ground floor, but the cleaning up had taken some time. Therefore, before he painted the ceiling, he filled in the extensive cracking that had resulted in the plaster. After that, it all went according to plan, except that he had to dash out and purchase some more paint before the shop closed on Saturday, having miscalculated on his original purchase.

Late in the afternoon of the following day, Dalmar was feeling pleased with himself. Just one more coat of gloss paint on the skirting boards, and he would be finished. However, this was not the easiest of tasks, bending down and crawling along on his knees, with his head to the floor. He placed sticky tape along the carpet edge, which speeded the brushwork up.

Mandy Pittstucker often did things, when the coincidence of thought combined with opportunity, seemed to suit. She was on her way back from London after a weekend visiting a girl friend from school days. Ahead of her was home in Bournemouth, her mother, and four-year-old son by a marriage that had only lasted two years. On impulse, she decided to call on an old flame. She loved to play the part of the unexpected visitor: it suited her personality. Actually, this man was not really an old boyfriend; they had never properly parted. Over the past two years, up until last Christmas, they had come together on the odd weekend. She, originally, met him when he was visiting the business where she worked. There had been an instant sexual chemistry between them, but unfortunately that was all. So, they enjoyed a sort of freedom from commitment with each other. His name was Dalmar Hunter.

She parked her M.G. open top sports car outside the man in question's garage and being a person of absolute honesty, took out her suitcase and headed up the path towards the house. The case was too heavy for her and she listed a little to the right. Her black, stiletto high heel shoes were not suited to the gravel and she kept making small stumbles. She had a bouncy, curvy figure and the cheeks of her bottom, showing a partial outline under a red velvet mini skirt, silently undulated from side to side. Above, through a pink jersey top, her breasts jiggled up and down. At this moment she was wearing a white silk headscarf, but her tight hair curls containing more black out of a jar, than naturally within, open-curtained a cheeky grinning face with a cute nose and dark made up eyes. Her complexion was still tanned, and her teeth showed a flaw of line below her upper lip. This made her look even more mischievous, and it was with just such an expression on her face, that she put down her suitcase and rat-tacker-tacked with a ringed finger on the stable door, which had been left slightly ajar.

This woke up Fly from his position under the alcove table in the sitting room. He wandered through to the kitchen – took one look at the grinning face peering at him above the lower half of the door – grunted – tossed his head in the air – and went back to his lair of solace.

Dalmar was painting the last strip of skirting board. The sudden intrusive noise made him miss and go over the top onto the wall. He cursed softly and quickly grabbed a cloth from behind his crouching position, in order to wipe the mark away. He carefully rose to his knees and then full height, shaking off the slight dizziness which the action caused, before descending the stairs. On entering the kitchen, he peered towards the half open stable door, showing complete surprise at the vision of Mandy Pittstucker before him.

She giggled at his paint-besmirched attire and asked, "Got a bed for a girl for the night?" The cheeky grin widened at the same time.

Dalmar laughed in greeting showing some embarrassment. "Err –

that might be difficult," he uttered. Her expression showed slight disappointment – but that was all. Dalmar cast his arms open. "Come on in anyway, Mandy. Marvellous to see you. How are you? By the look of you, pretty good – yes?"

"I'm okay." She had a Dorset county dialect, which was not too pronounced. After embracing him, gingerly, because of the paint, she gave him a sweet kiss on his lips, before removing her headscarf and shaking out her curls.

"Mandy...I've very nearly finished this." He pointed to the paint smears on his hands. "Come on up and chat. Then I'll get us both a drink."

"Okay," she followed him up the spiral staircase. Having visited his cottage on two previous occasions, she was familiar with it. "What are you decorating?"

"The main spare room: needed doing." While he finished off, they mostly indulged in small talk. But once Dalmar had poured them both a drink, they quickly found their old rapport, and talked mostly about the place where she worked and the colleagues, they both knew. All the while, Fly kept one eye open, as though watching them disdainfully. He showed not the slightest interest in Mandy, because he knew from past meetings that she only tolerated him. There was no real care.

Eventually she asked, "So – why can't I stay?" There was matter of factness and not regret in her tone.

"Well ... got a serious relationship going; since June. Funny really, if she were here, there would be no problem ... but ... because she isn't." He shrugged his shoulders to finish the explanation. "Gone to visit her folks for a few days. I've got to pick her up from the station tomorrow evening. I am sure you would like her." That part was true. What he was not sure of – was whether Suzanne would like Mandy.

"Oh well, I won't bother to phone home. Just have this drink and be on my way." She seemed to accept the situation. If she was feeling displeasure, nothing showed on what was a very expressive face. They talked for a good half an hour before Mandy got up to go. "May I use your loo – quickly?" Dalmar was about to say 'Of course,' but she had already made her way there. He went out through the kitchen and sat on the wooden bench under the glass overhang to wait.

When she had finished, she found him waiting for her outside. She asked him if he still had the handbag she inadvertently left behind on her last visit. She bought it while shopping in Winchester with him and had not, as yet, actually used it. "Oh yes - sorry, I had forgotten all about that." He went upstairs and brought the bag down, handing the strap to her so that she could put it over her shoulder. Then he picked up her suitcase and followed her along the path. Mandy, expertly, retied her silk scarf, ready for the wind in her hair once again.

Suzanne left her parents a day early without informing Dalmar. She had spoken to him on the telephone the night before and given him the time of arrival of her train at Southampton on Monday evening. The main reason for the premature return was because she sincerely missed him, coupled with an irritating annoyance over her mother's house rules entirely brought on by her new-found freedom. It would be an extravagance for her as she intended to hire a taxi from the station and surprise him, something she was quite confident would please her lover. It would still be early evening when she got there. The train was on time, although the journey had been a little crowded and uncomfortable, due to the doubtful calibre of the other passengers sharing her compartment. The taxi rank looked rather busy, but she did not have to queue for long and was soon on her way. Rather than give the driver an address he would not be familiar with, she told him to drop her at the Claymans Heron hotel. After about thirty minutes, the taxi pulled into the large gravel parking area outside the hostelry. She asked the driver to park on the far side, explaining that she was going to one of the houses nearby.

"This is where that serpent killed all them people, isn't it?" The driver remarked, after stopping the vehicle at her requested situation.

"Yes," said Suzanne. "Not very pleasant. What do I owe you?" It cost her a few pounds, but she reckoned it was worth it. As she pulled her suitcase out from its position in the rear of the car, she looked over the top of the taxi and glanced towards the garage by Dalmar's cottage. The evening sunlight on the chestnut trees was very attractive. She noticed the leaves had almost completed their transformation to their full autumnal colours. What else she saw – made her stop what she was doing and stare in consternation. Dalmar was placing a suitcase into the rear compartment of a small pale blue sports car, parked right outside his garage. A petite, pretty girl kissed him fully on the mouth while holding him tightly in an embrace. But even that was not as shattering to Suzanne as the sight of a bright yellow handbag, with a long shoulder strap, slung over the girl's left shoulder. Almost certainly the same one Suzanne had spotted on the floor in the corner of Dalmar's wardrobe. Its brazen colour clearly stood out against the dark laurel hedge by the side of the garage.

The girl climbed into her car and placed the bag on the passenger seat. The next thing, the engine was revving, and the vehicle reversed out of the small tarmac parking area. Dalmar waited until the M.G. Midget was pointing in the right direction, before raising a hand in a stationary wave.

Suzanne pushed her suitcase back into the taxi, jumped in next to it and said to the driver, "I'm sorry ... I've changed my mind. Could you take me ... to Cheriton ... please?"

"You sure miss?" The driver spun round in his seat, noticing distress in her voice.

"Yes ... please, let's go ... I'll give you the address when we get to the village. Do you know where it is?"

"Off the A272: other side of Winchester. It's going to be an expensive evening for you."

Before he drove off, he had to wait for a sky-blue sports car, driven by an attractive girl, as it accelerated past him. 'Hmmm,' he said to himself.

As Dalmar waved goodbye to Mandy he could have sworn that the taxi, which had just pulled up by the hotel – had not discharged anybody. 'Must be lost,' he thought.

Meanwhile – that taxi's suddenly fragile young passenger, was trying to face up to the unbelievable reality, that her world had just been covered over with a desolate, dark blanket ... The lights went out in her eyes.

CHAPTER THIRTY-EIGHT

"SHE DOES NOT WISH TO SPEAK WITH YOU."

All afternoon Dalmar watched the clock in his office. He was so looking forward to the hour when he could get to the station and wait for Suzanne's return. During his lunchtime break, he went to a department store in walking distance of the business he worked for. He purchased an expensive bottle of perfume which he and the sales assistant had carefully chosen. He thought that its citrus style aroma would suit his girlfriend well.

There is something exciting and romantic about a busy railway station when you are meeting a person that you long to see. It has a smell and atmosphere all of its own. While he was waiting for the arrival of his loved one's train, Dalmar remembered a childhood sensation concerning the edge of the platform. It was as though it heralded an abyss into a subterranean world: a terrifying, unknown world, from which there was no return. Tearing himself away from this reverie, he watched the pigeons fluttering in and out of the lofty metal roof structure, using the supporting rods as perches.

The Taunton locomotive arrived ten minutes late. This did not worry Dalmar; he had been on the platform for forty-five minutes preferring to be here than to stay on at his office. He tried to suppress a tingling feeling of excitement all over him – looking for that carriage door to open, and the adorable picture of his darling that would appear. One after another the doors swung out over the platform edge. Sometimes one person alighted with or without luggage: sometimes several people, or families with children. Dalmar, from his position in the centre of the long platform, kept glancing in both directions in an attempt to avoid missing the first sight of her ... She was not there.

While the train stood stationary and people were boarding, he began to look lost. Soon she would appear; she was playing a joke. All sorts of thoughts played through his mind ... But she was not there.

Three minutes went by before a whistle sounded. It went through Dalmar's head like an unwelcome alarm call. The train started to move. Urgently, he commenced a jogging type run to keep up with it, all the while scanning the inside of the carriages. He wondered if she might have fallen asleep ... She was not there.

As the train's rear-end disappeared beyond the web of railway lines, he stared after it quite perplexed. His next act was to go and sit on the same seat he had waited on earlier, for a full ten minutes. Perhaps she might appear from behind a pillar or hoarding and shout, 'Fooled you!'   She did not ... She was not there

Eventually, he went to enquire of a man collecting tickets if there was another train from Taunton due that evening. There was not. Really – he knew that.

He must get home and telephone Suzanne's parents. Was she still on that train for some reason? Her only method of contacting him would be to make a phone call to his home from another rail station. He must get there as soon as possible.

Very rarely would Dalmar drive recklessly, but he did now. He was very lucky not to have been stopped by a police patrol car. Thirty-five minutes later he arrived at his home with a skid from brakes applied too hard and late. Bursting through the stable doors with a double crash as they banged together from too exuberant a push, he swung into the small hall and reached for the telephone receiver. Then he had to put it back on its stand, because he had forgotten that his telephone book was in the kitchen. Having located it, he turned to the letter 'w' and read out the Westward's number while he dialled.

Suzanne's mother answered, "Taunton two, one, one, six, one." She spoke in a refined, middle-class voice.

"Oh, hello, Mrs Westward. It's – it's Dalmar," he said, trying to hide his agitation. "I don't want to worry you - but which train is your daughter on?" The strain in his voice showed.

"Ah … Dalmar … Yes," Would you hold on a moment." The tone of her voice told him that this was not a request – it was an instruction. A frown creased his forehead. It did not make sense. He thought he heard some distant muffled female conversation before she came back to the telephone. "Hello … are you there?"

"Yes."

"I am sorry – she does not wish to speak with you."

Dalmar was bewildered. "I – I beg your pardon … is Suzanne there?"

"Yes, she is, but she does not wish to speak with you." There was a short pause – and then, "Goodbye." The dialling tone replaced her voice.

Dalmar sat on the bottom of the stairs holding the telephone. He was absolutely stunned. The dawn of meaning made his brain numb. He heard her mother's voice saying those defined words, over and over again, 'She does not wish to speak with you,' and the final, 'Goodbye.' It took a full quarter of an hour before the awful realisation reached inside his head. Suzanne had ended their relationship. Desolately, feeling cold, he went like an automaton to collect Fly from his neighbours. What made it worse, or so it seemed, was the fact that he had not met Suzanne's mother; this made her voice appear even more distant.

"What's matter with you?" asked Janice Short, the normally serious lady looked unusually cheerful this evening. "Look's like you see'd a ghost," she cackled at him. Dalmar could not smile, but he gave Fly a huge hug when he bounded out to meet him. He thanked Janice, as always, and left. The worldly lady looked after him. 'Sum'at's amiss, if I'm any judge,' she said to herself.

Dalmar spent the evening cuddling his dog. The therapeutic effects of a loving pet in such circumstances are invaluable. Fly sensed some distress in his master.

As Dalmar's mind played on the matter, he began to see how it all fitted together. Suzanne's sudden whim to go and see her mother and father: even though they were both due to visit them soon. It gave her opportunity to part without a scene. Other men would not have left it at that. They would immediately have made enquiries as to why? They would probably have telephoned Tim or Christine to find out more. Unfortunately, Dalmar was not such a person. One hint that he was not wanted, and he would walk away.

Right now, to him, it became horribly clear that Suzanne had fallen out of love for him. Not an unfamiliar distress to this man. He had experienced it before. He did not know why? But this would make it the third time that when he had started to develop serious thoughts for a girl; at that point, she had gone off him. When the relationship was more casual, and he did not achieve those in love feelings, more perhaps a fondness, then *he* usually ended the alliance.

So Dalmar remained unaware of the desolation that had invaded Suzanne's life. Equally heartbroken, she had spent a tearful night at Cheriton making a hurried return to Somerset the next morning. The previous evening's taxi fares had left her bereft of funds. Tim had lent her some cash with which to purchase another rail ticket.

Dalmar could not help but discover that most of Suzanne's wardrobe was still in place in their bedroom. This struck him as odd and gave him some small hope, but he was not very optimistic. Unfortunately, the recent disappointment clouded his rationality. In reality, he believed it was the end.

For Dalmar earning his living the next day may have been difficult, but it was a blessing. For without that preoccupation, he seriously doubted whether he might maintain his sanity. He knew that ahead of him lay weeks, perhaps months of heartache. That familiar twisted knot, in the upper reaches of his stomach had returned after an absence of some years.

When he arrived home late in the afternoon, after collecting Fly, he was surprised to see a key lying beside a note under the stable door. He bent down and picked it up. Fly stood back with a puzzled expression on his face. The note read:

'Sorry about this intrusion.
Collected Suzanne's personal possessions. Clothes etc.
One returned key.
Regards.   Chris.'

"Well – that is absolute confirmation," Dalmar said aloud. It did not escape his attention that Suzanne would hardly have had time to post the key to her brother's house from Taunton. In other words, the matter had been fore planned. Entirely due to a devastating trauma in his childhood, Dalmar switched off. Self-preservation kicked in to ward off depression.

Fly stopped his welcoming tail-wag. It was as though he knew. Dalmar gathered a great deal from the use of 'Regards,' on Christine's note. A few days ago, it would have been – 'Love.'

Apart from one item, he could not find anything that Christine might have forgotten. Even Suzanne's clothes in the laundry basket had been removed. That one item was a dark blue velvet Alice band: the type that clips over the brow, pushing the hair back from the forehead. He found it lying on the floor in their bedroom, half hidden by the counterpane. Dalmar put it under his pillow. He was not in the least bit ashamed of doing so. In the corner of the room was a small table with a free-standing mirror placed upon it. Suzanne had used it as a dressing table. Lying there was the gift-wrapped bottle of perfume he had purchased for her homecoming.

That evening, much to Fly's disgust, our lovesick man started playing music. From his drink's cupboard he took out a bottle of whisky and another bottle containing ginger wine. He mixed a glass with equal portions of each. The drink is better known as a whisky-mac. After an hour or so, Fly retreated to the upper floor and stayed there. Dalmar's music system was a good one, especially when played loud. It had an excellent amplifier, and although the sound cabinets housed a normal set of tweeters and mid-range cones, the Goodman's Axiom twelve-inch base speakers produced intoxicating waves of vibrant, quality low notes.

At around one o'clock in the morning and after the twenty-third playing of Simon & Garfunkel's, 'Bridge Over Troubled Water,' Enid Johnson, who lived in a much larger house next door, decided that was enough. Her husband grunted at her, "To leave matters alone," but she was angry and climbed out of bed.

As Dalmar was singing *"Sail on silver girl"* at full throat, Enid banged on the stable door with her fist. Fly had a good sense as to what this was about. He stayed upstairs with his ears cocked. The force Enid used was enough to cause Dalmar to stop his rendition. He was standing in the middle of the sitting room. The whisky bottle was half-empty, and the ginger wine was virtually finished. He still wore the shirt and tie from his day's work, except that the shirt had become un-tucked from his suit trousers on one side, and his tie was not properly housed around the collar. Instantly, he knew that this was not a social call, but he was far too far-gone to instil immediate sobriety. He managed, after three attempts, to turn off the tuner-amplifier on his music system, bringing about an abrupt silence. He staggered out into the kitchen and opened the top half of the door. Dalmar tried to make out what was before him on the other side of that doorway. Enid wore a very upset, middle of the night face; her hair was in rollers, and she stood resplendent in a full-length pink nightdress. Fortunately for him and Enid, Dalmar's eyes would not focus on the apparition, which kept moving about in front of him.

Her voice, however, was strong and clear. "Now that's enough!" she shouted at him. "For God's sake – some of us have to sleep tonight. Go to bed will you!" She looked at the swaying bulk before her. His hair lay across his forehead, and what eyes she could see, seemed to be red-veined and squinting. In his left hand, he held a glass half full of a dark, amber-coloured liquid. Before turning away, she held up a partially open fist and pointed a finger. "Oh – and by the way, you can't bloody-well sing!" Dalmar managed to make out a hair netted, night-dressed individual disappearing into the gloom.

Anyway, it worked. The desolate man took himself off to bed, unwashed and still clothed.

The next day he had to contend with a bad hangover as well as his private distress. His constitution, when it came to a large consumption of alcoholic drinks, was poor. His suffering tended to be worse than that for the average man. Fortunately for him, he did not have to meet with anyone his senior during the day, but his staff, and particularly his secretary noticed he was not himself. She tactfully asked him if he required any painkillers. His reply was in the affirmative.

That was the only time that Dalmar allowed himself to indulge in the drowning of his sorrows, but the sorrow itself kept on and on, night after night. 'Bridge Over troubled Water' kept getting a thorough pounding, although he now resorted to the use of earphones. Also, on the menu were more of his favourite songs by well-known artists such as, 'I'll Never Find Another You', sung by The Seekers. When he thought he could risk a loud blast earlier in the evening, or at the weekend, he did so. Somehow, Fly began to understand just what the sorrow was about, although he would not have known why or where his mistress had gone. It was fortunate that his immediate neighbours loved the collie, as if he was their own pet, for he frequently howled along to the music.

One evening, Dalmar finally managed to remember to put the envelope containing Stephen Knopner's aerial photographs through the Forestry Commission office letterbox, after returning from his day's toil. He did not enclose any accompanying note.

As soon as the access to Yewhurst Wood was re-instated, Dalmar and Fly went back to their old trails. Some media crews carried out little excursions with film equipment to satisfy the public curiosity, but after a few weeks it all seemed to get back to normal. A different notice replaced the 'No Admittance' variety of the summer months. Walkers were asked to stick to the marked footpaths. Stephen Knopner and his staff had been busy with colour-coded posts to assist the public in this matter. As the weeks passed, no-one other than the usual local people carried on using the footpaths.

There was something sinister about the Red Adder attacks, which put deep fear into the hooligan element, so they kept away. Except for one group of lads after a Saturday lunch time session at a local pub. They were heard strolling up a main fire clearance route shouting abuse at an unseen enemy. Stephen had been expecting something like this, but rather than interfere, he let the exercise sober them up. They were last seen running, or rather stumbling for their lives as dusk was descending. None of them knew what had triggered their collective panic.

As the days went by, Dalmar gradually returned to his old life. He played squash with a few work colleagues and had a drink with them. His weekends were taken up with gardening, mostly fallen leaf sweeping, but most of the time was given over to the exploration of the countryside with his dog. He would sometimes drive some way, even into neighbouring counties, to explore a high ridge on down land, or a forest area, usually in a river valley.

The Christmas holiday drew nearer. As in the past, he would receive a couple of invitations from people concerned about his solitude. He had got into the habit of lying, telling them that he was going away. One of the things that Dalmar did like about Christmas Day, however, was the momentary effect on the environment. While nearly everyone cosseted themselves at their family gatherings, the normally busy roads and bustling streets were quiet. Therefore, he would drive around with Fly by his side especially through a main town thoroughfare, early in the afternoon when roast turkey was being served. It was a strange experience.

On the morning after Boxing Day, Yewhurst Wood was gripped in a breathtakingly beautiful hoar frost. After rising, Dalmar went out into the garden with Fly. The trees were dripping with ice crystals and the grass lawns looked as though they were covered in a silvery blanket. The heathers in the centre bed, breaking the line of the lawns, seemed to house their own miniature exhibition of strange sculptures in white. There was only one place to be, on a rare opportunity like this, in a wooded area. After splitting some logs from the stock in the little side shed, he and Fly took off in the Triumph roadster for the New Forest. Taking the road from Romsey to Cadnam, Dalmar drove down past Emery Down to the Christchurch road and after a few miles turned left onto the Ornamental Drive. He parked in the first car park he came upon. Fly was about to have a wonderful time. There were magnificent trees in every direction. Tall redwood, broad oak, angelic birches, stumpy yew, thick furs, hanging spruce and arrowed pine – all covered in white ice dust. Low mist added privacy to the scene taking away distant sight but not height, and that was the bonus here. This was why Dalmar had come. The great redwoods rose into the sky like giant steeples, and the cool mist at their base made the whole – ethereal.

Winter clothes suited Dalmar. In a strange way he complimented the collie. Today, he wore his usual blue jeans, but he wore a pair of walking boots, and his torso was clad in a heavy knit, black, polo neck jumper. To finish off the cold protection, he wore an open three-quarter length navy blue, woollen hooded coat; the type favoured by some yachtsmen. Most of the time, the hood lay down across his upper back.

The man and his dog walked for a few miles and saw no one. This was strange for a holiday time. They were in a well-known beauty spot. The reason became obvious to Dalmar after a couple of hours passed by. Somewhere, he had taken the wrong path. Fortunately, he had remembered to pocket the compass he kept in the glove compartment of his car. With knowledge that the Lyndhurst to Christchurch road ran from east to west, he took a bearing and followed it. The result was that they came out by that road, but some distance from where he had parked the Triumph. By the time they arrived at the car park, the light was starting to go and the silver frost, still in evidence, did not look quite so inviting. Fly flopped into the back of the roadster, and Dalmar headed for home and a to-be-born roaring fire. 'What a shame Suzanne had not shared that day with him,' he thought. Although he did not think she would have been too impressed with his navigation. A wry smile showed across his chilled lips.

That evening, after he fed Fly and cooked himself a supper, Dalmar lit the fire in the sitting room fireplace. This was one of his joys. The smell of the burning timber and the atmospheric glow it provided often persuaded him to leave the lights switched off. However, sometimes this occurred due to the frequent electric power cuts. A hangover from last winter's government imposed three-day working week, caused by industrial action in the nationalised coal mining pits and power stations. The fire, on these occasions, not only provided warmth, but, also, a method for boiling a kettle or heating a saucepan of food.

Dalmar sat on the floor with Fly lying by his side. His left arm lay across the dog's back, and his hand took comfort from the warm soft feel of the animal's coat. They stayed in that position for a long time, just staring into the embers. The only reason Dalmar had to eventually break the magical spell was because he needed to rise and put another log on the fire. He felt the exertions of the day in his tired legs as he did so. When he was satisfied with the state of the quiet combustion, he sat back down next to the sleeping collie, this time with a pencil and notebook. Then – over the evening – he wrote the following:

THE LOG FIRE

In colder lands with winter's season there is one great delight,
The comfort of the hearth-filled blaze from the raw, dark night.
Build the basket high with logs to keep us going an hour or two,
Then I'll while the long eve out and dream of tender days with you.

I pity the modern abode with fireplace for ornament only,
As we gaze at television, night after night - lonely.
For while the barren hearth remains in place no longer alive,
We cannot escape the memory of how we used to survive.

The Shy Avenger　　　　　　　　　　　Scardthomas

The flicker-putt of the hot embers I would never be without,
Nor would wish to from November to March - about.
The heady scent of ash, beech, and oak burning in the hearth
Gives the rural dwelling its timeless ambient heart.

When I have visited lush tropical areas in faraway lands,
I must eventually leave the coral reefs and golden sands,
To return to my country - with the allure it brings.
All I need is some dry wood - then the home bell rings.

   Before retiring to bed, he wrote a note to himself and left it on the dresser in the kitchen. It read, 'Order logs.'

PART TWO

1976

CHAPTER THIRTY-NINE

"AND WHAT IS THE MATTER WITH YOU, MR. ANTI-SOCIAL?"

On the Tuesday after the New Year holiday, Dalmar was about to drive off for work, sitting in his car waiting at the end of the lane for the road to clear, engine idling. A black Jaguar stopped on Brook Road right opposite. The driver's window opened, and David Andrews waved at him to come across. Dalmar cursed: it was raining. He got out of the car and put his jacket collar up while walking halfway over the road. "What's the matter?" he asked, squinting through the rain at a dry Dr Andrews, who was wearing some new, black-framed spectacles. These housed smaller lenses than his previous style.

"Good morning! Can you give a message to your other half for me?" David was half grinning at him, but Dalmar's face must have showed some emotion.

"Have I just said the wrong thing?" The doctor's countenance changed to a questioning expression.

Dalmar gave a slight grimace. "I'm afraid she left for pastures new ... or old ... not sure which. It was a while ago now."

"Well – bless my soul. Sorry to hear that." David usually knew when it was time to be tactful and this was one of them. "Well look ... it doesn't really matter. Remember that TV documentary they wanted to make?"

Dalmar recalled the conversation when Suzanne agreed to be interviewed. "Yes," he affirmed.

"They have put it off: something to do with winter being the wrong time." He paused a moment. "If I need to get hold of her later this year, do you have a contact number?"

"Yes, her parents' house in Somerset." Dalmar was getting wet and he had to get to his office.

"Many thanks. Will let you go. Bye." David raised his hand as he drove off leaving Dalmar standing in the middle of the road. There was a sudden toot behind him. A car was approaching. He quickly ran back to his sports car.

One evening, about a week later, Dalmar was in the act of preparing a meal for himself. He was not in the best of moods. The first signs that he was getting a cold were upon him. It was seven-thirty by the kitchen clock. A quiet tap on the door made him jump. Unusually for him, Fly started barking loudly and came skidding in on the linoleum floor. "Quiet boy! Come here!" His owner pulled him back by his collar, away from the stable door. "Sit!" The dog obeyed while panting forcefully, contenting himself with a low growl. His master gave him a stern stare. Fly went completely silent. Opening the top half of the door, Dalmar recognised someone whose appearance he was vaguely familiar with.

"Mr Hunter?" enquired the voice of a man of a senior age.

"That is I ... Mr Haddle, I do believe?"

"Ah, I was not sure if you knew me." Allen Haddle gave him a smile. "I have seen you out exercising your dog on many an occasion."

"How can I help?" Dalmar searched the man's eyes for a hint.

"Do you have a moment?" Allen edged forward making it obvious he wished to enter.

"Yes, of course, come in. Don't mind Fly, he is far more docile than your terrier," Dalmar said with a grin. Allen laughed in a concurring fashion. "Come on through to the sitting room." Dalmar ushered him into the hall and pointed to the open doorway on the left. He hoped it was relatively tidy. No dusting had been done for weeks. However, the removal of one magazine was all that was required to allow his guest an uninterrupted seat in the armchair. "Can I offer you a drink – perhaps?" Dalmar politely asked.

"Oh, no, no ... no," Allen answered waving his right hand vigorously in negation. "Although we have not met officially, I have heard of you from various acquaintances. There is something that has been bothering me." Dalmar looked at his visitor. Dressed in sensible, seasonal clothes of corduroy trousers and a tweed jacket, he looked casual despite the ever-present white collar and tie. Suddenly – Dalmar felt ill at ease. He had a distinct feeling that he knew what was coming.

Allen Haddle took a deep breath before giving the younger man a question, which was phrased in such a way, to give little doubt as to its meaning. It could not be evaded – save by a lie. "You are Simon Hunter's boy, aren't you? I refer to the Hunter family that lived on The Great Mile in the nineteen forties? The very same family, who due to a Red Adder, lost their pet spaniel in one year, and their eldest son in the next." Two hard, deep blue eyes focused directly on Dalmar's face. Those eyes had dimmed a little with age, but they had not lost their authoritative spell which the owner used when necessary. The kind of look he had put into practice many times when dealing with pet owners, who had obviously neglected their responsibilities. Dalmar, who had seated himself on the small settee adjacent, must have shown all that was needed in the expression on his face. "Ha!" exclaimed Allen, half rising in his seat, without dropping the direct look.

Dalmar took his time before replying. There was no point whatever in denying it. He had been asked a straight question. Honourably, he must answer in the affirmative. "Yes," he said.

"I knew it!" Allen thumped the armrest of the chair with his left fist. "I knew there was a familiar ring as soon as I heard your name mentioned, but it has taken my old brain an age to work it out." The retired veterinary surgeon was now quite excited. "I presume your parents dropped the use of your first name ... John?"

"Correct." Dalmar started to study the older man curiously. He could understand the interest, but there was something else: something very deep indeed. It showed in the agitated wringing movements of both hands, thrust up against the sides of his groin, on the inside of his legs.

"But ... why didn't you tell anybody? Especially with all the Red Adder business last year."

"Do you blame me?" Dalmar fired a curt question in return.

Allen looked a little taken aback. Then he nodded. "No. ... No can't say I do. The press would have pestered you." A thought suddenly occurred to him. He raised his right hand a little and lent forward. "Your discretion is safe with me."

"Quite." Dalmar acknowledged, in a tone that suggested he sincerely hoped so.

"You see," Allen went on, "You won't remember, but I attended to your family's dog after it had been bitten, and as a result I got to know your father quite well. We played bridge at the same club."

"I do remember." Dalmar's polite comment was virtually ignored. The memory was vague, but it was there.

"After your brother's death ... terrible tragedy," Allen shook his head from side to side almost deliberately. "Of course, you all moved away," he sighed. "Do you have memories of your brother?"

"Yes – quite a lot actually. We were very close; argued a lot, as brothers do, but very close. William was my hero."

"Yes, I see ... do you know – if it's not a frightful imposition – I think I will have that drink after all."

"Certainly," Dalmar stood up. "A glass of beer? Or perhaps – whisky – sherry?" He opened his eyes wide to amplify the question.

"Sherry, if I may. Do you have a dry one?"

"Yes, I won't be long." This gave Dalmar the opportunity to turn off the oven and so prevent his meal from spoiling. On the way he noticed two paws hanging over a stair about halfway up the spiral. Fly's head appeared from around the corner, looked at his master and growled. Dalmar ignored him, surmising that he could scent Allen's terrier.

Returning, carrying a small tulip shaped glass containing a very pale coloured fortified wine, and a small beer for himself, he handed Allen the former. He took a sip. "Ah, yes," and he smacked his lips quietly. "Just right – thank you. I believe your mother and father died very close to each other?"

Dalmar sat down and told him the sequence of events.

"And was there not a little girl?" asked Allen.

"My sister – Judy. She is in Africa with her husband." Dalmar gave a small shrug of his shoulders; we write."

"You ought to go and visit."

"A tiny smile crossed Dalmar's lips. "Someone else said that," he said. He gave out a quiet laugh at the same time.

"Well, you should take advantage of it."

"Said that as well."

"That someone wouldn't be a certain young lady, would it?" David Andrews had informed Allen of the breakup with Suzanne.

"Yes," answered Dalmar with a sigh. Then for the first time, he told another person what had transpired. He had no idea why he was divulging this. Allen Haddle was hardly someone he knew well.

"If I were you, I would not have left it there." Allen took another sip of his sherry.

"How do you mean? To me, it was a definite – bye-bye."

"It may look like that, but you might have upset her in some way. However, it is none of my business: just a thought." A deep frown temporarily etched itself on Dalmar's brow. Allen brought the conversation back to the Red Adder, "What is your opinion? Do you think it will reappear this year?" Then he added, just to clarify matters, "The snake I mean."

"Who knows?" commented Dalmar, forcing himself away from the troubling thought Allen had just thrown at him. "Going by past habits, it will probably depend on the local climate, don't you think?"

"Yes ... I thought that," Allen obviously agreed with him. "If it does, do you think it will be in the chestnut by the pond?"

"Ah – so someone does believe in the pond after all?" Dalmar heard his voice deepening with the effects of the onset of the cold virus.

"Well ... I am only going by what I have gathered," said Allen with an upheld palm gesture. They discussed other matters concerning the village for a while before Allen rose to his feet. "Anyhow, I must not take up any more of your time. I have to say I am very glad to have quizzed you, so to speak. I thought a lot of your father; he was a good man. Terrific integrity you know." He drank the last drop of his drink and put the glass on the coffee table.

"Yes ... I do know." Dalmar said succinctly.

"Of course you do, dear chap, forgive me." Both men smiled at each other. Passing through the kitchen, Allen commented, "Hope I didn't spoil your meal?" The aroma suggested something was in the oven.

"No, no," Dalmar relieved him of the concern. "Nothing that won't keep."

Before leaving, Allen raised the first finger of his right hand to his mouth and pursed his lips. "So, mum's the word, yes? About your identify?"

Dalmar thought for a while before saying. "If any official bods need to know," he shrugged his shoulders, "then okay. It is the press that would bother me."

"Fine," agreed Allen, "I quite understand. And thank you for the sherry." He hesitated before saying, "Do you mind if I call you John? It seems appropriate ... somehow. I will be tactful – of course."

Dalmar bowed his head slightly, "As you wish." Perhaps it was due to his recent romantic disappointment, but, really, the matter ceased to bother him anymore. "Allen?"

"Yes," Allen's face lit-up with a generous smile. Both men shook hands before the visitor vanished in the dim light along the gravel path.

Fly appeared from his chosen exile making low grunting barks at the door as Dalmar closed it. "And what is the matter with you, Mr Anti-Social?" He ruffled the hair on the dog's head. "Now for that supper."

For reasons Dalmar could not fully explain to himself, he felt relieved that his family connection to John the Red was out – although, hopefully, not too publicly.

A great deal of his poetry, at this time, was quite naturally melancholy. He found it rather masochistic to sit and write poems about unrequited love on a Sunday afternoon, or late on a weekday evening. But in other ways it helped relieve the pain. The fearful cold he developed, which lasted for a good two weeks further lowered his spirit.

The knots in his stomach were finally beginning to subside by March 1976. The love remained, but the pain was abating. This did not mean that if Suzanne were to suddenly re-enter his life, some feelings would have been lost. Quite the contrary, they would probably be all the more powerful. He did dwell, a lot, on the comment made by Allen Haddle about not accepting the separation without more explanation. But he was quite convinced that it would only make matters worse if he were to make delicate enquiries now; however discreet they might be. Anyway, he did not have the faintest idea as to how to go about it, and whenever he started to probe the unease, his mind always came back to the return of the key.

Some people would question his sensitivity and conceit over this matter especially in the early days of the break-up. Dalmar was the youngest of three children. Even the second child normally showed more competitive spirit than the eldest, and the third, often, even more so. But what had happened here was that the elder brother, his father's main pride, had died tragically, and, more importantly, unexpectedly. This altered everything. Dalmar found himself, not ignored, but very often having to go without the attention his tender years deserved. It made him feel as though the wrong sibling had died. As the years went by, he closed down his emotions in self-protection.

One of his poems, whilst moody, did not directly relate to his recent relationship. It was an explanation into a world where love affairs he had experienced before, also, made no real sense. He wrote 'Blue', as he titled it, in an effort to understand this phenomenon. He used a different style. A more contemporary method seemed to suit the subject. At first, he thought it might be the best thing he had ever done, but, after a few days, he was not so sure. 'Had he got it right? Could it be improved?' In the end, he decided to leave it with the spontaneity unimpaired.

BLUE

Blue lands on blue minds
wandering along a grey road.
Blue skies on blue eyes
passing out of clouds.
Blue waters on blue voices
waving goodbye.
Under the moon.
Still.
Space and forever.
I feel easy.

Blue times – remember.
I know her now,
flying in on the face of a stranger,
or wondering a friend.
Hello Blue.
The tried must be tried.
The hope of no hope,
to humble and balance.

Blue is the colour.
Blue is my mood.
Blue is ………..
Blue – on blue … on blue.

CHAPTER FORTY

"YOU MEAN – HE'S A THIEF?"

Dalmar awoke on Good Friday morning to the sight of a layer of snow on the ground. Pushing back the curtains of his bedroom window, he stared with his mouth partially open for quite a while. So, that was why Fly had roused him all skittish. The day before yesterday, the temperature had reached the low sixties – and now this! He scratched his head in wonder. The season of spring was well on; being the middle of April. He felt a tingling of excitement looking at the arctic landscape laid out before him. Apart from some hard frosts, there had been very little snowfall throughout the winter months. Generally, it had been mild and unusually dry. Another summer like the previous year and there were bound to be severe water shortages in some areas of the country.

The next day, the snow was still in evidence; so being a day in the middle of the Easter holiday when there would be less activity at Yewhurst Church, Dalmar and Fly wandered through the churchyard to take a look at the big trees all liberally spattered with dollops of white. They had left it rather late in the afternoon and dusk was descending rapidly. As they rounded a curve in the gravel path by two cedars, a magnificent sight greeted them. The big stained-glass window at the altar end was displaying all its radiant colours, brought about by some powerful lighting inside the church. The snow laden trees and gravestones gave off a cold atmosphere due to the grey twilight shadows being cast beyond them; but out of this came the great warming glow of the church window. Dalmar stared spellbound until the lack of movement chilled his bones. Even though he was dressed in his Lakeland wool jumper and wore an extra thick pair of socks under his boots, the cold came creeping upon him. Fly, with his marvellous long-haired coat, was not in the least discomfort. The sound of singing was coming from the interior of the church. 'Must be choir practice,' thought Dalmar. He made his way to pass by the entrance door before he intended dropping back down to the road and the return home.

It was Fly who stopped first. The great door, set back in its arched porch, abruptly swung open letting light and a sudden increase in the sound escape into the gathering darkness. A black-robed churchman came out, closing the door behind him with a loud clang, returning the singing to the volume of before. He swung his cape across the lower part of his face. It was Paul Sanders. Dalmar stopped to acknowledge his presence.

Recognising the man, although he had only seen fleeting glimpses of him and his dog in the past, Paul hailed him. "Ah, just the very person I have been meaning to have a word with. You are John Hunter? And is this your dog – Fly?"

"Yes, on both counts," Dalmar gave a distinctive grin to the churchman. His breath struck the cold air, causing small clouds of mist to form and evaporate instantly.

Paul smiled back, but it could only be seen in his eyes; the cape hiding the lower part of his face. "May I walk down to the bottom gate with you? I take it that is the way you are headed?"

"We are."

"Good – after you," Paul proffered his hand to signal to his new acquaintance to take the lead through the gap by the first rhododendron hedge. As he did so, with Fly following behind them, Paul said, "Really should have called on you, to be honest. I have been rather concerned having had a conversation with Allen Haddle, about a week or so ago."

"Ah ... yes," Dalmar thought pensively, wondering what was coming.

"I know you asked Allen not to say anything about your parentage, but he was worried about you. So please do not think badly of him."

"Well, that depends ... but go on."

"I understand – your young lady – has gone?"

"Yes." Dalmar bowed his head.

"Allen noticed that you seemed depressed." Paul suddenly raised his shoulders and thrust his head forward earnestly. "Look – if you need someone to talk to?"

Dalmar returned the vicar's gaze. Fly was whining impatiently a little way ahead. "Quiet boy," he commanded. Then the emotionally wounded man said, "Look – don't worry – the worst is over. Tell Allen the next time you see him – tell him that." Here, he let out a soft sigh. "Yes, I did feel low. But you have to get on with life. Anyway, there are many folk suffering a lot worse than a broken heart."

"Ah – right," agreed Paul, "but I meant what I said…"

"Thank you, Vicar," Dalmar interrupted him.

After a pause the clergyman added, "Okay ... Please call me Paul."

Dalmar gave a polite nod before saying, "Actually, there is something I would like a word about."

"Go on – I'm listening," said the vicar. The two men carried on conversing for another minute or so before they reached the lower gate by the drinking well. "There is no need to inform me when – just carry on," was Paul's last remark before they parted, one going towards the centre of the village, and the other, with his dog, towards the Claymans Heron. At the top of the little hill opposite the main church entrance, the choir could still be heard singing with obvious enthusiasm. 'Angels in the heights, adoring, you behold God face to face,' competed with the traffic noise on the road.

253

As the man and his dog passed a group of holly bushes the sound of the choir vanished, almost instantly. It was time to put Fly on his lead ready for the road crossing. The traffic was heavy in both directions. Dalmar detested the constant noise when it was like this.

The next day, Easter Sunday, the climate in the south of England fooled everyone, including the meteorological office. The snow had thawed by ten o'clock in the morning, and during mid-afternoon the temperature soared, in some areas, to sixty-nine degrees. Over the next fortnight, the weather returned to the pattern set in the early summer of 1975, except that it started earlier in the year: warm and dry with long periods of unbroken sunshine.

With the return of the hot weather during early May, rumours started to circulate in the village about the feared return of John the Red. Nothing reached Dalmar's ears and nobody, officially, had sighted anything. It was just gossip locally, or was it? A man, who regularly walked his two Labradors on the eastern side of Yewhurst Wood, claimed to have seen a giant serpent that frightened his dogs. However, the Forestry Commission did not take the story seriously, due to the fantastic description, and access to the woods remained open.

A week later, on the Saturday afternoon, Dalmar was in his garden catching up on the laborious task of weeding. Because of the excellent soil, unwanted greenery sprouted in the big shrub bed running in the lowest part of his property at an alarming rate. During the growing season it was necessary to use a hoe once a week, at least. Fly was lying flat out, under the silver birch, dog-tired. They had been to Butser Hill, the highest point in the county. It had been a good hike with the springtime sights and sounds on the chalk downs. The bleating of new-born lambs had been pleasing and Fly behaved himself admirably following his training in the Lake District. He had not forgotten anything, due, no doubt, to the inherent natural instinct of his breed. His owner showed his pleasure by giving him extra treats and cuddles.

At half past five, Dalmar got fed up with the incessant midge bites and made himself ready for a visit to a pub. He had a thirst that needed satisfying urgently. They had both partaken of quite enough exercise, so he put Fly into the rear of the sports car. As in the previous summer, the hood was rarely in place, and they set off for the other end of the village.

The Black Horse was not yet crowded and Dalmar fully intended to be gone before it became so. He ordered a pint of real ale and remained standing in one corner of the bar. Fly lay down across his feet. Shortly, some local men-folk drifted in. Most of them would be taking a quick drink before going home to their families. Three men in casual attire came and stood to one side of him. They were engaged in an intense conversation about a car rental business. There was something familiar about them. Dalmar was shocked to realise why. The voice of the shortest in stature was the bell ringer in his brain, with its distinct Scottish enunciation. This was the same man who had thrown a large proportion of a pint of beer in his face, last year in the Claymans Heron. He looked different without his business suit. The protruding belly seemed more pronounced in his sports style shirt. Dalmar recognised the youngest of the three as being one of the gentlemen he had seen in the Claymans, but the other fellow, he had not laid eyes on before.

He felt ill at ease and decided to drink up and leave. It did occur to him that he had no one to embarrass this time apart from Fly, that is. The younger man gave them a quick glance, obviously admiring the dog. Then he looked into the face of the owner. There was recognition there and his face developed an uncertain mask. He began to shuffle his feet, noticeably. Dalmar, meanwhile, drank the last of his pint and put the glass down on the counter. He was about to try and catch the eye of the landlord to mouth a thank you in leaving, but something about the oratory of the short man stopped him. He was talking about his son and his ability to take pint glasses out of pubs without anyone noticing. Dalmar was surprised that he had a son in his, he presumed, late teens for he certainly did not look old enough. Then he recalled that he was a managing director of a business. "Yes, he has quite a collection, you know," he said, pulling back his shoulders and thrusting his head forward as some proud fathers are prone to do.

"You mean – he's a thief?" Dalmar heard his voice saying this as though someone else was speaking.

The person for whom the remark was intended spun round to face the speaker. He saw the dog first, who had risen expecting something to happen, even if it was only to depart. His eyes travelled up the full height of the collie's owner and seeing a face that he had last seen in similar circumstances, his mouth came open. "Oh, come now!" ... he started to say. Meanwhile, Dalmar, almost casually, put out his right hand and closed it over the other man's wrist, which was holding a practically full pint of beer. He strengthened his grip so that the short man winced. Dalmar manoeuvred the captive arm over the bar. Then with his other hand he took the drink out of the managing director's temporarily disabled one and placed it on the bar. The other two men watched incredulously. Dalmar released his hold and stood with a fixed, piercing look into his antagonist's eyes; but not for long. It was so quick that the stunned witnesses hardly saw the initial movement. The senior executive went down onto his haunches and shot passed Dalmar's legs, pushing the puzzled Fly to one side, while desperately scrabbling away on his hands and knees. He left the pub, and, seconds later, the powerful motor of a large saloon car could be heard starting up and revving. There was a squeal of tyres before the vehicle accelerated away on the road.

The elder of the two men remaining said; "Well, I have never seen anyone talk to Halkins like that before."

Dalmar suddenly became apologetic. He half waved his hands in front of him. "Sorry ...   I really shouldn't have."

"It's okay," came a quick response. "He's actually very good at his job, you know."

"I don't doubt it." Dalmar gave both men a hesitant look. To his great surprise, they became keen to enter into a conversation with him, and there then followed an ardent discussion about the present recession in business, generally, and what was to be done about it.

Dalmar amazed them when he made the following statement. "Are you currently engaged in a redundancy program?"

"How the blazes did you know that?" asked the younger man, a regional operations manager who lived locally. "That is what we are about right now: bloody awful job. We have been sitting over a desk going from branch to branch on paper, in my patch, with an axe shaped pen. Apart from my office, there is at least one poor employee for the chop at all the other depots. Max here," he pointed to his colleague, "is my immediate boss. He and our MD are both staying at the Claymans. On Monday, I start in north Hampshire on the program we have come up with."

"Thought so," said Dalmar. "Can't say I envy you." He got ready to leave; making sure Fly was on his feet. "Take my advice. When they have got you to do the dirty work – watch your back."

"How do you mean?" queried Max with a worried expression on his face.

"I'll bet my reputation that one of you will be looking for another job within three months. And I'll tell you something else. Your boss may be good at his work for the current economic climate, but as soon as the good times come rolling back, he will be out, and the board will appoint a motivator. That is how the cycle goes. ... See you around." With that he left, leaving the two men dumbfounded.

"Thanks very much," whispered one of them quietly with a sullen look on his face.

"You realise – we are walking?" said the other.

CHAPTER FORTY-ONE

"WITNESS TO WHAT EXACTLY – WATER DIVING?"

One week later, on a Friday, during the evening, Dalmar went upstairs to open the windows in every bedroom. It was now the third week in May, and the heat of the day was trapped inside the house. It needed somewhere to escape. As he opened the window in the larger of the two spare rooms – he went completely still. From way out over the road and deep into the forest came a sound: the sound that sent fear running through many a soul who heard it. Because it was hot, most people had their windows open, so all over the village they witnessed the offensive, shrieking din. Stephen Knopner certainly did and went straight to the telephone to call Jonathon Shure in London, as he had instructions so to do. The closure notices would be going up around Yewhurst Wood tomorrow morning. "So much for my Saturday off," Stephen cursed to himself.

Dalmar stood looking out of the window, staring into the blackness away from the lights of the hotel. Fly came up, seeking reassurance. His master ruffled the hair around his neck: an answering half squeal, half grunt, came back at him. After some moments, Dalmar let out a very long sigh, and then he went into his bedroom and started sorting some clothes. He dug out a pair of old denim trousers. They had not been worn for a while and looked a little tired. He found a faded, dark blue cotton shirt to go with them. A rummage in his sock drawer produced a black woollen pair. He required these because he had decided not to wear his moccasins, choosing instead the fell walking boots he had purchased with Suzanne at Grasmere village. What he needed, on this occasion, was ankle support rather than fleetness of foot.

Next, he opened the cupboard under the stairs. He had to go down on all fours and reach into the farthest part before he found what he was looking for. Out came a ten-inch Bowie knife, encased in a black leather sheath, topped by a plain polished hardwood handle. He undid the retaining strap and pulled out the blue-steel blade. Good – the grease he had put on a few years before had done the trick. It was clear of rust. He had purchased this, probably illegal object, while he was visiting Montreal in Canada, during his seafaring days. He found it in a second-hand shop in a poor condition. Over time, he had carefully restored the knife so that it looked almost new, spending hours on the steel getting the pitted rust spots out with wire wool and oil. The leather sheaf had come up well with saddle soap. All the handle had required was a good polish. Right now, the next job was to get a sharpening stone out of his shed and hone the blade, until he was satisfied that it was dangerously razor like. Finally, he replaced the knife in its sheaf.

Then he extricated a pair of black swimming goggles from a drawer which contained similar oddments. He put the knife and the goggles on the kitchen dresser worktop. 'Now – where was his belt?' He found it hanging on a rail in his wardrobe, a two-inch wide, black, calf-leather belt with a solid silver buckle. This was important to him: it had belonged to his father. The family must be represented. The buckle was severely tarnished; so, he quickly gave it a clean and polish. There was one other item, which when found, he checked over as well as he could to ensure that it was working and loaded. He drank a cup of coffee, gave Fly a bowl of water and a couple of biscuits, before going early to bed, setting his alarm clock for five-thirty in the morning.

The intention was to get a good night's sleep, but too many things played on his fearful mind. The result was that he did not drift off until the early hours of the following day. However, when the alarm rang, he felt surprisingly alert and keen to get going. The trepidation had gone, to be replaced by outright determination. This was not for him: it was for William, his elder brother, who, in truth, he still mourned.

It was cooler in the morning. The sun had come up, and a slight mist hung about along the hedges and in the crevices of nature. Dalmar, with Fly by his side entered Yewhurst Wood at about six o'clock. When they got near to the entrance to the forest by the churchyard, he called Fly to heel in a hushed tone. He could make out some activity ahead. Man and dog skirted round some dense laurel growth so they could not be seen by what appeared to be forestry workers putting up notices. "So," said Dalmar to himself, "I am just in time." When he broke clear onto the main path, there was no one in sight. Dalmar spent some time looking up and down the firebreak, and then he scanned the tops of what tall trees he could see. Satisfied, he moved on saying to Fly, "Away!" The dog galloped off for a run, stopping and sniffing the ground every now and then.

Our trespasser's destination was the pathway consisting of a tunnel of hazelnut trees. He had some unfinished business with a certain pond. The springtime lusciousness was at its peak. New leaf blessed all the deciduous trees, giving a luminosity of fresh green lying under a lustrous blue sky. The mauve of the rhododendron bloom showed itself in abundance, and the grasses seemed velvety to the touch. Even the conifer army on the right periphery seemed to be at ease. There were white, yellow, blue and shades of red dotted here and there, especially along the verges: wildflowers advertising their pollen.

When Dalmar arrived near the north-east boundary of the forest, he found the tunnel entrance quickly enough. He stared at it for a minute or two. There was no point in delaying matters, he decided, so with Fly following behind, he set off. After fifty yards of the stooped gait, he tried to make a sortie through the hazels to his right. He did not get very far. The growth was just too intense. He returned to the tunnel and then repeated this exercise, literally every ten to fifteen yards. After about the eighth attempt, he managed to make some way off the path. Eventually, they broke out into a sort of clearing with what appeared to be long dried grass everywhere. It snagged around Dalmar's ankles and got wrapped up in Fly's four legs. He got cross with it and barked his displeasure. Dalmar persisted with his exploration, but all it rewarded him, in the end, was a view of a field with the backend of a farmhouse on the other side. Traversing down the side of the field brought him, as he expected, to the other end of the tunnel of hazel trees.

Perplexed and frustrated, Dalmar returned along the passageway to the main pathway. Once there, he sat down – about five yards from the entrance – and looked at it. He glanced at his wristwatch. It was nearly eight o'clock. This surprised him – had it really taken that long to carry out the exploration? He noticed that the ground that he was sitting on was already very dry. The lack of enough rainfall during last winter, following the dry summer which preceded it, together with the current spell of fine weather was really beginning to show its effect.

Just then, he heard the sound of a vehicle moving along the firebreak he had branched off earlier. Soon it came into view at the junction which Dalmar could see about a hundred yards away. He recognised the insignia on the Land Rover's side as that of the Forestry Commission. At first, it carried on toward Yewhurst Church and then abruptly stopped. It stayed there with the engine idling. Dalmar thought he could detect that the driver was looking in his rear-view mirror. Unexpectedly, the vehicle reversed all the way back to the junction, stopping, before a gear change heralded it going forward again – except that this time it was headed straight in Dalmar and Fly's direction.

Our man was not concerned. Any thoughts about him being somewhere – he was not supposed to be – had evaporated instantly. He had seen something very odd. The implications of that oddness were welling up in his mind. Those implications, perhaps because they were mostly unforeseen – were of enormous importance. Up to this moment, the whole John the Red, Red Adder business had been thought to be something to do with a freak of nature... But now ... He felt his stomach – go icy cold.

Stephen Knopner stopped the four-wheel drive almost on top of Dalmar. Fly jumped up from his reclined position and started to bark.

"Down Fly. Quiet!" Dalmar rasped out the command. Fly stood square in the path and contented himself by staring hard at the Land Rover. The noisy diesel engine was abruptly silenced.

"For someone who is breaking the law, you don't seem exactly concerned to see me?" asked an obviously annoyed forest officer, as he climbed out of the vehicle. He had been up early and was not too pleased. His ranger's uniform was already creased from the exertions of the day. He and Dalmar had not met since the death of Ginger Styles last year, and, by the tone of his voice, Stephen did not seem to wish to renew the acquaintance, not at this moment that is. "After the photographs I let you have a loan of ... can't see why you should still have an interest in this neck of the woods?"

Dalmar did not look at Stephen. He hardly seemed to know he was there, except that he gently held up a hand to silence him. All the while, he carried on studying the area by the entrance to the tunnel. Finally, Dalmar spoke. "As to that, the reflection of trees in water can hide a small pond from aerial photography." He still did not look in Stephen's direction.

The simplicity of the answer stunned Stephen. The man was probably right. On the other hand, to establish the whereabouts of a pond was not the main reason for the flight being chartered. His facial expression went serious again. "You haven't answered my question. Why are you disobeying the law? And please tell your dog to stop growling at me like that!" Fly's aggressive attitude *was* a little off putting.

"Sit!" said Dalmar still staring ahead of him. The dog gave up the theatricals and sat down, immediately inclining his head away from the two men. It had been after considerable solo debate that his master had decided in favour of taking Fly with him this morning, but if asked why he would not have been able to give a satisfactory answer.

It was not the tunnel entrance that Dalmar was so intent on. It was the rhododendron bush next to it. What had first captured his eye was half an inch, no more, of wood without bark-covering near the base. The stark, pale cream of the unprotected stem was obvious. Otherwise, there seemed to be nothing out of the ordinary. The bush looked as though it was in the flush of spring, but, if one looked further, the leaves were drooping a little. And if you studied the large plant even longer, as Dalmar had just done, there was something about the way it was rooted to the earth ... or lack of it.

Dalmar got to his feet. At last he turned to acknowledge Stephen. "Good morning," he said. Then he made his way toward the rhododendron.

"And?" came Stephen's reply. He was beginning to get cross.

"Actually, illegal presence or not, I am very glad you are here. You see – I need a witness, and somehow I don't think my dog – will suffice."

"Witness to what exactly – water divining?" The sarcastic edge to Stephen's voice was at its hardest: an obvious reference to the illusive Secret Pond.

Dalmar said nothing. He went up to the bush and studied it at close quarters for a few seconds, before bending down and stretching his arms out to take a grip, low down on each side. Then he lifted the complete bush clear off the ground. He expected it to be heavy. But it came up almost too fast.

"Stone me!" uttered a loud voice behind him.

Dalmar stood up to his full height, and, still carrying the bush, shuffled to the left until he felt he was exactly opposite the hazel tree tunnel entrance; then he bent at the waist and released the rhododendron. As it plopped and settled on the ground, he stood back.

"Great tits!" exclaimed Stephen. The tunnel entrance had disappeared, and in the place where the bush had been – was another opening to a hazel tree tunnel that looked almost the same, except that it curved away to the right.

"That is more as I originally remember it," commented Dalmar. At exactly the same moment, Fly began a low growl. Not the same growl he had given Stephen earlier. It was lower in note – somehow more serious. His owner ignored it.

Inserted into the ground where the bush had been was a galvanised bucket half full of water. The lip of the bucket was flush with the ground. 'Funny - I do not recall seeing that before,' thought Dalmar. It was only a matter of moments before he discovered how. Placed into some of the front hazel trunks was a flat, circular board. Dalmar slid it out and plonked it over the bucket's aperture. It covered it with room to spare. He looked at Stephen, and not being satisfied scuffed some old leaves and other material over it affecting a perfect camouflage.

Stephen stared incredulously. "Well ... after you," he suggested, and backed it up by giving the other man a gentle prod in the rear.

"Thought you might say that," said Dalmar with a slight chuckle. And so, he led the way. Both men had to stoop, for if anything, this tunnel was even lower than the other. The way went around a bend to the right, and just when you thought you must come back onto the main path, it straightened out.

After about two hundred yards, Dalmar clapped his hands. Stephen had little time to shout, "What the!" before the sound of ducks flapping their wings over to the right and a little ahead, brought joy and intense relief to Dalmar.

He half turned to the crouching Stephen, "Ducks," he said with an empty expression on his face. "Ducks live near water." Then he made a motion as though carrying a divining stick.

"Alright, clever-dick, let's see this bloody pond of yours first – eh. By the way is that knife legal?"

Dalmar just shrugged his shoulders in answer. They had only gone a few more yards before he found what he was looking for. It was not a path, but there were definite signs that animals or people or both, had made a rough route off the passageway. Dalmar pushed back some hazel branches with his right forearm and followed the way through a large growth of long grasses. It was then that Stephen said to him, "You do know your dog isn't with us?"

"No, but I half expected it. He'll be waiting on the main path – I hope."

"You don't want to go back for him?" queried Stephen.

"Nope," He turned to look at the forestry man. "It's okay, he has done this before." He half squinted his eyes at Stephen to make sure he took in his next comment. "Trouble is. He usually does it – when the Red Adder is nearby."

Dalmar got the reaction he was hoping for. Stephen stopped in mid-stride and his mouth opened partially with a look of sheer concern all over his face, and then he said, "Oh shit!"

Soon they came up to the bases of a group of European larches. Dalmar made a point of fingering the new, light green needles. "There are no larches in this part of Yewhurst Wood – apparently." The forestry boss had already spotted them from a way off and was expecting this.

"Absolutely: quite right. These must be plastic," he said with a fake sneer.

"Ah; of course, how stupid of me." Dalmar pushed his way between two of the trees in question and climbed up onto a rise of grey granite rock. Reaching the top, he turned around and held out a hand. Stephen coming up below looked at him with a very weird expression. "You may need this. Might be a bit of a shock," said Dalmar.

Stephen ignored the out-stretched hand and climbed up beside him, looking at the granite rock with complete puzzlement. He raised his head and said, "Blo-ody hell!" The first and last parts of the expletive were dragged out. He had good reason. Before him – lay a sparkling, clear water pond. The purity of the water was obvious in its very appearance. It had a sort of lead crystal look about it. Most of the ponds in this part of Hampshire have a dark peaty form. This one looked like a pool from a mountainous district.

Christine Westward had remarked, when she first saw it, that it must look wonderful in the spring. She was right. In broken clumps, interweaved by the granite, were bluebells in full bloom. This glorious sight, backed by larches, stretched two thirds of the way around the circumference of the pond, on its elongated shape. A large clump of rhododendron took up the rest. The bushes were covered in a mass of mauve flowers, and snugly fitted in amongst it was the trunk of a sweet chestnut tree. It rose with its classic shaped leaf, the undisputed boss of the area. All this was reflected in the water making it look as though you could walk on it. Stephen took it all in. Immediately he regretted his earlier sarcasm. "I owe you an apology," he said meekly.

Dalmar turned his head toward him. "Not me ... my ex-girl-friend – maybe."

"Well – do it for me."

"You can do your own grovelling. Anyway – as I said – ex-girlfriend. I have not seen her for months, and I am not likely to."

"She was a nice girl." Stephen changed the subject. "Well, here it is – the Secret Pond. It's certainly lived up to its name."

"Yes – we've been fooled, haven't we? And quite deliberately. Someone, and I mean a human being, did not want anyone else to know about this."

"Uh, uh, but don't read too much into it: probably a tramp's home. Let's look around. I'll bet we'll find evidence of a den somewhere. We have come across vagrants' shelters before you know."

"Would a tramp go to the bother of all that camouflage? I doubt it somehow." Dalmar was not convinced about that theory. "And why wasn't it in place when the girls came here?"

"Obviously, our tenant forgot to close the door after him, or ... he was here... watching," suggested Stephen.

Dalmar felt a chill go through his body. The thought of an unseen party spying on the girls swimming did not please him. But he dismissed this quickly. "You are forgetting something."

Stephen, who was making his way over the rocks to try and traverse around the pond, stopped, turned and cast his head towards Dalmar. "What?"

"You see that chestnut?"

Stephen looked at it. It was right across the water from him. "Yes, a beautiful specimen it is too."

"Well, it was from that tree that the snake attacked Christine Westward. She was swimming under it."

"Really ..." Stephen gave it a thorough further look with renewed interest.

"Do you think a vagrant would share his house with the Red Adder?"

"Ah – see your point." Stephen rubbed his chin. "Yes – will have to think on about that. Anyway, come on. Let's do a search of the area?"

"Just a moment, do you mind if I thoroughly look at that tree before we go near it?"

"Carry on if it makes you feel more secure. I'm going ahead." With that, Stephen started to make his way around the pond in an anti-clockwise direction. Dalmar finished his detailed scan of the chestnut long before the forest officer arrived near its overhanging branches. Sometimes, Stephen could not navigate his way immediately next to the edge of the water due to heavy growth, particularly blackberry bramble. He then had to make a detour. This was never easy due to the lower growing thorns and tall grasses that obstructed his legs.

Finally, Dalmar looked away from the chestnut; however, he did not feel completely satisfied. There were too many blind areas in which even a fairly large snake might be hiding. He also knew that it would not necessarily be red in colour and might blend in with the dark tones of the trunk and branches. Anyhow, he started after Stephen who had broken out into a less dense area coming up under the tree. Nevertheless, the forest officer had to go right around it, away from the water. Shortly afterwards, he disappeared from sight. Dalmar, who was following almost exactly in the other man's footsteps, because the way had been partially cleared by him, heard the start of another, "Great ti..." coming from his direction. This was followed by, "Come and have a look at this lot!"

Well before he caught up with him, he nearly trod on something, which Stephen had missed. It was a lady's soft casual shoe, or rather used to be. He spotted the other one, making up a pair, partially hidden by a clump of bluebells. Dalmar realised who they belonged to – immediately. He kicked them under some shrubbery. Christine would hardly want them back.

He found Stephen in a standing 'thinkers' position looking at something very odd. Dalmar made a little grunt of surprise. Tucked around the back of the chestnut behind a semi-circle of larches, were what appeared to be two large rabbit hutches – one on top of the other. On drawing closer, the two men noticed that the bottom hutch had lost its top, and the two had been joined together. This measured about six feet in length and eight high. The lid had an overhanging layer or two of heavy duty felt. The base half of the end nearest the pond was a door. It was wide open. Someone had gone to a great deal of trouble putting a very fine steel mesh over the top and sides of the cage, including the hinged door panel. Most of the interior of the housing was packed with bales of straw, a considerable quantity of which had been broken up.

"Are you thinking what I'm thinking?" Stephen's question sounded flat in the strange scenery.

"I would say that something rather nasty hibernated in there last winter," Dalmar answered him.

"Yes – I am beginning to realise what you meant earlier. It looks as though Jonathon may have been right."

"Sorry?"

"Well – at that conference we had at the Claymans last summer, Jonathon Shure mentioned the possibility that the Red Adders might have been brought about by a person, in some way. They never took it any further because our science officer, Wilfred Blyte, blew his top at the suggestion, accusing Jonathon of being a television prima donna. I think Wilfred is going to be somewhat chagrined. Serves the know-it-all right." Stephen huffed after he said the last words before adding, "Mind you, I know the evidence is mounting up, but it is not conclusive yet."

"It isn't still in there, is it?" Dalmar's question made Stephen jump back from the side of the cage. Both men looked around for the same thing at the same time: a stout stick. Stephen found the ideal article, which had fallen from the chestnut and started prodding the bales through the open door. There was no sign of any movement.

Satisfied, Dalmar lifted one end of the straw. Seeing nothing untoward he replaced it and went around the other side to do the same. Abruptly, he placed a hand inside and retrieved a small fragment of eggshell. "This may well be that evidence. I think you had better see what your science officer can make of it." Then he added. "Thought a prima donna referred to a female?"

Stephen shrugged his shoulders before taking the eggshell piece. "Well done - thanks," he said, putting it carefully in his over-flapped shirt pocket. "What do you reckon to these marks?" Stephen pointed to some dark areas on the wooden base strut of the bottom cage.

"Looks like acid burns," said Dalmar bending down to rub his finger along them.

Stephen was of the same opinion. "Strange," he commented with a quizzical expression. They had a good look inside the rest of the cage but found nothing else. Someone appeared to have carried out a cleaning up operation. "Do these snakes shed their skins?" asked

Stephen.

"No idea. And if they do, I don't know at what time of year. Good thought though. Shall we have a look around?" suggested Dalmar. They agreed to do so, exhaustively searching for anything unusual, but whoever was involved seemed to have done a very good job at leaving as few clues as possible.

Stephen went back to the subject. "I still think this is the work of, shall we say, an intelligent vagrant. It makes sense he wouldn't have his bedchamber too near, but it might not be that far away. It would be handy for him to be close to the water. I'll get my chaps to do a thorough search. We have done enough for now. How did you spot – the rhododendron thingy – by the way?"

"Where the bush had probably been chopped, a small area of white was showing indicating missing bark," explained Dalmar. "The person responsible had covered the other ends with mud, but he must have missed this one. Otherwise, we would still be none the wiser and you would have packed me on my way." Stephen smiled ruefully at him.

"I'm a bit worried about my dog; do you mind if we head back to the path?" asked Dalmar. He realised that he had left Fly for rather a long time, and, as there was a strong possibility that a nasty snake was about, he suddenly felt anxious.

"No – I was going to suggest we make a move," said Stephen. Wonder if Ginger spotted this water? There is the top of the Scots pine he fell from – over there – look."

Dalmar followed the line of view from Stephen's outstretched hand. He considered the question for a little while before saying. "Certainly would have done – if he had had the chance to turn his head. Unfortunately – he was prevented from doing so." Then he thought for a second or two. "But - I don't know might have."

CHAPTER FORTY-TWO

"SEEN ANY FISH IN HERE?"

Dalmar and Stephen completed the circumference of the pond by pushing through the undergrowth in the opposite direction to that which they had come. Arriving back by the main conglomerate of granite rock, the forester, who was in the lead, carefully avoided treading on some bluebells in full bloom and placed his right foot on a rock by the water's edge. He left his left leg trailing so that he could bring his elbow onto his knee, and peer into the water with a hand on his chin. "Seen any fish in here?" he asked.

"No;" Dalmar paused before adding, "had a really good look though." He came up beside Stephen and tried to look into the depths of the pond. The reflections of the trees and bushes did not help; using their hands as shields, both men tried to shade out the sun, now beginning its climb into the sky. "Nothing," said Dalmar after a good while, "Nothing that I can see. How about you?"

Unbeknown to Dalmar, Stephen had visibly stiffened. "What the hell is that!?" He pointed into the water right by him. The bottom was a good depth, probably four feet or more.

Dalmar moved his head to look into the pond nearer the forester. At first, he could see nothing, and then he thought he could make out a triangular shape like a ray or flat fish. There was no time to study it further. The object, dramatically, got larger. Stephen withdrew his pointing hand, and his shoulders went back. A giant viper's head burst out of the water! Any sound that it made was lost in the harsh scream that Stephen let go as the jaw of the creature, dripping water, partially closed over his leg, just under the knee. Although tough, the material of his ranger's working trousers was not thick enough to protect him from such enormous fangs. Unfortunately, his boot had not been long enough either. Dalmar jumped back away from the pond edge as the horrid, sinister looking head and neck disappeared back under the surface. Stephen stumbled and started to fall backwards. Dalmar grabbed him around his waist. "Oh Christ!" Stephen yelled, "It hurts like hell!"

Dalmar transferred his hold to an under-arm support. "Stay like that," he said. "Just while I take a quick look."

Stephen coughed out a struggling, "Ok-kay," while Dalmar rolled up the trouser on the wounded man's right leg. There under the kneecap was a single dark bloodied hole.

"You are lucky; it only got you with one fang."

"Oh really! I'm going to dance – with bloody joy. Oh w-wow – what a bonus! ... Jesus wept – it hurts!" He let out some gurgling noises signifying intense pain.

Dalmar let down the trouser leg and went back to supporting Stephen under his shoulder. "Right, let's get back to the Land Rover. I presume you have a field telephone on board. We'll call an ambulance. Get some anti-serum into you, and you will be doing the two-hundred meters hurdle in a couple of days."

"Boll-ocks!" said Stephen. "Come on – let's go. Where's that bloody creature got to?" Almost as though announced, a huge snake, in excess of fifteen feet long, came out of the water on the far side of the pond. It was not red, but a dirty brown colour with large black zigzag markings on its back. That was all that the two awestruck men saw, for it meandered at lightning speed across and over the rocks – to be lost from sight among the larch trees. Stephen, momentarily, forgot his pain.

It was extremely difficult for Dalmar to support the injured man and get him back to the hazel track. But then things got very hard. The tunnel was not wide enough for two men to go side by side. Dalmar went in front, practically on his hands and knees, and Stephen draped his arms over his shoulders and sort of hopped along with his bearer. It seemed as if the stronger light at the end of the tunnel would never appear, but, eventually, one man in agony, and another with an acutely aching back arrived at the pathway.

Dalmar, immediately had to prevent Stephen from trying to sit down. "No!" He almost shouted at him. "Must stay on your feet until we get you into the Land Rover, then you can rest. Okay?"

Dalmar was now perspiring profusely. He brushed moisture from his brow to stop it dripping into his eyes. Then he put his arm under Stephen's shoulder and more or less carried him over to the motor. He propped him up against the side. "Stay there," he ordered while he opened the passenger door wide. Dalmar placed his left arm under Stephen's legs and lifted him onto the passenger seat. He located the seat belt and made sure Stephen was harnessed in tightly. "I am going to try and get through to your office," he said finally.

Stephen grunted at him.

Dalmar went around to the front of the vehicle and opened the driver's door. 'Good,' he said to himself, Stephen had left the keys in the ignition switch. Before getting in, he yelled at the top of his voice, "Fly – come!" He waited a few moments, but there was no sign of the Collie.

He was about to get in the Land Rover when, out of the corner of his left eye, he noticed that Stephen was staring ahead through misty eyes – horror written all over his face. Dalmar followed his gaze. John the Red was in the centre of the pathway, with its head raised up some three to four feet off the ground, and about fifteen yards away. The

The Shy Avenger   Scardthomas

enormous snake was looking at them without making any movement. It could have been a sculpture. Now it was red, almost all over. Not a bright cherry red – deeper in tone – much deeper: the colour of blood when seen in depth.

There it was. To some, it would appear magnificent, but to the two men watching – it was terrifying: a gigantic snake with an air about it of outright aggression. Its head started to sway, ever so slowly, from side to side: its predatory eyes seemed to possess nothing but loathing for the on-lookers.

Dalmar's first thought was to start up the Land Rover and run the thing over, but he was quite sure it could, when necessary, move extremely fast. It would be able to take evasive action and might even strike at Stephen through the open window. He had no time to think about closing that window, for, as though reading Dalmar's mind, the snake lowered its head and the whole massive length started to move slowly towards them, using the side-to-side motion of the legless reptile. As the head moved and triggered the first 's' shape in the front of the body, it seemed to ricochet down the rest of its vast length, before the front commenced the motion all over again. Dalmar quickly considered starting up the vehicle and going into rapid reverse, and again he rejected the idea. In among these thoughts lay extreme anxiety for his dog. He did not call his name again. Now was not the time for Fly to make an appearance. He hoped that the animal was somewhere on the route home.

There was only one solution. Dalmar accepted it in a surprisingly cool manner, considering the awful theatre of the situation. If he perished, then so would Stephen – almost certainly: a family man. He stepped out in front of the Land Rover and advanced five yards towards the snake. It was now a mere twelve to fifteen feet from him. Dalmar could see the malevolent profile of its head: the broad triangle with dark, corrugated flutes under the line of the mouth, and stark, ugly scales above it. The long, flicking forked tongue was going in and out almost seductively, and, at the same time, seemingly, vibrating. Those evil-looking amber eyes heralded the body that must have grown immensely, since last witnessed by a surviving human being. Fleetingly, Dalmar noted the over-sized scales all over its body. To him, they appeared prehistoric. It was as long as any venomous snake anywhere in the world. But what made it totally different was its huge body. Due, possibly, to the loose folds of skin on the underside, the girth of the main body made it look like a gigantic python. The only narrow parts were the neck and the tapering tail. Even then, that neck was extremely chunky.

When it reached to within a couple of yards, it stopped and raised its head. Dalmar immediately felt into his left-hand jean's pocket and took out the pair of goggles. Quickly, he pulled them over his head and secured the circular glass cups over his eyes. One of the lenses started to mist slightly with the effects of the hot moisture from the perspiration on his brow. He ignored it. One good eye would have to do. The snake was not deterred by these actions; it started the staring routine. The reptilian eyes turned to a pose of complete immobility. Dalmar unclipped the strap on the Bowie and drew the weapon from its sheath. Holding the knife in his right hand, with the blade opened towards the monster reptile, he started to inch his way forward. He was not ready to return the stare just yet. He had to get a little nearer.

Unknown to Dalmar, Stephen, half- conscious – was witnessing all this. Too weak to do anything himself, he watched, with much apprehension, the intense drama before him. The reptile gave off an appalling air, as though it was telling the two men to prepare for their final moments of existence.

Dalmar continued with his stealthy advance, at the same time swaying his head from side to side, so that the snake was unable to line up a trajectory for the venom propulsion. Everything had gone silent around them. The occasional birdcalls of the woodland had stopped. Dalmar remained focused on the snake's head. When he was satisfied that he was near enough, he halted his advance and corrected his stance to an astride crouching position. This close to the ghastly reptile, Dalmar experienced an enormous urge to drop the knife, turn, and run. Bracing himself, he placed his left foot a little ahead of his right and held the knife hand wide and back. Now ... he returned the snake's stare.

Far sooner than the highly tensed man expected, the mighty viper's mouth opened enough to expose both fangs. Then came that amazingly loud 'STUTT'! The sound and action from the reptile's head had a power about it like a high voltage electric current shorting out. Both lenses of Dalmar's goggles received a splash of yellowish liquid across them. His left hand flew to the goggle straps, tearing them to the ground. At the same time, he lunged forward with his knife. He stopped in mid-thrust. John the Red did not wait to see the result of his spitting attack. It struck with the speed of a bullwhip and the force of a jackhammer! The fangs came at Dalmar at waist height. He had a split-second in which to swivel his hips and avoid them. The snake recoiled like a broken hawser and struck again, this time aiming for where his target's hips had been. Dalmar swivelled the other way, and the Red Adder missed. It recoiled just as fast, and, without hesitation, struck out, lower down, going for Dalmar's left leg. The incredibly teed up man leapt into the air and the Red Adder missed again. It recoiled once more.

Dalmar felt a massive wave of fear envelope him. The first sight of the giant snake, on the track, barring their way had been awesome enough, but now he realised that this reptile had a power about it that made it virtually impossible for him, alone, to defend himself. Dalmar became acutely aware that the snake had the ascendancy in the attack. It would only be a matter of time before a strike struck home. Somehow, he must turn the situation around ... or perish.

Then, unaccountably, the snake seemed to hesitate. Dalmar was desperately trying to formulate a plan in which he could stab the oncoming head during an attacking thrust. He knew he would never have sufficient reflexes to beat it in retraction. He half hoped that the next onslaught would, once more, be aimed at his midriff, and this time he would meet it with steel!

Dalmar was not sure when he first noticed what started as a blur, way away in the background – moving very fast towards them. He is also unsure as to when he noticed that the blur became a ball of black, tan and white. But at some stage in those dramatic seconds, he became aware it developed into a sure running collie, coming up at full speed behind the serpent, head thrust forward with teeth bared!

Dalmar had no time to cry out in an attempt to stop Fly, because the snake's head suddenly rose up in the air. John the Red looked as though it was going to hurl itself high onto the defending man's torso. But the dog was there. Fly's jaws closed around the conveniently raised red neck, and although that neck was far too wide to get a complete grip, his teeth had sunk in – and he was not going to let go! In confirmation of this, he kept up a persistent ferocious snarling. Dalmar watched as the ghastly reptilian creature started to writhe, using its immense body. He was sure it would only be a short time before Fly would be forced to release his hold and suffer a fatal strike. Then came that dreadful noise as John the Red opened its mouth wide, and let forth a hideous high-pitched, hissing shriek!   It completely drowned out Fly's growling. Dalmar hurled himself around the back of the conflict and trapped the writhing snake between his upper legs. As he squeezed his thigh muscles together with all his might, he became aware of its massive strength. He could hardly believe the force with which it tried to counter the pressure he was exerting. He plunged the Bowie down across the snake's neck, angled, just behind Fly's growling mouth. He pushed down and sawed, down and sawed, down and sawed, backwards and forwards. Disgusting spurts of blood erupted. From behind, Dalmar could feel and hear the body and tail of the giant snake thrashing about. The ground beneath his feet reverberated with the thudding impacts, and, amazingly, severe quantities of dust rose into the air around them. The huge serpent sent a massive surge of power through its coils, and Dalmar fell awkwardly to his right, causing him to lose his hold on the knife. He managed to retain his grip with his legs while being bucked up and down as though on a manic seesaw! Dalmar desperately flailed around on the ground with his right hand feeling for the knife. Then – he realised – almost stupidly, that it was still embedded in the reptile's neck.

Fly, in the meantime, was miraculously still holding his bite, all the while snarling fiercely as the red snake hissed and hissed non-stop in its efforts to shake him off. Dalmar managed to get himself upright again and recommence his sawing action with the Bowie. It seemed an age: backwards and forwards, over and over again. He felt as though his arm muscles would seize up.

Without warning, the interminable hissing suddenly stopped. Almost at once the snake's body went still. Dalmar kept on cutting, blood was flowing freely now. He pressed together still further with his legs, until he realised that there was nothing to fight against any more ... He had severed the head from the body.

Withdrawing the knife, he threw it on the ground. Then he patted the still growling Fly who had not let go his hold. "All right boy – all right!" Dalmar was panting with the shock and exertion. "All right!" He took hold of the dog and started to pull him away, "Drop it boy – drop it!" Dalmar's tone was beginning to show intense relief. Finally Fly opened his jaw and the terrible head of John the Red fell to the ground. An exhausted man embraced his wonderful pet and cried dry tears into the soft coat on his back.

As Dalmar rose to his feet, remembering the urgent situation concerning Stephen, the wounded forester came into view through the still swirling dust clouds. He was still conscious and was staring at the scene through the Land Rover's windscreen, a look of sheer wonder on his face. When Dalmar approached him, he managed a few words. "That was ... well done. That was ..." But the talking was too much for him, and he went quiet and lowered his head.

Dalmar went around to the back of the vehicle. He released the retaining straps for the canvas flap and rolled it up, clipping it into place at the top. Then he pulled the pins for the rear panel and let it hang downwards. "Fly – in!" Dalmar pointed into the Land Rover. Fly, who was standing right behind him leapt aboard with one bound. He came up behind Stephen and started to nuzzle his ear. The forester did not object.

Dalmar climbed into the driver's seat and took a green telephone handset off its hook. It sparked into life at once with a crackling noise. He pressed a switch marked 'transmit' and spoke into the mouthpiece. "Stephen Knopner calling base ... Stephen Knopner calling base – over." He pushed a button to access the receive position.

A woman's voice came on the loudspeaker. She was speaking from the Forestry Commission office at Chapp. "Stephen? That doesn't sound like you – over?"

"It isn't. My name is John Hunter. The Red Adder has bitten Stephen. Did you get that – over?"

"Oh no!" Understandably the lady sounded in distress.

"What is your name?" asked Dalmar followed by, "Over."

"Maria – Maria Parsons. Over."

"Right Maria. The bite is below the knee, and I hope it is only about half the usual potency. Fortunately, the snake did not make a very good strike on him. I think Stephen will be all right as long as we get an ambulance as soon as possible – over." He said all this without confidence and hoped it didn't come across in the tone of his voice.

Maria Parsons grasped the urgency and put her distress to one side. "Right, I will phone for one – over."

"Good. Tell the ambulance service to go to Yewhurst Church car park. If it comes from Winchester, they will pass the Claymans Heron on their left. After that, tell them to slow down and look over on the right-hand side of the road. Look for a tree with a white painted ring around the trunk. That is the entrance to the car park." He paused to gather breath. "I will be there, in Stephen's Land Rover, with him on board. Okay – over?"

"Got it," said Maria. "Over and out."

"No – hold on – this is important. Make sure they understand that the casualty has been bitten by *The Red Adder,* and make sure they bring some anti-venom serum with them, also make sure there is someone on board that ambulance who knows how and where to inject it." Dalmar paused again. "I think that's it ... get off Fly!   Over"

"Got the bit about the serum, but what's that about a fly – over?"

"Don't worry – just my exuberant dog. Deserves to be; he is a hero – over."

"Oh"... there was a sound like anxious breathing. "Okay, over and out."

"Over and out." An arm with a distinct tremble, replaced the handset on the receiver in the Land Rover.

The urgent matter having been attended to; John Dalmar Hunter retrieved his knife. As he came near to the body of John the Red and the dismembered head, he half expected some part of it to come to life, such was the sinister aura that surrounded it. He wiped the Bowie in the long grass near the edge of the path. When he picked up the swimming goggles, he became unsure as to what to do with them. The venom on the glass had to be kept away from Fly, in particular. Then he had an idea. Gingerly, he held them out in front of him and hung them over the radio aerial protruding from the Land Rover's wing. The poisonous deposits had already lost their liquid look.

Dalmar gave Stephen some encouraging words as he jumped back into the driving seat and started the ignition. Almost immediately, he got out again, and extricated a tiny silver camera from a trouser hip pocket. He approached the snake's body parts, and brought the little lens to his right eye, squinted, and pulled on the shutter, a left to right action. He did this three-times before climbing back into the Forestry Commission's vehicle.

CHAPTER FORTY-THREE

"NOW – IT DOESN'T MATTER ANY MORE."

Dalmar, although familiar with a four-wheel drive vehicle, knew it was going to be a bumpy ride. They juddered about while he searched through the gears with much graunching. Fly showed his displeasure by barking at him while he turned the Land Rover around. "Be quiet boy, this is difficult enough as it is without your assistance." Dalmar tried to minimise the lurching by keeping the wheels out of badly rutted areas. When they got to the main firebreak, this became near impossible, and poor Stephen had to suffer frequent bucking bouts which caused him discomfort. But he suffered it stoically, clenching his teeth most of the way.

On arriving at the gate by the road, the policeman on duty obligingly opened it for them, thinking it was a normal Forestry Commission vehicle going about its business. As they passed through, the driver said, "Thank you, Officer," and carried on without stopping. The policeman gave him a funny look, because although Dalmar's attire was liberally covered in dust, he did not look like a typical forestry worker. Just as the vehicle started forward, he gave an even funnier look, and made an unintelligible shout when he saw the sight of a man, apparently slumped over in the passenger seat. Dalmar turned right onto the road, and, immediately right again into the church car park. The policeman closed the gate quickly and ran to investigate, even though there was another officer on duty there.

Dalmar called out through the open window of the vehicle to this policeman, as soon as he had driven close enough for him to hear. "Look out for an ambulance coming along the road, please. I've got the Forestry Commission boss here. The Red Adder has bitten him." The policeman did not say anything. He had been caught in the act of taking the first mouthful from a chicken sandwich. Hurriedly, he placed the remainder on a clean mossy area of ground and came running up.

"Can you say that again?" There was a totally confused expression on his face as he looked at Dalmar's sweat lined features. The other constable arrived, but he was naturally more interested in the groaning figure in the passenger seat. Obviously, Dalmar had to explain in more detail. Once the matter had been related, the policeman who had been guarding the gate went to watch for the ambulance.

Dalmar heaved himself out of the Land Rover. He was appalled, but not surprised to see the upper parts of his jeans covered in blood, and, unfortunately, some on the driver's seat he had been sitting in. He was too late to stop Fly helping himself to the chicken sandwich. The dog had been taught never to take food from anywhere, other than ground level.

"Are you hurt?" the policeman enquired, pointing to the state of Dalmar's trousers.

"No," he answered. "That is the snake's blood." Any further questions on that matter came to a halt as the policeman spotted Fly devouring the rest of his sandwich. Dalmar shrugged his shoulders unsympathetically. Fly considered that the tasty morsel was clearly intended for him. He showed his appreciation after he swallowed the last piece, by rolling his lengthy tongue over his upper jaw.

Because of the time taken in getting to the car park from the attack site, altogether ten minutes, the ambulance arrived inside another twelve. A period usefully employed by Dalmar in removing some of the dust embedded in his dog's hair, all the while keeping a wary eye on Stephen Knopner. The ambulance driver had made extremely good going from Winchester, the city being eight miles away. Maria had been successful; not only were there two ambulance service men on board, but also a young doctor. The same young doctor who had attended to Christine Westward and been at hand in the forest when Brian Dace and Rattlesnake Ben had been killed.

He went straight up to the injured man with a syringe at the ready, located the area of the bite wound, and the injection of anti-venom serum went in above the knee. Dalmar let out a long, "Pheeew!" One of the policemen looked at him with a great deal of consideration, wondering what kind of ordeal they had just been through.

However, this was not the end of the medical emergency. Stephen had to be conveyed to Winchester Hospital quickly, so that the body could rest while the fight for recovery took place. They brought a wheelchair from the ambulance. The patient would not be allowed to lie flat on a stretcher to ensure that the bite wound remained below his heart. The uniformed paramedics lifted Stephen out of the Land Rover and placed him in the chair. Then they wheeled him across to the ambulance and winched the chair to the level of the floor. They were just about to pull him in, when he started to demand something from one of them. As a result, an ambulance serviceman approached Dalmar and said, "He is asking for you."

The doctor said, "Quickly now," looking at Dalmar, and then he climbed into the ambulance ready for the rear doors to be closed.

Dalmar went up to Stephen, who beckoned to him to come close. He spoke in a hoarse whisper. "On the field telephone…"

"Yes," said Dalmar.

"You – you gave your name – as *John* Hunter?"

"Did I?" Dalmar showed the surprise on his face.

"Mistake – was it?" Stephen's voice was weak.

"Not exactly … it's a long story. I'll tell you when you get back to fitness."

Dalmar could not have said anything worse. As the ambulance man tried to close the last half of the door, Stephen grabbed hold of Dalmar's shirt with both hands, and with a grip that surprised him at its tenacity said, "No! Tell me now. I want to know … tell me." Stephen had rapidly, over the last hour, become aware of a significant mystery concerning Dalmar. It was not just a case of involvement today; he was sure there was a giant yesterday as well.

Dalmar kept it short. "You have been informed about the snake attacks of 1947 and 1948?"

"Yes."

"You know that the first human casualty was a young boy?"

"Yes."

"That boy's name was William Simon Hunter … my elder brother." Dalmar let it sink in. "My first names are John Dalmar. After the tragedy, my parents dropped the first name because of the connotation with John the Red."

"I see," Stephen looked satisfied. He let go his hold on Dalmar's shirt. "Now – it doesn't matter anymore." His voice became weaker, and Dalmar hardly heard the next bit, but he could read his lips. "That is why you called yourself John…'

Dalmar, Fly and the two policemen watched the ambulance, sirens blaring, blue lights flashing; disappear round the bend of the road by the hotel.

"Excuse me Sir, do you work for the Forestry Commission?" asked one of the officers.

"No, no, just a member of the public giving a hand," replied Dalmar

"Are you going to take this vehicle back to Chapp?" The same policemen asked. He was confused as to why an ordinary member of the public had been in a position to come to the assistance of Mr. Knopner but left it at that for the time being.

"Yes, but there is another job to do first." He looked at the police officer. "You wouldn't care to help – I suppose?"

This policeman was not stupid. "Firstly, it depends on what assistance you require? And secondly it must not involve me leaving my post."

"I see," said Dalmar. "Well as for post abandonment, I shouldn't worry too much about that. You see the reason why you are stationed here – is no more. The Red Adder – is dead."

"Is it?" There was obvious joy in those two small words.

The other constable looked pleased as well. "What – you mean – after today, there will be no more of this boring duty," he said. "That's great – hey Bill?"

"Maybe, but we take our orders from someone else, can't take *your* word for it," said Bill. "Sorry … What is the problem though?" In truth, he was still sulking over the loss of his chicken sandwich.

"I need to go back, in this vehicle, and collect the body of said Red Adder." Dalmar thought to himself, actually, in the end it was hardly an adder of any description. "It is only about half a mile into the forest. I think I've got the hang of driving the Land Rover. Don't need to use the four-wheel drive: too dry. Disengaged it coming down the hill – went much faster." Dalmar added, "Don't think Stephen appreciated it though."

"Oh, come on Bill, I'll go if you won't. Anyhow, I can watch both entrances without any problem. Hardly needs the two of us," said the other policeman.

Bill was not entirely convinced. "Why can't you do it on your own?"

"Because it will be very difficult – you see – we are talking of a snake about fifteen to twenty feet long and – big in girth. It is a heavy so and so."

"What!" exclaimed Bill. "Good God!" He looked even more perturbed now – but after a few moments, he said, "Oh – all right, but let's get on with it. The ambulance service may have informed our lot about this, and I want to be back here before any top brass arrive."

So, Bill sat alongside Dalmar as they travelled swiftly up the fire clearance. The Land Rover yawed about a lot on the hard, rutted clay surface and Fly barked his disapproval once more from the back. They got to the top of the hill and set off down to the second path crossing point. Several times Dalmar had to apply the brakes as the vehicle gathered too much speed. He drove straight over onto the narrower track and proceeded along the grassy way feeling apprehensive. Although he knew the snake was no more, there was something about seeing the body parts again he did not like. After he had informed Bill of its size, the policeman did not appear to be looking forward to the task either. "I'll leave the head to you," he said frankly.

When they arrived by the entrance to the hazel tunnels, there was no sign of the large reptile, which Fly and Dalmar had recently killed. The two parts of John the Red – had gone.

276

CHAPTER FORTY-FOUR

"IT'S BEEN NICKED?"

"So ... we have no snake's remains, just a lot of blood on the ground and certainly a bucket full on your trousers. I hope, for your sake, the witness to this morning's events – survives." Bill, the policeman, made this pronouncement as Dalmar drove him back to the church car park. "I shall have to ask you for a statement in due course Sir – you understand?"

"Yes," Dalmar answered him. Secretly, because of what had been discovered today, he was quite sure the police would be taking far more interest in this matter, imminently.

As they arrived back at the gate by the main road, the other policeman came up to the Land Rover's open window. "Well ... where is it?" He asked peering over the driver's shoulder into the back of the vehicle. All he saw was a prone collie.

"Gone," said Dalmar.

"Gone ... how can it have *gone*?" he asked.

"Gone," repeated Dalmar. "Don't ask me where? Just some blood deposits – that's it."

Bill climbed out of the vehicle and came around to join his colleague. "Like he says Alex, nothing there at all."

"Has it recovered and gone to ground?" asked Alex.

"It was headless," stated Dalmar.

There was a pause. "What – you mean ... it's been nicked?" Alex asked finally, looking at both of them in turn.

"Looks like it," confirmed Bill.

"But why – who would want it?" questioned Alex, his face showing incredulity.

"Search me," said Bill. "Thing is what do we do about it. Report a missing dead snake?"

"May I suggest you leave it with me?" Dalmar volunteered.

Both officers shook their heads. "Well, when I say that," Dalmar added by way of explanation, "I am now going to return the Forestry Commission's vehicle. I will, of course, give them a full report. I mean the snake effectively belonged to them didn't it? And I wouldn't be surprised if it's in the hands of their chaps anyway. Probably came across it while we were getting Stephen off to hospital." Before finishing, he gave Bill and Alex a positive look. "If it makes you feel any better, why don't you radio through to your headquarters and report the matter. They can contact the forestry office at Chapp, and everyone who should be – will be in the know – okay?"

Alex looked at Bill and returned the questioning glance by nodding.

277

"Okay, but first I need your personal details," said Bill. He took a notepad and pencil from his tunic pocket. Dalmar gave him his full name, address and telephone number.

"What's this?" asked Alex, reaching for an object hanging at the bottom of the Land Rover's radio aerial.

"Don't touch them!" Dalmar shouted at him. Alex instantly withdrew his hand, just in time. "They are swimming goggles."

Dalmar was about to explain further, but Alex stopped him. "Forgive me," he said. "Do forgive me, but why have we a pair of *swimming* goggles hanging over our aerial? Is it some new fashion accessory that I haven't heard of?"

"There's snake venom on them," Dalmar informed the officers.

Both policemen stepped backwards and stared at the goggles. After a period of silence Bill said, "Sorry?"

"It spat at me," said Dalmar reaching for the field telephone. "Just realised – should have informed Stephen's office that he was successfully dispatched to hospital. They will be anxious."

"So," came back Alex. "The Red Adder spat at you while you were wearing goggles?"

"That's right. Hunter to base – Hunter to base – over."

Alex took off his helmet and scratched his head. Bill rubbed his forearm over his right eye. "It seems to me that the sooner you make that statement – the better," he remarked.

"Hello John, what's the news – over?" Maria's voice came through the telephone speaker clearly.

"Stephen was packed off to Winchester Hospital about half an hour ago. He has had the anti-venom injection, so we must hope for the best. Oh – and he was still able to talk before he left – over."

"Right," Maria sounded relieved; "We've all got our fingers crossed here – over."

"Have any of your men radioed in about finding the body of a large snake – over?"

"No ... I would certainly know if they had! Mind you, we only have one other field radio out today, and it isn't in Yewhurst Wood," she finished. "Over."

"Okay, I am on my way round to you with Stephen's vehicle. See you in a little while – over."

"Thank you – will look out for you. Just park it up outside the office. Over and out." The radio receiver crackled and went quiet. He started the engine and glanced into the back of the Land Rover. Fly looked to be fast asleep.

"Be seeing you both," Dalmar nodded at the two officers. Both of whom gave him a knowing look as he pulled out onto the road. Alex even managed a little grin.

Dalmar was grateful and a little puzzled as to why neither of the constables had challenged him over his knife. They would have been bound to have noticed it.

When he arrived at the Forestry Commission's office, he left Fly asleep, and went inside. There were two ladies present. One, whom he presumed was Maria, sat with her back to him at her desk. She was looking over her shoulder. The other lady stood by her side. She had on a plain lemon cotton dress, with a wide white belt around her waist. Her blue eyes were watery, and her soft hair looked a bit untidy, as though she had been disturbed from something. "Are you Mr Hunter?" she asked in a rather feeble voice. Both women gave his blood-soaked jeans more than a cursory glance, not to mention the dangerous looking knife in its sheath dangling from his belt.

"Yes – John Hunter." Surprised at himself he added, "Some people know me as Dalmar."

"I am Susan Knopner, Stephen's wife." She held out her right hand in a rather coy way. "My husband has talked of you." Susan had a roundish soft featured face, fairly full lips without lipstick, and gentle blue eyes. Her pale blond hair was natural.

Dalmar shook her hand with a tender pressure. "Very sorry about Stephen," he said to her, genuine concern in his eyes. Turning, he looked towards the other lady. "You must be Maria? You did well," he said.

She gave him a nod without rising from her desk. In the circumstances there was only a flicker of a smile on her face. Dalmar considered that there was a strong Mediterranean look about her: quite a young woman, probably not out of her twenties. "Thank you," she said. "I let Mrs Knopner know as soon as I could. She has just arrived."

Dalmar gave Susan Knopner a very sympathetic look. He thought he could recall that Stephen had three children. She must be very worried. He felt the need to explain in greater detail. "The snake struck out from underwater just by the bank of a pond that your husband and I were looking into. It bit him below the knee."

"Do you know what ward they have taken him to at Winchester?" Susan asked. She was obviously anxious to get to the hospital. A Red Adder bite was usually fatal.

"No, I don't – I'm sorry." Dalmar had not thought to ask the houseman in the ambulance. He was about to say that Christine Westward had been taken to the Victoria Ward last year, when he remembered that ward had been used for intensive care patients, so he merely suggested that she ask at the accident and emergency reception.

"Right. I must go to him then. Goodbye." The poor woman looked extremely agitated. She briefly waved a hand at Maria.

Dalmar stood aside for her. He half wondered whether he should offer to give her a lift, but she was gone before he could suggest it. Anyway, he doubted the insurance on the Land Rover included him as a driver. Her car had been parked in the road and they heard it motor off. "Where are her children?" Dalmar enquired of Maria.

"With a friend. Just as well for now. They don't know of course," Maria said biting her lower lip. There was a slight southern Italian accent there. It had not come across on the field telephone. Normally, thought Dalmar, that face would be a smiley one: large mouth and all. He handed over the keys of the Forestry Commission's vehicle, and, while drinking a cup of coffee Maria had made him, related the bare facts of what had happened. Secret ponds and other matters would be of no interest to her. Before he left, he went and retrieved his swimming goggles. He explained what they were about, and she found him a plastic carrier bag displaying a well-known supermarket's logo. He placed the goggles in the bag and tied a knot with the handles to seal it.

"I suggest you let your science officer know about these. Stephen was telling me you have one. I don't want them back. It is a reminder – I really do not need."

"Wilfred Blyte. I'll let him know," said Maria. "Why were you asking about a snake's body?"

"We killed the Red Adder. But when I went back for the remains after getting Stephen off in the ambulance, it had vanished. So, I wondered if one of your men had come across it?"

"That is good news – about the snake," she said, and a full smile suddenly illuminated her face. "That is *really* good news." Suddenly her face went serious. "Err – your trousers, are you hurt?"

"No, no, this is the snake's blood." He pinched the cloth with two fingers as though amplifying the point.

"And where is your dog? You said something about him being a hero?"

"He's sound asleep in the back of the Land Rover. Yes ... played a big part in helping us kill the snake." He gave her a smile while handing back the empty cup with its saucer. "Thank you – that was *very* welcome."

Poor Fly was not very keen on being awoken to start walking once more. After they passed through the gate of the Forestry Commission's office, Dalmar continued straight down the road ignoring the turning to the left, which was his normal way home. He ambled around the bend until he could see the front of Ma Hessil's cottage. The billowing smoke from a bonfire was coming from her back garden. This was exactly what he had expected to see. It had a strong scent in the afternoon air and seemed to have the aroma of something other than burning vegetable matter. Well *if* that was John the Red going up in smoke, one thing was certain, Ma Hessil could not have carried its body all the way here on her own. He turned on his heel and whistled for Fly to follow.

Dalmar strode home with his dog by his side. There was an upright, square shouldered look about him, and his stride was full. No more fearful glances were cast towards the forest. He gave a cheery wave to Bill and Alex, the police officers, who had joined forces in the rear of the church car park. They acknowledged him from a distance. He wondered if they had officially heard anything yet.

Next on the list was a long soak in his bathtub. Before that, he gave Fly a wet towel treatment: a very wet towel treatment, much to the collie's disgust. It was not just because of possible blood deposits, which, amazingly, seemed to be non-existent. He was more or less certain the snake could not have made a cursory strike on him, but he wanted to be absolutely sure.

Afterwards, Dalmar ran the bath water and climbed in. He washed himself thoroughly with a good soaping all over and shampooed his hair before reclining as near full stretch as he could. The bath, however, was not long enough and he had to settle for his legs being bent at the knee.

The hot water relaxed him, and at one stage he felt the heavy eyelids of sleep descending. He shook them off and started to run through the day's events in his mind. Something kept prodding inside his brain. Something that was not right. There was only one-way to discover what it was, and that was to go through every moment: re-live it all in his mind. It was when he got to Stephen's remark, after he suggested that he make a thorough scan of the sweet chestnut by the pond – that an urgent alarm bell kept triggering. The forest officer intimated that he had not known that it was from that tree that the Red Adder attacked Christine. 'Now why was that so important? Why did it not balance with recent history somewhere?' He gave up after a while and continued with his reverie. The problem would be solved some other time, no doubt.

When Dalmar finished a bath, while still partially immersed, he liked to coil the chain attached to the plug around his big toe and pull the plug out. He then set himself the trial of flicking the plug, still held between big toe and first toe, so that it would exactly loop over the cold tap and hang there, swinging on the chain. He had to achieve this before all the water drained out of the plughole, which made it necessary to accomplish the task within a few tries. On this occasion he made it on the third flick. The conscious effort took his mind away from the day's dramatic events.

By the time Dalmar had dressed in clean clothes, with the denim and soft-shoe look in evidence again, it was late afternoon. He fed Fly before doing anything else. Then he picked up the telephone and dialled a number. He managed to get through to Winchester Hospital and was informed that Stephen Knopner was comfortable, but they would continue to keep a very close eye on him. The poor man had to remain in a position with his legs below waist height, so that his heart was well above the bite area. To achieve this, they had put him a wheelchair. He would have to stay like that – all night.

What really cheered Dalmar was that Stephen was not being kept in a ward for intensive care patients. When he finished the call, Dalmar was relieved for the man's sake, his family's sake, and for his own sake. Stephen was the only other human witness to the death of John the Red, and, once again, with no body…

Half an hour later, the telephone rang. It was Dr David Andrews. "Congratulations! I have just heard," came an enthusiastic voice in the earpiece.

"Ah," acknowledged Dalmar. "About the Red Adder – yes?"

"Absolutely! – How ever did you do it?"

"It wasn't me – it was my dog."

"No! What a wonder dog. How on earth did he manage it?"

"Got him from behind – around the neck. Gave me enough time to use my knife."

"I see." David thought about this for a while, before going onto another matter. "Been in contact with Winchester Hospital – Stephen should survive without any nasty side effects... Maria at the Forestry Commission – tells me the snake came out of a pond, is that right?"

"Yes – after we found the Secret Pond. The beast was lurking under the surface."

"You found the pond ... my goodness! Look – too many questions – need to see you. Jonathon Shure will certainly want an audience. May I arrange a meeting? And – by that I mean probably tomorrow – Sunday. Any good?"

"Yes – been expecting it, but I wonder if we could kill two birds with one stone?"

"Go on."

"At some stage I have to make a statement to the police. Quite frankly rather than go to a police station ... well ... would it be possible for that retired chief inspector to be in on the meeting?"

"Sounds like a really good idea," David concurred. "Chief Inspector Wilkins. Tell you what – give me about an hour and I'll get back to you. All right?"

"Fine, I'm not going anywhere."

"Call you later then – bye."

Dalmar used the next hour to get himself something to eat and partake of a much-needed glass of beer. He felt massive relief, and an inescapable feeling that some enormous responsibility had been lifted from his shoulders: a responsibility that had been with him from a young age.

When the telephone rang, he was more than ready. David's voice came over the line loud and clear. "Dalmar – hello again. If you can make it around seven p.m. – tomorrow – at the Claymans – we will have the chief inspector and Jonathon. Can you?"

"Yes," said Dalmar.

"Right, I will meet you at the hotel reception desk. We have reserved a room there."

"Fine – and thanks – thanks a lot."

"All right, see you tomorrow." The doctor rang off.

Dalmar poured himself another drink. The tall glass soon frosted up and he cradled it in his right hand. With Fly at his heel, he went outside and strolled slowly up the gravel path, coming off onto the lawn by the apple tree, which was covered in pink and white blossom. Fly snuffled at his feet. Dalmar turned and looked back down the narrow lawn before it finished at the heather bed, sharing its patch with interspaced red azalea. In the foreground, off to the right, was the breath-taking sight of a big rhododendron bush in full bloom: an all-white bloom. He studied it for a long time, now and again taking a drink from his glass. Then he went inside and came back with a notebook and pencil. He wrote down the following, while his glorious dog lay on the grass, with his head resting across his master's feet.

THE WHITE RHODODENDRON

Let me live through another May, so I may see Old Rhody bloom again.
And so it is that every June the tide of beauty does remain,
Firmly bedded in my hungry-seeking, colouring mind.
The wealth of memory summed up in seasonal time,
Of a peat-loving bush with dark forbidding leaves.
At the bottom of my garden, her flowers dotted with honeybees.
Her pyramided blossoms heaped from crown to low, down low.
And when I open the entrance gate and amble up the path,
I wonderingly look upon this herald of summer's task.
She is my beauty, my flower of the Spring.
She makes me forget – every lone, troublesome thing.

CHAPTER FORTY-FIVE

A POLICE MATTER.

Sunday was another fine and dry day. Dalmar left Fly guarding the house at a couple of minutes before seven o'clock and ambled over to The Claymans Heron. He walked stiffly. The exertion of holding the snake between his legs, the previous morning, had caused muscle discomfort testament to the extreme pressure he had been forced to use.

David Andrews and Chief Inspector Wilkins were waiting for him. After greeting each other and getting a firm pat on the back from a very cheerful, so-called retired policeman, all three went upstairs to room 103 where they were told Jonathon Shure was already in residence. The bedroom had been converted to a small conference room. Jonathon had not physically met Dalmar before, so they introduced themselves. "Well done," said the zoologist straight away. "Who knows how many lives you might have saved this coming summer. We all owe you a great debt. Or is it your dog? Or both?" He finished with a generous smile.

"Fly, my collie, is the hero." Dalmar confirmed.

"Looking forward to hearing about it," said Jonathon. He produced a tape recorder and set it upon the desk. "Anyone have any objection?" He looked around to inspect the faces of the three men.

"Could I have a copy?" It was Inspector Wilkins.

"Of course, Chief Inspector, I was going to suggest it," Jonathon replied.

"Good, it will save me having to take notes. Can we stop all this rank stuff? My name is Peter."

What followed was a request to Dalmar to recall everything that happened to him the day before, from the point when he entered Yewhurst Wood in the early morning, to the time he left the Forestry Commission's office in the afternoon. This he did, hoping he had not left anything out. There then followed several questions.

First in was Chief Inspector Wilkins. "May I ask what conclusions you drew from the deliberate attempt to cover up the footpath to the pond?" Dalmar noticed a change in the man's tone from the bonhomie of earlier.

"That it was done by a person or persons wishing to hide the location of the pond from anyone else."

"And why do you think they did that?" continued Peter.

"To hide a site for the breeding of experimental reptiles." After Dalmar said this, Jonathon raised his eyebrows and gave a pointed look in David's direction. The doctor had been a witness to Wilfred Blyte's outburst, after the zoologist had suggested the possibility of human interference at the conference here last year. He received a recognition nod from David in return.

"Do you have any idea who might be responsible for this *experimental breeding*?" asked Peter.

"No – I'm afraid not. Stephen see... that is Stephen Knopner ... seems to think it might be some kind of brainy vagrant." Here Dalmar shrugged his shoulders. "But that is for him to elucidate."

"Of course," added the inspector. "Apart from the so-called rabbit pens, the straw inside them and a fragment of eggshell, did you find any other evidence of experimental breeding?"

"No. Incidentally, that fragment of eggshell was in the top pocket of Stephen's shirt." A sudden thought ran through Dalmar's mind. 'The shirt might have been washed and the fragment destroyed.'

"Don't worry. The Forestry Commission at Lyndhurst has it," Jonathon assured him with a slight chuckle. "Stephen wouldn't rest until he got some action on that, apparently. Went on about the bloody effort that had gone into getting it, etc." They all laughed at this. Dalmar could imagine the scene. "What's the latest on him, by the way?" asked Jonathon looking at the doctor.

"Off the danger list: on the mend. Bet you he will be back at work by mid-week," David informed them. "While we are on that subject, Dalmar ... sorry – Peter have you finished?"

"For now." The policeman half-raised his right hand.

The doctor asked, "Did you do anything to Stephen after the bite? Medically that is?"

"No. Just tried to get him out of there in an as upright a position as possible," answered Dalmar. "From information broadcast after your conference here last year – I gather a tourniquet is not a good idea?"

"Correct," David confirmed. "If some of the poison has already travelled up the body – and it almost certainly would have done – interfering with the natural flow of the bloodstream could make matters considerably worse." He continued with another question. "What about those noises the snake made by the way? You know – like the one Jonathon has on tape."

"Sorry, forgot to mention that. It made an extraordinarily loud hiss when my dog got hold of it, and virtually hissed nonstop while we were trying to kill it – but that was all. Nothing like the racket normally associated with the Red Adder."

"Just as well," explained David. "The press didn't pick up on one of the facts that came from Mary Taylor's autopsy." Here he hesitated before saying, "Both her eardrums were perforated." Dalmar flinched and screwed up his face.

Jonathon was next with some questions. "May I ask why you did it?"

"Sorry – what?"

"Why did *you* go into the forest yesterday, shall we say – with intent?" clarified Jonathon.

"Oh – I see. Well ... I heard the snake from my bedroom window the night before." Dalmar shrugged his shoulders. "Felt it was time."

"Dalmar," David's tone was conciliatory. "Would you mind telling these two gentlemen about your family's connection?" David received a questioning look from Dalmar at this. The doctor raised a hand and pursed his lips, "Allen told me," he said by way of explanation. Needless to say, the other two men looked exceedingly curious.

Dalmar developed a resigned countenance. "In 1947, the Springer spaniel that was attacked by a similar snake belonged to my family, and, in 1948, it was my elder brother William Hunter, who was killed while riding his bicycle on the Great Mile."

Jonathon let a low whistling sound escape through his teeth.

"I have one more question," said Peter. "I don't suppose you know anything about an anonymous letter sent to the Forestry Commission, last year, concerning the burning of one of these Red Adders?" The inspector stared straight into Dalmar's eyes. Dalmar felt guilty and thought about his reply for far too long. "Well?" came the inevitable prompt from Peter.

David gave a small cough of embarrassment before Dalmar finally gave his reply. "I can tell you that some local people, by that I mean ancestors of real local people, not wealthy second home occupiers or senior forestry employees, but relatives of the farm workers who have existed in this area for a few hundred years…" Dalmar paused and then carried on, sure of what he should say; "Well – they believe that unless John the Red … and I say that in preference to the Red Adder … is destroyed by fire, he will reappear. I was privy to information that the snake shot by Jim Pearce, after the death of Ginger Styles, was taken from the woods and burnt by one or more of these people." Dalmar came out of his crouched position leaning over the table. He sat back with his shoulders straight.

"You have not answered my question," insisted Peter. "Do you know anything about an anonymous le…?"

"I know that a letter was sent in order to inform those that needed to know, so that they would not be under the impression that there was more than one of these snakes on the loose."

Jonathon was privately impressed with this.

"Do you consider that the same fate, incineration, befell the beast you and your dog slew yesterday?" Peter sounded as though he were referring to a dragon.

"I do," replied Dalmar. "As I have said, some of the forestry workers are local folk. They used to be farm workers, or certainly their fathers were. These lads would have the same sympathies about John the Red. After all, the bush telegraph is in place, isn't it? In the shape of the Forestry Commission's own short-wave radio system."

"All right. That will do for now. But I must warn you that if this matter ever gets into a court of law, you may be asked to give far more information – under oath." Peter gave Dalmar a serious look. The interviewee felt like a very naughty schoolboy, and, for a moment, he looked like one. The inspector turned to Jonathon. "Matters have altered now. We will be roping off the area – by the Secret Pond, in order to carry out a thorough investigation. Fatalities have occurred due to the breeding of these snakes, and therefore we are now conducting a multiple manslaughter investigation." He then added almost in a whisper. "Possibly – murder."

This had suddenly gone way beyond David Andrew's desire to be involved. He kept unusually quiet. Dalmar was already aware of the seriousness of the situation. He realised the implications from the moment he had discovered the un-rooted rhododendron bush.

Jonathon was effectively relieved of his responsibilities, as the person in charge of the Red Adder anomaly. It had become a police matter. There was no point in discussing when the restriction notices, applicable to Yewhurst Wood, would be withdrawn. Dalmar knew there would be two disappointed constables, who would not be going back to normal duties – just yet.

"Are you staying the night here?" asked Peter of Jonathon.

"Err, yes, I have to see Charles Brewster tomorrow: meeting him up at Chapp. Do you need me?"

"Not for me to say. Another officer will be taking this case over: an active one. Don't know who it's going to be yet. Shall I let them know you are around for a couple of days?"

"Yes. Hoping Charles will let me go and see what Wilfred Blyte, the Forestry Commission's science officer, has come up with, on that eggshell fragment."

"Sorry," said Peter. "Been impounded I'm afraid, or rather, it is now Queen's evidence."

"Oh," Jonathon did not look too perturbed about this news. "Yes of course – it would be. In that case I shall be returning to London on Tuesday."

"Right – and you two gentlemen. Not going anywhere – holidays or what-have-you?" Both David and Dalmar shook their heads. "Right – good – well I have no further questions." He held out his hands. "Anybody – anything else?"

As soon as Jonathon had ascertained that there were no other queries; he switched off the tape-recorder and rewound the spool before taking it off the machine and handing it to the chief inspector. He said that he did not require a copy but asked if he could have it back when the police had finished transcribing it.

"May I have a private word with Dalmar?" Jonathon was determined not to have all his plans thwarted. "Scientific matters, I assure you. Nothing to do with the police investigation."

"Of course," acquiesced Peter. "Is the Zoological Society going to feed us?"

"I suppose so," grinned Jonathon. "Why don't you and David go down to the bar? I'll have a quick word with Dalmar, and we will meet you there shortly. Then we can all go to the grill."

"Hope you don't mind if I pick your brains?" Suddenly the policeman looked un-authoritative. "Would someone mind telling me – just what is anti-venom?" He directed his question at the zoologist.

"You would be amazed how many people don't know the answer to that," said Jonathon with a wry grin. "I honestly think most of the general public think it is made up in a laboratory, like a medicine. Well – obviously there is some laboratory work involved, but the stuff is obtained by milking a snake's venom. And that means exactly that: the fangs are agitated, by encouraging it to bite on a suitable container. The venom is then diluted and injected into an animal, such as a horse or goat. As the animal builds up immunity to the venom, the dose is increased until the animal creates a blood rich in antibodies." Reading a furrow of doubt on the face of the chief inspector, Jonathon explained further. "Antibodies are blood proteins which are created to fight such things as blood poisoning. That, of course, is what the viper's venom is. The antibodies collect in the serum that is separated from the red blood cells. Following purification, this anti-venom serum is ready for injection into a person suffering from the effects of a poisonous bite." Here Jonathon open palmed both hands. "It follows that we need an anti-venom serum for every group of poisonous reptile. The anti-venom for a puff adder, would be useless if you had been bitten by a king cobra; or, for that matter, a scorpion."

David butted in at this point. "The serum used to treat Christine Westward, initially, was that used for a common adder, but what ultimately saved her, was some serum to treat a far more dangerous viper's bite. It was driven down from London during the night."

Jonathon added to this. "What we had standing-by for the observation team's operation, Jack Kanton brought with him from Australia in a special refrigerated container. It is used to combat the very nasty venom of the death adder, which is one of the world's most lethal snake's, and, probably, the nearest in terms of toxicity and quantity to our Red Adder. Recently, it was used to great effect – to treat Stephen Knopner That lot any good?" finished Jonathon, looking at Peter.

"Yes, indeed. Thank you – I feel considerably more au fait with the matter now," confirmed a grateful Inspector Wilkins. "Right, come on doctor, buy this poor old pensioner a pint, there's a good chap." Peter grabbed hold of David's arm a little too enthusiastically, causing his spectacles to work loose around his ears. David stood up and adjusted them. He raised his eyebrows, looking at Jonathon and Dalmar as the two of them departed.

When the door had closed behind them, Dalmar studied Jonathon's face to see if he could guess as to what might be coming. "Strange really," the zoologist had a wry questioning expression about his body language. "Those two seem to have taken it for granted, that the surviving Red Adder of last year, was the very same one you beheaded yesterday?"

Dalmar felt an instant rapport with Jonathon. "Do you know – a similar thought occurred to me, although I reckon it had more to do with a lack of interest in my description of the Red Adder. I suppose the emphasis is now on this mysterious breeder. I believe it *was* the same snake that attacked Christine Westward in July of last year, simply because its main habitat appears to have been the Secret Pond." Here, Dalmar stopped, and pondered his thoughts. Jonathon did not press him. He waited patiently. "You see, Suzanne Westward said that the snake that attacked her sister-in-law was about six feet long. She based that estimate on the sight of it swimming and then climbing out of the pond. We know that various people have questioned this length as a possible exaggeration. I think – that it was far from an exaggeration – because of the meander movement. I reckon its actual length was probably more like eight to nine feet. We do not have any surviving witnesses to its size when later on in the year it attacked Brian Dace and the American. Apart, that is, from a couple of vague aerial estimates from members of your observation teams. Am I right?"

"Yes, one of them thought – three to four metres," answered Jonathon. "But please – go on."

"Well, I reckon that by then it was over twelve feet in length. You see – the snake that we killed yesterday was – believe you me – *very* long. As I said earlier, I have a recollection of thinking in excess of fifteen feet, but I don't really know why I came up with that figure. It was the kind of overall size you would associate with a large boa constrictor. I read in a newspaper that the attack on Private Dace must have come from the air, and that those two witnesses thought the snake's flight could have been in the region of a quarter of a mile. I am sure you would agree that for a snake to glide that far, it would have to be wide in girth to have the width of skin folds required for - well ... lift?

"That occurrence has not only puzzled me but also every gliding snake authority in the world," added Jonathon.

"Oh well, something that cannot be explained." Dalmar said with a sort of finality.

"As yet – maybe. Let us hope there will be more answers to come. Do you think this breeder *is* a vagrant?" Jonathon threw the question at Dalmar. He had not expected it, and it was certainly significant as far as the police were concerned.

"If so – he has been a tramp for a very long time. When did it all start – 1947?" He gave Jonathon a very knowing look. "I don't think so." He wanted to confide with this man about Ma Hessil and her story. But he had given his word, and it was not yet the right time to break it. Jonathon, on his part, knew that Dalmar was in the know about something, and he had hoped he would open-up, but he could sense that it was not to be.

"I think the answer lies with someone who lives locally?" was all Jonathon would say. "You may be able to help with one other matter. Your clothing – some of it had the snake's blood on it – yes?"

"I've been expecting this. The jeans I wore. The top half was covered."

"Can I have them?"

"You certainly can. They are sitting in a carrier bag in my fridge."

"Great. I'll arrange to collect them off you."

"Okay. Tell you what; I'll leave them in my garden shed. I don't lock it. You'll easily find it opposite the stable door entrance to my cottage. The second one down the lane that runs along that side of this hotel." Dalmar inclined his head in the direction referred to.

"Thank you – and what about your knife? That must have been liberally coated in blood?"

"Yes – and it has been liberally washed with soap and water. That knife is special."

"Really – I've heard that somewhere before." Jonathon said ironically.

Dalmar wrinkled his brow in puzzlement, but he made no comment on the matter, instead moving on to another thought. "Sorry about the eggshell fragment," he said, and looked genuinely so.

A huge smile spread over the zoologist's face. "Actually, I already knew about that. What the police don't know is that Wilfred Blyte owes me, and a certain pair of swimming goggles is awaiting my pleasure at Lyndhurst. Dalmar returned his smile.

After that, they left the room to join David and Peter at the bar.

"I have a thirst like a dry sponge," said Dalmar feeling his throat.

"It's all that talking," said Jonathon with mirth.

They took their drinks to a table in the grill restaurant. Over a plate of breaded plaice and chipped potatoes, Peter approached Dalmar concerning the subject of a press release. "Have heard you are a bit shy of the media, which I can understand, but the sooner this is out, and I am referring to the death of the Red Adder, not your family's personal history, the sooner it will be over. What do you say Jonathon?"

"They will want to interview you and," Jonathon smiled ruefully, "take numerous photographs of your collie. But that should be that. Quite honestly, I should give them the lot, your family's unfortunate involvement and so on. They will label it as 'sweet revenge' or some such phrase. If you don't tell them, someone will spill the beans and they will be back."

"I guess so," said Dalmar.

David coughed on a mouth-full of chips. "What … you don't mind?" he asked.

"Wouldn't say that, but I agree – let's get it over with." Jonathon and Peter smiled at each other, for David had sworn that there was no way Dalmar would talk to the media.

"Your line is personnel management, I believe?" Jonathon asked Dalmar, deliberately steering the conversation away from snakes.

"It is. I work for a Southampton based firm: D.S. Containers. Not too big an outfit. Suits me."

"Really!   … We used them last year for a shipment;" Jonathon looked at Dalmar with added attention.

"That must have been from the Congo?" suggested Dalmar.

"Almost. It is more often the other way round nowadays. We are sending the results of our breeding back, to where they belong. So, it went to the Congo." The other two men at the table expressed an interest in this repatriation, and a lively discussion ensued.

As soon as Dalmar arrived home, he extricated the bloodstained jeans from his fridge and put them in the garden shed.

He spent Monday at his office. If he was honest, he felt a sort of anti-climax. The drama of the weekend somehow made what he was doing awfully humdrum. It was necessary, he realised that, but there was an atmosphere about his brain, which gave him the feeling of having just returned to work after a long illness. It was the only way he could describe to himself how he felt. His working colleagues were familiar, but somehow, also strangers.

When he drove the T.R.6 into the private close alongside the Claymans Heron, late that afternoon, hood down so that his upper frame was visible to all, those feelings disappeared in a dazzling mass of light and sound. In front of him was a dreadful sight. to him, it was the equivalent of being in the centre of a crowded football stadium as the only player. To another person, it would be a horde of pressmen and photographers. He had been caught completely by surprise. He had assumed that there would be some sort of official announcement by the police first. Unbeknown to him, there had been.

"John Hunter?" one of them shouted over the throbbing sound of Dalmar's sports car engine. He knew he would not be able to park by his garage and made no attempt to do so, coming to a halt in the middle of the lane.

"Yes," Dalmar answered without getting out of his car.

"May I have a word?" asked another man.

"Can you talk to the Chronicle?" shouted a female voice.

"Mr Hunter – over here!" bellowed a reporter while puffing at a cigarette. These were just some of the many shouts directed at him all at the same time. Also, accompanying this was the constant clicking of camera shutters. Some of which seemed to be right on top of him.

He held up his hands. "Ladies and gentlemen!" he said with raised voice. Suddenly there was a sort of mini hush. He took advantage of it. "It isn't me you want to see ... It is my dog."

There was an instant clamouring of "Yes!" and "Where is he?"

Dalmar struggled out of his car and closed the door, almost having to shove some people out of his way. "If you would all wait here. Please do not follow me. I have to enter another person's property where Fly is being looked after. I promise I will be back with the dog directly." He finished by nodding at them all, in general, vigorously, in a pleading manner. Fly is going to love this, he thought.

A terrified Janice Short handed over an exuberant dog almost reluctantly. The next half an hour was all his. He was patted and petted by every journalist and photographer there. He was asked to pose on tree stumps, on the bonnet of the Triumph, with his master in various stances and, best of all for Fly, because it involved numerous enticements with biscuits, leaping in the air.

There then followed a sort of impromptu press conference in which Dalmar related the events of the previous Saturday, being careful not to embellish anything. There was intense interest when he told them that he was the younger brother of a boy that had been killed by a similar snake in 1948. The media knew nothing of this, and it therefore became a major part of the story. Obviously, many of the reporters wanted to know what had happened to the dismembered body parts of the snake. Dalmar had already prepared himself for this, although he had not expected it this evening. When he was asked, he shrugged his shoulders, exaggeratedly, without actually saying anything.

Two outside broadcast television crews were present. Dalmar found this part nerve-racking, knowing he was on camera, but not so, Fly, who literally lapped it up. His master was very grateful for the way the collie diverted attention from him. He was looking magnificent in his colours of white, black and tan against the evening sunlight. Janice must have given him a good combing during the afternoon.

The next morning, in the post, came the first of the paperwork that Dalmar had been expecting from the Hampshire Constabulary. It was a transcript of the statement made by Suzanne Westward at Beech Cottage, after Christine had been attacked last year. He considered that the chief inspector must have secretly recorded it to achieve such accuracy. Retired or not, he had not taken any chances. They wanted Dalmar to read the document through and sign it to confirm his agreement with the contents. Also, they had transcribed his statement from the other evening to print, and they asked for his signature on this as well. He did as instructed - making sure all the papers were posted back that day.

CHAPTER FORTY-SIX

SHE ABSOLUTELY KNEW.

Suzanne Westward put three mugs of hot coffee on her aunt's brass tray and carried it into the sitting room where her uncle Reginald was waiting. "Just the ticket," he said as she placed it on a low table by the three-piece suite. She shoved a folded evening paper aside with the corner of the tray as she did so. He repeated the same phrase most evenings when she brought in their late evening drinks.

She had spent a miserable winter in Somerset. Her mother beseeched her to go out and find some work, rather than mope about the house all day. But she had not been in the mood, even if her mind might have been taken off her despair. She sought solace among some of her friends; one friend had been most understanding.

Christmas had been better because Tim and Christine had spent a greater part of the holiday with them. The year before they had gone to Christine's parent's home, so, fortunately, it was his mother and father's turn. At last, the glum face was replaced with something nearing normality, and smiles were witnessed on her countenance now and again.

In mid-April, she went to stay with her aunt and uncle in the Lake District. After a couple of weeks, she started to get bored. One of her favourite haunts was a commercial art gallery in Grasmere. They sold paintings, prints and artists' materials. She got to know one of the ladies who had a part time job there; initially by chatting to her while she carried out her duties, and later meeting her for morning coffee in a restaurant next door. Then Suzanne received some luck. The other part-time receptionist at the gallery had to leave, because her husband needed to move south with his employment. After a hint from her new friend, the woman who owned the business offered Suzanne the vacancy. She took it at once and was soon engrossed for two days a week learning her duties.

One Tuesday in June, she found herself almost skipping to work. She felt a great deal more positive about life than she had done for a long time. The incessant bleating of new-born lambs on the low fells pleased her. It was a rare day in the English Lake District, for there was not a single wisp of cloud in the sky. The crisp glint of the sunshine bounced off Grasmere Lake and captured the beauty in her face. Her eyes had at long last returned to their former sparkling glory, and her marvellous dark hair gave off a texture of the finest deep-toned velvet. She wore the softest of blue dresses, slightly flared at the hip.

Her lady employer was also in a cheerful mood. She asked Suzanne to manage the shop on her own for an hour, as she had an appointment in the village. Almost immediately, Suzanne became engrossed attending to a framing order brought in by a young gentleman. It was quite a complicated task involving a few pieces of artwork. Inadvertently, he left his newspaper behind when they had finished. She did not spot it straight away, being occupied in checking the order details. It was therefore too late to run after him. 'Oh well,' she thought, 'perhaps he will call back.' She picked it up in order to put it in a more obvious place by the shop doorway. It was a broadsheet paper folded in four. When she turned it over, she spotted a large photograph of a collie. Then she read the headline which was hidden under the fold. 'FLY, THE HERO.' She breathed in sharply and caught hold of the paper in haste, straightened it out, and read the article. It started in bold print: 'Collie crucially assists in the death of the Red Adder. The scourge of Yewhurst Wood is no more.' Suzanne's mouth went dry. The article then went on to tell the story of the previous Saturday's dramatic events. When she came across her former lover's name, her heart jumped. Fly had attacked the snake at the time when his master was facing up to it. She remembered how frightened the animal had been when she and Christine had their terrible experience. Understandably, she felt a longing to pet him as she had done so many times last summer. 'And Dalmar, allowing himself to be interviewed!" she thought. That was amazing in itself. She was very surprised, and a little hurt, to read on and find out that he was the brother of William Hunter, the young boy who was tragically killed by a snake in 1948. According to this newspaper, it appeared that Dalmar's first name was actually John. All this explained his distaste for the subject of John the Red. But why had he not told her? Another memory flashed into her mind. The occasional letters, delivered by the postman at his cottage, addressed to a J.D.Hunter. She never did get around to asking him about those.

There was a picture of Stephen Knopner in a hospital bed surrounded by his wife and three children. 'Hmm,' thought Suzanne, 'maybe he will be a little less critical now.' She would not wish a Red Adder bite on anyone, but she reckoned it might have taken the tone out of his sarcasm.

What got to her more than anything was the sudden re-emergence of her feelings for Dalmar. There was no picture of him. It occurred to her that his part was intensely courageous. She had not quite finished the article, (it was one of those that continued on page two) when she became aware of a figure standing over her. It was the young man who had returned for his newspaper. She apologised with embarrassment and immediately flunked an attempt to refold it. Then she thought that she was being silly and explained to the customer that she knew the dog in the photograph.

During her lunch hour she went to a newsagent and purchased a copy of all the daily newspapers she could find. Back at the gallery, her employer was curious, so she told her the story playing down the romance aspect.

That evening she scanned all the papers looking for coverage of the incident. There were three photographs of Dalmar, all of them with Fly. She felt her stomach tighten. When she had finished, she borrowed a pair of scissors from her aunt and set about cutting out all the relevant articles. Then she carefully folded them so as not to put creases in the wrong places. Later, she asked her uncle if they could watch the main news broadcast on the television. When she saw Dalmar and Fly filmed outside their home, she felt tears welling in her eyes. They were not tears of sorrow ... They were tears of joy. Behind all this – she was not aware – but the feelings of injury over her disrupted romance – had waned – for reasons she really did not understand. They just had.

The following weekend, Dalmar took Fly with him to the Bush Inn at Ovington. He planned to let his dog have a run along the banks of the river Itchen, and then treat himself to a pint of beer afterwards. The pub was bound to be fairly crowded on a Saturday, at lunchtime, but this did not bother him. He would be able to pay for his beer and then drink it by the riverbank away from the majority of the inn's clientele.

He parked the Six at the pub car park and then walked directly along the road by the river, taking the first left-hand turn towards an old mill. They went up a hill on a narrow road until they joined a wider lane at the top. By going downhill for a quarter of a mile, they found a path that took them back to the valley and the chalk stream, which brought man and dog onto a glorious riverbank walk. There were two swans with their new cygnets on the water, and ducks of many varieties. The new leaf on the abundant willow trees produced cascades of a sharp light green, like numerous drapes hanging out over the river. Added to this, in the water itself, the deeper greens of the weed blankets trying to push the fast-flowing current aside, helped to create the perfect fisherman's stage.

Fly, naturally, had plenty to drink from the river itself, but Dalmar needed something rather more potent. He purchased a pint of a well-known local brew and took it back to the narrow bridge that spanned the river. The dog was allowed to run loose provided he did not stray too far.

The inn car park was, by now, practically full and other vehicles were starting to park along the narrow access road. Most of the people visiting the pub would be having lunch, either in the restaurant or ordered from the bar. Those with children would take up the tables outside on the lawn areas. Such a lovely early summer's day with unbroken sunshine brought more than just those with children to utilise the gardens. One such foursome was Christine and Tim Westward, and a neighbour married couple, whom they had got to know. They were seated at an old primitive style wooden table which had survived some misuse over the years. From here, Christine had a clear view of the bridge on which Dalmar was leaning. He had his back to her, with his posture in a hunched position, craning his head to look into the water; his drinking glass angled dangerously toward the river, balanced on one crooked finger in the handle.

Christine said, "Excuse me," to their friends who were chatting with them. She nudged Tim, who was sitting alongside her; "Look." she said.

Tim raised his head, surprised. "What?"

"Over there on the bridge. Isn't that Dalmar?" As Christine gestured in that direction their two friends turned their heads to look, curious.

"You could be right," said Tim. "Can't be sure," and then after a small pause. "Yes – it is. I would know that footwear anywhere."

One of their friends, the man, jokingly asked. "Is he a Red Indian?"

"No," said Tim before adding, "used to be my sister's boyfriend." And as the thought occurred to him, "Oh – and if that is him, get your autograph book out. He is the man who was in the press recently. You may even have seen him on television: the slayer of the Red Adder."

"Wow!" said their lady friend. "Can't see a lot of him, but he does look tall, dark and handsome."

"He is," confirmed Christine.

"Oh yes?" commented the lady's husband.

"I am going to go and say hello." Christine said looking at Tim. "Shall I invite him over?"

"Go on then," Tim did not argue with her although he had mixed feelings. Dalmar had given his sister a broken heart, but, on the other hand, he had almost certainly saved his wife's life. The brief story of which, in Christine's absence, he related to his neighbours.

To get to the bridge, Christine had to go out of a side gate by the inn and walk along a path which directly led onto the footbridge. Dalmar was still leaning over it, only now in a more upright position taking a gulp of his beer. Christine felt a little apprehensive as she got nearer. "Hello," she said.

Dalmar knew the voice instantly. He spun round – nearly spilling his drink. He received a double surprise because Christine was six months pregnant. "Good gracious!" he exclaimed. "Congratulations!" Then he smiled. He felt really glad to see her. Being with child had made her face fuller than he remembered. It lessened the squareness of her jaw a little, but her radiant beauty still made her stand out from the crowd.

"And what brings you to this neck of the woods?" She came up to him, lent over her bump and kissed him on his left cheek. Dalmar had not expected this. He felt pleased.

"Just a change of scenery," he replied with a chuckle. Before she could ask about Fly, the dog made a sudden appearance coming from the other side of the bridge. He knew her at once and demanded to be petted.

After Christine had stooped to him and said lots of "Hellos", Dalmar sent him away in recognition that it might hurt Christine to hold that position. She looked grateful but added quickly, "Come on – he does deserve a hero's welcome."

"I know – he has been getting a lot of that lately: probably gone to his head. But seriously – *this* is more important," Dalmar pointed to

Christine's tummy. "When is the baby due?"

"Oh, another three months yet, but I'm over all that morning sickness bit. Feel really good now."

"You're blooming – able to enjoy the pregnancy. How is Tim?"

"Come and ask him for yourself. We are with some friends in the pub garden."

As soon as Christine mentioned that they were with friends, Dalmar knew he was going to make excuses. "Ah," he glanced at his watch. "Look – I'm really sorry – but I promised someone..."

"A girl-friend?" Christine had a slight twinkle in her pale blue-green eyes as she asked the question.

Dalmar looked at her. "No ... I ... I don't have anyone – now."

Christine had been about to start the preamble before saying a farewell message, but there was something in the way Dalmar replied to her inquisitive remark that stopped her. "Just wondered – that's all," and then almost too casually, "Thought perhaps you might be seeing one of your – many?"

"Sorry?" Dalmar furrowed his brow.

"Well, I don't want to press the point, but you were caught red-handed by Suzanne." Christine waited to see the guilt spread over his face.

"Christine," he said, looking acutely embarrassed – rather than guilty, "I don't know what you're on about?"

"Oh, come on. She saw you with some bit of stuff outside your house. You were actually seen putting the girl's suitcase in her car."

Dalmar's jaw dropped. A memory came flooding into his mind. He said, "Mand ... Mandy Pittstucker."

"Ah – so she does have a name." Christine needed more confirmation though. "You were caught out. Suzanne came back to you a day earlier than expected. She wanted to surprise you. It turned out she was the one who got the surprise, and, incidentally, had to suffer a monumental broken heart as a result." Her face looked suitably disapproving.

"The taxi that didn't discharge its fare." Dalmar almost murmured.

Now it was Christine's turn to say, "Sorry?"

"Oh no." Dalmar's face suddenly blanched. Christine thought he was going to stumble.

"What's the matter?" she asked urgently. "Are you thinking what I think you are thinking? If her taxi had arrived a couple of minutes later - Suz would never have known?"

"No ... no ... no - you don't understand." Dalmar was deeply saddened. "I'm sorry ... please. You are so wrong. Oh dear – so wrong."

"What?" she pleaded. "What is it?"

"Yes – that girl – an old friend ... she did want to stay. But I said no because I was in a relationship. She had only been at my house for about an hour." As Dalmar finished these words it was Christine's turn to gasp and feel emotional. She knew; she absolutely knew, that from the way Dalmar had just spoken, he had been telling the truth.

"Why didn't you try and contact Suzanne?" Christine asked this almost knowing what the reply would be.

"I did. Her mother told me that she didn't want to speak to me." Christine knew it would be pointless to ask why he had not persevered.

Because neither of them was sure what to do in the circumstances, they came together in an embrace: an embrace of friends in need.

"Look," said Christine. "I believe... from the way you are acting, that you are still in love with Suzanne. I cannot speak for her. She has been *very* badly hurt. But..." Christine held out her hands and placed them on either side of Dalmar's face. "For heaven's sake – write to her and explain. Please! Do it soon. She is at her aunt and uncle's in the Lakes. Do you have the address?"

"Yes," he said – in a quiet voice.

"I hope we will see you soon." Christine gave a long, deep look into his eyes, before taking her hands off his face and touching his arm lightly with her right hand. Then she smiled, turned, and walked away.

Tim looked up as his wife re-joined them. Their friends had gone to the bar to purchase some more drinks. Not seeing Dalmar with her, he glanced towards the bridge. There was no sign of him. "Well?" he said.

"Oh Tim, I think there has been the most awful misunderstanding between Dalmar and Suz. I shall have to phone her this evening." She told her husband, word for word, of the conversation that had just taken place on the bridge. Their friends, Pat and Mary, returned in time to hear Tim let out a sharp whistle through his teeth. Christine had to give them a brief resume.

"Pity he's gone" observed Mary. "I should like to have met him."

"Hmmph," uttered Pat. "Just because he is handsome *and* a celebrity." He pouted appropriately.

"Not just that," grinned Mary. "He sounds like an interesting man."

"He is," said Tim. "And a good friend. Who knows, maybe you will get your wish – in the not-too-distant future."

CHAPTER FORTY-SEVEN

SEEMED TO ACCENTUATE ALL HIS SENSES.

That evening Dalmar hoped with all his being that Christine would contact her sister-in-law to tell her of the encounter at the Bush Inn. He wrote a short letter to Suzanne expressing his regret about what had happened. He explained the events as they had transpired and made a written promise that it was the truth. He did not ask for a reconciliation. Instead, he finished a short poem on a separate sheet of paper and inserted it in the same envelope.

SUZANNE.
The sound of the music fading tells me I should away,
Over the hill that looks on us to the plains of yesterday.
I hear the mountains calling and a vale with water clear,
Reminds me of a velvet cheek and single droplet tear.

On a rolling down of chalk, I first met her on high,
And felt deep emotion under the ever-brooding sky.
Music that stayed above us caught my wondering mind,
With ardour never stilled by the tragedies of our time.

Now it has all gone through replaced by love-lost sighs,
I will never see again the girl with lights in her eyes.
Unless, I hear the music sounding out over that distant hill,
Then I shall know it's you, coming back, dearest, to fulfil.

Dalmar placed the two sheets of paper in an envelope; wrote Suzanne's name with her aunt's address on it and put it in the kitchen ready to post in the morning.

When he rose on the Sunday, the air was clear, and the sun shone in a brilliant sparkle: unexpected dew covered everything. On impulse, he took Fly up to Farley Down, and, after parking the car walked up to the monument with a deep melancholic feeling, for he had come here purely because this was the place where he had first met Suzanne. Strangely, at that very moment a strong breeze sprung up, even though there were no clouds in evidence.

The man and the dog took up a position on the edge of a steep, tufted grass slope. They were alone. Fly, standing proudly, let the gusts cool his handsome body. He held his mouth open, with his long tongue undulating to a healthy pant. His eyes were bright and clear. The strong breeze seemed to accentuate all his senses.

Dalmar stood by his side, his dark hair blowing back from his brow, and his denim covered chest thrust forward in a fruitless attempt to push the element back. He looked across the southern Hampshire countryside toward the coastal towns. In the far distance a transparent haze hovered above the mid-blue tones of the sea. With a lover's hope, softly, he recited his poem.

In Grasmere village, a young girl received news via a telephone call that left her trembling. She did not know whether relief, frustration or even regret caused it. Whatever it was, it would not go away, and she was still suffering the next morning. To compound the problem, she had been debating whether to accept an invitation to dinner on Saturday, from the gentleman customer who had left his newspaper in the gallery. She eventually decided that it could do no harm and accepted. But on the Tuesday morning she rushed downstairs when the post came, to see if there was anything for her. There was not ... She went to work trying to camouflage her disappointment by adopting a fake, jaunty air.

Early on Wednesday, her aunt brought her a letter that had just been posted through their letterbox. She recognised the writing. Trembling all the more now, she opened it. First, she acknowledged the familiar address on the top of the notepaper and then she read on:

19th June 1976

'Dear, dear Suzanne,

I hope by now that you will have heard from Christine of the tragic coincidence that befell us. An old girl friend of mine called to see me on that Sunday evening. She asked to stay. I said that would not be possible. I gave her a drink. We had a chat, and then she left. That is when you saw us. This, I promise, is the truth. I am so very sorry for any pain it may have caused you. If it was anything like that felt by yours truly, I am desperately unhappy you experienced it.

With all my love,

Dalmar.'

There was the familiar style in which he wrote his name. She started to cry. As she put the letter on her bed, having read it at least three times, another piece of the same writing paper, which had been placed behind, fell to the floor. She picked it up. As she read the poem, her hands simply would not keep still. She could hear Dalmar's tender masculine voice reading it to her, resonating through her head.

Christine's prophecy, that one day her turn would come, had come true.

As Dalmar arrived home on Wednesday evening, he was in the act of getting out of his car, when he became aware of a figure standing looking at him from the direction of the copse of chestnut trees. Once upright, he turned to look. He recognised the features of a fairly well-known actor, whom he had heard lived in the village. "I know we have not been introduced," said Thomas Hurn in his deep voice, "But I was just on my way into the Claymans to partake of a wee dram, when I saw your car pull in. I wondered, as we are near neighbours, and I've heard so much about you, whether you would care for a tipple?" He advanced towards Dalmar and held out his hand. "Thomas," he stated as though that were all that was necessary.

Dalmar, after returning the handshake, did not know why but he answered "Yes," immediately. "John Hunter. Sounds like an excellent suggestion." He closed the door of the Triumph. "I need to do one thing though. Collect my dog from this house right here," he pointed with a finger, "and quickly feed him."

"Okay. What can I get you?"

"What are you having?" replied Dalmar.

"Whisky and soda."

"I'll join you," said Dalmar agreeably. Thomas let out a broad grin, before heading back towards the entrance of the hotel.

It took Dalmar about fifteen minutes to collect and feed Fly. He quickly took off his tie and went over to the hotel bar without his suit jacket, leaving his dog behind with an apology and promising a walk later. He found Thomas Hurn talking to David Andrews, although it rather looked as though there had been some good-natured bantering going on. "Here you are," he welcomed. "A large whisky and soda. Hope it is to your liking?"

Dalmar said, "Good evening," to David as he took a sip. "Great," he said savouring the whisky. "Thank you. Well now, what are you both chatting about?"

"What else?" replied David. "The Red Adder mystery – of course."

"Ah. Do you know how the police investigation is going?" Dalmar directed his question at the doctor.

"Not really. Don't even know who is in charge. Probably the chief constable – I should think."

"Bound to be on a matter of this importance," added Thomas. He seemed to have already acquired a healthy suntan.

"I can tell you that they have roped off the area by your pond," said David. "Going over it thoroughly – turning over every fallen leaf – apparently."

"From what you tell me ..." here Thomas looked pointedly at the doctor; "They suspect somebody in the village of breeding these snakes. Is that right?"

"Well – I think it is more likely to be someone who lives in the area."

David answered taking a drink from an orangey coloured glass. "But - I don't suppose it need necessarily be so."

"Without a house-to-house search, any result is going to depend entirely on something that our mysterious breeder may have left behind, however small," commented the thespian.

"Exactly," confirmed David. "I imagine, if they draw a blank, an every property search is a distinct possibility."

"Naa – the bird will have flown by then. All evidence destroyed, I shouldn't wonder – if they haven't done so already," said Thomas with a conclusive air. "John," … he turned towards Dalmar wishing to come to the purpose of his invitation. "I was wondering, considering your history, if I may put it like that, if you happen to know the identity of the poet?"

"Sorry – not with you there," said Dalmar reaching for his glass with a puzzled look on his face. Even though he had taken off his suit jacket, he could feel perspiration on his brow. Now they were into June, the days were getting longer, and with them came warmer evenings.

"The poem about John the Red?" Thomas explained.

"Oh." Dalmar had heard about Thomas's prowess at reading it, probably from Suzanne. "No – sorry – don't know."

"How disappointing," said Thomas. "Felt sure you might." He thought for a moment before adding, "Of course there isn't any reason why you should, when I think about it. Your family moved away from the area in the late forties I believe?" Dalmar nodded. "It is probably the last thing you would want to have knowledge of."

Dalmar nodded confirmation to him.

The three men chatted for some time with Dalmar purchasing a return round of drinks. The immediate professional commitments that Thomas was about to be engaged upon were interesting. After this, they left to go to their respective homes.

At work the next day, the local Southampton press pestered Dalmar. His company wanted to make as much of the story about his dog as possible, realising the advantageous publicity. He had to go along with it, and reluctantly agreed to bring Fly into his office the following morning. Some of the female staff were thrilled.

Julia Thornton had now been officially declared missing, presumed dead. A full year had gone by since she had mysteriously disappeared from her home and life in Yewhurst. The police were completely mystified, although there were several theories as to Red Adder involvement.

CHAPTER FORTY-EIGHT

BOTH MEN GAZED AT EACH OTHER.

During the early evening, the very next Sunday, Dalmar decided to wander up to the church with Fly. He had to take the dog for a walk, but his real intention was to spy on any police activity. What he found pleased him. A notice had been posted in the church car park stating that limited access to Yewhurst Wood would be restored as from Monday. All the plantations would be out of bounds; the only pathway where access would be denied was the one in the northern part of the woods. Dalmar knew this to be the narrower, grassy way that led passed the Secret Pond.

On his return, and some two hundred yards away, he caught sight of Allen Haddle, arriving home with his white terrier. Even at this distance, Fly still growled. Dalmar waved politely, and he received a similar gesture from Allen, who was just about to open the gate onto his drive, flanked on each side by juvenile sweet chestnut trees.

Dalmar continued on his way, telling Fly to be quiet. Suddenly – he stopped. The collie looked round and waited patiently with an appealing cocked ear and quizzical expression. His master did not move. He was staring hard into the ground. Eventually, after several seconds that seemed an age to the waiting dog, he turned around and looked back. Allen was still there ... looking directly at him. Both men gazed at each other. Dalmar could see, even from a distance, that Allen had a questioning attitude about him. After a short demur, Allen Haddle swung his gate open, beckoned Jupiter in and disappeared down the snug hill towards his front door.

The dawn of realisation for Dalmar had started a minute ago. The sight of Allen by those chestnut trees had provided the trigger. 'Could it be? Could it possibly be?' As the seconds had stacked up, he became more and more certain. He remembered the details of a conversation that had taken place at his cottage last winter, between himself and Allen Haddle. That problem that had bothered him when he lay in his bath, after he and Fly had killed the Red Adder – concerning something Stephen Knopner had said, about not knowing from which tree the snake had attacked Christine Westward. What had been not quite right somehow – now became frighteningly clear. He needed to check some details to be sure.

Dalmar literally ran all the way home. His face was a fixed mask of deadly gravity. On-lookers from the Claymans Heron could not help but stop what they were doing, and stare at the running man with his dog joining in at full gallop.

When he arrived at his cottage, Dalmar looked up the Hampshire police headquarters' telephone number and dialled it. He asked whom he should speak to in connection with the Red Adder case. He was told that the chief constable was not there, at this time, but he could speak to a Chief Inspector Grant. Dalmar explained that he did not wish to right now, but he would almost certainly do so later in the evening. He left his name and telephone number and rang off. Following this, he hurriedly but deliberately checked the details of Suzanne Westward's report about the attack on her sister-in-law from the copy sent to him by the police.

Turning to his dog he said, "Guard the house Fly," and left, closing the stable door behind him. He strode with purpose, a long striding fast walk, with his face set as though carved in granite. When he got to the Haddle's gate, he pulled back the handle and swung it open, closing it behind him with a loud clang, and without turning his back advanced towards the front door. He closed his right fist and banged three times.

There was a long pause before Jean Haddle opened the door. Normally, she would have been smiling, but the loud thumping had annoyed her. She wondered why the doorbell had not been used: it was in a prominent position. "You must be John Hunter;" she addressed the serious looking man in her doorway. "Allen said to go on up to his study." Dalmar expressed no surprise, even though there seemed little reason why he should be expected. He looked blankly at Mrs Haddle, not because he did not understand, but purely because he did not know where the study was. She realised his dilemma and pointed up the staircase leading straight off from the hallway. "Go to the top of the stairs, and then to the far right-hand corner of the landing – that's it." She uttered the last two words in a higher note than the rest of the sentence, as though announcing a scene from a play.

Dalmar, rather rudely, brushed passed the confused lady and climbed the staircase without hesitation. He found a closed door at the other end of an ample landing area, which housed a solitary oak hat chest. On one side of this chest an antiquated hardback novel was precariously hanging over the edge. A copy of Charles Kingsley's Westward Ho. He knocked with the knuckle of his first finger. It was a purposeful knock that sounded echoic in the empty, spacious area.

"Come in," came a clear, immediate reply.

Dalmar opened the door and entered. Allen Haddle was seated side on to him in front of an antique roll-top desk. This looked as though it had been well used. It had been polished regularly, but, on closer inspection, showed the years of mishaps from spilt drinks and falling objects. Nevertheless, it was full of character giving away a history in the patina. One fact was quite obvious; its owner kept it tidy, very tidy. The numerous pigeonholes were full but stacked neatly with labels and drawing implements. Several of them contained small instruments of various kinds. All the side drawers, which formed on each side of the bureau, its main support, were closed. Behind this desk, in the far corner, was what appeared to be an old American icebox. Allen was studying Dalmar's face, searching all the while, with his deep blue eyes. It was an uncomfortable, chilly stare. "May I have a word?" Dalmar requested. He waited to be asked if he would like to take a seat.

"Of course, dear fellow" replied Allen, and he pointed to a two-seater settee of a dull fabric, which lay up against the wall adjacent to him. Dalmar strode over and lowered his rather tall frame to sit down. It felt too low and put him at a disadvantage. He tried leaning forward, but that seemed worse. Realising that this could be used as a deliberate ploy of Allen's, a trick often used by men of small stature, he moved to the other end of the piece of furniture by means of a quick shuffle, and stretched his long legs out to one side, almost as though he were about to put his feet up on the settee. Then, he half reclined against the armrest. The result was to transfer his height into length, which really, was just as effective.

As he glanced about, the overall sparseness of the study seemed out of character for its owner. On the walls, the usual framed photographs of school or college days were totally absent. In short, there was no display whatever of matters concerning personal history: nor even qualification documents. A large bookcase took up one area, and presumably, contained volumes on veterinary matters. There were no colourful dust jackets belonging to modern publications: all looked period. Next to him, by the settee, was a dull cream coloured two-door cabinet. It was tall, and had an ominous looking padlock attached across some strong brackets. 'He doesn't want anybody meddling in there,' thought the visitor. Dalmar was rather expecting the offer of a drink, but there was no sign of it. He decided to get down to the reason for his uninvited, but, apparently, expected call.

"I ought to explain," Dalmar started, "that something has been bugging me of late, in connection with John the Red. Earlier this evening ... I realised what it was."

"Go on," said Allen Haddle. The serious tone to his voice matched his guest's. The dim lighting emanating from a single Angle-Poise lamp, housed on top of the roll-top desk, created a disheartening atmosphere.

"When you came to see me about my connection to the Hunter family ... you asked ... if the snake were to reappear this year, did I think it might be in a tree by the Secret Pond?"

"Indeed," agreed Allen "and you were surprised, I thought, that someone actually had faith that the pond existed."

Dalmar nodded. "I had an envelope from the Hampshire Constabulary the other morning. Inside was a draft of the statement made by Suzanne Westward, concerning the Red Adder attack on her sister-in-law." 'Was he imagining things, or did Allen's right eye start a slow twitch?' "I have had to return the original, of course, but they gave me a copy, and I have just verified one part in particular." Dalmar became aware that Allen's demeanour abruptly changed. He had not noticed it before, but a low growl from the well under the roll-top desk, behind Allen's feet, brought attention to the curled-up shape of Jupiter. The terrier's head was raised, and his top lip was stretched back in a snarl. Undeterred, Dalmar continued. "It is the bit that relates to the actual snake attack. I was not present at that time, making Miss Westward the only witness. She said that she did not actually see the snake land on her sister-in-law, but she believed it came out of a tall tree, some of whose branches overhung the pond." Dalmar stopped talking and looked at Allen. Both men had tight eye contact.

"Yes, that is what David Andrews told me," Allen's voice was slow and precise.

"Yes – it would be, because he was present when Miss Westward first mentioned it. So was I." Dalmar deliberately lowered the tone of his voice. At the same time, he narrowed his eyes. His dark brown hair, a little tousled from his recent running, hung over his brow. The jaw was set so that only his lips moved as he spoke. "Why then ... did you ask me? ... If the Red Adder returned this year ... did I think it might be found living in the *chestnut,* by the Secret Pond? Not just a tall tree – but quite explicitly – a chestnut."

Allen Haddle stiffened in his seat and sat more upright. He brought back his legs and tucked his brogue-clad feet under the chair. Jupiter growled. Dalmar, severely, continued. "How could you have known that there was a chestnut by the pond? Miss Westward made no mention of a particular tree, only a reference to its height." Allen stared at a point somewhere under his inquisitor's chin. He started a slight up and down and side-to-side movement of his head, as though studying a chessboard, after his opponent had called 'checkmate.' He made no reply. "Unless," Dalmar sounded unstoppable, "you had been to the Secret Pond yourself?" ... But stop – he did. He knew, instinctively, that he had said enough. The silence was absolute ... historically.

CHAPTER FORTY-NINE

"WAS IT MAGNIFICENT?"

What Dalmar could not know was why the question about the possible reappearance of the Red Adder had been asked by Allen Haddle, in the first place. It was purely because he was desperate to find out how much Dalmar knew. Later, he had regretted asking it, sensing he might have made a serious mistake.

"It is time I told the story." The voice seemed to come from a different human being than the Allen Haddle that Dalmar knew, even of his brief acquaintance. It had not taken Allen long to come to this decision. He had thought about bluffing his way out of it – 'slip of the tongue' or a similar excuse. But no – it was just a matter of time before the police would make a connection. And – if anybody deserved to hear his confession – it was the person sitting opposite him right now. Allen settled himself into a more comfortable position in his leather chair, and his legs came out from their hunched position. Jupiter relaxed with a low whine.

"During the war," he began, "I was lucky, some people might think, in that my services as a vet were of more importance to this country than going off to fight abroad. The Ministry of Defence employed me to look after our local farm stock in principle. You, no doubt, can see the importance of that?" Dalmar made an abrupt nod. "The thing was I had this other interest, not herpetology, which I think you may suspect. No ... I was fascinated by artificial insemination." He stopped here to risk a look into his guest's face. What he saw – he did not like. Dalmar still possessed that hardness of expression. His brow seemed permanently creased in a deep frown. The eyes were slightly closed, and he was clenching his back teeth causing muscle tension in his cheeks.

Allen carried on, hopeful that he could soften matters – in time. "Anyway, I met Jean in 1942, and we got married two years later. We bought a house in Eastleigh, at the top end of Arbuckle Road, and shortly after that I was able to return to my practice, although, at the time I was only a junior partner. After the war I found it hard to get back to balancing the books, if you know what I mean. Of course, one had to swim or sink." Haddle paused momentarily; a clock chimed the hour somewhere in the house, and muffled voices could be heard from a television set downstairs.

"Almost immediately, I set about working on my hobby. I won't bore you with the science of it all, but after a great deal of theoretical work, I concluded that reasonably primitive life would be the easiest sphere in which to start my experiments. The trouble was that whenever I thought of the method with, for example poultry, the reason for any insemination was pointless, because I was transferring one primitive life form into another. After exhaustive research – and I mean exhaustive. It wasn't just a case of taking books out of the library; my thirst for knowledge took me to London, Edinburgh, and Paris. In those days it was not in any shape or form addictive. It was just an honest endeavour, to improve my abilities at a subject that genuinely interested me.

I believe a turning point came when two important things happened. The first was the diagnosis, sadly, that my wife could not bear children. An undetected infection of the womb made it a definite impossibility. Like most young and healthy married couples, we wanted our own children, but…" Haddle went silent, deep in pensive thought, before shaking his head slowly and then resuming. "The second event was the beginning of an idea. Simply explained, I came across a species, with which I believed I could experiment with a great chance of success. The broad species was reptilian, and the most likely to produce dramatic results were egg-laying snakes. The simple structures of their being, with various defensive and aggressive attributes were the principal reasons, but also, far more importantly, I made a scientific discovery, which may go with me to my grave … it depends."

Dalmar said nothing. He knew he was supposed to. But he remained silent.

"Anyhow, matters got to the stage where I required a field of operation, as I termed it, but where? You see, carrying out experiments on incubating eggs may not need a great deal of space, but I had to have secrecy, and I knew Jean would not tolerate live snakes in our house, or in a shed in our garden for that matter. I was confident that my new species would soon outgrow cage apparatus suitable for indoor habitation. I believe certain people have a loose theory that a Malayan golden tree snake, which they think escaped from Southampton Zoo in the mid-forties, may have mated with our common adder. In actual fact, they were not far wrong. I stole that snake from the zoo. It was terribly easy. One day when they were feeding in the reptile house, I simply sneaked in while the door to the rear of the glass cubicles was open and helped myself: carried the thing out in a shopping basket. At one stage, I caught it sticking its head out, forked tongue going like mad. Fortunately, nobody noticed." Haddle smiled.

"The process was to drill a tiny hole in a snake's egg and further fertilise it with other snake's active sperm by injection. To achieve this, I kept a live female cobra, obtained by arrangement with an old college friend who lived in India, plus this male golden tree snake and several male adders. Also, being a veterinary surgeon, I had the necessary equipment in ultra-fine drills. As you can imagine, things were hectic immediately after the hibernation period. Keeping and obtaining supplies of feed, namely tiny rodents, was often very difficult. But after contacting a new herpetologist society, I managed to get that sorted out." Dalmar glanced in the direction of the old fridge. "Yes, you are right," Haddle nodded at him, "Still going strong too." He paused briefly, gravely thinking to himself. "Back to the problem of where to have an outdoor laboratory. I walked a hundred miles, I should think, searching for the right place. Couldn't afford to purchase a plot of land, and it had to be away from curious eyes. Obviously, I needed to keep the entire matter secret. If anyone were to find out what my real motives were; I could see there might well be trouble. Apart from anything else, I had in my charge an extremely dangerous snake: the king cobra. It is well known that this breed of snake is responsible for more human fatalities than any other, by far. What is little known, or certainly was then, is that its glands can contain a large quantity of venom: enough to kill an Asian elephant."

Dalmar could not hold himself back any longer. "Forgive me," his voice had an edge of sarcasm with it, "But why was it necessary to carry out these experiments with dangerous snakes?"

"Because I wouldn't prove anything without doing so!" Haddle snapped back at him, as though he were talking to a first-year veterinary student. "Don't forget that the whole business was still a ploat." Temporarily, he had forgotten the necessity to appease his visitor.

"Sorry?" said Dalmar. "A pl..."

"A ploat." Haddle gave him an impatient glance. "An idea without foundation, or to be more precise something improperly theorised," he said sternly, as though that were sufficient explanation, at the same time shaking his head from side to side. "Anyway," he continued, "my experiments required a species with good defensive capabilities, so that in the end I could arrive at the greatest capability of all – attack!" He finished this with flushed cheeks and excited eyes. Dalmar wondered whether Allen's raised voice might attract the attention of his wife.

After a brief interlude, during which he calmed, Allen Haddle carried on. "I found what I was looking for on a hunch. I attended to a client's cat not far from where your family used to live. While in casual conversation with the lady of the house, she boasted how lucky they were to have woodland at the back of their home, most especially because no one ever went there. Naturally, I investigated. I found a large area of about four acres of unmanaged woods. It was what I came across in the middle of it that clinched the matter, an unused shed, big enough for my purposes. Obviously, there was clearing and shoring to do, but nothing that a hammer, saw and some planks of cheap timber wouldn't solve. So, by the early spring of 1947, I was ready. Inside the shed I built four glass containers, each four feet long, and placed then on strong supports."

"Where was the access to this shed exactly?" asked Dalamr.

"No harm in telling you now. Way down the other end of the woods from your family's house. It was tough; I had to do all the carrying on foot. Those glass aquarium-like containers, even in pieces, were very heavy, I assure you." At the time, Dalmar would have been too young to venture that far into the woodland, and he doubted if his elder brother or sister ever did, so they would have been completely ignorant of the goings on behind their home.

"This was the amazing thing; I had success with my very first try. Two inseminations into a cobra egg, and I got one baby snake. All the incubation warming was supplied by a couple of car batteries powering a small tube heater, under a bed of straw."

"Did you require much heat?" Dalmar asked casually.

"Ah – you have to remember that both the cobra and the tree snake hail from somewhat hotter climates." Secretly, Allen Haddle was encouraged by what he thought was interest. "But you are right, combined with straw to substitute a shallow buried nest, it was only necessary to ensure protection against a late frost." Allen paused while waiting for some reaction from Dalmar. There was none. Undeterred, he continued. "The egg hatched during the night. I didn't even see the first signs of a crack appearing. I arrived one afternoon and saw the broken eggshell, and then came across the little reptile hiding under the straw. I whooped with joy. I have to admit that this exuberance was quelled somewhat because it could be just another cobra. But then I realised that although tiny, our hatchling was not like any species of snake known to me. I studied it in wonder."

Haddle stopped here and re-arranged his feet. Jupiter did not stir. "Well, it grew, oh dear me, did it grow. Now this was no real surprise, after all, its mother might reach fifteen to sixteen feet in a few years, although at the time she was only about seven feet long. The fathers – well – the common adder and the tree snake are titchy really, neither of them would grow to any great length. The interesting thing was that our youngster possessed the head of a viper, in other words, the adder's head. Not the golden tree snake or the cobra's. After four weeks it started to develop the loose skin, a vital part of the flying snake's make-up.

One day something happened, which gave me my first concern. I was attending to the tree snake at the time, giving its house a good clean and replacing the water, when our new arrival, for its size, made a very loud hiss. I investigated the container and blow me down if it hadn't turned a bright red. I can tell you it looked very bad tempered, and I kept my distance. This behaviour was important. Snakes are not hostile unless they are after prey or on the defence. So, what had caused this to happen? Anyhow, after a few minutes it ceased the aggressive actions, and gradually returned to its normal colour. By now, it had acquired a distinctive zigzag marking on its back, like an adder." Allen Haddle was in full flow. This was the first time in nearly thirty years that he had had a detailed conversation with another human being about his obsession.

"At the end of May the snake was already four feet long, and I was becoming alarmed. I found it difficult to clean out the glass box because it started to behave in a very unfriendly fashion. One day, I opened the container just to give it a small mouse, when it reared up and started to go red from the neck down. Then it struck; fortunately for me, hitting the wooden top strut of the box. I dropped the mouse and jumped to one side. It was a terrible mistake. I should have slammed the lid shut immediately. Too late, it was out. As I shrank back into the other side of the shed, it made its escape through the open door, and was gone with ferocious acceleration. I remember how the speed of its departure – amazed me."

He paused for breath – and to look pointedly at his visitor. "Of course, you know the rest." Allen glanced at Dalmar, hesitating for quite some time before adding, "I'm afraid ... I was secretly pleased that it survived the winter of 1947/48 in hibernation. Particularly as it was one of the hardest winters on record."

"That is all very well," commented Dalmar. "It won't bring my brother back." Haddle glanced at the floor, saying nothing. "What happened to the body of the snake Big Harry killed?"

Allen gave Dalmar a pointed look at this question. "I recovered it." He continued to stare before saying. "Gave it a decent burial – and I have no intention of telling you where."

Dalmar hardly moved a muscle, indicating that he was not in the least bit interested. What did not seem to occur to Allen Haddle was the effect on Dalmar and his sister of their brother's death: the frequent nightmares. To them the Red Adder represented all that was evil. "You must have continued with your experiments," said Dalmar. "There was something about 1959, apparently, and then we have the last two years?"

"Yes – but look what I had achieved? I had to go on. You could say that those poor people would have died in vain otherwise."

"Haven't they anyway?" Dalmar said provocatively.

Haddle ignored this, although, there was that twitch in his right eye again. He went silent for a while as though trying to make up his mind whether to continue.

Out of the corner of his eye, Dalmar noticed that at the far end of the room, the window looking out over the rear garden was prevented from displaying the evening sunlight, due to the existence of a double layer of net curtains. Under the window was a large marble slab raised up on table legs. It looked scrupulously clean. At one end, stood an old but valuable looking brass microscope, and beneath the marble table was a set of narrow draws, like a miniature plan-chest. Dalmar wondered what information lay within.

Allen's voice came back – slower than before. "Well, of course I lost my shed. There was far too much activity going on around the Great Mile for me to carry on there. I cleared everything out, before it could be discovered, and found myself back where I started. Unfortunately, I had to get rid of the king cobra; the Malayan golden tree snake died anyway. It took another ten years before I could get going again. Jean and I moved to this house in 1956, bought it from new, and naturally started to enjoy walking in Yewhurst Wood, as indeed, you do now. And, I daresay I came across the Secret Pond, as you call it, in much the same way as you did, except that it was many years earlier. The Forestry Commission was not in charge at that time, and they hadn't started planting. That happened later. Fortunately, their eventual plantation didn't reach my secret area. I, myself, planted some young larches to help prevent anyone discovering the pond. This time, instead of operating from a shed, I used large rabbit pens with a fine mesh to keep the inmates in. And I removed the glass breeding aquarium, in each case, as soon as it became redundant. It was a lot simpler, and I could hide the big hutches fairly well..."

Dalmar interrupted him. "How did you manage to do that without being spotted? The number of visits you would have had to make – the materials you needed to convey?"

"Easy," replied Haddle. "Did it after sundown. Once you have familiarised yourself with the geography, by daylight, all you have to do is drive in at night. There has always been a good track down there, and when it was really muddy, in the winter months, I didn't need to go." Dalmar offered up his right hand in acknowledgement. "Anyhow, I carried out the same experiment in 1959, importing the cobra and tree snake, legally, this time, and was overjoyed to get another result. But I cursed myself later – didn't appreciate the brute's strength. Having witnessed a strike and received alarming results concerning the potency of the venom when analysed, I should have been more alert. I was always very careful, but I hadn't realised just how strong my creations were, physically. This one literally broke out. Must have twisted the mesh with its mouth and escaped. I never saw it again. And then a fox or some wretched animal damaged the other containers and broke them; so, there was also a King cobra on the loose. The tree snake would not have been dangerous. But nothing was ever sighted – who knows." He waved his hands aside. "There then followed several years of failure. This is where the climate factor comes in. Up to now, I had been lucky, in that all the experimental years had started with very fine weather."

"Why didn't you move the operation to another country?"

"Ah," Allen squinted at Dalmar over his large nose. "Wouldn't have worked – needed to be carried out in a temperate climate situation." He paused before saying. "To tell you the main reason – would give too much away – sorry." Dalmar shrugged his right shoulder.

"I don't know why, but after that I decided to stop the experiments. Until that is some fifteen years later. My old friend who still lives in India; only been back to this country a couple of times, I believe, contacted me, and asked if I would like a M'fezi or Mozambique spitting cobra. Couldn't resist it, and the tree snake species was easily available. So, as everything else was still in place, apart from renewing the batteries..."

"What about the adders?" interrupted Dalmar with suppressed anger. "I mean it surely is not that easy to get hold of an adder?"

"It is – if you are a vet. Even in retirement," Allen answered. "Just have to know the right people. I did have one problem though. I noticed far too much activity, for my liking, around the pond. For instance, you didn't see me one day, but I saw you; although, I think your young collie was aware of me. Didn't know who you were? Knew the forestry chaps didn't go there – but a dog walker; that was too dangerous." He shook his head vigorously. "So, I came up with a method to disguise the entrance. It was highly fortunate that there were two identical looking paths, of a sort, close together."

"The fake rhododendron." Dalmar interjected.

"Indeed – as you say – the fake rhododendron."

"How often did you have to replace it?"

"Surprisingly – only a couple of times a year. Let's face it; there is a plentiful supply near at hand. Originally, the path leading to the pond was not at all obvious. In fact, a casual passer-by would hardly have noticed its existence. The other path was far more apparent, but I suppose my coming and going over the years made a difference. That is probably how you came to discover the pond yourself.

"Did you get any trouble from vagrants?"

"None at all. I knew some took up residence, if you like, in Yewhurst Wood for short periods of time. But none, to my knowledge, ever ventured that far into it. Yewhurst Wood covers several square miles: most of it unused by anyone other than Forestry Commission employees.

"What about water supply for the rhododendron? I saw the sunken bucket..." He broke off – realising the answer.

"The pond," said Haddle, with a superior smirk on his face.

"What did you do this time? There were two successful births – yes?"

"Correct – although one was positively minute when it hatched out. But still it survived, until that is, the forestry man shot it." Dalmar did not flinch. Haddle must have known that he was present on that occasion. "Mind you, things started to go wrong right from the start. I was working behind the pond when your ex-girlfriend and her sister-in-law came blundering in. All that shouting and splashing. I got very angry – but I couldn't declare myself, for that would have given my secret location away. Looking back, I realise it was my own fault for leaving the gate open, so to speak. You see – I was starting to get careless. Didn't think anyone would come along. I was only going to be about a quarter of an hour: just dropping off some food. Anyway, do you know what I did? I got so annoyed – I just had to let off steam..."

"You let them go," said Dalmar icily.

"That's right! Or rather I let *it* go. The smaller one was already free." Haddle's eyes appeared to protrude from their sockets. Saliva was starting to show in the right-hand corner of his mouth, and his lips had lost some of their colour. "Soon sorted them out, I can tell you!"

"Some people might call that attempted murder." Again, Dalmar was impassive, and his voice seemed to be getting even harder.

"Call it what you loike," Haddle's voice whipped back. He was now at his most aggressive and had lost interest in pacifying Dalmar. "Those stupid girls could have wrecked moi life's work in foive minutes!" He was almost spluttering the words out. Dalmar could have sworn he slipped into a mild local dialect. Jupiter woke up and got to his feet. He cowered away from his owner and went right over to the far side of the room, locating a corner under the marble top table, which hid him from view. Dalmar had the feeling that he had done that many times before when experiments went array.

It was at this moment that Dalmar realised that his life might be in serious danger. It had not occurred to him before. He was responsible for killing this man's greatest achievement. 'You could say – his baby?' Slowly Allen's left hand reached toward the second drawer down on that side of the desk. With two fingers he pulled back the drawer a fraction, and then he stopped. There was a long moment of silence, before he withdrew his hand.

Gradually, Haddle's pulse rate seemed to subside, and eventually he carried on with his story. "After that catastrophic episode, there was nothing for it but to clear everything out – batteries and incubation heater: the lot. I left the hutches intact so that I could return later in the year with some straw. If any of them survived the summer, they would need it for hibernation. Of course, after a few days only one was still alive. It got too difficult for me to visit the pond, what with all the security at the entrance gates – not to mention alert forestry personnel." Allen stopped and stretched his neck muscles by moving his head from side to side exaggeratedly, before proceeding. "I thought that the winter months would not require any attention from me – but..."

"This could answer my next question," said Dalmar. His tone had become a little less antagonistic.

"You want to know how that winter growth occurred?" asked Haddle, raising his head once more to look at his inquisitor. "I visited the cages one day in November, and, to my utter amazement, found the snake awake. A dash to a butcher in Romsey for a rabbit nearly resulted in discovery when I returned. Fortunately, whoever was driving a Forestry Commission Land Rover at the time failed to spot me. I was actually in the act of removing the rhododendron bush. Anyhow, after that, I paid regular visits and often found John either awake or in a state of drowsiness. He ate a lot of rabbits; I can tell you. Of course, I didn't quite grasp how big he was getting, but you saw the result. Magnificent wasn't it?"

"Oh yes," replied Dalmar, not troubling to hide his sarcasm. He was surprised at the reference to John. "Forgive me for making the observation – but those cages would never have held the beast that attacked Stephen Knopner and myself."

"You don't need a cage when a snake is hibernating. All it wants is a refuge. Anyhow, after March, I left the door open."

"I see," said Dalmar.

"Good." Haddle sighed. "Well – that's something – you agree it was magnificent?" Dalmar wanted to remind him of all the people those snakes had killed, but he decided that it would be pointless verbal retribution. The man was mad. He was hanging over his chair now, his arms loose by his sides, head lolled forward. Suddenly, he came upright. His face had transformed. It wore an almost sadistic, straight-lipped smile. "On that final encounter," here – his eyes became ice-blue slits. "Was it magnificent!?"

"You mean – was it terrifying?"

"Yes, yes, whatever – go on. Tell me – was it the most – terrifying, living creature you have ever seen in the flesh?" He was obviously desperate for information that only Dalmar could give him. This desire, probably, was the main reason why he had made his confession to Dalmar; the most important witness to the snake's last moments alive.

"Yes," said Dalmar.

Haddle's face was nearly comical. He sat bolt upright and looked at Dalmar incredulously. "Is that it!?"

Dalmar shrugged his shoulders. "What do you want me to say? Yes – it was terrifying."

"But – it had all those defensive attributes. It … it … it had the most toxic and possessed the greatest quantity of venom of any living snake on this planet – bar none." While raising his voice – Haddle stuck out a pointing finger from a stubby fist. "It could project its venom with deadly accuracy, and at a great range. It could hypnotise its prey. It could glide vast distances. It was fast and strong. The fastest and the strongest – I'll wager. But the most important facet of all was its extraordinary aggression. Maybe it was territorial; I don't know. But that fierce attacking force within its physiology was … just beautiful!" He finished with a big smile on his face, head swaying about all over the place. Then he quietened without warning, appearing to be out of breath. Abruptly, his face took on the look of outright excitement. His eyes bulged alarmingly, and the veins at the side of both temples were throbbing noticeably. He sat forward in his seat, so that his trousers became too tight around the crutch. "What about the sound it made. Did you ever hear anything so menacing? They reckon at least two victims – died of sheer fright after experiencing that at close quarters." Haddle sat back in his chair, staring at Dalmar, waiting for a reaction. All he received was an impassive and irresolute expression. After a while the eager look on Haddle's face subsided.

Starting with a half sigh, Dalmar said, "Shall I tell you what was the most frightening? *The* most frightening aspect of being face to face with your creation." He waited for an answer.

"What! Yes – tell me." A look of intense interest returned to the older man's countenance.

"Its notoriety," said Dalmar. Haddle changed his expression to one of puzzlement. "That's right – its reputation: the whole John the Red thing. They won't remember you for your cleverness. They will remember the story." That was almost cruel, and Dalmar knew it. "Anyway, I am not sure that you went forward with your experiments."

Haddle looked as though he had been hit in the face by an unseen hand. "What are you saying?"

Deliberately, Dalmar adopted a casual tone with his reply. "Well ... when I eventually came face to face with the Red Adder." Here he gazed straight into Haddle's eyes. "I had the distinct feeling that I was looking at a being from the past ... not the future."

Allen Haddle looked defeated as though he had been forced to agree with something that had been troubling him for some time. He let out a long, deep sigh. "I knew the pond had been discovered before I heard the news about John's death: saw that the bush had been moved while taking Jupiter out late on the afternoon of your ... adventure ... What are you going to do now?" He asked the inevitable question.

"I have an appointment with a police chief inspector." Dalmar did not really care whether Allen believed him or not. "By the way ... Julia Thornton…?"

"She was too damn nosey." This was said without the slightest aggression. Then he waved both hands in front of him. "But ... it does not matter. I don't wish to discuss that," he finished with finality.

Eventually, after several seconds, Haddle reached out his left hand and slid open fully, the second draw down on the far side of his desk. He withdrew from it, a British Army, Second World War, officer's revolver. Transferring it to his right hand, he pointed it at Dalmar's chest. "You understand … I am going to have to use this?"

Dalmar looked down the barrel of the gun. He could see the ends of the shells in the unengaged chambers. They would be old, and there was a chance that one or two would be dud. He felt calm. Slowly rising to his feet, he said, "Don't you think there has been enough killing? Up to now you have kept your wife out of it. Be a pity to ruin that."

"I wouldn't..." began Haddle and he advanced the revolver a few inches. Dalmar ignored him, and before Allen could do or say anything further, he turned his back and quite purposefully strode towards the door.

If Dalmar had tried to disarm him, Allen Haddle would have opened fire without hesitation. Dalmar was the killer of his creation. But because he did not, Allen's sanity started to return, and with it, reason: the reason of a man who had cured countless animals of ailments. The reason of a man who had brought tears of joy to children on seeing their pet, under his care, survive; and comforted them when a painless death had been the kindest thing to do. Then the feeling went past sanity, and, like matter being swallowed by a black hole, his life's work started to disappear into an end ... A terrible end.

Something caught Dalmar's eye on the way towards the door. It surprised him that anything would in the circumstances. Nestling on the second shelf of the bookcase, partially hidden, was a small deep black frame. Inside, behind glass, set on a backing cloth of maroon baize, was the unmistakable design of a dark bronze Victoria Cross: the medal awarded for extreme gallantry to members of the British armed forces.

Jupiter had one eye open. The dog seemed to be studying the drama before him, in an off-hand sort of way. Dalmar kept his back to

Allen Haddle all the while. If he had turned, he would have seen that the revolver had already been lowered. Allen's shoulders had dropped, and his eyes seemed to have sunk deep behind closed lids. The man was in despair.

Dalmar opened the door, walked through and closed it behind him. He ran down the steps, three stairs at a time and was gone out of the front door before Jean Haddle had risen from her seat by the television. Although she had heard raised voices from her husband's office from time to time, something on the television had held her interest, preventing her from going to investigate.

Dalmar charged up to the gate and vaulted it. Then he ran his fastest across the lane and down through the Claymans Heron hotel car park.

Floyd Hemming was smoking a cigarette outside the hotel entrance. He recognised Dalmar as he hurtled towards him. Although he did not know him personally, they had spoken on several occasions, simply because he was a local resident. "Everything all right?" he half shouted, as Dalmar came alongside. The running man turned his head to make a wave of acknowledgement, and then changed his mind, skidding to a halt in the gravel.

"May I –use your phone – to call the police?"

Following Dalmar's exit from their house, Jean Haddle dashed up the stairs as fast as her legs would allow. She opened the study door, and a little short of breath, peered at her husband sitting in his chair. Jupiter hiding in the well of the desk was strangely quiet.

Fortunately, there was no sign of the revolver "What a rude man!" she said with emphasis. Allen was staring straight ahead – studying ... something abstract. "My dear," she said. "What is it? What's the matter?" She went closer. Never in all their years together had she seen him looking like that. His face was ashen. The lips were drawn tight, and there was nothing but misery in his expression. "Has Mr Hunter upset you?"

After what seemed a ridiculous spell of time, he spoke to her. "My darling wife," Jean knew that he had never addressed her in that way before. It was not the wording. It was the tone.

"Yes dear?"

"Please ... could you get me a large whisky?" His eyes turned up, at last, and they were almost pleading in their expression.

"All right dear – I won't be long." She did not ask any questions but went to do his bidding. In their dining room she opened the top portion of a large, dark wood antique Court dresser. They had a good selection of drinking glasses. She took out Allen's favourite Waterford spirit tumbler and filled it half full of an expensive Scottish malt whiskey. When she returned, her husband was in much the same position. The facial glumness had not deserted him. If anything, he looked worse. She handed him the drink without saying a word.

"Thank you. Would you mind leaving me alone for a few minutes? I'll be all right." He could not smile.

"Are you *sure* Allen? You don't look very well to me. Perhaps you should go and lie down?"

He took her hand and rubbed it gently with his. "I'm ... fine. Look – I will come downstairs and join you soon. There – and take Jupiter with you. It is time for his biscuit" She took her hand away, smiled at him, and left the study with the terrier snuffling at her heels.

For several minutes, Haddle did nothing but take the occasional sip of his whisky. He sort-of washed the inside of his mouth before letting it trickle down his throat. But his eyes hardly moved. They seemed to be unseeing in their trajectory. After a while, he detached a piece of writing paper from a pad. His fountain pen was located in a compartment among the creative apertures of carpentry throughout the desk. He unscrewed the top, and, on a scrap of paper, tested the nib to ensure ink was flowing properly. Then he wrote the following:

June 26th, 1976

I, Allen Jules Haddle, take my life.

No other person is involved.
The reason will become apparent from information passed
by the undersigned, this day, to a John Dalmar Hunter Esq.

His handwriting was neat and steady in line. He finished with his usual signature and placed the sheet of notepaper on his desk, by a blotting pad, before putting away the pen.

Taking some keys from another partition in the desk, he rose and went to the large cream cabinet. He unlocked the padlock and gathered together a hefty bunch of papers. These he took over to the marble table and made a point of ensuring that they were all together in a neat pile. He lent forward and pulled back both sides of the double net curtains. Outside, dusk was drawing in. He opened the window wide. There was a box of Swan Vestas matches on a shelf situated to the side of the table. Sliding open the lid, he extracted a single match with its distinctive red tip, struck it, and set light to the papers. Using a metal rule, he kept the small fire in reign. As the flames grew higher, blackened pieces of burnt paper lifted off and sailed out of the window. In a few minutes there was nothing left but a heap of dark ash. He closed the window. Then he crossed the room and took up his position in the chair by the roll-top desk and continued to drink his whisky.

Intrusively, there came the sound of vehicles pulling up outside the house. Unhurriedly, he felt for a key in his jacket pocket. Once found, he unlocked the top right-hand drawer of the desk and took out a sealed cream-coloured envelope, which had the single name, Jean, written in his handwriting in the centre. He placed this envelope next to the blotting pad, and leant it against a small, chrome postal weighing machine, which was in a prominent position.

Then he retrieved the handgun from the desk drawer, where he had replaced it following Dalmar's exit. He put the end of the barrel to his right temple.

After Dalmar had made the call to an almost disbelieving Chief Constable at the Hampshire police headquarters, Floyd Hemming invited him out onto the terrace for a drink. The two men had been in intense, hushed conversation for the past twenty-five minutes. They were now looking over towards the Haddle's house where two police cars, having been driven fast passed the hotel, had suddenly turned sharp left to come to a skidding halt, scattering small stones over the gravel lane. Plain clothed and uniformed policeman hurriedly disembarked, and the sound of thudding doors being closed drifted across to the watching men.

Shortly after that, Floyd thought he heard a gunshot. It sounded muffled … as though it came from inside the house.

Dalmar was sure that it was indeed a gunshot. He bowed his head.

CHAPTER FIFTY

SHE WAS NOT AWARE OF IT.

Dalmar spent most of Saturday morning in an interview room at the county headquarters of the constabulary in Winchester. By arrangement, they sent a car to collect him from his home.

Allen Haddle was found dead in his office when the police called on him, the evening before. Despite the suicide note, there was nothing that could alleviate the dreadful distress to his widow. The next morning, she boarded a car with an unknown relative, and went away to an equally unknown destination. The terrier went with them. Jean Haddle was never seen in Yewhurst again, and the press were not able to locate her.

One of the problems facing the police, was what exactly should they tell the media? Before Dalmar left their courtesy, they decided to make an announcement after the coroner's hearing, which had been scheduled urgently for the following Thursday. There was no doubt – as to the cause of death.

Dalmar learnt something that he was not aware of during his visit to the police. "Did you know that we found a note on the body of Captain Young?" Chief Inspector Grant asked him. Presumably, due to the terseness of the question, he was testing for some kind of reaction. All he got was a blank look. Dalmar had to think as to who Captain Young was. Then he remembered Ma Hessil talking about the vagrant's body, which had been found in the forest last year. He asked if that was who they meant, without disclosing his source. "Yes – and keep this to yourself. We don't want it to be common knowledge yet. The note, the words of which were cut out of newspapers and magazines, and then pasted on a piece of paper…" He hesitated, "Hold on – I'll show you."

Inspector Grant opened a buff folder and sorted through some documents. He handed Dalmar a clear plastic folder containing a scrap of brown paper, the type used for wrapping parcels. It showed the creases of crumpled use. The words were laid out haphazardly, although, in line – as it should be read:

come   to   YEWHURST WOOD   on June 6th
IF MY Name is   not familiar   note the date
use   access   opposite   hotel
JOHN

The script used for Yewhurst Wood, looked as though it had been taken from a map, due to its pale green coloured background. Dalmar scratched his head before developing a puzzled frown. "In the light of what happened yesterday – got any ideas?" asked the policeman.

"Absolutely none," answered Dalmar. He shook his head in confirmation. "I'll give it some thought though."

"Needless to say – after recent events – we are not entirely satisfied with the coroner's verdict – death by misadventure."

Dalmar nodded.

They wound up the interview after Inspector Grant implored him to let them know if any further revelations came about. It was then that Dalmar remembered something. He hesitated before declaring anything. The sharp-eyed inspector noticed. "You ... seem unsure about..."

"Yes," Dalmar interrupted him, "Towards the end of the – err – discussion with Haddle, I asked – or rather – I think I merely mentioned the name of the lady who went missing from Yewhurst, about a year ago."

"Julia Thornton?" Chief Inspector Grant looked very interested.

"He replied – something about – 'was a nosey' ... can't remember the exact words, but what stuck in my mind was the use of *'was'*. Mind you, she has been declared missing, presumed dead, so why shouldn't he use the past tense? But, then again, it wasn't that: it was the way he said it, and then – refusing to discuss the matter further..."

"Anything else?" asked the inspector.

"No."

Dalmar left the police headquarters to be driven home, quietly dreading the coroner's inquest.

It actually proved to be less of a gruelling affair than he had expected. Although serious, the hearing seemed to possess an unreal relaxed atmosphere, from start to finish. Perhaps this was because the Coroner's voice was of a soft quality, giving out calmness. Dalmar had to stand and relate his evidence for a full hour. Due to the gentle promptings from the coroner, he was fairly sure that nothing had been left out. Among other things, they wanted to know how he had formed his suspicions about Allen Haddle's involvement with the breeding of these snakes? When he had first realised that a human being or beings were involved, rather than the official line of a freak of nature? Why did he take it upon himself to go and see the suspect instead of leaving it to the police? To this, he replied that he did not really know, possibly it had something to do with his family's involvement nearly thirty years ago.

There was not much doubt as to the coroner's verdict – suicide. Allen Haddle died by taking his own life. There would now follow a continuing police investigation. This police inquiry would be trimmed down and designated 'not urgent,' the cause for any concern over future loss of life being no longer an issue.

Due to the sensitive subject of the Red Adder victims, and interest from zoological societies and other scientific concerns with regard to Allen Haddle's experiments, all material, when finished with by the police, concerning those experiments would be returned to the Hampshire Coroner's office. Nothing would be released without the authority of that office.

The media were given the basic facts, but Dalmar's name had been kept out of the official news release, at his request.

Suzanne Westward enjoyed her Saturday dinner date. The young man took her to the restaurant at The Wordsworth hotel in Grasmere. His name was Douglas McLennan. Originally from Scotland, his family had been sheep farmers in Cumbria for four generations. At the end of the evening he asked Suzanne if she would like to see the farm at the weekend; he promised to show her some new-born lambs. She agreed at once.

Her new part-time employment was much to her liking. On other days she helped her aunt with housework and spent a great deal of her time walking the fells. She was trying to summon up courage to start painting in watercolour – having already purchased some paper, paints and brushes. She knew that the only way to capture true colour was out in the open air. What took nerve was to pick a spot, sit down and do it. If a curious walker should come and have a look – let them. And if they made comments, be honest, and tell them that she was very much a beginner. She knew that soon she must have a go, for her favourite season, early summer, was coming to an end.

The next Saturday came upon her all too quickly, and she still had not made her initial location study. When Douglas called to collect her for the visit to the farm, she was cross with herself and looked so. He was worried that it might be something to do with him. She put his mind at ease and explained. This, of course, gave him a perfect excuse to continue their friendship. By now he could not disguise his fondness for her. "Let us paint together?" he suggested. This was exactly what Suzanne needed: a companion to take out the solitary embarrassment.

She enjoyed her guided tour of the farm, particularly the lambing sheds. If Douglas was looking for a future farmer's wife, Suzanne would, in all probability, not be the most practical choice. Her fondness for the fragility of a baby animal might well be rather too romantic. But, for now, she could indulge herself with the cute woolly beings.

Suzanne could not imagine why she had not expected it, but she was caught completely by surprise. After Douglas finally managed to extricate her away from a little lamb with black feet, she was ushered into the farmhouse kitchen to meet not only, Mr and Mrs McLennan, but also two sisters and a further three brothers. She had to partake of a high tea, which her stomach did not require, of newly laid boiled eggs, buttered toast and a cake that had so much fruit crammed into it; the sides were bursting in several places. After the initial conversation pleasantries, Suzanne handled the curious questions about her background and present circumstances fairly well. The McLennan family was, evidently, reasonably well off. However, this wealth was no longer acquired by farming practices. Nowadays, the most profitable income was derived from self-catering holiday chalets. They owned a purpose built complex of five units, situated on the farm, a sensible distance from their own home.

All the children had attended private school and three of them were still doing so. There was no trace of a Cumbrian dialect, or, for that matter, a Scottish one. She thought perhaps she could discuss farming in the Lake District, but they did not seem to want to answer her questions, replying with short nonsensical phrases such as, "Now – there's a thing."

When the hour came for Douglas to drive her home, Suzanne was relieved. A further problem occurred after her escort parked his car outside her aunt and uncle's house. She was not ready for kisses and cuddles just yet, but he clearly was. He embraced her across the front seats of the car. Suzanne wriggled free and gave in to a kiss on the lips, more to end matters, than anything else. She agreed to accept a telephone call from him soon.

Entering the cottage, her aunt called a greeting from the living room. Suzanne responded and said she would be down to see her in a minute. As she climbed the stairs – she stopped halfway up, deep in thought. Douglas was a nice man, and she must be careful not to take advantage of him. It seemed – she was not ready for a new romance.

The next morning, her aunt knocked on her door while she was still in bed, enjoying the pleasure of that half-awake feeling, yet knowing you do not have to rise just yet. She came in with a cup of tea and a page from the Sunday newspaper. "Look at this, my dear," she said urgently, pointing out a small headline to a column of print near the bottom. It read 'RED ADDER BREEDER COMMITS SUICIDE.' "Would you believe it? One man responsible for all those deaths. I should think he *would* do himself in." She passed the page to Suzanne. She pushed herself up on one elbow and placed a pillow behind her head. Her dark hair fell against the white cotton on both sides of her face, and her shining eyes, as though illuminating her intense curiosity, homed in on the article.

"Did you sleep well?" her aunt asked, going over to open the curtains. Suzanne did not answer. She was reading, and very deep in thought. She had one arm crooked around a large teddy bear, the one that Dalmar had won for her at the fun fair last summer. As she read, Suzanne rubbed her lower arm. She was not aware of it, but it was the very same spot where Allen Haddle had held her when he demonstrated the two bite techniques used by snakes, over a year ago in the Claymans Heron.

Aunt Maggie studied the pretty, sleep-downed face with curiosity. She had never been able to talk to her niece about Dalmar Hunter after the break-up. Her sister had told her what had happened. 'Perhaps – unfinished business,' thought Maggie to herself.

CHAPTER FIFTY-ONE

"NOW ... REST IN PEACE."

Ten days later, on a Wednesday evening, Dalmar was ruminating over the ups and downs of recent times. Three days after he had sent Suzanne the poem, he started to post watch. A rare happening for him but he kept it up for at least two weeks. His initial optimism, which he felt since speaking to Christine on the river bridge at Ovington, gradually dispersed as each day ended, bringing a dreadfully disappointing reality once again. Right now, he was stretched out on his settee wearing only a pair of shorts. Usually, the first thing he did before taking Fly out for his early evening walk, was to rush upstairs and tear off his business suit, shirt and tie, and get into a comfortable pair of jeans and light cotton shirt. After the walk he would take a bath, and, in the hot weather, spend a while in just a pair of shorts until the coolness of the coming night forced him to put his shirt back on. He was in the very act of doing exactly that when the telephone rang. He heard Christine's voice coming through the earpiece, and his emotions somersaulted. "Sorry to disturb whatever it is you are up to?" came a cheeky remark.

"Putting on a shirt – actually," said Dalmar innocently.

"There you are then – what did you take it off for?" This was followed by a soft string of giggles.

He let out a, "Hmmph."

"Reason for the call;" there was a slight hesitation. "Could you possibly be near a telephone, preferably the one you are talking on now – Friday week?" And then almost as though forgotten, "In the evening?"

Dalmar did not know what to say. 'Why?' the thought crashed through his head. He hardly dare hope. "Okay." He heard himself reply.

"Good. That is all for now; except ... do you still take Fly out in the early evening?"

"Yes, as soon as I get in from work. Usually on Friday, I have a pint with a couple of colleagues from our office. But I can skip that if you want?"

"Yes please ... so when do you ... when will you be at home after taking your dog for a walk?"

"Around seven…"

"Great. Bye then."

"Bye," said Dalmar putting the telephone back on its stand, and feeling a complete idiot for not asking ... why? But he was damned if he was going to telephone back to find out. After a few moments, Fly witnessed him cursing to himself aloud. "Help ... I have to wait a whole nine days ... just for a phone call!" And then after a further few minutes, he realised that it was worth it. It was very definitely – worth it.

The next morning Dalmar's post watch recommenced, more out of a distant hope than any real expectation. He received an envelope addressed to J.D.Hunter., Esq. bearing the Zoological Society's logo. The neatly typed letter inside was from Jonathon Shure. It was an invitation to visit his office at Regents Park for the forthcoming Monday. All expenses would be reimbursed, and lunch would be provided. Dalmar was the sort of person who did not like passing up on a worthwhile experience. This was one of those possibilities, and during the day he got his secretary to acknowledge the invitation and accept.

The following day's post produced an airmailed envelope from Rhodesia. Now, this was exciting for him. It had to be a letter from his sister. So as not to tear the flimsy paper, he used a knife to slit the sides. He opened it and read as follows:

'Salisbury, Rhodesia
June 1976.

Dear JD,

Word reached us recently of the death of the latest Red Adder, and your part in it. Ever since our dear brother was killed by one of those horrible snakes, off and on, I have felt a kind of burden around the back of my neck. I knew there was nothing there really, but it felt as though there was. You were probably too young to feel such things, especially in the early years.

Hearing just last night that with the death of the snake's creator, there will be no more of the horrid things, that strange and unwelcome feeling has been lifted from my shoulders. It must have taken great courage to do what you did. I am not sure it was wise, but I am very proud of you. All those people who live in Yewhurst, especially those with young children, must be very grateful. Oh – and not forgetting Fly – we hear! I hope I get to see him one day.

More newsy letter following shortly. Must dash now. Going to a barbecue at Tom and Celia's farm.

Well done, my dear brother.
William is avenged.

Your devoted sister,
Lots of Love. Judy.'

"Thoughtful and nice," said Dalmar aloud. "Still a bossy-boots though."

The letter prompted Dalmar into carrying out something else. Saturday morning found him, with Fly by his side, driving up the old London road and on through to Buckinghamshire. Just after noon, he located a florist in the high street at Gerrards Cross and purchased twelve white tulips. After that he drove to St. James Church, with its distinctive tower and dome, and parked the car under the shade of an elm tree. He walked up The Driveway to the cemetery. With Fly panting behind him, a short walk took him to a grave marked:

Simon Michael Hunter
1898 - 1969
And his beloved wife Margaret Judy
 1901 - 1970

He placed the tulips in a container, set into the grass surface of the grave. Then he went to the rear of the church and found a rain-butt with a small watering can by the side of it. Locating a tap, low down, he turned it on and partially filled the can, before returning to top-up the container. Finally, he stood at the foot of the grave and called Fly to heel. Dalmar bowed his head and remained silent for a moment before saying out loud, "Now ... rest in peace."

When Monday arrived, Dalmar got out his best suit, dark grey with the faintest of mid-blue stripes and a white shirt. The tie he selected was a plain deep blue. Leaving his car at Winchester rail-station meant he had to put the hood up for the first time in weeks. The London train arrived at Waterloo a mere five minutes late, and he joined the queue for taxis just outside the station. After a short wait, he was on his way to Regents Park.

Jonathon worked for the Institute of Zoology, and Dalmar expected him to have a palatial office on the first floor of the administrative building at London Zoo, but he did not. His office was a pokey little room on the second floor. It was, however, neat and tidy. The zoologist greeted him warmly and said how grateful he was that he had come to London. He explained that another trip to Hampshire was just not possible for him, at the present time, due to three important conservation programs he was working on. As always, he was at his sartorial best, dressed in a light grey suit of fine-weave material to fit the climatic conditions. There was no air-conditioning in his office, and only a slight breeze crept in from a small opening in the top of the double-paned window. Below them, not far away, a monkey's screeching could be heard. Jonathon looked fit and well, the greying hair lying softly but neatly against his scalp. He liked and respected Dalmar and it showed, with the frequent smiles that he bestowed upon his guest.

He asked his secretary to get them both coffees. She could not resist congratulating their visitor on the successful outcome of his tussle with the Red Adder. They had not met while she assisted Jonathon at Yewhurst, although, since then his name had often been mentioned. Dalmar had tasted better coffee, and it turned out to be one of those drinks that he wished he had declined. During the day, the reason for the lack of luxury became apparent. The society placed rather more emphasis on work achievement than petty comforts.

Dalmar was asked to re-tell the details of his encounter with Allen Haddle. The process was subjected to thorough tape recording. Jonathon checked the equipment with a voice test before trusting it. Again, Dalmar tried to relate the events word for word, as best his memory would allow. No interruptions took place even though the telling must have taken some considerable time.

When he had finished, he asked Jonathon if anything useful had been recovered from Haddle's study? "With regard to his breeding programs, all we have are his instruments, which tell us very little other than probable method," replied Jonathon. "The real stuff, his documents, lay in a heap of ashes on top of a marble slab. There was sufficient evidence visible in those ashes to confirm this."

Dalmar remembered the table by the window. 'So, he had chosen not to divulge any of his secrets. Probably just as well,' he thought to himself. While on the subject he voiced his opinion to the zoologist that the Red Adder's eyes seemed to be like those connected with lizards, or even crocodiles, rather than a snake. He described the oval, yellow sclerotic coat and the vertical, elongated diamond shaped pupil. "Quite frankly the beast was like some unknown, frightening creature from the past."

Jonathon nodded in his guest's direction. "I agree. But, brought up in scale – they are not too dissimilar to that of a large viper. When Private Dace was attacked – you know the glide it made? – presumably, from the top of a tall tree – we are not sure from where – but there is an out of place Sequoia that would fit."

"Yes" affirmed Dalmar.

"The distance it covered has to be around a quarter of a mile. That is amazing: something quite out of this age. I mentioned to you before, I believe, that most experts consider it impossible?" Dalmar confirmed this with a nod. "Also – when Ginger Styles got venom in his eyes – has anyone ever considered how the, admittedly smaller snake, managed to climb to the top of a Scots pine!? It has virtually no branches lower down."

"You know – I wondered about that," said Dalmar.

"Perhaps it didn't climb ... perhaps it descended there by flight from another, taller tree?" Jonathon explained. "I don't know whether you noticed, but they, the Red Adders that is, usually seemed to travel from the tall trees near the church to the Secret Pond. The top of those trees is the highest point in the area. The Wellingtonia, in the churchyard, for instance, would, despite its great height, be easy to climb due to the abundance of protruding branches. Taking the starting point as the pond, I would suggest that the return journey, if you like, was probably made by gliding."

"Ah."

Jonathon raised his right hand a little, to introduce a change of subject. "There *is* still an unanswered question. The matter of the note found on the body of Captain Young?" Jonathon gave Dalmar an enquiring look while he asked this question.

"Yes. Did the police tell you about that?" Dalmar asked, intrigued.

"They did. Who told you?"

"The same source. No doubt wanted to see if I made any reaction."

"Yes, I see, although can't understand why they thought you would be involved. Anyhow – you know the smaller snake we have just referred to?"

"Yes."

"Well, everybody who saw it reckons it was only four-foot long. Am I right?"

"There-abouts – yes."

"In which case, it would have been portable. Captain Young was killed on June 6th, the anniversary of the 'D' Day invasion. This has got to be more than coincidence. Captain Young led the same regiment of marines that Sapper John Head was attached to, on D-Day 1974, when he was killed in action. According to Stephen Knopner, John the Red is supposed to be named after that man due to a family grievance. It could be," here Jonathon picked up a pencil and twiddled it in his hands, "that our breeder actually released it at the time and place of that attack. Mind you – he would only get one chance; can't see him catching it again."

Dalmar took this in before making the comment. "But why on earth would Allen Haddle – wish any harm to this – Captain Young?"

"That," said Jonathon, "is *the* question: if he did. But I can tell you this; the police found a fine mesh cage with a carrying handle in Haddle's garage. Nearby was a black cloth with a hole in the middle. This cloth, presumably, was used to hide the contents of the cage when in use. I expect he inserted the handle through that hole."

"And used the cage at night," added Dalmar.

"Precisely," said Jonathon. "Although – it did occur to me that it could have had an innocent use. After all, he had been a practising vet and might have used it to convey a timid animal. The police made the comment that that is what people would think. He was covered both ways in all kinds of instances with his obsession, due to his profession. Anything else you want to ask me?"

Dalmar had already decided not to mention any suspicions the police might have about Haddle's involvement with the disappearance of Julia Thornton. Instead, he altered the angle. "Well, the obvious interest lies in the method. Or shall I put it this way? Did Allen Haddle make a scientific discovery of note?"

"Ah," Jonathon gave the matter a few moments thought before replying. "If he had chosen a different species of reptile to experiment with, we might now be lauding his praises ... maybe. You see, it isn't just a matter of insemination; there is the involvement of the world of genetics. Do you know anything about that subject?"

"I'm afraid not," replied Dalmar, "only the very basics."

"Depending on how you look at it, to date, that is all most of us are aware of. Unfortunately, we shall probably never know just what it was he discovered, but I have a feeling that it might have been significant." He paused before adding. "Great shame. Allen Haddle, undoubtedly, was a very clever man."

Dalmar made no comment.

Suddenly Jonathon got to his feet. "Come on; let me take you down to our canteen for some lunch. You can meet some of my other cronies. They will certainly want to meet you;" he finished with a smile.

Dalmar rose from his chair. "I have a request?" he said. Jonathon stopped in his progress towards the office door. His visitor produced a small tubular object from his jacket pocket. "On this film there should be three photographs of the Red Adder – after it had been killed."

Jonathon almost leapt across the office towards him. "You wonderful man!" he exclaimed. His face had broken into a marvellous toothful grin.

Dalmar held up a hand. "There is one condition." There was no apology in his tone.

"Oh," said Jonathon, suddenly looking disappointed. 'Was this going to be a demand for some sort of personal remittance?' he considered.

"When your organisation has finished with it; I should like – perhaps the best of the photographs – will leave it to you – released to the press: the highest bidder. All proceeds to go to Brian Dace's widow."

Jonathon, showing relief, took the proffered undeveloped film; looked into Dalmar's eyes and said. "You have my word."

"Also, as things stand, I probably could be prosecuted for withholding evidence." Dalmar looked Jonathon straight in the eyes. It was not an aggressive look – being more concerned with trust. "The provider of that film is anonymous."

"Again – you have my word."

The eminent zoologist rather showed off his heroic celebrity over lunch in the Zoo cafeteria. Quietly, Dalmar was amused at Jonathon's attempts to tempt him with one of the hot meals on offer, whilst settling for a sandwich himself. However, the aroma was enough to suggest otherwise, so Dalmar also chose a sandwich. He was a little overawed at being introduced to many important professors of their calling. But he found it all interesting, and Jonathon gave him some time afterwards, showing him details of the zoological conservation projects the institute were currently working on.

On their way down to the reception office, Dalmar remembered something. "Did you get anything of use out of my jeans?" he asked.

"Wondered if you were going to mention them," replied Jonathon. "Actually – yes. The blood group was from a snake unknown to any in existence today. But I guess we all knew that. It is just a sort of confirmation. Oh – and as to the venom spatters on your swimming goggles."

"Oh yes," said Dalmar.

330

"Well, thank your lucky stars that it didn't get you. The most potent venom ever known." Jonathon then added almost as an aside. "I have to tell you that if it hadn't been for you and the efficiency of the ambulance service, Christine Westward would not be alive today. Stephen Knopner's bite was a different matter. Really odd – the biggest snake – yet the smallest bite – practically nothing. Must have been saving itself for the main event ... you!" Both men laughed.

Using his right hand in a short sweeping movement, Dalmar pushed back the lock of hair that had fallen over his left eye. "I wonder," he said, "if the last Red Adder reached that incredible length in such a short time; what size might it have reached if it had been allowed to live its full life span?

"One of my colleagues reckons double. Myself – I can see why he has that opinion. We know that its growth rate was phenomenal. After your conversation with Allen Haddle, we can assume it went from a baby to a length in excess of six feet in four months! There is something else though, which no one else seems to have spotted."

"And that is?" asked a curious Dalmar.

"Its intelligence." As his guest made no comment other than showing a quizzical brow, Jonathon enlarged. "It attacked a human being, more or less, whenever it had an opportunity. Now – what about the shoot day and several days when the observation teams drew a complete blank. Why?" Dalmar still did not volunteer a remark. "Well – I think it knew when the odds were stacked against it – and in those circumstances stayed quietly well out of the way."

"Pheew." Dalmar was beginning to see the importance of this line of thinking.

"At the time of your re-discovery of the Secret Pond, I am sure you didn't consider it to be just a coincidence that you were both bent over the pond exactly where the snake was submerged, prior to Stephen being attacked?"

"Well ... actually..."

"I think it more likely that when you arrived in the immediate area, the Red Adder hid in the water, coming up for air with a hardly noticeable snout now and again." Jonathon paused briefly. "It literally shadowed the two of you by using your reflections in reverse." The zoologist looked at Dalmar standing by the entrance door. Sunlight from the glazed upper part of it gave him a halo effect around his head. "If that snake had survived for another year or two – it would have been extremely fast moving, certainly able to outrun a man, especially through terrain such as that in which it was living. Its venom would be able to kill in seconds. Its strength would have given it other powerful weapons should it have needed to use them. Add to that, severe aggression, and now – intelligence" ... Almost as though it was of no importance, Jonathon said in a low voice, "A more frightening being – it is hard to imagine."

Dalmar could not help feeling how much Allen Haddle would have enjoyed those remarks.

He left Regents Park with a small bundle of brochures, which gave him some reading material on the train journey home.

When he laid his head on the pillow that night, he could not help but dwell on the fact that there were only four days to go before he might receive a telephone call from a certain person. He tried to dismiss these thoughts for fear of disappointment. But he could not, and they kept him awake – long into the night.

Allen Haddle's body was cremated at Southampton on Wednesday morning. Apart from the funeral directors; present were his widow, two of her relatives and the deceased's solicitor. Jean Haddle had deliberately kept the event secret. Her husband did not appear to have any surviving relatives. Allen left Jean, if not wealthy, wanting for nothing. But that was of little comfort to the sad, distressed soul. By one of those strange coincidences, the skies clouded over that morning. For the first time in several weeks, sunlight was not in evidence. This gave the scene outside the crematorium, for the small group that waited for the coffin, the atmosphere – it deserved.

CHAPTER FIFTY-TWO

"WHAT DID YOU DO THAT FOR MISTER?"

As Dalmar drove back to Yewhurst, late on Friday afternoon, he felt decidedly skittish. This was the state of mind that had been with him all day. It was, he knew, because he would be receiving a phone call at around seven o'clock this evening. He did not know quite who was making that phone call. He was fairly certain it would be Christine again, but he had every expectation that it would be to give him some good news concerning Suzanne.

To all his colleagues at work, it seemed as though he was in a very good mood. None of them knew the reason, although a serious attempt to find out was attempted by two fellow executives, who usually had a drink with him after work at the end of the working week. Instead of expressing disappointment that he would not be joining them, he was unmercifully teased. Most of the ribbing he received was of the 'I hope she's worth it?' variety. Or 'don't start a precedent; show her who is boss' etc.

After leaving his place of employment, driving his open top sports car through Southampton was a distinct pleasure, and he beamed at unknown pedestrians inanely. He could not resist a burst of excessive speed after passing through the built-up areas. The creation of wind through his hair was intoxicating. Taking a less frequent route home, he took the T.R.6 on a camber ride through some twisting lanes. There seemed to be music in the air.

As he drove down Brook Road, his mood changed, abruptly, to one of apprehension, and then a mixture of the two. He had not the slightest appetite. Normally, he would be planning what the evening meal would be. Sometimes, he did some preparation in the kitchen before taking Fly out. There would be none tonight.

When he collected the collie from his neighbours, a strange thing occurred. He was about to take his leave from Janet when he received a smile, which, usually, he would consider to be an initial approach from a lady with seduction in mind. He blinked at her and left hurriedly. 'Must have imagined it,' he thought, and then fervently hoped that he had.

Leaving the stable door to his kitchen open, he rushed upstairs and changed into his denim jeans, shirt and soft leather moccasins. It was a lovely feeling to get out of his business suit and hard-heeled shoes; especially in hot weather, such as now. He also washed his face and hands, splashing some of his favourite aftershave lotion around the sides of his neck. Then he cleaned his teeth. As he put the toothbrush back in its holder, he stared at his reflection in the mirror. 'What had possessed him to do all that, just to receive a telephone call?'

Fly was ready for his walk. As soon as they had crossed the road, Dalmar said, "Away!" and off he bounded. They took the usual route towards the church.

To his surprise, he came across a large group of people, apparently, dressed ready for a party. They came chattering through the trees on all sides of him. Or rather, while the adults stuck to the path, several young children were charging hither and thither through the woodland. Fly barked at them, taking up their playful zest with enthusiasm. His master rebuked him gently. "Down boy." But no one seemed to worry, and the fine-looking animal received only admiring glances. Dalmar thought that the grown-ups seemed to go out of their way to smile in greeting, and there was a lot of giggling from the ladies once they had passed by.

A little further on, he stopped to gaze into the topmost reaches of a large beech tree. In the evening sunlight, the young dainty leaves were translucent on their outer edges, giving a pleasing lime coloured hue to them. To appreciate the majesty of the tree, it was best to stand close by the base of the wide trunk and look straight up the smooth olive bark, through branch after branch and layer upon layer of leafy frondage, until, after a considerably dizzying height had been reached, the blue sky appeared as a haphazard pattern created by the multitude of those leaves. It was a beautiful sight.

When he lowered his head, he saw yet another group of people, a little way ahead on the path: by the look of it a family. They too were dressed ready for some sort of celebration. The men were in formal suits and the ladies in colourful dresses. This time the children were older, probably in their teen years. All of them were looking at Dalmar.

"Nice tree?" said the eldest man.

"Yes," acknowledged Dalmar. He smiled knowingly before saying, "In a world where the balance of life is maintained by the art of eating one another, we need such as this."

"That's deep," replied the man in a slight country dialect. "But I'm sure you be right. Good eve'nin to you," he said as the party continued on their way.

'Must be some sort of do at the Claymans,' thought Dalmar.

After that, he went to check on an important matter in the churchyard. Near the junction of the gravel paths by the Wellingtonia, a previously unmarked grave possessed a new headstone. Inscribed in black lettering on the shiny new marble was the following inscription:

Here lies
William Simon Hunter
1938 -1948.

"Good," said Dalmar to himself, "I'll be back soon – with some flowers."

He took Fly down the main fire-break path for a while, and then cut along a lower path that would eventually bring them behind Beech Cottage.

On the way, he noticed his dog cocking his ears and swore he could hear a large amount of people, including the high-pitched voices of young children, heading down the path from the church to the hotel.

Fly looked marvellous, running ahead of him as they proceeded down a grass covered narrow course, some way to the rear of Tim and Christine's previous home. His long flowing tail was displayed behind him, and he held his head high with a strong pant, his legs springing powerfully on the turf. Every now and then he would turn and bark impatiently at his master who was dawdling taking in the scenery. 'He has such a proud face,' Dalmar thought admiringly.

As they came up towards the rear of Beech Cottage, Dalmar stopped and looked ahead. About twenty to thirty yards away grew a great bank of young silver birch trees. They were packed tightly together. Even so, this season's bracken was growing beneath their canopy at an abundant rate. The strip of trees disappeared to the right joining on to the main pathway. Fly stood patiently by his side wondering what purpose his master was about.

Without warning, Dalmar started to quote verse, although in a subdued tone. A vivid childhood memory had come into his mind. He recalled his brother, as though it might be yesterday, and something that he used to do – very well.

"Five hundred silver soldiers with five hundred silver spears,
Lay fast before my path on that bright summer's day.
They were the guard of nature to the inner forest tiers,
And from their outer circle made to bar my way."

Suddenly, Dalmar took one step back, and then with a roaring sound charged headlong at the birches. Fly jumped to one side, taking avoiding action, and stared at his owner as though he had gone berserk. Dalmar aimed between two of the unfortunate trees and turning slightly sideways on at the very last moment, covered his head with his right arm and placed his shoulder so as to push his way through. At the same time, he jumped a little forcing his feet and ankles into the bracken. He managed to make some headway for several yards, breaking through a small amount of the tree lines, before his foot fouled a hard, raised root, and he tumbled to the ground with a loud grunt. He turned over and lay on his back, the bright green ferns closing over him; its distinctive scent invading his nostrils to bring back memories of long ago.

Thinking to himself, he was sure of one thing. William could have stayed on his feet and gone the whole distance through the depth of the birches, twisting and turning, crouching and leaping with precision timing. He came to the conclusion the sport was best attempted by a young boy with the acquired skills. Fly watched his master reappear from the tree line with green smears all down his denim jeans, and a big grin on his face. His hair was dishevelled, and he had a scratch above his left eye, which had started to bleed. This and everything else Dalmar instantly forgot, on hearing a young boy addressing him from the path ahead.

"What did you do that for mister?" The boy would have been about eight years old. He wore a pair of pressed grey trousers and a white, long-sleeved shirt, with a tie that had gone slightly crooked on the knot, showing the top button of the shirt. His hair had probably been dampened, for it was smoothed down in an attempt to make him look smart. His face gave away the feeling that he was not used to looking tidy. Beside him stood a younger girl with long brown hair, and the face of sweetness personified. Both of them had great big wide eyes upon him.

Dalmar decided not to lie. "I was trying to be a boy again," he said. "Actually – bit silly really – not really a summertime thing." Relieving his master's discomfort, Fly started to pad over to the children, head bowed expecting attention.

Around the corner of a bunch of young hawthorn trees, walked the parents of the youngsters. They were in time to see their daughter embrace the heavily frilled neck of the collie. "Is this the dog that killed the snake?" she asked in a clear, adorable voice, looking up at the tall man as he approached.

Dalmar smiled at her, and then in the direction of their mother and father, who were looking at him sheepishly. No wonder, considering his appearance. "Yes ... he is," he confirmed.

"Gosh," said the boy and joined his sister in petting and cuddling Fly, who showed his appreciation by gruffing affectionately.

"Come along you two, we are already late," spoke the children's father, with a broad grin on his face. "I expect you will see the dog again soon." Brother and sister reluctantly obeyed and the four of them went on their way with lots of backward glances. Dalmar waited until he saw they had crossed over the road, and then started to follow them.

A sudden thought made him glance at his watch. It was five minutes past seven. 'Drat,' he said to himself, 'My telephone might be ringing even now.' Quickly he called to Fly, checked that no traffic was approaching, and jogged over the road.

When they reached the other side, the dog suddenly came to a slithering stop on the gravel of the hotel car park. It was so abrupt that it made Dalmar take notice and come to a halt as well, grabbing the pole of a signpost to steady himself. Fly seemed to be sniffing the air intently. His head was straining towards their house. His ears went from half-cocked to a complete arch, and without any kind of warning he went forward into a fast trot. Dalmar called after him, "Fly ... stay!" For the first time, ever, the collie blatantly disobeyed him, letting go a short sharp bark, which either inferred 'come on' or 'sha'n't'. The dog increased his speed to a full track run. There were a lot of people gathered around the hotel entrance and in various stages of approaching it, including the family he had just spoken to, together with numerous comings and goings from traffic. Fly ran straight past the lot going at full pelt scattering small stones everywhere. But he did not get any cross looks; only from his master who was actually more amazed than angry. Dalmar slowed his pace to a walk as he came adjacent to the hotel entrance, feeling rather embarrassed, with head angled away from the on-lookers. He knew he must be imagining it, but he felt that nearly everyone was watching him. There was so much whispering going on. 'Must be some celebration,' he reckoned. He was relieved to reach the moderate shelter of the trees, which led to the lane by the farm cottages. There was still no sign of his dog, but he did notice that the latch gate entrance to his garden appeared to be slightly open. His brow crinkled, for he was sure he had shut it when they left, and Fly would have jumped clean over the fence.

When he reached the gate, he could hear the disobedient animal giving welcoming snuffles and whimpers to someone. He looked down the length of the garden and his heart all but stopped. Before the heather patch, Fly was sitting with his long nose buried under the dark hair of a young woman's head. A front paw was on her left shoulder and his tail was wagging very fast from side to side, across the short grass. The girl's eyes were tightly shut, as she held the collie in a fierce embrace around his cuddlesome neck with both arms, and a look of utter bliss upon her face. There! There in front of the white rhododendron ... was Suzanne.

Dalmar felt such intense emotion he could not speak. He opened the gate and stepped onto the gravel path. Then he moved silently forward onto the lawn, bending his head under the lower branches of the apple tree, until he was only a few yards away from them.

Suzanne opened her eyes and looked at him, starting from his moccasin shod feet and working upwards to the green smeared blue jeans, up, up to his denim covered chest and those wide shoulders, and then – onto his face. A face that looked on hers with tears welling in his eyes, radiating a love so strong that she knew she might never see the like again. She rose to her feet leaving her left-hand dangling for Fly to lick. Sensing the happening, the dog moved a little away, watching them both quietly. For Dalmar, a vision of Suzanne had taken on celebrity status, because he had to accept that he might never see her again. So, now, he was in awe of her immense attractiveness. Visibly he took her in, dressed in attire that looked as though she was on her way to a dance. A glorious cobalt blue dress hugged her figure and she balanced this with a pair of blue leather, not too high-heeled, shoes. There was the sapphire brooch, exactly as he had brought it to his memory so many times throughout the long winter. There was that glorious near black hair cascading down the sides of sun-blessed cheeks. There were those neat little rows of small, dark freckles under her eyes. She smiled broadly at him, and there was that mouth that he had fantasy kissed through his pillow hundreds of times over the last lonely months. And as she smiled, so came into being those dimples on either side of her mouth – and there – looking directly into his, were those fabulous twinkling eyes, blessing him with her love.

Great oceans of emotion flooded over them; their thoughts were blanked out by a tidal wave of sentiment.

He held out his hands to her, and she threw herself forward and pressed herself into him, so that he had to hold her slightly off the ground. They held each other tightly, cheek to cheek, not saying a word, but feeling everything. The deep love within sending messages back and forth mind recording the moment, just for the two of them. And now Suzanne openly cried silent tears to join his, her shoulders trembling in evidence. Fly, studying them, was not perturbed. He knew his mistress had returned.

After a long time, Dalmar gently let her down until her feet touched the cushioning grass. She brought her head round to him and they looked upon each other's tear-sodden faces. She brought a hand up to lightly touch the blooded scratch on his forehead, but he shook his head, as if to tell her it was no matter. Their mouths found one another and started a kiss that went on and on and on. Eventually, Fly got fed up and started to whimper. They broke off and consoled him with their first spoken words, not to each other, but to him.

Finally, Dalmar had to say something to her. He spoke softly. "I don't understand – Christine told me to expect a telephone call, which I hoped and prayed would have something to do with you. But this?"

Suzanne put a single finger to his lips and then kissed him again. "Your presence is required young man," she said. As she spoke, the once familiar tones of her voice entered his head like a glorious symphony, and the scent of her completed the ultimate thrill for all his senses. "Tim and Christine are over in the Claymans." And then, as he still looked perplexed, she took pity on him and added, "All will be explained – shortly." She received a slight frown in return, but he was not going to argue with anything she said right now: nothing at all.

"All right but look – I shall have to change. Been playing in the woods, I'm afraid," he said with a slight guilty air.

"Is that how you got that scratch?   It's quite deep you know. Better bathe it."

"Yes – I won't be long. Are you – are you going to keep me company?"

"Of course," she said. "Lead the way."

Naturally, despite their embrace, they were both very shy of each other. It had taken Suzanne a great deal of courage to do what she had just done. But she had been determined. Dalmar went and busied himself cleaning up and getting ready, while Suzanne renewed her affections with Fly, and when Dalmar had finished in the bathroom, she went in and quickly repaired her sparse amount of makeup. Just a couple of dabs with a tissue, amazingly, were all that was necessary.

After about ten minutes, Dalmar came down the stairway dressed in clothes that surprised Suzanne. She had assumed he would opt for his smarter denim attire, thinking they were only going for a drink, but he had picked something up from the way she was turned out and wished to compliment her. He was dressed in dark blue moleskin trousers and had replaced the moccasins with a pair of black leather casual shoes. The shirt was made of light cotton, coloured a shade of paler blue than his trousers. Also, he was now wearing his gold wristwatch. Suzanne did not say anything, but she was secretly pleased, knowing what was coming.

"Okay," said Dalmar. "Just one more thing to do. Must feed Fly, and then I am ready."

"No need for that," Suzanne touched his arm before explaining. "I have been instructed to ensure that Fly accompanies us."

"But they don't allow dogs in the Claymans," said Dalmar looking worried. 'Just who was doing the *instructing* anyway,' he pondered?

"Tonight - they will, trust me, you will see, and he is going to be fed – I promise."

Dalmar looked even more worried. What was going on? The trouble was he knew that he had to go along with it. He was not going to let this girl out of his sight just yet. So, he lowered his eyes to the ground and made acquiescence obvious with his facial expression. Suzanne grinned fully: she knew he was hers.

As though in understanding, Dalmar, Suzanne and Fly walked with their heads, often turned to each other, but otherwise held up, down the garden, through the chestnut trees and across the car park to the pub entrance of the Claymans Heron. Dalmar opened the outer door and went in. Then he pushed the inner one with his shoulder and held it for Suzanne and Fly. The dog hesitated, wondering whether this was really happening. "Come with me," Suzanne cajoled him. He did not require a second invitation.

CHAPTER FIFTY-THREE

SO THAT WAS WHAT THAT LOOK HAD BEEN ABOUT.

"And about time!" hailed a familiar voice. It belonged to Timothy Westward, who was standing by the bar, a totally unabashed smile illuminating his face. Some evening sunlight from the window caught the very top of his reddish hair, giving a bizarre look to the crown of his head. Christine, sitting on a tall bar stool and supporting her large tummy was smiling all the way to their hearts; she was so overjoyed at what she saw. Dalmar could not recall seeing her in such resplendent attire before. She was wearing a glorious pink maternity dress, which had a definite air of exclusivity about it. Even Tim seemed to be in a suit that might be reserved for special occasions.

None of them cared who was looking. They greeted Dalmar as though he had been away fighting a war. He, of course, was very embarrassed, but he managed to do his usual trick and get Fly to take most of the attention. Tim's greeting had a double-edged meaning, which had not escaped Dalmar's notice. It told him a lot. It told him that as far as Suzanne's brother was concerned, he, at least, approved of the possible renewal of his relationship with his sister.

"Come on now, Dalmar, you are not driving, how about a nice big drink?" Tim invited.

"Thank you, Tim. I could do some serious damage to a pint of beer,"

"And what about my dear, darling sister?" There was a smirk on his face as he said this, "What is your disgraceful tipple to be?"

"A large bucket of iced water, which I can douse you with – brother dear." Suzanne crinkled her nose at him.

"That will do," said the peacemaker, Christine, raising her eyes to the ceiling. "White wine Tim – please."

"Okay, sure you wouldn't like a triple measure to save time? You usually drink it as though it were a glass of lemonade." With that he turned his back on his sister to order the drinks from the barman.

Suzanne glowered at the back saying, "That – is a total falsehood." The trouble was she would like to have done something much more dramatic, such as whacking him hard on his buttocks. But she dare not, for fear of upsetting the evening's arrangements, and she knew that Tim was perfectly aware of that.

After they bought their drinks, Dalmar was most keen to find out how Christine's pregnancy was going. Following a scan, she knew she was not having twins or anything out of the norm, and she wasn't giving anything away as to what sex the baby might be. Anyhow, she felt fine, and everything was going nature's way. Dalmar had to agree that she looked totally serene. She seemed to be completely at one with her world.

While all this was going on, Dalmar noticed that his companions seemed edgy. He began to have suspicions again. 'Something was going on, and why was Tim dressed in a suit?' It made him feel somewhat underdressed.

It was Christine who brought the situation to the fore. She slowly got off the stool and took Dalmar by the hand. "Suz," she opened, handing her sister-in-law a small dark blue evening bag she had been looking after for her, at the same time grabbing her own from the bar, "You are in charge of Fly; better keep him on his lead for a while. Come on," she said, looking into Dalmar's face. "Bring your drink – we have a little surprise for you." Dalmar cast a worried look in the direction of Suzanne, who had her face fixed in a downward stance, so as not to give anything away. Meekly, he let himself be led. He gave up trying to attract Suzanne's attention, and instead cast a hopeful glance at Tim, who was doing the opposite, staring at the ceiling and executing a false whistle. Dalmar grimaced. They passed through the bar into the hotel foyer and reception area. He failed to notice a member of the bar staff scoot out ahead of them. "That's a nasty scratch on your forehead?" Christine observed, raising the hand that held his a little of the way, as though pointing at the wound.

Dalmar smiled, "Took a tumble in the woods: I was telling Suzanne; playing – I'm afraid." Christine gave him a knowing grin. "Where are we going?" he asked anxiously.

"Right here," she pointed to some closed double doors in front of them. "You going to do the honours Tim?"

"Sure thing." He advanced to the middle of them, grasped both handles and waited. Dalmar was not aware how it happened, but he now found himself holding Suzanne's hand, who was standing firmly by his side with Fly next to her. She gave her escort a reassuring look, but nothing more. The trouble was – Dalmar knew those doors to be the entrance to the main conference hall. A sudden feeling of sheer apprehension enveloped him.

The doors opened. Christine nudged him in the back to enter. The first thing he became aware of was a large room laid out for a banquet. There were twelve long tables occupied by rows of people ... looking at him! Glancing up, he dimly became aware of a ceiling carpeted with different coloured balloons. The table immediately in front of them was almost entirely made up of young children. The whole room sat in total silence. They had all turned in their seats to watch the party enter. As

Dalmar, Suzanne and Fly walked in, all as one rose to a standing position, making the sound that goes with it; moving chairs, grunts, coughs and squeaks from over excited little boys and girls. From an additional far table, where there were a few seats still vacant, came a strong, clear voice. It was Floyd Hemming, the hotel manager. "Ladies and gentlemen – will you please welcome our guests of honour, John Hunter and his marvellous Collie – Fly. Hip, hip!"

"Hooray!" cheered the reply raised in a raucous sound that was heard by everyone in the hotel.

"Hip, hip!"

"Hooray!"

"Hip, hip!"

"Hooray!" At the end, the children's higher pitched voices could be heard over the adults, such was their enthusiasm. There then followed hand clapping which developed into the stamping of feet, with some boisterous types banging their hands on the tables.

Dalmar felt excruciatingly self-conscious. He did not know what to do. Fly, on the other hand, started to bark his approval, which prompted much laughter from those nearby, although some held out their hands to let the animal know that they were not laughing at him, but with him. Fortunately, he seemed to get the message.

Abruptly Suzanne tugged at Dalmar's arm. He looked down at her with help written all over his face. She started to lead him towards the farthest table. It seemed to be endless, that walk, and he tried to return all the smiles and greetings as he passed so many people by. He did recognise his neighbours. So that was what that look had been about. He could make out the huge grin of Jim Pearce somewhere in the giant collage of smiling faces, and there were the three teenagers who sometimes took Fly for a walk.

Suzanne led him to the middle of the furthest side of that distant table and told him where to sit. To his relief, she sat beside him, still holding onto Fly's lead. Tim and Christine took their places in the same row. As they did so, everyone else resumed their seats; except one man, and that was the person next to the lady on Dalmar's right, Floyd Hemming. He hushed the applause and general cheering by waving both his hands up and down. Then, in a raised voice said, "I think perhaps we should start by explaining a few things to our guest of honour." He turned a conciliatory face in Dalmar's direction. "John – or as some of us know you better – Dalmar. The owners of this establishment have laid on this evening's entertainment to celebrate the final demise of the Red Adder. As the person who brought that about, the entire population of our village salutes you and your dog – for outstanding bravery." The manager turned his attention to everyone in general. "This is a party for everyone who lives in the village of Yewhurst. We are going to start with a meal, and, later, all the tables will be moved to the sides, so that the evening may be finished off with a disco dance. Fly has not been forgotten. Our chef has prepared him a dinner of best fillet steak! Together with his favourite biscuits." There were general mutterings of appreciation from various sections of the audience. "The only other thing I am going to add for now – is – enjoy yourselves – and bon appetite." Floyd sat down to more applause.

Right opposite Dalmar and Suzanne were David and Dorothy Andrews. At the other end of the table sat Paul Sanders with his wife. Next to the Andrews were Stephen and Susan Knopner. Most of the others, Dalmar did not know. He was pleased to see Christine and Tim take their seats to his left. Many of those seated on his table were smiling at him. With his head half-bowed, he tried to acknowledge them all.

The lady on his immediate right spoke to him as the general settling down of all those present took place, and they relapsed into their previous conversations. "Are you okay? Was it a terrible shock?"

"I have never been so terrified in my whole life!" replied Dalmar, although, he inwardly was aware of an underlying feeling of excitement mixed with sentiment.

"Oh dear – even worse than the snake?" But the lady did not wait for a reply. "I'm Jan Hemming, by the way, Floyd's wife." Dalmar shook her hand from his seat. "Now, let me see, you have met David Andrews of course, but you may not know his better half, Dorothy?" He lent across the table and shook hands with them both. He could not recall ever meeting Dorothy personally.

"Don't tell me we managed to keep this little lot a surprise?" David enquired; eyes showing wide open under his spectacles. He looked like a television barrister, rather than a physician, being dressed in a very smart dark grey suit. Even Dorothy had broken away from the country doctor's wife image, and wore a plain, albeit, expensive looking dress.

"Yes," said Dalmar. "That is until a short while ago. It was obvious something was afoot but…" He broke off and waved an arm indicating the whole room. "Nothing like this!" Under the table, he felt Suzanne's hand searching for his. She had been talking to her brother before being distracted by Jan's conversation and greeting the Andrews.

While all this was going on, Fly remained tightly sandwiched between Dalmar and Suzanne's legs, probably wondering what was happening. The answer came quickly. Two young girls appeared behind them. "Ah – well done you two," said Jan turning to them. "These are our daughters, this one's" she said touching a girl of about thirteen on the back of her ponytail, "Joy … and this is June." Jan transferred her hand to the younger of the two. They were both smiling coyly at Dalmar. June had a cute gap in the centre of her upper teeth "They have been looking forward to this for days," explained Jan. "With your permission, may they take Fly away for his special meal?"

Dalmar grinned back at the two girls. He patted Fly on his nose and gave Suzanne an acknowledgement, as she handed over the lead. "Away you go boy. You are a very lucky dog." Fly rose to his four feet, looking excited. He was quite hungry. It was past his suppertime, and he went off willingly, sensing that there was food somewhere at the end of this. As the Hemming daughters walked proudly with their charge past the tables, there were lots of murmurs and admiring glances in the trio's direction.

Dalmar became distracted by a conversation going on across the table between Christine Westward and Stephen Knopner. Stephen had already introduced his wife, Susan, to those immediately opposite them, and was now expanding on an idea. "You see Christine; you and I are the only people *ever* to have survived a Red Adder bite. I think we ought to set up an exclusive club. What do you say?"

"All right," said Christine, putting on an I'm important look.

"Good. What we must do is to hold our Annual General meeting at the poshest restaurant in the county. Agreed?"

"And who is going to pay for it?" queried Tim with a dubious expression.

"The taxpayer, of course," answered Stephen, "who else?" Even though he was wearing a suit, he still managed to look scruffy. His tie was slightly out of position, but the dishevelled appearance was mainly due to his mop of wiry hair.

"Sounds good to me," said Christine.

"Actually ... there is something I would like to say before this meal gets under way," said Stephen, turning his attention to Suzanne. She only partially returned his gaze. "When you good people first told me about all this business after Christine here had been bitten." He paused and looked at the ceiling before returning his eyes to look at the people opposite him. "Quite frankly, I thought you were a bunch of raving nutters – high on pot!"

This was like the release of a safety valve to Dalmar. After all the recent nervous tension, it only needed something to set him off. And that something had a lot to do with the expression on Christine and Suzanne's faces, coupled with what Stephen had just said. It started deep in his chest, rising in waves of guttural laughter. Everyone nearby could not help but join in, even if they had no idea what had caused the hilarity. The more they joined in, the worse the effect on him. Suzanne desperately tried to quell it by pulling on his sleeve, but it was too late. The spasms had to run their course. He might have calmed down quite soon, if it were not for the fact that he happened to glance in Stephen's direction through watery eyes. That man was drumming the fingers of his left hand on the table, with the other hand cupped under his chin supported by an elbow, and the expression on his face said – 'When you have quite finished.' This set Dalmar off again, while pointing a finger at Stephen, which rose up and down with the laughter. Eventually – he calmed down after the forester, finally, resorted to turning away from Dalmar and looking at the nearest blank wall.

"As I was saying." Stephen, at last, was able to continue. Once again, he turned his gaze upon Suzanne. She had hold of Dalmar's left arm, which had stayed in place since the middle of the laughing fit, and she decided that now was not the time to let go. If anything, she held on more firmly. Stephen carried on with what he wanted to say, "I had serious doubts about your collective sanity. You can hardly blame me. I knew nothing about Red Adders or John the Red. To have it thrown at me that there was this fantasy type pond in the middle of the forest, unrecorded on any map, unknown by anyone working for us; and that this good lady," he pointed to Christine opposite him, "had been attacked by a six foot long, cherry coloured snake." He raised an open palm in the air, "Well." Nobody made any comment, although some smiled ruefully.

"However, I soon began to realise, especially when I recognized the calibre of that gentleman;" here – he stabbed his left hand's forefinger towards Dalmar, "there was something very sinister going on. But that does not excuse me from a sad disrespect to you Christine, and most especially for doubting the word of the young lady sitting next to you."

He rose to his feet. Stephen Knopner was not Suzanne's favourite person, but she lived in hope that her attitude might change as she did with anyone who made her feel uncomfortable. She felt sorry for his wife and family after their recent trauma and was looking forward to getting to know Susan later in the evening. Her feelings towards that lady's husband were about to change dramatically. Stephen had risen to his full height. Most people would have remained stooped, so as not to attract attention. Then he looked down, straight into Suzanne's eyes. "I wish to offer my apologies for any bad feeling that I may have caused." The statement was remarkable, because the terminology was out of character for its spokesman, as though it had been heavily rehearsed. When he resumed his seat, he took up a head bowed posture.

It was David Andrews who started it. A light handclap: one that did not attract the attention of everyone in the dining hall, but loud enough for all those seated close at hand to be aware of. Except for Suzanne, all those nearby, including Dalmar, joined in. Suzanne, from a half standing position, her mouth forming a shy grin, leant across the table, and held out her right hand. Looking up, Stephen grasped it and shook, a little too enthusiastically. His wife clasped both hands to her face, and when she took them away, revealed a wide smile right across it.

CHAPTER FIFTY-FOUR

"WE SALUTE YOU BOTH."

The children's table was the first to get their initial course. They were having a different menu, with more accents on fun and the kind of tasty treats youngsters like. The only adults at this table were volunteer hotel staff. Two of Stephen and Susan's children were present, and most of the boys and girls who lived in the village. They were having a wonderful time with plenty to eat and drink. Also, several party toys had been provided as well as a good supply of crackers. The grown-up's meal consisted of a four-course dinner. Nearly everyone ate sumptuously, and those that did not relish a particular dish kept quiet, instead, indulging in the abundant supplies of alcoholic drinks, which were all the more appreciated by the imbibers, because they were not paying for them.

On Dalmar's table, there were also a husband-and-wife teacher partnership, the local councillor and his wife, together with Paul and Catherine Sanders. Floyd and Jan Hemming, from their central position, divided their conversation between the Sander's end and the Westward's. Tim was supposed to be seated directly opposite Stephen, but because Christine had altered the place settings, so that she could sit next to Suzanne, he found himself able to get to know Susan Knopner.

As they worked their way through the meal and the wine eased any awkwardness, there was no doubt all the adults were enjoying themselves. Judging by the whooping and hollering coming from the children's table, they were too.

When Floyd had been given a tip-off by a member of his staff that all the grown-ups had been served coffee, following the repast, he rose to his feet. Taking a spoon, he tapped loudly on a large glass jar full of white, oval-shaped mints. Gradually, silence descended over the whole room; that is, unless one counts the odd child's snigger. "Ladies and gentlemen. Please may we have some hush? Our vicar, The Rev Paul Sanders is going to say a few words."

Paul pushed back his chair and stood up holding a small piece of paper in his left hand. His normally ruddy complexion seemed calmer in the dimmed lighting. His haircut was as neat as ever, and he had an air about him that suggested great pleasure in what he was about to say. "Citizens of Yewhurst," he began and there was a spontaneous handclap from several proud members of the audience. "We have assembled here together this evening to honour one of our number, who has carried out an act requiring the utmost valour. Many years ago, some of you experienced the sadness of lost ones caused by a terrible reptile that lived in this neighbourhood. In fact, our guest of honour is himself a kinsman of one of those families. Last year, there was more suffering caused by a similar source." Here, he cast a respectfully lowered head in Dalmar's direction. "If it were not for John Hunter's courage and tenacity, and, I understand, his dog's as well, we might even now be mourning another severe loss. "Sir ... we salute you both." Paul raised his glass at this point, and then gathering what they were supposed to do, everyone in the room stood, except for Dalmar: Jan had a hand pressed down on his right shoulder and Suzanne was doing the same on his left. Paul proposed a toast. "John and Fly." One and all raised their glasses and repeated the toast as they took a sip from their drinks. The youngsters watched, fascinated.

After that, and when everyone had re-taken their seats, Paul, remaining standing said, "John, we wanted to give you something to show our appreciation. After a great deal of discussion, we decided that a memento, such as a local scene picture or an artefact would not be appropriate. So, all the village residents have contributed to our gift to you. Also, we have had some considerable assistance from local businesses. Their names are printed on the back of this presentation folder." He held it up high, so that everyone could see. "You are going on holiday in four weeks' time. Now..." again he inclined his head in Dalmar's direction, "This has been cleared with your employers. In fact, I think you will find their name on the folder." He jabbed a finger at it. "Your destination – is a superb three-star hotel on the Island of Skye, off the west coast of Scotland. Your room has a marvellous panoramic view across the sea to the Island of Rhum. You will be able to explore the unique scenery of Skye and the Cuillin mountains." Paul paused for breath. "One of the reasons for this choice was to enable you to take your dog with you. After all, he deserves a reward as well." Dalmar nodded as several supportive comments were clearly heard. "The hotel management has assured us that it is perfectly in order, in fact, they are very much looking forward to greeting him. The holiday is for two people. Having said that; there are a number of us who are delighted to see a certain young lady by your side." Suzanne blushed and lowered her head. Dalmar turned to give her a reassuring embrace around her waist. Prompted by Paul's remark there were several "Here here's," from those that knew the guest of honour more intimately. Paul Sanders left his place at the table and came around to stand behind Dalmar, between him and Jan Hemming. He handed the folder to the recipient saying, "There is also something else in this little parcel," which he produced from his jacket pocket. "It is for Fly, with our grateful thanks – may God go with you." There then followed enthusiastic general applause from the entire assembly.

While this was going on Paul handed Dalmar another envelope. He had to raise his voice above the handclapping. "In here are two tickets to the opening night of Thomas Hurn's new play, in London's West End. He couldn't be here tonight but sends his best wishes. Wanted you to have these." The recipient mouthed a 'thank you.' He was a little awed having never been to an opening night before.

Dalmar waited for the applause to die away. He had to wait a long time. He knew that he need not respond, but he pushed back his chair and got to his feet. Everyone fell silent in anticipation. Suzanne looked up at him – anxiously. He waved both main presents in the air, one in each hand. "Thank you for these ... thank you very much indeed. Although, I must say, the reward seems rather on the generous side." As he placed them on the table in front of him, several people shook their heads vigorously. Dalmar ignored it, continuing, "I can tell you – already – I am looking forward to that holiday. The Isle of Skye happens to be on my wish list of places to visit one day." Murmurs of gratification were heard all across the room.

Dalmar had quite a strong speaking voice. He knew how to project his voice. "This is a celebratory occasion and I don't wish to impair that mood. The Reverend Sanders has already mentioned the sadness experienced by some families over loss of life caused by the Red Adders, as far back as 1947." Dalmar paused. "I wonder if you would allow me to propose a toast – in memoriam."

Actually, for some time now, this recognition was something that, in Dalmar's mind, had not been given. This evening suddenly presented an opportunity, which might be taken further later, in the shape of a memorial plaque perhaps.

"Ladies and Gentlemen, would you please raise your glasses." Everyone stood, including the children. Dalmar gave out the salutary words loud and clear so that no one would be in any doubt. "The victims and their families!" It was accepted and repeated by one and all. Dalmar sat down immediately after this. He did not particularly want to soften the serious air by making some statement encouraging them all to carry on enjoying themselves. He considered it right to let this naturally happen.

Most of those present entered into private thoughts concerning their own family connections, past and present.

Following a short spell, Floyd Hemming rose to his feet to make a final announcement. "After about half an hour, to give you all a chance to finish your coffee, we are going to move the tables to the sides of the room. The lights will be dimmed, and a disco will begin and go on until midnight. A bus has been laid on to take the younger children home. We will let the parents know when it arrives." Floyd smiled and sat down to the last applause of the evening.

This was also a signal for those that wished to move from their present seats and go and chat to someone else. A lot of that went on, although nothing much changed on the speaker's table, until that is, a young man with a thick country accent came and tapped Dalmar on the shoulder. "Beggin' your pardon sir, but me great auntie 'would loike a word we'you." Dalmar turned to look at the youth. He was grinning right across his face and obviously felt self-conscious, whilst pointing to an old lady sitting at the far end of the third table back. It was Ma Hessil resplendent in a dress liberally covered with a design of large chrysanthemum blooms. Dalmar turned to Suzanne who was talking to David and Dorothy. He whispered in her ear, "Just going to have a quick word with someone – be back soon." She half turned to acknowledge him, at the same time continuing to pay attention to Dorothy.

"Yes, the Lakes are one of our favourite haunts. David gets quite fit after a holiday up there. Mind you, I like the clothes shops." She smiled guiltily at Suzanne and hunched her shoulders.

"Spends an absolute fortune on woollen this and woollen that," commented David. "That's why I get fit; have to drag her onto the fells just to get her away from those shops! Did you say you work in a gallery in Grasmere? Think we know it. Not far from the Wordsworth Hotel, bought a painting there a couple of years ago: hangs in our lounge. You know the one dear?" He looked at his wife for confirmation.

"That's the place," said Suzanne. "Mind you, I don't know whether I'll be going back just yet. They'll have got someone else by then."

"Good," said David. What he meant by that didn't require explanation. They had a long discussion about Cumbria, and after some minutes Suzanne glanced over to see if Dalmar was on his way back.

She saw him leaning over close to Ma Hessil, who was trying to tell him something against all the general babble. Suzanne noticed her hair was just as willowy as ever and standing out starkly against her skin was a liberal application of bright red lipstick. Suddenly, Dalmar straightened up, looking at the old lady incredulously. Ma Hessil's expression was serious, but at the same time showed puzzlement. Dalmar leant forward again and seemed to be talking to her earnestly, as if seeking verification on a matter. Then he smiled to her and left with a raised hand in acknowledgement. Several people wanted to stop him on his way back, and he politely had a quick word with them all, in turn, but Suzanne could tell from his body language that he had urgent business elsewhere.

At last, he was free and came around to her side. "Sorry to interrupt you, but I need to talk to you David," he said, looking at the doctor without waiting for a reply. "Floyd," apologies for this," for he too was in deep conversation with a member of the teaching profession. "Is there somewhere we could have a chat, somewhere relatively private?"

Floyd thought for a moment, glancing at his wife. "Sure ... let me see. Let's go to reception and see if any of the hotel rooms are free. Jan – keep the show running darling." David and Floyd rose to their feet.

Dalmar then turned to Stephen. "Sorry, think you ought to sit in on this." It had been easy to catch his attention because of the interest that the small disturbance had created. "And Tim, I need your moral support." He gave Tim an appealing look. Dalmar blew Suzanne a kiss, saying he would be back as soon as possible, and please could she look out for Fly. "Save the first dance for me," he said with an encouraging smile. The ladies watched their men go with varying degrees of perplexity on their faces.

CHAPTER FIFTY-FIVE

"I TAKE IT – THAT IS A NO?"

Immediately following their partner's' departure, Suzanne chose the moment to go and sit in Stephen's place, so that she could have an introductory chat with his wife. "Did your husband suffer much from the bite?" she enquired.

"Let us say, he made the best possible use of it in terms of attention seeking," Susan replied, with a super smile. Normally she had quite a morose expression, but when she smiled, a mighty door opened onto her more cheerful personality. Christine, Jan, Dorothy and Suzanne all laughed and begged to hear more.

Floyd Hemming went behind the reception counter to see one of the girls on duty. David, Dalmar, Stephen and Tim loitered by the desk. "Did we give you much of a shock?" Stephen asked Dalmar, with his elbow planted at one end of the counter. He was grinning mischievously.

"Yes, you B – did," was the reply.

"Good – that's what I like to hear," Stephen seemed delighted.

"How's your leg by the way?" This question came from Tim, directed at the forestry boss.

"Oh, all right, gives me the odd gyp – you know – not *too* bad." Before Stephen could get any sympathy, Floyd returned.

"All the hotel rooms are taken gentlemen it appears we are full. But look – the rear restaurant is not being used. It is only in operation for breakfast and special functions. We can grab a corner in there. That okay?" he asked, glancing at Dalmar.

"Sure," said the principal guest, "as long as it's distant from prying eyes and ears."

"In that case, it should be fine. It is right away from any activity." Here Floyd held up a hand. "Before we go in, give me a moment to organise some coffee." He made a gesture indicating that they should wait where they were.

Nobody saw the figure, obscured by a postcard-stand at the other end of the reception desk. This person silently went ahead of them along the corridor, down a group of steps, and into the hotel breakfast-room.

Soon our five men found themselves by a table around the corner at the far end of the restaurant. A large double bank of full-length windows lay to their fore, magnificently draped in giant embroidered curtains, depicting traditional rural farming life.

They took seats at a table laid up for six, presumably for breakfast the following morning. "Must try not to disturb anything," said Dalmar pointing at the cutlery.

"Absolutely," agreed Stephen, promptly, with a protruding elbow knocking a knife and fork on to the floor with a loud clatter.

"His mother disowns him;" Tim commented.

"No matter," Floyd placated the guilty party with his hands and told him to leave it.

Stephen and Tim took off their suit jackets and placed them over the backs of the chairs. It was a warm evening and therefore a little uncomfortable in formal attire.

A waiter arrived with a tray of cups, saucers and a pot of coffee. There was also a little jug full of cream and a bowl of Demerara sugar. "Shall I pour?" said Floyd. There were no refusals, so he proceeded to fill up five cups. They all helped themselves to cream with only Stephen having sugar. He dipped his teaspoon into the bowl but instead of depositing its contents into his cup of steaming coffee, he clipped the side of the cup with the spoon and spilt the sugar all over the saucer and onto the tablecloth. "Bollocks!" he said.

"What are you going to do for the finale?" asked Tim. Stephen scowled at him.

When the waiter had gone, David was the first with his curiosity. "What's this about?" he asked.

Dalmar looked at him before glancing around the corner, and at the entrance to the restaurant to make sure they were alone. "David, do you happen to know if Allen Haddle had any relatives living in the area?"

The doctor did not answer straight away. When he did, it was with deep thought. "Do you know ... I really cannot recall anyone."

"What about – say thirty years ago?"

David again went into a reverie. "I am trying to remember any details about his parents. But I can't ... nothing at all. Strange, he never mentioned his mother or father? Perhaps his family lived away from here. He must have come to the area when he took up a position at the veterinary practice."

"So – definitely no immediate family?"

"What are you driving at?" David turned the questioning around.

"I take it – that is a no?" said a determined Dalmar.

David smoothed the hair on the back of his head with his left hand, at the same time palming his right hand out in front of him. "Yes – none that I can remember. My wife told me that they sometimes had a nephew to stay during the summer holidays, a young boy. But he would have been from her side of the family. Most of her kin hailed from Wales."

Dalmar shrugged his shoulders. "Nobody else here knows of any - I suppose?" The tone was almost appealing. Both Tim and Stephen shook their heads.

"What of it? If he has ... sorry had," Stephen commented opening his eyes wide.

"Well ... it appears he did have a relative living in the village, that is, up until the early nineteen-fifties ... A sister." Dalmar was almost matter of fact in his tone.

"You're joking?" said David with extreme puzzlement. "I'm sure I would have known ... I mean he never mentioned her ... perhaps my wife..."

Dalmar interrupted him; "His sister's name was Doris Head." He let the words sink in. Both David and Tim immediately grasped the sensational connection.

Stephen wondered why they were both looking so incredulous. Then he remembered who Doris Head was, the wife of John Head, whose first name had been used to label the Red Adder. "Great tits! Wasn't that?..." He decided he did not require the others confirmation of this. He could tell by their faces.

As the implications dawned on Floyd, he leant forward and made a sudden move with his right elbow: a little too sudden. His cup half full of coffee, turned over in its saucer, and the resultant spill overflowed onto the tablecloth. "I'm glad *you* did that," said Stephen without sympathy. Floyd cursed, but decided to leave it and merely righted the cup in the flooded saucer. A waiter would have to change the cloth later.

Dalmar continued. "Ma Hessil has just told me, and, incidentally, she was staggered that I didn't know. Doris's maiden name, apparently, was Haddle, or 'Addle as she called him. She did say that she had been *very* surprised to find out that the root cause of John the Red's existence was that very lady's brother, although I think she still believes there was witchcraft involved. Apparently, Allen had been really kind to his sister after her husband, John, had been killed in the D. Day invasion. Sometimes he would visit Doris every day, and he always made sure she never wanted for anything. He even got very concerned about her hatred for Ma Hessil and her husband. Often tried to mediate, or 'meditate' as she put it, but I'm sure she meant mediate." Dalmar paused, quickly recalling something. "Come to think of it – that explains the Victoria Cross I saw in Haddle's study – just before he shot himself. Must originally have been the property of John Head. You remember Tim, Ma Hessil telling us he had been awarded it posthumously?"

"Yes – but just a sec," replied Tim. "I am sure that when my wife and I first met Allen Haddle, about this time last year – right here in that bar." He pointed to the restaurant exit. "He denied all knowledge of the John the Red origination. He said something like, 'I don't know where that story came from,' and..." Tim hesitated, trying to remember, "when we asked him about Ma Hessil ... well you would have thought he would have mentioned his sister's involvement. After all, Doris used to be her neighbour."

"You were in Allen Haddle's study just before he shot himself?" Stephen was looking at Dalmar – astounded.

"What's that?" said Tim, suddenly recollecting Dalmar's recent words.

Floyd and David, who seemed to have an ear to everything, enlightened them. The other two said nothing, choosing to stare at Dalmar in astonishment.

"Anyway," said the doctor, bringing the conversation back to where it was. "You're right Tim – Allen always claimed that he knew nothing of the John the Red business. But there is something that doesn't add up here. If Allen was Doris's brother, why didn't he speak with a local dialect? I can assure you – that Doris had a very strong accent."

"He had elocution lessons." It was Tim again. "Ma Hessil told us that Doris's brother had taken elocution lessons, didn't she Dalmar?"

"Oh, and when was that?" David Andrews asked with a curious expression on his face. "That is – when did you have this little chat with Ma Hessil?"

"Err – umph," uttered Dalmar looking at Tim with squinting eyes.

Tim put his hand to his mouth and said, "Oh pooh!"

"Ah hah!" David pointed a finger between Tim and Dalmar. "Just as we thought, that is Jonathon Shure and I, you two have had some assignation with old Ma Hessil we didn't know about. Am I right?"

"You could be," Dalmar came in quickly, and if you want to know any more, you will have to promise us that it won't go any further. And don't worry – it won't incriminate you." He looked at David knowingly.

"Now what's all this about?" asked a confused Floyd.

David went quiet, torn between his professionalism and sheer curiosity. His curiosity got the better of him. "All right – I promise," he said with a sigh.

"Cross your heart and hope to die?" said Tim with a sly smile.

"Uh oh, this is good," said Stephen smirking and nudging Floyd in the ribs at the same time.

"You had better tell him," suggested Dalmar, looking at Tim. So, he did, starting from Ma Hessil's telephone call, one morning late in the summer of last year, and the subsequent meeting at her house that evening. He told them that he had taken Dalmar along, more as a witness than anything else, but it turned out she had been half expecting his presence anyway. Then he related her story, or as much of it as he could remember, occasionally prompted by Dalmar.

"That reminds me of something," said Tim suddenly looking at his collaborator. "She called you John when we took our leave of her. Well – well – well, she knew more than the rest of us – huh?"

Dalmar lowered his head and then almost immediately raised it again. "Sorry about that," he said, although he was at a loss to understand how Ma Hessil had known his first name.

"I am sure you had your reasons," Tim simply remarked.

When Tim finished narrating the story of their meeting with Ma Hessil, the doctor drew a hand across his brow, took off his glasses, looked at the lenses and put them back on again. "Phew!" he said. "Tell me, when did this meeting take place?" Tim thought for a while, before giving him an indication that it was some time after putting Beech Cottage on the market, following the death of the reporter, Mary Taylor. "So," said David, "you two wouldn't have had anything to do with a certain letter delivered to *this* gentleman." Here David inclined his head at Stephen.

Tim buried his face in his hands, and Dalmar said quite openly, "What letter?" His face was poker blank.

Stephen, with his mouth wide open, was pointing an accusing finger at them. David shrugged his shoulders and said, "Oh well, never mind, in the light of what I have just heard, I would probably have done the same. I have to say to you all that learning that Allen Haddle was responsible for all this business – made me feel a complete fool. My father knew him well. They were good friends. We must have had Allen and Jean to dinner at our house on at least ten occasions. We visited them regularly as well. Incidentally – I have never seen the inside of that office of his – often wondered why he was so secretive about it." He changed his tack suddenly. "Jean was a delightful woman. It is very sad. She has cut herself off from Yewhurst. Dorothy tried to contact her through one of her relatives, but she was ignored. Suppose you can understand it – the shame – but I thought she might at least have said goodbye to my wife. We are both so shocked about Allen. There was never any inkling that he had this bizarre hobby – none at all." David looked across the table at Dalmar. "Tell me – what made you suspect him. It was sudden, wasn't it?"

Dalmar replied with a question. "You know their house has a chestnut tree on either side of the entrance gate?"

"Ye-s," said David.

"The night he shot himself, I was returning home having taken Fly for his evening walk, when I saw Allen by his gate. He had obviously just returned from taking his terrier on a similar mission. We acknowledged each other from a distance. As I carried on my way home, the combination of seeing the chestnut trees – and him, answered a puzzle that had been nagging away in my brain for weeks. The revelation came flooding into my head."

Dalmar related the details of Haddle's slip, when he mentioned the chestnut at the Secret Pond, during a conversation between the two of them while he was visiting his cottage. "Unfortunately, I had not thought anything of it at the time. Later, I read the transcript of Suzanne's statement to the police, which made no mention of a particular tree. But it wasn't until I saw Haddle standing under those chestnut trees by his gate, that it hit me. Now I knew that he was the breeder. He had been around in 1947 and 1948. He was involved. I knew it was him. David ... I hadn't known the man anything like as long as you, but I can assure you - you should be grateful – you never knew – the *other* Allen Haddle."

There was a lengthy pause in the conversation before Stephen raised a question with a look of high regard on his face. "So, you went and challenged him at his home?"

"Remember my brother?" Dalmar raised both eyebrows as he made the comment.

"I see," came Stephen's short response.

"I really think the important matter that concerns us all – is just what was Haddle responsible for?" Dalmar was not changing the angle of the subject on purpose; he was the one who would have to contact the police with this latest information.

"How do you mean?" Stephen was getting interested.

"Well, did he release one of last year's Red Adders – near Captain Young, on 6th June last year? Was it him who sent the note to the captain?" Dalmar challenged them. "Let us recall who this old soldier was – none other than – the commanding officer of the platoon in which John Head and Bob Hessil served."

"Just a tick – what note? I'm lost now," said Stephen, scratching his head.

"Same here" said Tim. Floyd expressed lack of knowledge as well. David had been informed about the note, but he left it to Dalmar to explain to the other three.

"Are you intimating that Allen Haddle – deliberately bred these snakes as part of the revenge package for the death of his brother-in-law?" suggested Tim.

"I doubt that it is as simple as that," Dalmar answered him. "In my opinion, he started out as a genuine hobbyist of a rather odd sort. Yes, he should not have experimented with very dangerous reptiles, but that is how he got his kicks. I believe that after the death of Peter Hessil and his fiancé, the John the Red thing just sort of fell into place, and he carried on with it to please his sister. After the snake had been driven away from the Great Mile in 1947, he told me that he had no idea where it might have gone. I believe him here. It is hardly likely that he engineered that particular tragedy. It was more probably a coincidence, which convinced Doris that the Red Adder was her husband reincarnated. Allen simply went along with it, and later, took it to ultimate lengths. So much so, that even after her death he carried on with the horrid business."

"He could have influenced the death of Ma Hessil's husband," said David Andrews. "I diagnosed a stroke after his body was found in Yewhurst Wood, in the summer of 1959, and I said at the time that his face wore an expression of abject terror."

"And then he caused the death of this Captain Young. Game – set and match – as far as avenging his sister's husband – yes?" queried Stephen.

"Not quite," Dalmar came back. "Ma Hessil was still alive. We know that there were two of these snakes around last summer. Could he have released one to get Captain Young? Recaptured it, and released it again to attack Ma Hessil, only to end up with her dog instead? One of the snakes was quite small, and the police found a portable cage in Allen's garage."

"If that's the case," said Tim; "he must have been close at hand when Paul Sanders, my wife and sister and I, helped her that afternoon."

"Except that his house is only just across the road from where it happened," commented David.

"You could be right," agreed Tim. "Probably laid in wait for her."

"Blimey!" exclaimed Stephen. "Would you ever. What a nasty man."

"Of course," Dalmar glanced at them all in turn, "if Ma Hessil had been killed, this evening's little surprise might never have come to light. That, surely, is a motive?" David screwed up his lips and the others all made various nods of assertion. "However," Dalmar said looking at all four of them in turn, "I don't suppose we will ever know for certain. I personally think it more likely that he did release the smaller of the Red Adders to get Captain Young, and that it stayed in the area for a while, which is why Ma Hessil's dog was bitten. You see – Allen Haddle told me he released the *second* snake, the big one, when your wife and sister," he glanced at Tim, "were swimming in the Secret Pond. Apparently, he was annoyed at the noise they were making."

"What!" exclaimed Tim.

"Quite," Dalmar gave a slight nod of his head in sympathy.

All of a sudden, Stephen sat back in his chair. "He didn't breed any more of those damn things last year, did he? I mean could there have been *three*? One for the dog: one for the captain – the big fellow; and what about the attack on Ginger? Hold on that makes *four*."

Realising just what it was that Stephen was implying; David, Tim and Floyd's faces showed outright alarm.

"Don't worry, there aren't any more out there," Dalmar's calm voice instantly caused all of them to relax their postures. "When I questioned Allen Haddle about the number of experimental baby snakes bred last year, I can unequivocally say that he confirmed to me that there were two. One of which was much smaller than the other: a fact – born out in recent history. The Red Adder that killed Ginger was the very same that killed Captain Young and Ma Hessil's spaniel."

"There is still one thing that bothers me." The comment came from the doctor. He had a distinct frown right across his forehead. "Allen's wife, Jean, would surely have known about his sister? In which case, I cannot imagine that the subject would never have come up in our conversations together: if not with me – certainly with my wife?"

"Unless ... she didn't know." Dalmar's tone bordered on the authoritative.

"You mean his wife didn't know her husband had a sister?" Tim looked amazed.

"But surely not. What about their marriage? ... Doris must have been present?" asked David, hesitating for a full half second. "Although I seem to remember – it was before I knew them well – they got married in Paris – quiet ceremony – I believe."

"Not only did Allen never inform his wife about the existence of his sister, but, also, his sister never knew he married Jean, or anybody, for that matter." Dalmar informed them in a quiet but definite manner.

"What! How on earth do you know that?" asked a now completely bewildered David. The faces on the other three men looked amazed as well.

Dalmar spread his hands, palms out, up in front of him, closed his lips and opened his eyes wide. "Because – Ma Hessil had no idea he was married – said something about him having a fancy woman, although there was a rumour spread by a village postman, but it wasn't taken seriously apparently."

After everyone had taken this in, Dalmar altered the line of the discussion. "Tim, did you find out who paid for Christine's private room at the hospital?"

Tim straightened his back at this question. "Do you know, I had forgotten all about that," he said. "No, still none the wiser, except that it definitely wasn't any of Christine's relations – or mine." Dalmar looked directly at the doctor.

"No, no, wouldn't be permissible. I believe Dorothy sent some flowers. Hope she received them?" David looked for confirmation from Tim who was desperately searching his memory.

"Ah – yes – there was a bouquet, but it had no note attached. They were a mystery as far as we were concerned. Sorry."

"Oh – it doesn't matter. The label must have fallen off. Just hope they cheered the poor girl up," David added.

"So, we still do not know who paid for that private room. Perhaps that *is* something the police might come up with," Dalmar conjectured.

"Oh no ... you don't think Allen Haddle coughed up for it, do you?" Tim looked aghast at the thought.

"Several people have asked me if this whole business had anything to do with the disappearance of Julia Thornton?" said Floyd Hemming.

"No harm in telling you," answered David. "It will be common knowledge soon. The police are going to dig up Allen's garden."

"Bloody hell!" exclaimed Stephen.

"Would have thought that a waste of time," Tim said, pointedly. "If he did her in, it is somewhere in that forest she's buried. Needle in a haystack."

"Just a mo..." said Floyd. "Are you saying Julia died from a snake bite?"

There was quite a long silence before David said, "There is a thought that this might have been direct murder. Something to do with her knowing too much."

Before anyone could make any further comment, a sheepish-looking waiter appeared from around the corner. "Excuse me, Sir," he said shuffling up to the table. "Your wife wondered whether you would come and say goodbye to the children."

At first Dalmar said nothing, but Tim nudged his elbow before commenting. "What's all this, been a secret wedding?"

Dalmar looked up to see that the waiter was, in fact, addressing him. "Ah ... right ... yes – of course." He looked at the others who were all smiling at his confusion.

"Mr Hunter isn't married George," Floyd said to the waiter. "I think you are referring to his lady escort."

"Beg pardon sir ... the lady seemed most anxious. The children are in the bus, and they would like to say goodnight."

"Naturally," agreed David. "I think we have finished. I suppose it will be another visit to see the Chief Inspector for you?" He looked at Dalmar for confirmation.

"Afraid so. Will try and contact him in the morning."

They all rose from the table, collected jackets and made their way out of the restaurant to join the corridor leading to reception.

On the way, Stephen touched Dalmar on his right arm. "I'm taking my brood on in our car: Susan's driving," he quickly added for he had consumed several glasses of wine. "But that doesn't mean you are getting away with it. They will want a goodnight kiss as well." He smirked at Dalmar, as he made his way toward the conference hall to catch up with his wife.

Nobody had noticed the toecaps belonging to a pair of tan coloured leather shoes, which were poking out from under the base of the curtains hanging over the floor length restaurant windows. The owner of the shoes waited patiently until the waiter could be heard departing with a tray. One of the drapes twitched and an eye looked out between a tiny gap in the middle. Seeing no one in the restaurant, a hand pulled back the curtain, and there stood Jack Tuppence, the reporter, with the biggest smile on his face he had ever displayed in his life. He had quite an exclusive, but he desperately needed to write it all down before he forgot the details or muddled them up. He quickly weaved his way among the dining tables, out into the corridor, and, without being spotted, slid silently into the gentlemen's toilet.

CHAPTER FIFTY-SIX

"I'M VERY PLEASED YOU DID."

Suzanne and the two Hemming girls were waiting by the main door with Fly, who jumped up to greet his master. "Hello boy," said Dalmar. "Have you been thoroughly spoilt?" Joy and June nodded in confirmation, with big grins on their faces.

"See you in the disco," said the elder one before they both ran off to re-join their mother.

"Afraid you have a bus load of kids waiting for you out there," said Suzanne with a mischievous smile.

"Oh, that's no bother," he said, much to Suzanne's surprise. "Bet you they would rather say cheerio to Fly though. Is that the present for him in your hand?" She was holding onto that and the holiday folder, plus the other envelope. Dalmar took Fly's parcel off her and gave her a gentle wink, and then he opened one of the double doors and ushered the collie out with him. He had a shrewd idea what might lie concealed in that parcel, or something very similar. The bus was right alongside. Suzanne gaped as he leapt on board, turned around and told Fly to follow him. The balloons had obviously been released from their lofty perch in the dining room, judging by the quantities of the colourful things that were bobbing about inside the bus. The children were having a great time biffing them about.

Suzanne watched as the visible top half of Dalmar's body moved to the centre on the inside of the bus. He seemed to be encouraging those children at the back and front to gather around as best as they could. Now he could be seen, amidst the bobbing balloons, opening the parcel. Inside was an extremely attractive black leather collar. There were two brass plaques, inlaid to the leather, at each end. The inscription on the first gave the dog's name, and the other one read, 'THE SAVIOUR OF YEWHURST 1976.' Dalmar read it out to the children. Then he bent down to Fly, removed his old collar and put on the new one. To a prompt from Dalmar, all the children cheered. After that, he and Fly had to extricate themselves from the chaos. Fortunately, there were a few mums and dads present who helped calm down the still excited but rapidly tiring boys and girls. When Dalmar and a furiously tail-wagging Fly finally managed to disembark, Suzanne joined them to wave an exaggerated goodbye as the driver slowly drove the coach slowly.

"Dalmar," Suzanne touched his arm, "shall I take Fly back to your house? He must be tired out by now, and I'll put these holiday tickets in a safe place, while I'm at it."

"Sure you don't want me to." Dalmar thought that perhaps he should.

"Quite sure: wait for me inside. I won't be long. They are just about to start the dancing." Looking through the glass door, she noticed a figure she recalled from last year: it was Jack Twopence making his way over to the hotel bedroom staircase. Briefly, she wondered what he was doing here. No press people had been invited to the evening's celebration. She dismissed it from her mind and looked down at Fly's neck to admire his new collar.

"While you are there – put this in a safe place. He was wearing it when he attacked the Red Adder." Dalmar produced the old collar from his trouser pocket, at the same time handing her a door key.

"Oh – right," she gave him a perceptive smile and ambled off with the collie. The dog's head was looking over his shoulder at Dalmar, not with an expression of anxiety, but one of 'bad luck old chap.'

Tim, meanwhile, had gone to join Christine in the main hall. All the tables had been moved to the sides of the room, releasing the polished wood dance floor. At the far end, a small stage housed the disco electronics, and an extraordinarily handsome looking fellow was preparing the late evening's entertainment. Stephen and Susan had their two children with them and were ushering them outside. Dalmar was introduced to the two boys. They seemed to hero worship him. Their two-year-old sister had had to stay at home with a baby-sitter. Dalmar promised the brothers that he would call and meet her sometime. On the way out, Stephen took Dalmar's arm and held him back a little. He said, "All joking aside – thanks for what you did out there." He pointed a hand towards the forest on the far side of the road.

"Well, one could say that if I had not been where I was on that day – you would not have been bitten." Dalmar looked serious.

"And 'one' could say," said Stephen briefly taking off Dalmar's English, "if that were the case, the Red Adder would be still alive, and might have claimed another life or two by now: probably my staff." The two of them shook hands with a meaningful firm grip, before Stephen led his family away to find their car.

At that moment, Dalmar spotted Suzanne making her way back through the wooded area by his cottage, so he waited for her, and arm in arm; they encountered David and Dorothy Andrews. "You off too?" asked Dalmar.

"Yes," replied the doctor, adjusting his glasses. They had fallen onto the end of his nose. "I'm on early surgery in the morning."

"Oh, too bad," said Suzanne. She smiled at Dorothy who made to give her a polite kiss.

"Now look, you two," said David, "we are very glad to see you together," here he pointed at their intertwined arms. "Very glad indeed." He further directed a finger at Dalmar and looked into Suzanne's eyes. "This man has had a face like an overturned bucket since you've been away! So please hang around." Then he smiled and leant forward to give the girl a kiss, before shaking Dalmar's outstretched hand with enthusiasm. Dalmar was rather gentler when he said goodbye to

Dorothy.

No sooner had they departed than a whole bunch of the older guests came up to take their leave. Dalmar and Suzanne found themselves saying thank you after thank you and polite going away phrases over and over again. However, the amount of grateful and endearing comments they received were greatly appreciated. At the very end came Paul Sanders and his wife. As neither Dalmar nor Suzanne had met her before, they spent a little while chatting, until; eventually, they had gone too.

Not all the less sprightly people departed; some fully intended to join in with the younger element and indulge in a good bopping session. As Dalmar and Suzanne entered the banqueting suite, the lights were suddenly dimmed and some were switched off altogether, completely changing the atmosphere. They found Tim and Christine waiting for them at the rearranged seating. A man's voice came over a loudspeaker system. "Good evening ladies and gents my name is Rick Landers, and I am your D.J. for tonight. We are going to kick-off with some new numbers, so let's get going!" Up to date popular music pounded everyone's eardrums, and the dance floor filled remarkably quickly. Dalmar found himself whisked into action by Suzanne. She had good rhythm, swaying her hips and moving her feet with a relaxed ease. She had never seen Dalmar dance before and was not in the least surprised to see that he was rather awkward and ungainly. Like a lot of tall men, he could not balance his height with the required movement. Fortunately, he did not seem embarrassed at all and entered into the spirit of the event. By his very attitude, he allowed her to take the spotlight.

Christine managed a few dances, but, after a while, she felt uncomfortable carrying the extra weight, so she sat down. Tim and Dalmar took turns to chat to her and have a go on the dance floor with Suzanne.

During one softer record, while dancing with Dalmar, Suzanne managed to make herself heard above the beat music. "Sorry about all the secrecy before tonight, but that is the way the village wanted it. I know you are not very happy at being the centre of attention."

Dalmar looked into her eyes. "If it meant seeing you again, I would do anything." He smiled and his teeth flashed, caught by a bright, narrow beamed light. She loved those teeth; remembering the top layer that were almost straight, but not quite.

"Anything?" she said, her eyes sparkling.

"Anything," he replied, putting a serious mask on his face, and then smiling at her again.

After an hour and a half, Tim caught Dalmar's attention. He took him on one side away from their table, when both he and Suzanne had returned from a long dance. "Sorry, Christine needs her beauty sleep. I am afraid we are going to have to head home."

Rapidly, Dalmar realised that his world might be about to crash. Unless he could persuade Suzanne to see him again – perhaps she had only agreed to partner him for this evening, even though she seemed very keen up till now. "Of course," he replied. "The poor love must be exhausted. I will come out and see you all off." He had to shout above the music.

Tim went to get Christine and Suzanne. Then all four of them made their way back through the hotel foyer, and out into the refreshing night-time air.

Dalmar was desperately trying to think about what he should say to Suzanne. His brain just would not function. The whole evening had been one incredible time spot in his life: how was it to end – with nothing? He put his hand on her waist, which intimated something, at least. It was all very well other people discussing a holiday for the two of them, but what about her thoughts on the matter. "When did Ma Hessil and her friends leave?" he asked, making conversation.

"While you were having your meeting, she came up and gave us all a kiss. Quite an experience, I can tell you," remarked Suzanne at the same time wrinkling her nose. "Said she had to go because her 'skoi - arctic- arrgh' was playing her up. "Incidentally, what were you men gassing about?"

Christine was walking a little way behind her husband as they made their way to their car. "Don't worry Suz, I'll get it out of Tim later… Dalmar, if you are going to ask us back for coffee. Sorry. Not tonight." She turned to him looking weary. "Anyway, you have to stay until the death – I'm afraid. They will be most disappointed if you bunked out now." She smiled weakly at him.

Dalmar half-raised a hand, "Yes – I understand that" he said. This made matters worse because now he did not know how to follow it up. The coffee business had not been expected and put him off track. However – if he were to say, 'In that case, we will postpone coffee'… but it sounded pathetic in his mind. He was very aware that he owed Christine an enormous debt of gratitude, but now was hardly the time to thank her.

"So – we will see you both for lunch tomorrow?" It was Christine speaking. Dalmar felt Suzanne stiffen by his side. He was not at all sure that he had heard her sister-in-law correctly. But her voice started up again. "Thought we might go to the Bush at Ovington for a drink first. We have some friends who are dying to meet you, Dalmar. A really nice couple. Live next door but one to us." She smiled encouragingly at him.

Tim had reached the Morris and was busy locating a key in the lock. Christine put out a cheek for Dalmar to kiss her goodnight. This he did in a daze. She turned her attention to Suzanne. "And don't look at me like that, Suz. It has taken a great deal of effort to get you two together again. There is *no way* we are letting you part now, not even for a few hours." The two girls kissed each other with Suzanne apparently tongue-tied.

Having got Christine safely into the driver's seat, Tim came up to Dalmar with his hand outstretched. "Welcome back," he said. Dalmar wanted to hug him in gratitude but contented himself with a gentle but definite squeeze in the shake. "Night Suz," said her brother. He disappeared around the other side of the car and got into the passenger seat. Dalmar and Suzanne, hand in hand, watched as they reversed out. Christine opened her window and shouted, "Dalmar – hope you have a spare ... oh it doesn't matter - of course you have." There was a mischievous grin on her face. And then they were gone. For the second time that evening, Dalmar and Suzanne came together in a long kiss.

Back in the discothèque things were into the final half an hour of the show. The two lovers watched the dancing for a while and finished off the drinks Floyd Hemming had given them earlier. Finally, it came to the last dance before the disco was due to close-down at midnight.

Grateful for the slow number, so that they could hold each other, Dalmar and Suzanne floated lazily back and forth across the floor. Now they had eyes for no one else. Just at that moment, Suzanne had hers tightly shut. She stretched up and spoke softly into his ear. "Thank you for the poem: I love it," she said, meaning every syllable.

"Oh ... just-as-well," he said with a chuckle. She replied by squeezing him tightly around his waist.

When the dance finished, Floyd and Jan came up to them. "Now would be a good time to make your escape," Floyd suggested.

"Don't you think we should say our goodbyes to everyone?" Suzanne looked concerned.

"By the look of some of them, they wouldn't be capable of knowing who they were saying goodbye to," said Jan. "All that free liquor." As if in confirmation, a young man, very unsteady on his legs, suddenly pitched forward onto his girlfriend's lap, causing great merriment among their friends. Some of them may have been intoxicated, but there was no nastiness anywhere. It was all good-natured.

"If you are sure," said Dalmar.

"We insist, actually," said Floyd. "Go on – get out of here."

Dalmar smiled ruefully at him, and Suzanne was secretly glad. "We have to say a gigantic thanks to someone," suggested Dalmar.

"No – no," Floyd quickly stopped him. "My company received a lot of good business from John the Red. Trouble was – it felt a bit like blood money – so this is our way, in some small measure, of paying back – you see?" Dalmar nodded politely.

"Anyhow, the real thanks go to you and Fly," commented Jan. "I hope we are going to see lots of your doggie. Got to carry on the business boom somehow." They all laughed cheerily, and then our reunited lovers slid quietly out of the hotel doors, across the flood-lit gravel car park, and were soon lost from sight. They strolled slowly, his left arm over her shoulder, her right arm about his waist, loving the closeness of each other.

"Phew, what an evening," said Dalmar, breaking the silence. You must be tired. Have you come straight here from the Lake District?"

"Yes ...." She stopped, and by placing a hand against his stomach, so indicated that she wished him to as well. They were just in front of the gate leading into the garden. She looked up at him. "You and I have a lot of catching up to do," she said. "What have you been doing since last I saw you?"

Dalmar bent his head for another kiss. Afterwards, he said in a low voice, "Thinking of you." They fully embraced, holding each other tight, during which Dalmar whispered in her ear, "I love you Suzanne. Please stay with me."

When they entered the house. Fly came into the kitchen and made a fuss of the girl, but not for long, he was too weary, and retreated to his place in the sitting room.

"Why didn't you tell us about your brother?" Suzanne asked.

Dalmar looked into her eyes. He knew he must tell her the truth. "Fear," he said.

"Not sure what…?" Suzanne did not have time to finish the query before Dalmar cut in.

"Fear. I thought that if my relationship to a victim of John the Red was known, people would expect me to be some sort of avenger. You see, all our youth, my sister and I were sure we hadn't heard the last of John the Red. Don't ask me how. Neither of us know – it was just – an atmosphere … Fear – very nearly stopped me coming to live here."

"I'm very pleased you did." At the same time as she said this, Suzanne raised her face for another kiss. It was a kiss she wanted to give him for his honesty. His answer had completely absolved him from any petulance that she had previously felt. He returned her kiss with passion. "Mind you," she said softly, "I am not sure that I could ever get used to calling you 'John'?"

He smirked. "My mother and father stopped calling me by my first name after the title, John the Red, was coined." Dalmar gave a small shrug with his shoulders. "My sister always called me J.D. – ever since I can remember. Still does."

"Do you know what they are calling you – in the village?"

"No."

"The shy avenger." Dalmar thought about it, and then laughed softly. "Tell you what," said Suzanne, "let's have some coffee upstairs. I'll use the bathroom and see you up there in a little while, all right?" Her face wore such a sweet smile. He nodded to her, reading from her question that she wished him to take his time.

After cleaning the small amount of make-up from her face, she located a new toothbrush in the cupboard under the sink. There always used to be one there, she remembered. Then she left the bathroom and went upstairs to their old bedroom.

She was sure that this was what she wanted to do, but she did so wish any niggling doubts would go away. Suzanne considered they might well do so, in time. Had he been telling the truth about that girl who called on him that awful Sunday evening, for instance?

On the little table by the window there was a small, gift-wrapped parcel. She wondered who that was for.

Suzanne smiled to herself: men never could puff up a pillow. Dalmar's attempt was just as pathetic as usual, referring to the side of the bed nearest the door; the side he slept on. She gathered his pillow to her to do it properly.

In that moment ... any doubts vanished forever. There, nestling against the white sheet was her blue Alice band. She put down the pillow and picked up the familiar object. She caressed the soft nap of the velvet with the nerve ends of the first three fingers of her right hand. Behind her, she heard the subtle chink of two mugs being carried together, and a low creak as the bedroom door opened a little further... She turned to him.

THE END

THE SILVER BIRCH RUN

Five hundred silver soldiers with five hundred silver spears,
Lay before my path on that bright winter's day.
They were the guard of nature to the inner forest's tiers,
And from their outer circle made to bar my way.

Only pleasing minds may enter the busy tree throng,
For paths are shown to those of us who softly tread.
The melancholic lyric of the lilting forest song,
Comes to the folk who dwell among the leafy bed.

Placed into the way of the untrod destruction bent,
A multitude of briars form a gigantic web.
They scratch at the limbs of the loathsome descent,
And send them scuttling home gouged red.

Five hundred silver soldiers, with five hundred silver spears,
Hail all those that have made the silver birch run.
To escape unscathed, a master-skill of master-steer,
So, honour the fast runner of the woodland sun.

JOHN THE RED
(THE RED ADDER OF YEWHURST.)
1947/48

There is a straight mile of road run along by oak and beech each side,
That lies beyond Yewhurst Hill where the Red Adder does reside.
It was a hot summer's day and the snake lay high among the trees,
Looking down on mossy way through the myriad of leaves.
Tom, the spaniel, was padding softly along the path,
Easy walk for an old dog over the short aftermath.
A flash of red cast through the air! It came from out of the sky.
And old Tom howled his last … then lay down to die.

It was three hours later when young Judy went in search of Tom,
Listening now and then after she called his name to come.
But no sound did she hear, and her calls became long wavering with anxiety,
'Till she came across his body and sat down to cry long tears of pity.
Now the vet said, 'Old Tom died of a terrible snake poison.
The like of which he had heard not before, nor could reason.'
So, a strange and fearsome mystery hung about this area of land.
People talked about Tom's death and how he died by a strange hand.

The Sunday following the French family were picnicking under an oak tree,
Enjoying sandwiches and fruity things, laughing in their
freedom busily.
They had no knowledge of the events that had happened before.
Nobody sought to warn them for the tale was not news anymore.
Now Mr. French went to the ditch to bury their unsightly rubbish.
They held the countryside to the law, not they litterbugs to punish.
Mrs. French screamed when she saw her husband's ghastly face,
And nasty red snake fall and disappear into the bracken, no trace.

The Shy Avenger

Scardthomas

Paul French died within the hour though the ambulance came quite soon,
A local householder having telephoned the local hospital before noon.
The snake had been seen, but from the description no species was known.
'A Red Adder,' they said. 'Dangerous and deadly', and here was one alone.
The whole neighbourhood now knew of the terrible peril on The Great Mile.
The locals barred their doors and kept a look out all the while.
And thus, the frightening legend of John the Red was born,
To bring a dark cloud to all about each worrying morn.

The summer passed by and soon brought the autumn dew,
And nothing more was seen of John the Red anew.
Nobody walked the mile alone anymore. The word went out to steer clear,
For a man and a dog had died a horrible death that year.
The winter snow came and went and talk of John gradually ebbed away,
But some feared for the end of the long sleep and out of hibernation day.
'Perhaps,' they said, 'He'd died or gone away. We've heard the last of John.'
One man ventured forth to walk the mile and won five pounds of Ron.

Young Billy had a new bicycle: a birthday gift from dad.
Now in his tenth year he loved to ride through the woods, brave lad.
A track ran along by the road for nearly all the mile.
Billy could get up a fair old lick and ride his bike in style.
It was a lovely sun-lit spring day and Billy was preparing for a run.
Faster and faster went his machine until he imagined he was doing a ton.
John the Red from a high branch leapt and Billy shrieked in pain.
The vile serpent of the mile had mercilessly struck again.

After Billy's funeral, fear turned to anger amidst the neighbouring countryside.
Fury became hate. They determined to hunt the snake and so turn the tide.
On the appointed day a hundred men with guns met to carry out the deed,
Dressed in high boots, large hats and tough suits of tweed.
They started at one end of the mile, moving slowly forward in a row.
Two hundred eyes peered into every tree, looking for the thin red foe.
They went up one side of the road and down the dim-lit other,
Never wavering from their task, staying close together.

The great hunt proceeded all day long and several small vermin died.
Many disturbed birds flew off choosing somewhere else to hide.
Constantly the men scoured the land and even searched the bracken.
Looking whilst fearing for themselves, knowing anything might happen.
Several tall trees were climbed by courageous young men,
In the hope of spying from above, the snake in some secluded den.
But at the end of that long day, all returned home wearing a heavy frown.
For no matter what they did, no trace of John the Red was found.

The local Council, when they heard of the failure of the great hunt,
Stepped in and said, 'We have the answer to rid us of this runt.
The red snake lives in the oak tree from where it did twice attack.
Science tells us so – we have no doubt of that.'
A gallon of spirit was poured into a hole in that poor tree.
A great blaze started. They claimed John had been fried. Everyone was free.
And the people believed them and walked the mile once more.
Indeed, not one further attack occurred. John the Red was gone for sure.

The Shy Avenger

Scardthomas

In the centre of the village about a mile from where the story has unfolded,
Lay an area of woodland over by Budd's barn, up to now secluded.
It was decided to clear this parcel of land to provide extra for a farm.
Seven people started work with axes and saws, busy but calm.
There was Charlie, Stan, Malcolm, Cynthia, Hazel, Lucy and Big Harry.
All with one purpose to occupy their minds as they toiled happily.
As each tree was felled, a great bonfire was seen to blaze,
And smoke drifted on the air adding to the late summer's day haze.

Now Peter, who lived with his folks up at near-by Chapp
Saw the smoke and passed a message with the newspaper boy, young Jack,
To his beloved sweetheart, Susie girl, to arrange a walk that eve.
'Let's go by Budd's barn and at the bonfire embers my arms you'll receive.'
So, with his thoughts on romantic pleasure, he lived his working day,
Longing for eventide and the bright smile of Susie to come his way.
'If all went well,' he thought, 'I'll choose tonight and ask her hand
In marriage to me. How proud I'll be, there's no fairer than Susie in our land.'

The two lovers never returned home that night.
Their mothers and fathers were angry, thinking they had eloped, not right.
'What earthly reason could they have for doing such a crazy thing?
Surely, they had nothing to fear, for them the wedding bells would ring.'
Yet this was odd for no provision or clothes had they taken along,
And anger turned to concern among their next of kin and friendly throng.
Charlie and Stan discovered their bodies wrapped together by a dead fire,
Their faces masked in pain. What fate caused these youngsters to expire?

The Shy Avenger   Scardthomas

Great tragedy. The doctor knew at once the cause.
He found fang penetration marks with nasty swollen, purple sores.
There was no mistaking the faces of Peter and Sue twisted in pain.
That terrible viper, John the Red, in his new lair, had struck again!
And this time a double blow to such an innocent couple.
A halt was called to the work by the barn: no point to incite trouble.
Poor Stan would have none of it; his fear was mighty to the extreme.
Who could blame him? John was a frightening killer, so incredibly mean.

But Big Harry was not a man to be frightened off by John,
And with his wife, Lucy, he persuaded the rest to carry on.
Plans were made to post two guards while they worked on desperately:
One with an axe and one with a gun, watching all the while, acutely.
The next day the intrepid few began, not without many a pause of dread,
To cast fearful glances at the branches that lay above their heads.
All day long they toiled and hard work replaced unease by and by,
Until one pine remained: a giant that stood one hundred and twenty feet high.

It was very clear to all as they looked at this great tree,
If John was still about, somewhere up there, he lurked menacingly.
Charlie and Malcolm took the big saw to the base of the tree's large trunk,
While the rest watched aloft, with Big Harry and his axe ready to jump.
Lucy, who was standing, eyes straining, trying to perceive any sign,
Up high among the evergreen leaves of the dying pine,
Had one split second to save her life, when suddenly, she saw a red blur.
Flying through the air - descending fast towards her!

In that time Lucy did not know what made her jump and start.
A dire feeling told her something evil was approaching lightning fast.
She froze – rooted to the ground! John landed not two feet away!
Her mind was in a daze and her body started to sway.
She tried to scream, but her voice had gone, lost by shock and fear,
As John made to make the strike: her death was surely now so near!
Out of the air, a mighty arm wielded the axe incisively true!
Crashing it to the ground! There lay John the Red – in two!

A great cheer rose from the hill. It was heard from miles around.
The curious went out to meet the workers homeward bound.
But Big Harry stopped and retraced his steps to the place.

The Shy Avenger — Scardthomas

'Folk must see John's body,' he thought, 'face to face.
Then we'll all be free from the dreaded viper we all feared.
We will burn him on this piece of land that we've just cleared.'
But – when he came up to the place where the joy of now had been born.
His face paled ... for the two parts of John ... had gone.

Printed in Great Britain
by Amazon